Praise for
The Spanish Brand Series

MARCO AND THE DEVIL'S BARGAIN

"[There are] powerful themes of disease, infertility, strength in the face of loss, and kindness between individuals whose cultures are at war. Though la viruela is, in some ways, the story's main character, the love between Marco and Paloma, equal parts strong attachment and mutual high regard, takes emotional center stage, a satisfying oasis of beauty in the midst of stark harshness."
—Publishers Weekly

Grade A: "There are some series which need to be read in order if they are to be understood. Carla Kelly's Spanish Brand series is not one of these. Although I didn't read *The Double Cross* first, as I should have, I still managed to fall head over heels for Marco and Paloma. To me, that is a good testament to Ms. Kelly's amazing writing. I can't wait to get my hands on another one of her books."
—Alexandra Anderson, All About Romance

"I found this book a pleasure to read, the characters well-formed and credible. Her knowledge and understanding of the era are excellent. I look forward to her next in the series. Highly recommended."
—Historical Novel Society

"Kelly's ability to transport the reader into the unsettled Spanish territory of New Mexico is remarkable. From the daily life on the ranch to the travels into the wild, every word and action is well researched and natural…. With historical events such as smallpox and Native American threats and alliances driving the plot, *Marco and the Devil's Bargain* is a well-rounded story that is sure to please."
—Tara Creel, The Deseret News

"A fascinating and different premise, with an arrogant English physician as the antagonist, and Comanches as surprising allies—a romance in the middle of a really good Western novel."
—Roundup Magazine

THE DOUBLE CROSS

"[*The Double Cross*] packs a full story with plenty of frontier action and believable, sympathetic characters. I'm already looking forward to the next entry in the Spanish Brand series, but until then I will content myself with rereading *The Double Cross*."
—Heather Stanton, All About Romance

5 Star Top Pick: "Life at this time was hard and unpredictable, and this beautiful love story interwoven with history makes for an outstanding read."
—Lady Blue, Romantic Historical Reviews

"Kelly skillfully invites readers to share in this romantic adventure that is played out amidst scenes depicting the harsh landscapes and living conditions on the frontier–all punctuated with an assortment of unsavory characters pitted against the heroic."
—*ForeWord* magazine

"[An] unforgettable story of honor, love and redemption."
—The Historical Novel Society

"Engaging and highly entertaining, *The Double Cross* is Carla Kelly at her best. I can't wait for the next book in what promises to be an amazing series."
—Carla Neggers, *New York Times* bestselling author of *Saint's Gate*

"The characters, even the secondary ones, are real and lovable. Even through some darker themes, Kelly's smart writing breaks through and the adventurous heart triumphs."
—Tara Creel, *The Deseret News*

"One of the things Ms. Kelly does best is show ordinary people living lives of extraordinary grace, and that's a treat."
—Darlene Marshall's Blog

"Carla Kelly's vivid storytelling plunges the reader into a tense, hypnotic tale of love and courage in *The Double Cross*. A dangerous land filled with memorable characters springs to life and stays with you long after the final paragraphs."
—Diane Farr, bestselling author, Regency Romance and Young Adult Fiction

PALOMA AND THE HORSE TRADERS

PALOMA AND THE HORSE TRADERS

THE SPANISH BRAND SERIES

CARLA KELLY

CAMEL
PRESS
Seattle, WA

Camel Press
PO Box 70515
Seattle, WA 98127

For more information go to: www.camelpress.com
www.carlakellyauthor.com

Cover photograph of horses by Michael Mogensen
Cover design by Sabrina Sun
Map and brands by Nina Grover

Book Paloma and the Horse Traders
Copyright © 2015 by Carla Kelly

ISBN: 978-1-60381-990-9 (Trade Paper)
ISBN: 978-1-60381-991-6 (eBook)

Library of Congress Control Number: 2015940251

10 9 8 7 6 5 4 3 2 1

Printed in Canada

In loving memory of Laurie Browning—dear friend,

dear reader, dear sister.

Simply said, you are missed.

Books by Carla Kelly

Fiction

Daughter of Fortune

Summer Campaign

Miss Chartley's Guided Tour

Marian's Christmas Wish

Mrs. McVinnie's London Season

Libby's London Merchant

Miss Grimsley's Oxford Career

Miss Billings Treads the Boards

Mrs. Drew Plays Her Hand

Reforming Lord Ragsdale

Miss Whittier Makes a List

The Lady's Companion

With This Ring

Miss Milton Speaks Her Mind

One Good Turn

The Wedding Journey

Here's to the Ladies: Stories of the Frontier Army

Beau Crusoe

Marrying the Captain

The Surgeon's Lady

Marrying the Royal Marine

The Admiral's Penniless Bride

Borrowed Light

Enduring Light

Coming Home for Christmas: The Holiday Stories

Marriage of Mercy

My Loving Vigil Keeping

Her Hesitant Heart

Safe Passage

The Double Cross

Marco and the Devil's Bargain

The Wedding Ring Quest

Softly Falling

Non-Fiction

On the Upper Missouri: The Journal of Rudolph Friedrich Kurz (editor)

Louis Dace Letellier: Adventures on the Upper Missouri (editor)

Fort Buford: Sentinel at the Confluence

Stop me If You've Read This One

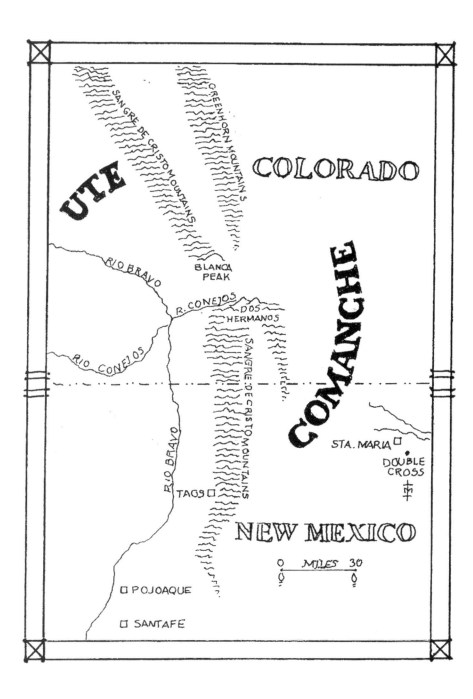

Juez de campo

AN OFFICIAL OF THE Spanish crown who inspects and registers all brands of cattle and sheep in his district, settles disputes, and keeps a watchful eye for livestock rustlers. In the absence of sufficient law enforcement on the frontier of 18th century New Mexico, a royal colony, he also investigates petty crimes.

Contents

Chapter One

In which Marco packs for Taos, Paloma gives advice, and surprises him

IN MARCO MONDRAGÓN'S MIND and heart, he loved his wife, Paloma Vega. She was bone of his bone and flesh of his flesh, but why, in God's name, did she have to be so solicitous while he packed for his trip to Taos?

"Husband…" she began, and he knew that amused look in her eyes, that spark of lurking humor that had already gotten them through crises both domestic and foreign—domestic in the royal colony of New Mexico, and foreign in the kingdom of the Kwahadi Comanche to the east.

She held up the loincloth that he had thought to stuff among his smallclothes and other things that Christian gentlemen wore to distinguish themselves from savages.

She surprised him then, as she often did, even though they had been married for more than three years and he knew her better than anyone. Grinning now, she moved up close and gave a gentle tug on the family jewels. "Big Man Down There, you want to hang loose, do you?"

She called him by his Comanche name, the one given by Eckapeta, the Comanche woman whose tipi he had shared with Paloma during their memorable trip to Palo Duro Cañón. Word had a way of getting around in Comanche encampments, and that was his name. He never told any of his New Mexican friends, but he couldn't help but take pride in the compliment, if only with Paloma.

She patted him there again, and he wanted to close the door to their bedroom and sport a bit in that quiet afternoon time. Wanted to, if not for their son Claudio, who slept on their bed where she had settled him after a prodigious nursing. And little Soledad Estrella—Soli—sang to her dolls in the next room.

Afternoons of casual coupling were long past. Thank goodness for nightfall, when the children were fed, sung to, and asleep in that room that he had kept closed, after his first family died of cholera while he was away inspecting brands. The room was a riot of color and activity now, good for playing and giggling and then sleeping, in that worn-out way of the young.

Then he and Paloma could find their own bed to laugh, talk, make love, and argue a bit, as needed. Quiet times with Paloma, scarce now, were even sweeter. His life had gone from orderly desolation to one overflowing with abundance, chaos, and occasional confusion. He loved it.

And there was that loincloth. He took it from her and returned the skimpy bit of deerskin to the spot next to his smallclothes, which he planned to shuck as soon as he and Toshua were out of the district that he administered as *juez de campo*. Summer was the best time to ride nearly naked. Paloma had no idea.

He gave her that look down his long nose, the one that always made her laugh. She did so now, but quietly, after a glance at their sleeping son. "It's August and there is no one to impress between here and Taos," he said. "It's time for the jewels to swing free. You can't imagine the comfort."

She laughed again, then turned wifely. She spoke into his ear, her words tickling him. "Just have a care that the sun doesn't scorch you in spots not usually exposed."

She kissed his ear, then darted out of reach when he grabbed for her. "Hold that thought," she whispered, and blew him a kiss from the doorway. "It's time for Soli's bath."

Marco followed her to the door of their bedchamber. He watched as she went into the children's room and held out her hand for Soledad. When Soli was on her feet, Paloma nodded to the little one, only seven months past her second birthday. Paloma clasped her own hands in front of her not-quite-so-slender waist and stood there with all the lovely dignity of the Spanish matron she had become. Deeply appreciative of Paloma's mothering skills, Marco smiled as Soli imitated the graceful gesture.

They looked at each other, mother and almost-daughter, as Paloma gently instructed her cousin on her place in the world of women, even little ones. *How did Paloma know to do that?* he asked himself, admiring the ladies in his life.

"Time for a bath, my dear one," Paloma told Soli, and glanced at Marco. "*Hija*, remember to give honor to your father."

He managed not to laugh as Soli dipped him a small curtsey, then started at a walk down the hall to the room where the servants washed the clothes and the children. Her dignity lasted until the exuberance of childhood reasserted itself. Soli picked up her skirts and skipped toward the kitchen, Paloma following.

His wife had asked him to fold a blanket next to Claudio, so he would not roll off their bed. He complied, tucking blanket rolls on both sides of their son, eight months younger than his sister-cousin.

Marco stood a moment in profound gratitude, observing the child they had prayed for, during those many months when it did not seem that Paloma's body would ever nurture a baby. "God is good," he whispered.

Paloma returned a few minutes later, having surrendered her cousin to the care of the woman who had wet-nursed Soledad, spirited away from the dead house full of smallpox where her parents had perished. The Pueblo woman had lost her own child shortly after birth. She had relieved both sorrow and full breasts by willingly suckling the infant daughter of Alonso Castellano and his wife Maria Teresa Moreno, gone more than two years now.

Because she had no other, Soli knew who her mother was, the darling woman coming toward Marco now. Through her own morning sickness and increasing awkwardness as their own baby grew inside her, Paloma had nurtured and loved her infant cousin. To understand the deep love of a woman for a child, Marco only had to turn his head each morning and look at the woman who shared his pillow.

Once Perla *la cocinera's* grandson had been placed into service watching their sleeping baby, Marco and Paloma walked toward the *acequia*, where the waters of late summer were less generous than in early spring. Theirs was a dry land, a land both harsh and dangerous. It was a place for *bravos* who wanted land grants of their own, which King Carlos willingly allowed, because the king did not like his New World possessions empty and idle.

This stroll near the irrigation ditch had nothing to do with preparations for his journey to Taos. There was no need to give this capable wife of his any instructions. His *mayor domo,* Emilio, knew his business in the fields and corrals, and Paloma could handle everything else. He had to admit that she was gracious and more diplomatic with the people of Santa Maria who came to him with questions of brands, or water-sharing, or petty crimes and misdemeanors. A *juez de campo* could not have a better partner than Paloma Vega. She had spoiled him with her abilities, and he didn't mind in the least.

On Paloma's shy advice, they avoided his former office, which had become the temporary home of his dear Comanche friends when they visited. "I think Toshua and Eckapeta are saying goodbye in there now," she whispered to him.

"Tipi time, eh?" he teased, and gave her a little pat on her thankfully not so skinny rump.

"You'll get your time," she promised, and was true to her word. Once all the servants had been formally convened for his parting words and blessing before a journey, and their children slept, Paloma loved him with that ferocity he adored, reminding him that she didn't like being left behind and that she would miss such moments until he returned.

"It's just a quick trip," he reminded her, when she curled up close to him, not bothering to hunt for her nightgown. "I wish I had time to break two horses to a team, but I don't. Rumor says the horse traders are bringing some good horseflesh to Taos."

"You won't drink too much," she admonished.

"Do I ever?"

"Well, no, but a wife has to give advice," she replied, ever practical.

"You're not going to warn me about wenching?" he teased.

"Of course not." She kissed his chest. "You know where you sleep best."

No argument; he did.

She chuckled; she knew him. "No gambling?"

"Maybe a little. I'm hoping Governor de Anza will be in Taos, at least to open the fair. Letters are well and good, but I can tell him how matters stand in Santa Maria. Kwihnai has kept his word, and we have had no troubles from the Comanches for nearly four years."

And yet. No sense in worrying Paloma, but in the last few weeks Marco had felt a certain unease, maybe because Toshua stood longer each night, looking to the east. When questioned, the Comanche merely shrugged.

"Should we not go to Taos?" Marco had asked Toshua only yesterday.

"We will go, but we will not linger," Toshua had replied.

When pressed, Toshua had admitted his own concern. "I see many horses in my dreams," he had said, then shook his head, as though to ward off foolishness. "But aren't we going to Taos to find horses?"

"Are there riders on these dream horses of yours?" Marco had asked. "It's just a horse herd?"

"No riders," Toshua had replied, almost a little too quickly to suit Marco.

His fingers in Paloma's pillow-soft hair, Marco tucked away any misgivings. He knew Toshua would never leave the Double Cross if there was something in the wind, both for his own wife's sake, and Paloma, whom he called his little sister.

Marco's eyes were starting to close now. He knew from sweet experience that one or the other of them would touch and stroke in the middle of the night and there would be more of this love that made him the happiest husband, father, and *juez* in his district, perhaps in all of King Carlos' New World possessions. Time to sleep, except he had a question.

"Will Eckapeta stay here while Toshua and I are gone?" One never knew about Eckapeta. She might surprise them a day later on their journey by joining them, or she might return to her people on the Llano Estacado. Lately, though, the attraction of little ones to caress and tend had kept her close to the Double Cross.

"Eckapeta says she will teach me to bead."

"What will you make, my love?"

"Probably a mess. I do not have deep wells of patience these days."

He silently agreed with her, just thinking of a typical hectic day on the Double Cross. Feeling Paloma relax in his arms, he smiled into the darkness, happy to be the author of her satisfaction. His eyes closed, as testament to her own mattress skills.

But first, he had to ask his usual question. He assumed he would get the usual answer. He asked it before every trip, in order to sound like a thoughtful fellow. He understood marriage politics as well as the next husband.

"Anything in particular you would like from Taos, *mi corazon*?"

"Actually, there is," she told him, which made him open his eyes in surprise, since she never asked for anything. "You've been so busy this past month that I don't think you noticed."

"Noticed what?"

"Aha! I didn't get my box of monthly supplies from the storeroom," she said, her voice muffled against his chest. He knew she was shy about some things.

He may have been lulled into a near-coma by Paloma's love, but he was not a slow man, by any means. He tightened his grip on her shoulders and hugged her closer, even if it was August and hot. Was it possible for a husband to feel even more blessed and grateful? Did the law even *allow* such happiness?

"When, Paloma?" he whispered into her hair.

"Let's see: it's August now, and in July we did find a few quiet moments." She laughed outright. "Your servants probably admired your diligent attentiveness in the hayfield. Some diligence!"

He remembered that afternoon when Paloma came along with the house servants, taking food to the men in the field. She had stayed behind, and one thing led to another, as those matters often did.

She was counting on her fingers now. "I'm thinking April, when the lambs and calves are born," Paloma said in her quiet way. "I really need another servant to help with Soli and Claudio, since I will be even busier." She rested her head against his chest again, and he felt the dampness. "I have prayed to Santa Margarita."

"And she listened?" he asked.

"I know she did," Paloma told him. "Her feast day is July twentieth, in case you have forgotten, and that was when we were in the hayfield." Her low laugh vibrated on his chest. "She knew we wanted more than one child from our bodies. It was not too much to ask."

"No, it wasn't. I'll find you another servant," he promised, "someone good with children, since our other servants have their own duties."

Marco put his hand on Paloma's belly, touched to find her own hands there already, cradling and protecting a baby so tiny that no one but its parents was aware of its existence.

"Horses and a servant," he whispered. "Paloma, *te adoro.*"

Chapter Two

In which big and little Mondragóns are not pleased

WITH A CREAK OF saddle leather, Marco bent down from Buciro to give Paloma a final kiss. "I don't like *adios*," Paloma whispered into his neck.

"It's only Taos, and I will behave," he told her. "We'll be there in three days, maybe four, if we dawdle."

"Go with God then, husband," Paloma said as she stepped back. She raised her hand to Toshua. "And you, my friend and brother."

Toshua nodded. He bent down and touched her head, then touched Claudio in her arms. "Eckapeta will watch over you now."

The Comanche must have noticed the unease she thought she hid so well, because he smiled, a rare occurrence. "I'll keep Big Man out of trouble."

He exchanged glances with Marco, who laughed, telling Paloma all she needed to know about just how soon Marco would be bare and in his loincloth, once they left the Double Cross.

Marco's expression turned tender. Paloma looked over her shoulder to see Soledad in Eckapeta's arms, struggling to get down and follow her dear papa. Marco blew his daughter a kiss, then turned his attention to Paloma again.

"Be easy. Take care of yourself and the little one we cannot see yet."

She knew she would do as he asked, because their servants would insist upon it. She had discovered early in her marriage that Marco never kept a secret. Before she was even out of bed that morning, he had been up, taking their joyous news to Sancha and Perla first, and relying on them to spread it throughout the Double Cross before breakfast. Before her master was even out of sight, Sancha would be bullying Paloma to lie down and prop up her feet.

The prospect had its appeal. Paloma relished the idea of being firmly coerced into rest by Sancha, the family housekeeper who had come with Felicia, Marco's first wife, and who extended her devotion to Paloma. Even now, with the sun still low in the east, she was already tired. How did a baby no bigger than her smallest finger command her whole body? God's mystery.

She watched the men ride to the open gates, just the two of them, because Kwihnai had kept his promise and reined in his warriors in return for the gift of smallpox inoculation that Marco and Paloma had taken east to the Texas plains nearly two years ago. Still, two men seemed too few, when one of those men was the husband she adored. Paloma calmed her fear by considering the two riders, both of them warriors seasoned by warfare but governed by caution.

My darling leaves his guards for us, she thought. She gave Marco the medium-sized curtsey that custom dictated, the best she could do with their son in her arms. In turn, Marco made the sign of the cross over her and their children and blew her a kiss. The kiss was not part of the ritual, because most Spaniards were circumspect people. Paloma smiled and waved, thinking how they had changed after their months in the Comanche winter camp in the sacred *cañón*. Marco kissed her in front of the servants now, which would have astounded his parents. *These are modern times*, Paloma thought, pleased with her man.

When Marco and Toshua rode through the gates, which shut behind them, Soledad started to cry. Startled, Claudio turned around in her arms to stare at his sister. His lips began to tremble.

"No, son," Paloma said and gently turned his face into her breasts. She watched as Eckapeta put her hand over Soli's nose and mouth and gave her head a little shake. After a gasp to breathe and a shuddering sigh, the child went silent. Eckapeta set her down, knelt beside her, then gathered her close, so there would be no hard feelings.

In another moment, Soli wriggled out of Eckapeta's loose grasp and walked purposefully toward Paloma. She clung to her mother's skirts, then tugged on them until Paloma set Claudio down beside her. In another moment they were cross-legged and playing with blocks on the veranda, the crisis over.

After making certain that Perla's little grandson would sit with her children, Paloma walked with her dear friend into the house. "I wish you could cheer me up as fast," she said.

"Just think! You have your whole bed to yourself for a while," Eckapeta said. "No one to steal your blankets or put cold feet on your legs."

"But it's August and hot!" Paloma couldn't help her tears, which more than her late monthly told her she was with child again. "I miss him already!" she wailed.

With an amused expression on her pockmarked face, Eckapeta gave her the same treatment she had administered to Soledad. She pinched Paloma's nose shut and put her hand over her mouth. The little shake of her head was accompanied by a kiss on the cheek. Paloma brushed aside Eckapeta's hand and laughed, her own crisis over.

There was no point in trying to restore her matronly dignity; Eckapeta knew her too well. Paloma sat down on the carved chest just inside the house. "It's not just for me," she said. "I know how uneasy my husband is when he and I are not in the same place. He tries not to show it, but the fear remains. I doubt it will ever leave him entirely."

Eckapeta sat beside her. "Then you will have to stay very busy until he returns," she said. She stood up, took Paloma's hand and pulled her up. She gave her a little push in the direction of the kitchen. "Sancha will keep you busy, and *I* will watch my children."

Paloma felt tears well in her eyes again. "In the Indian way, are they your children?" she asked, feeling shy in the face of such love.

Eckapeta only nodded, because her eyes were filling, too, which touched Paloma right to the center of her body. She swallowed, then threw all dignity to the wind as she wrapped her arms around the Comanche, a gesture her own mother, dead at Comanche hands, never would have understood.

Eckapeta returned Paloma's embrace. "Toshua and I gave up our daughters to the Dark Wind, which scarred my face. Our son was captured by Apaches on his first raid." She buried her face in Paloma's hair and rationed out one sob. "They paid, because Toshua's vengeance was terrible, but I felt no relief."

She held herself off from Paloma, her face so serious, her eyes searching for something deep inside Paloma. "Know this: I will defend your children to the death because they are mine, as you are mine."

They touched foreheads, then Eckapeta released her. "Get busy now! And listen to Sancha when she orders you to rest while our little ones are sleeping. Go on." She gave Paloma a gentle swat for good measure.

ONE DAY. TWO DAYS. On the third day, Paloma woke up and looked automatically for her husband lying beside her. Instead, she saw a pretty little miss with eyes as blue as her own. Paloma held out her arms and drew Soledad close.

"You miss him, too, *mi hija*?" she asked.

Soli nodded, but she did not cry this time. She was already learning the hard lessons of life on the edge of Comanchería. Paloma cuddled her close and waited for the next family member to pad down the hall. Soon Claudio rested against her other side. Paloma sang them a lullaby that her mother had sung to her, one barely remembered. Some of the words may have been wrong, because it was in the *idioma* of the Canary Islands, where Mama's own mother had been born.

The tune always soothed Paloma's heart, and today was no exception. Her breasts were full and she thought about nursing Claudio, except that Eckapeta had told her it was time to wean her son, now that another baby was on the way. Claudio had been drinking from a cup for several months now, so cutting him off completely was more of a trial for Paloma, who relished the comfort of a baby at her breast. Some months from now, she would feel that tug on her nipple again, the sudden rush of milk, and the satisfaction of nursing another Mondragón.

She looked at her son, admiring his sweeping Marco eyelashes and light brown eyes. His nose probably wouldn't be as long as his father's, but he had the same dimple in his right cheek and the same long fingers. The only trait of her family she saw in Claudio was his downturned lips, which reminded her of another Claudio, the uncle her baby would never know, dead so long ago near El Paso.

Her eyes went to the odd-shaped hide on the wall where she and Marco had pressed her family brand, the Star in the Meadow, after he had found it in the cave in Palo Duro Cañón—iron evidence of the Comanche raid that had ruined her life.

She kissed Claudio and then Soli. Ruined? No. She understood now how something terrible was occasionally the gateway to something better. *I would never have met your father, had I not suffered such loss*, she thought, looking from her son to her small cousin. *Blessed be the holy name of Our Lord.*

"Where is Papa?" Soli asked.

Paloma smiled, pleased as each day seemed to bring more language to her cousin's child.

"Papa is probably nearly to Taos. He is going to buy a team of horses to pull a carriage."

"Why?"

The eternal why of children. Paloma considered a satisfactory answer. "He wants us to be comfortable if we visit your Aunt Luisa, or go to Santa Maria."

Amazing that less than three years ago, the idea of her going anywhere without many guards was unheard of. As it was, Paloma couldn't remember when last they had taken a full complement of armed riders to Santa Maria. Maybe peace really had come to Valle del Sol.

Her answer must have satisfied the two-year-old mind. Soli nodded and snuggled closer to Paloma. Her eyes closed, and soon she felt warm and heavy.

"Papa," Claudio said with a sigh.

My sentiments exactly, Paloma thought. When both children slept again, Paloma eased herself out of bed and dressed. She walked to the chapel, relishing the quiet time to pray for Marco and Toshua's safety as well as their own protection in this district so far away from Spanish power, or what remained of it. She rested her hands on her belly and prayed for the new child.

She spent a longer time in the storeroom off the kitchen, pleased to see the fruit of summer's labors in bins and barrels, and the *ristras* of chili peppers hanging in ropes from the rafters. She sniffed the boxed rows of gleaming candles, then backed away, queasy from the odor of tallow. The beeswax candles smelled more fragrant, but even those upset her stomach.

She must have looked a little fine-drawn when she came into the kitchen and nodded to Sancha. The housekeeper appraised her, then reached for the cracker box. Silent, her eyes lively, Sancha handed her several *biscoches*, then followed them with water still cool from the *olla* on the shady back porch.

"Four months of this before I feel better," Paloma said with a sigh.

"Such is the lot of women," the housekeeper reminded her. "What will we do today?"

The crackers worked their magic and her stomach settled. Paloma looked around the well-ordered kitchen, where all business was conducted in the family. She breathed the fragrance of apples and quince. Nothing pressed on her mind today, so she took another sip of water, content, except that Marco was not there.

"I believe Eckapeta and I will take the young ones to the river. Could you prepare us a little *almuerzo*?"

* * *

MARCO AND TOSHUA ARRIVED in Taos after a long three days of traveling, made more comfortable for Marco by discarding leather breeches and linen shirt for his doeskin loincloth. Toshua trapped three rabbits, fat from feasting on the bounty nature offered as autumn approached. Even Paloma's *posole* wasn't as good as rabbit bits toasted on a stick over a *piñon* campfire.

Or so he told himself. Marco would have given it all up for restful sleep in his own bed with Paloma beside him. Only three days and he missed the wife of his heart. No doubt he was softening into middle age.

Even Toshua remarked on his companion's long silences. The Kwahadi removed his own rabbit tidbits from the stick, set them on his tin plate, and sprinkled salt on the meat, just a little pink the way he liked it. "Friend, a man cannot spend all his time in the company of women," he commented, sitting back on his haunches.

"I believe this man could," Marco said. "I sleep better in Paloma's arms."

"Then there is no hope for you," Toshua replied, with just the hint of a smile. "Even now, when she is soon to be puking in the morning, and not exactly eager for your embraces?"

You won't hear it from me that she remains eager, Marco thought. "Even now," he said, salting his own rabbit. He wondered how much to say, how to explain an uneasiness he didn't understand. It was a feeling above and beyond his usual fears, born years ago when he had come home to find Felicia and their twins dead of cholera. This was different.

How, he could not have said, beyond a pricking of the caution he had learned through a lifetime of living on the edge of danger. Some sense above the other senses warned him of danger, and he had ignored it, in his eagerness to find a team of horses and maybe get away for a few days from the grind of work.

And so he worried. What was supposed to be a carefree journey to Taos in the casual company of a friend had turned into wormwood and ash. All he wanted to do was go home.

Now they were in Taos, with the great annual fair spread out before them. Marco had donned his clothes again before they arrived, and he had made his visit to Governor de Anza, a particular friend. They had chatted for a few minutes about change and turmoil and Indian dangers before the governor had been called away to open the trade fair.

Marco had watched, uneasy, as de Anza spoke the usual words, both conciliatory and adamant, to the various Indian nations assembled. Wearing his most elaborate uniform and preceded by an official bearing the royal mace, de Anza offered ten days of unlimited commerce, after reminding the Indians of the Truce of God, which must not be disturbed, on pain of disbarment from future trading opportunities.

"You must honor the Truce of God and trade in peace with your enemies," the governor had intoned. "If you do not, Taos will be forever closed to you and you will not trade your hides, pelts, and horses for metal, knives, and blankets to keep you warm. You men, raise your arms and swear it!"

White and Indian swore their allegiance to the truce which would last from that day for ten days. They swore also to leave peaceably and not lie in wait to ambush. "Go then, and enjoy this time," Governor de Anza shouted. "God bless us all."

A priest—obviously new to the colony because he looked so frightened— blessed the assembly, swung a little incense around and shook some holy water, then retreated to the thick-walled church. A great shout rose up as the fair opened.

With some pride—Paloma would scold him if she knew—Marco couldn't overlook the deference given to him and Toshua, whose exploits on the frontier were well-known. He and his strange friend walked past displays of silver and turquoise jewelry spread on blankets, knives of fine workmanship, and metal pots that Eckapeta would love to take to her friends camping on the Llano Estacado.

Though miserable, he put on a proud face for friends and acquaintances. He wanted to see the stone walls of the Double Cross. He wanted to see Paloma standing in the doorway with their children beside her, maybe even both in her arms, because she was a fond mother. He didn't belong here, and he felt Taos closing in on him.

He stopped in front of a pottery display. Toshua stopped, too.

"Friend, let us go home at first light," Marco said quietly. "We can get horses later."

Toshua gave him such a look—not one of disgust or irritation, but understanding. *He knows I am troubled*, Marco thought with relief. *He isn't going to question me.*

"Toshua, something isn't right. Do you feel it?"

"I do."

Chapter Three

In which a carefree afternoon is less so

PALOMA KNEW WHERE SHE wanted to take their outdoor lunch. Months earlier, she had suggested to Marco that it was time for their little ones to play by Rio Santa Maria, where shallow waters created the ford. Trouble was, with summer and sheep, cattle and crops, there had been no time.

Eckapeta knew the spot and nodded her approval, as Perla packed bread and cheese in a cloth sack. She added dried plums and bits of peeled cactus to the basket. With a smile, Sancha gave Paloma a small crock filled with goat's milk and a smaller sack of cheese. "Marco tells me you are eating for two again," she whispered, as she made a little sign of the cross on Paloma's forehead.

Just the thought of an excursion, no matter how modest, vanquished Paloma's queasy stomach and lightened her mind, taken up with worry for her husband. "Remember how we promised ourselves in May that we would do this very thing?" she asked Eckapeta, as they walked to the horse barn, swinging Soledad between them. "*Mira*, here is August." She laughed. "Pray I do not imagine one hundred tasks I should be doing today, as soon as we are out of sight of the *rancho*."

"Would you wish yourself single, starving, and under the thumb of your uncle in Santa Fe?"

"You know I would not!"

Paloma stood still while Eckapeta lifted her small son into the cradleboard already on her back, the one that Eckapeta had brought back from Palo Duro last winter.

As the Indian woman steadied her, Paloma put foot to stirrup and swung herself and her son onto the back of her quiet mare. The saddle was Comanche, too, and comfortable. She had thought about dressing in her Comanche deerskin, with its convenient, thigh-high slits for riding, but reasoned that there were no men along, so no one would stare if she raised her skirt high.

No man around except Emilio, who merely rolled his eyes, then handed up Soledad to sit snugly in front of Eckapeta. Telling them to keep an eye on the sun's passage, he walked back through the open gates, the little yellow dog in his arms. After Andrés' sad death caused by smallpox inoculation two years ago, the dog had turned his loyalty to the new *mayor domo*.

Paloma looked back at the Double Cross. It had taken several years for her to grasp that what was Marco's was hers, too. She waved to the guard, who patrolled the ledge along the high wall, then turned her attention to the fields, where late corn still grew. The barley had been cut, along with what little wheat Marco had planted—just enough for their own use.

The sheep and their growing lambs grazed under the watchful care of two shepherds and their black and white dogs. The mature sheep had been shorn in May, their wool clips packed into bales and stored, ready for the Santa Fe market in the fall. Another season was turning, leading to winter, when bitter cold, wind, and snow would scour the harsh landscape.

No fears, though, because Paloma knew she would be warm and safe inside the walls of the Double Cross, kept there in comfort by the dearest man in her entire universe. She would knit and sew, and tend their children, and rest, so another baby could grow. In love already with this child she could not see, she patted her belly.

Eckapeta's chuckle told Paloma that her dear friend had seen the gesture. "Am I silly?" Paloma asked, suddenly shy.

"No. You will pat and caress and talk to the one inside, and he or she will come out already well loved, as Claudio did."

As the women exchanged a glance, Paloma felt an unexpected wrench, wishing her mother and father and her brothers, long dead now, could know of her great fortune, or at the very least, know that she was alive and well. *Does this longing ever go away?* she asked herself as they headed toward the fork in the road.

The perfect spot was as perfect as ever, and only half a league from the hacienda, a gentle slope to the river but little used because it was all Marco's land. After a few minutes, the horses were grazing nearby, and Soledad was heading to the river, towing along Eckapeta.

Claudio clapped his hands when Paloma took him from the cradleboard. Sitting on her lap, he nuzzled her breast, letting her know he wanted to nurse.

With a small sigh, she handed him an earthenware cup and poured in a few finger's worth of goat's milk.

He gave her a look that combined equal measures of dismay and then acceptance, because he was thirsty, and in truth, he already knew that drinking from a cup was easier. He took the cup and drank deeply, all the while assuaging her heart as he leaned against her, secure in his world, even if Mama had decided, for some reason, that his nursing days were over.

When he finished, she took his hand and led him to the river, where he played in the wet sand beside his only slightly older cousin, the one he called sister.

"We'll teach them to swim, when they are older," Paloma told Eckapeta.

"Teach me, too," her friend said.

"I thought you knew everything," Paloma teased.

Eckapeta shuddered. "Not this! Don't you fear what might swim below the surface?"

Paloma shook her head, secretly pleased that there was one skill—probably only one—that she could offer Eckapeta. "You might brush against a sleepy turtle or have your toes nibbled by minnows. There aren't any bad spirits."

The Comanche woman's expression told Paloma everything she needed to know about The People and water. "Well, never mind. If you fall in, I will save you," she said.

A few more minutes and Soli began to yawn and tug at her eyelids, which meant sand in her eyes. She shed a few tears until Eckapeta silenced her with no more than a stare. They stripped the children, washed them, dried them, and took them to the shade of a cottonwood back from the bank. New clothes went on, and then bread and cheese found its way into eager hands. Soli sighed with pleasure at the peeled cactus bits.

Eckapeta lay down and put her hands behind her head. The little ones snuggled on either side and soon slept. Paloma unbuttoned her bodice. "If I won't frighten you, I'm going to swim."

Drowsy, Eckapeta moved her hand to show approval. Paloma stripped and walked to the water. In another moment, she was floating on her back. Since the current of August bore no resemblance to the current of June, which roared from the Sangre de Cristos full of snow melt, she drifted along, always staying in sight of the tree.

She remembered the July haymaking afternoon that turned into baby making, and wondered why neither of their children seemed to want to start life in a bed. *Why, indeed?* she thought. *All I ever need is Marco, and he is portable.*

She laughed out loud, perfectly content, until she started thinking about all there was to do before the official end of summer. She had an excuse now to take life easier, but she knew the monumental effort required by everyone to prepare for winter. *I do hope you find me some more help for the babies, Marco*, she thought. She floated along and touched her belly, recalling with no regret her much slimmer waist.

The days of starvation were over and she was fertile. Throw in the loveliness of a husband like Marco, and a woman could not ask for more, especially in the royal colony of New Mexico, where life was hard. She was truly blessed, and she knew it.

"And I have friends," she said softly, as she saw Eckapetta hurrying toward her.

Paloma stopped, and let her feet swing down to the shallow river bottom. Eckapeta was running now, looking over her shoulder. Alert, Paloma started toward the shore at a half swim, half run. Eckapeta had a towel in her arms, which she wrapped around Paloma as soon as she clambered up the slight rise.

Eckapeta pointed with her lips, and Paloma saw the dust cloud—one not created by the fickle wind, but by many horses. She grabbed the towel around her and dried herself as they ran back to the trees, where the babies still slept.

Paloma threw on her clothes, grateful her hair was still confined by a ribbon. She scuffed her feet in her shoes, her mind a blank. Better not to even think about who this might be.

"Have they seen us?" she whispered.

"I don't think so," Eckapeta replied, her face stern. "We would only attract attention if we mounted our horses, so I will lead them into the *bosque*. Get the little ones."

The single cottonwood had been a prime location for a nap, but it offered no protection. Paloma glanced toward the growing dust cloud then resolved not to look again. With a hand on each small chest, she pressed lightly and spoke softly, waking her little ones and warning them at the same time.

She didn't think Claudio was old enough to understand, but she knew Soli was already a good child of Valle del Sol, born into trouble and raised to be wary.

"My love, you must be ever so quiet now. Follow Eckapeta and the horses and do as she says," Paloma whispered. "Go now!"

To Paloma's relief, the child did exactly as she was told, moving purposefully on sturdy little legs and without a glance back. Ready to put her hand over her son's mouth, Paloma scooped him up, along with what remained of their gathering that Eckapeta had not snatched. She ran after her daughter and crouched with her in the welcome shade of the clump of trees.

Eckapeta led the horses farther in, tied them, and left them. She hurried back and led Paloma and the children a little deeper, searching for the best place. When they were settled and both children were on Paloma's lap, their faces turned into her breasts, Eckapeta climbed the tree with the agility of a much younger woman.

"What do you see?" Paloma asked, after a pause that seemed to stretch for hours.

"Many horses and a few riders. Maybe they are going to the trade fair in Taos," Eckapeta replied, making no effort to speak quietly. "Still, we will stay here until …."

She stopped. After another long pause, Eckapeta spoke again, quieter this time. "But they are being followed by Nurmurnah, The People. Don't move or make a sound. These are not Kwihnai's people and I fear them."

Paloma did as she said, bowing her head over her darlings, keeping them silent. She wished that Marco was there to wrap his comforting bulk around the three of them. Calmly, she tucked the foolish wish away and prepared to fight to the death for her children.

Eckapeta was too silent. "Tell me what you see," Paloma pleaded.

She could have screamed with the silence, but she only clenched her jaw tighter. Claudio began to whimper, so she opened her bodice and nursed him; weaning could wait. He suckled and was comforted, while Soledad burrowed closer.

Paloma closed her eyes, remembering blessed moments of nearly four years, moments that would never have been hers, if Marco Mondragón had not ridden to Santa Fe to take his yearly records to the governor, and gone in search of a little dog to keep his feet warm at night. If this was all the joy she would know, it was better than none at all. She thanked El Padre Celestial for his kindness to her and put her terror away, too.

To her relief, Eckapeta nimbly retraced her way down the swaying cottonwood and joined her. She put her hand gently on Paloma's neck and gave her a little shake. "Be calm, dear one!" she murmured. "The smaller dust cloud has met up with the horse herd. I think they are fighting. They are closer to Santa Maria than to us, so let us ride for the Double Cross."

Silent, Paloma picked up Claudio and ran with him to her horse, Eckapeta close behind with Soledad in her arms. The Comanche woman helped Paloma put the cradleboard on her back again, stuffed in Claudio, then heaved them onto Paloma's horse with no fanfare. Eckapeta handed up Soledad next and Paloma seated the little one firmly in front of her.

"Ride and don't look anywhere but ahead of you," Eckapeta ordered. "I will follow behind you and stop anyone who might see us." She took out the knife she wore in her belt at the small of her back. "Go!"

Paloma jammed her heels into her normally sedate mare, which started in surprise at such unexpected treatment from her mistress. She was not a speedy horse, but maybe she sensed trouble. Perhaps she smelled strange horses. Whatever the reason, the mare shot away from the *bosque* and thundered toward the place where the road forked toward the Double Cross.

"Fun, Mama!" Soledad said as she leaned back against Paloma, enjoying the wind in her baby-fine hair.

"Yes, fun," Paloma said as she crouched lower in the saddle, wishing she could turn herself into a Comanche rider. Her skirts billowed well above her thighs. She knew Marco would tease her if he were here, but he was not, so she struggled to keep her tears inside.

Thank the Almighty that the guards were watching. As she raced toward them on her energized mare, the gates swung open to receive her and her babies. Emilio ran into the courtyard, summoned by a cry from one of the guards. The big patrol dogs began to bark, which made Soli put her hands over her ears and mutter something that sounded surprisingly like what her papa might say at such a moment.

Emilio struck the iron bar that dangled from a chain, which brought Sancha and Perla from the kitchen garden and into the courtyard. Paloma handed down Soledad, who still had her hands over her ears, and Perla helped Paloma from the saddle.

Paloma eased out of the cradleboard and handed it to Perla. "Take them into the kitchen. I will be in there in a moment."

Not waiting for an argument from Sancha, who would insist that she come too, Paloma followed Emilio up the ladder to the parapet, where three guards had gathered. She looked where they looked and saw, to her relief, Eckapeta bending low over her horse, riding fast.

The gates closed behind her as soon as she was through them. In one smooth motion, she dismounted, let the reins drop, and climbed up the ladder without even drawing a deep breath.

She put her arm around Paloma in a gesture so tender that Paloma felt all her love and concern, but her words were to the *mayor domo*, who watched them both.

"I believe I know these Kwahadi," she said, only then betraying that she was slightly out of breath.

"Is that good?" Paloma asked.

Eckapeta shook her head. "Their leader, a man named Great Owl, had words with Kwihnai last winter in the *cañón*. He was angry because Kwihnai has sworn to your husband never to attack Santa Maria again, or anywhere in Valle del Sol. Great Owl and his band rode from the *cañón*, and we have not seen them until now."

"Will there be trouble? Paloma had to ask, even though she could read

Eckapeta's expressions well. *I don't want trouble without Marco close by*, she wanted to say. *Please tell me all is well, even if it is not true.*

"There will be trouble, Paloma. Let us prepare."

Chapter Four

In which Paloma is proxy for her husband, the carefree fair-goer, drat his hide

"WE WILL KEEP YOU and your children safe," Emilio said, after a long look at Eckapeta, who stared back at him with an equally impassive gaze. "By the Virgin, I promise you."

Paloma nodded to Emilio, thinking how kind he was to spare her tender feelings, and also grateful for Eckapeta's unvarnished honesty. *He sees me as a fearful woman and Eckapeta sees me as a warrior, ready to fight to the death for my children*, she thought. *Our ways are different.*

She held out her hand to the old man, who had faced a lifetime of uncertainty, living in Valle del Sol, that farthermost outpost of Spanish civilization in New Mexico. "Tell me what I need to do," she asked, even though she already knew what course to take.

"The Comanche moon is rising again," he told her. "You will need to go underground tonight."

Paloma nodded, feeling suddenly like the fearful woman Emilio already thought her. Marco had taken her once to the hiding place under the chapel floor. She could almost smell the close air again and feel the dampness of the earthen walls.

"Very well. For now, though, we women will stay indoors and out of your way." She took his hand. "I know you will do everything in your power to keep us safe."

"On my honor and by all the saints who have ever heard of this colony, I swear to you that we will."

"Since you will all be watching from the parapets, we will bring you food," Paloma assured him.

"All anyone wants is something to do," she told Eckapeta when they reached the kitchen. "Even Soledad here." She knelt by her daughter, who clutched her skirts, fearful. "My dearest, I have a pile of napkins. Will you fold them if I show you how?"

Soli nodded. Paloma sat her on the bench at the table and folded one napkin into a square and then folded it again. She repeated her actions, then Soli put her hand on Paloma's arm, stopping her. As Paloma watched, her daughter folded the next napkin. The corners didn't match exactly, but she handed it to her mother, the fear gone from her eyes because she was busy.

"Exactly right," Paloma said, and kissed her cheek. "Finish these for me, and Sancha might have a treat for you."

She left her daughter with the stack of napkins and carried Claudio to the room he shared with his sister. After a dry diaper followed by a long cuddle, she put him into his crib, where he snuggled and then slept.

Sancha took food to the men on the parapet, and Perla bullied Paloma into eating a big bowl of *posole* she didn't really want, not with her queasy stomach. Paloma ate as she was bid, not certain if her nerves or the new baby were to blame. Eckapeta shook her head at the offer of food, which made Paloma smile to herself, because Perla didn't bully the Comanche woman.

"Who is Great Owl?" Paloma asked after she swiped the last scrap of tortilla around the bowl—maybe she'd been hungry, after all.

"He is a troublesome warrior, never content to be under Kwihnai's eye, no matter how light the control," Eckapeta said. She leaned closer. "It is said that he and his warriors even killed some Kiowa, our close brothers on the plains. This is not done."

"You … you recognized him?"

"Yes. He wears the headdress of a great horned owl. His horse wears a similar face mask. I am not certain which is more frightening."

Such an admission from the bravest woman she knew sent a chill down Paloma's arms. She sighed, wishing Marco would materialize suddenly. "Would that we knew what was going on in Santa Maria."

"I have noticed that trouble has a way of making itself known. Be patient."

As sundown grew near, two riders carrying Spanish lances approached from the direction of Santa Maria. Emilio brought the news himself, as he ushered the soldiers into the kitchen. Perla wordlessly pushed food toward them before they even delivered their message.

Eyes on the bowls of steaming *posole*, the corporal wiped his mouth with the back of his hand. He gave Eckapeta a wary look, then turned his attention to Paloma.

"Señora Mondragón, where is your husband? We have an urgent matter."

"He should be arriving in Taos today. He went to the great fair."

"*Dios!* We need him here," the corporal continued, evidently also thinking that the *juez de campo* would appear if summoned.

"Tell me what has happened in Santa Maria," Paloma ordered. "My friend and I saw something while we were at the river today." She gestured to the table. "Try the tortillas."

The corporal and private needed no more encouragement. The corporal ate quickly, then put down his spoon. "Some horse traders on their way to Taos were set upon by Comanches." He glanced at Eckapeta warily, as a child might observe a strange dog. "The … the Comanches killed one of the traders and got away with a few horses, but the private here wounded one of them."

Such initiative would astonish Marco, Paloma thought, looking at the younger man with some respect. "You captured him?" she asked the private.

He glanced at the corporal, as though seeking approval to speak. "Yes, señora. I brought him back to the garrison, where he is now imprisoned."

"The others?"

"They could be anywhere, and that is a worry," the corporal said. He turned his attention to Paloma. "We need someone to interrogate the Comanche and thought maybe," he lowered his voice, "this woman might help."

"What about the horse traders?" Paloma asked. "Surely someone among them speaks Nurmurnah."

"They don't want to waste a minute on their journey to Taos, and Comanches can be stubborn." He hesitated, then shrugged. "Our sergeant is uncertain."

Those are two understatements of the century, Paloma thought. She looked at Eckapeta, noting well the woman's sour expression. "What do you think, my sister?" She spoke the Spanish word for sister, not wanting the soldiers to doubt for a moment her tie to Eckapeta, if they thought they might try coercion to get her to translate. "Should we help the garrison in Santa Maria? It is your decision."

"See here now, we need her!" the corporal burst out. "She must cooperate."

Everyone in the room looked at the corporal, even the private. He had half-risen from the bench, but he sat down again. He frowned and looked down at the food in his bowl, mumbling, "That is, if she will help us."

Eckapeta looked at Paloma. "*Nami*, I will do as you wish, if you will accompany me. I won't ride alone with these two fools."

The two fools made no comment.

"Very well," Paloma said, after she stuffed her fear into a cupboard and closed the latch. "Emilio, please find us two fresh mounts. Fast ones."

Eckapeta followed the *mayor domo* out the kitchen door. Paloma went to her room and changed into the riding habit her husband had commissioned for her from Aldonza Rivera, Santa Maria's dressmaker since Señora Saltero had been carried off by smallpox two years ago. She glanced in the mirror, and a worried woman stared back.

She looked in on Claudio, who slept soundly. Soledad glanced up from her toys in the *sala* and her lip trembled when she saw her mama dressed for riding. "I know that Sancha has more napkins for you to fold," Paloma said, picking up her daughter. "I will be back before you miss me."

Soledad threw her arms around Paloma's neck, proving the comment false. Paloma kissed her and gave her to Sancha, then hurried out of the hacienda, already regretting leaving her darlings.

Emilio looked like a man ready to argue when Paloma said they would be safe with the two soldiers. "You know that garrison as well as I do, señora," he said.

"I do, *estimato señor*. I also know that my husband looks to me to carry out his will when he is not present."

Let's see if he'll buy that, Paloma thought. He knew better than anyone on the Double Cross the way she and the *juez* worked together. "The *juez* would expect you to keep his children safe, and you know I am in good hands with Eckapeta," Paloma continued. "Give me no argument, Emilio. We will not be long. Don't let down your guard."

What could he say? Paloma swung herself into the saddle, reminded that in a few months, she wouldn't bend so well. She rode close to Eckapeta, and wished, as she always did, that some of the other woman's enormous capability would rub off on her.

They rode at a steady trot, eating up the distance with no words spoken. The private kept his eyes on the swivel, which earned an appreciative grunt from Eckapeta. "This one will live long in Valle del Sol," the woman said at last. "The corporal, probably not."

"The corporal is watching, too," Paloma said. "How are they different?"

Eckapeta pointed with her lips. "See the fear on the corporal's face? It masters him, even though he speaks brave words. The other soldier looks interested, but not afraid. And see how loosely he carries his lance? He's ready, but not in a white-knuckle way."

In Santa Maria, they passed the church, located at the head of the plaza. Paloma saw four men in the cemetery, two with shovels. She veered her horse toward the burying ground, wondering if these were the horse traders. She looked beyond them to a milling horse herd, and knew she was right.

The corporal protested when she dismounted, but Paloma ignored him. He remained on the road, but the private followed her and Eckapeta. The traders were stinking, bearded, and greasy to a man. She chose one younger man only because he had blue eyes like her own.

"Señor, a word please," she said. "Are you bound for Taos and the trade fair?"

"We are," he said, taking off his flat sombrero, one like Marco wore. "And you are—"

"Señora Mondragón, wife of this district's *juez de campo*, who is now in Taos for the fair," she replied, acknowledging his bow with a slight nod of her head. "This man you have buried—"

"My father, Paco," he said, "or rather, the man who called me his son. I am Diego Diaz, and we are horse traders, come most recently from the land of the Utes."

"I am sorry for your loss," she said.

He had a pleasant voice and good diction, something that contrasted with his rugged appearance and his stench. She could barely see his face through a beard that probably hadn't been trimmed since Noah set sail.

He stepped closer, which made Paloma think he did not want to be overheard by his comrades. "No particular loss, señora. We palavered with these Comanches several leagues from here. They wanted four horses as some sort of tax to pass through their land, and Paco Diaz, my sort-of father, would not surrender them. Now he is dead," he finished simply. "Here endeth the lesson."

"You are so casual," she couldn't help saying.

"Paco found me years ago, and that is all," Diego said with a shrug. "We bought these horses at great cost, with the design of selling them in Taos. Our plan has not changed."

"You are a plain-speaking man," Paloma said, wondering how she could admire such a heartless fellow. She folded her gloved hands on the saddle's pommel and considered him. *He lives in a harsh land, too, Paloma*, she reminded herself.

"You are riding to Taos now?" Better just to change the subject.

"As soon as the dirt is tamped down on this grave," he assured her. "It is still light and we can get some distance. How far? Three days? Four?"

"Three, if you move along," she said.

"Well, then," he said, as if to dismiss her.

The grave was packed down. She had no reason to keep the man, because she did understand business. She backed up her horse, then stopped.

"Señor Diaz, a favor, please, since you are going to Taos."

He put his hat on, mounted, and came close to her horse. His eyes might be blue as her own, but the face was a hard one, with thin lips in a thin line.

He was as dark as Eckapeta, whether from nature or from lack of bathing, she couldn't tell. Still, he might do a small thing for her.

"It is this: when you reach Taos, please locate my husband, Marco Mondragón, *juez de campo* of Valle del Sol. Tell him there are strange Comanches in his valley. Tell him to come home immediately."

He grinned at that, which threw a few years off shoulders that had probably born too many burdens. "Señora, let a man enjoy Taos!"

"I can tell you are no husband!" She skewered him with a look. "I greatly fear it when Comanche my friend Eckapeta does not trust are loose in Valle del Sol. Tell him that, too. *Please.*"

Maybe he heard the pleading in her voice, this hard man, and was moved a little. Paloma knew she could probably hope for no more from men who traded regularly with Indians and lived on the fringes of society themselves. His face grew suddenly grave, as he inclined his head. "Señora, I understand what Comanches can do. Believe me. I will find your man and send him home."

Paloma saw his sorrow, and it touched her heart. Rough he might be, and smelly, but he must have had his own experience with Comanches, one beyond the hasty burial of this man he didn't entirely claim. Paloma touched her heart and extended her hand toward him.

"I know you will. Go with God, Señor Diaz."

He reined in his horse to look at her. "Señora, I do not remember the last time anyone told me that."

"Then you need to keep company with better people," she said quietly and made a small sign of the cross. "Hurry, now. Please hurry."

Chapter Five

In which Paloma discovers how fast a horse can move

Eckapeta didn't need to voice any misgivings about the encounter with the horse traders; Paloma had enough of her own. All she wanted to do was wheel her horse about, race back to the Double Cross and her babies, and fort up. She knew her husband well enough to be certain that would not displease him. She also knew the *juez de campo* in him, and continued to the garrison, riding quickly, ready to waste not one minute more than necessary in Santa Maria.

The corporal and private had arrived at the garrison first. From the terrified look on the sergeant's florid face—rumor had it he did nothing but drink—he already knew that Marco Mondragón had left the district.

He came to meet them at the gate of the garrison, shifting frightened eyes from side to side. *And this is what the viceroy in Mexico City thinks will protect us?* Paloma asked herself in disgust. *I would sooner trust my housekeeper.*

She dismounted and motioned for Eckapeta to do the same. The sergeant leaped back when the Comanche woman passed in front of him, and Paloma heard smothered laughter from two soldiers lounging at the gate. Was the state of affairs here so wretched that the sergeant's own men thought him a fool?

"As you can see, my husband is not here. He has gone to Taos for the trade fair," Paloma said.

Still the sergeant's eyes darted behind her, to the right and left, as though still searching for the man of courage she was married to. Paloma looked at him with pity, because he was well beyond his capabilities, assigned to a place that demanded bravery and quickness of mind.

"Sergeant, you remind me of days when I would come into a kitchen full of dishes to be washed, thinking that if I stared at them long enough, they would all disappear. The *juez* is gone to Taos and nothing will change that."

She said it softly, not wishing to shame him further in front of the men he was supposed to lead. Not for nothing had her mother taught her the best manners.

Her words, even quietly spoken, seemed to recall him to his duty, however much he wanted to avoid it.

"I need his advice," the sergeant said. It almost sounded like a pout, as though it was her fault Marco was not in Santa Maria to take charge.

"We will do what we can for you," Paloma said. "Your corporal said you needed an interpreter."

"Oh, oh, yes, that was it. This woman here?" he asked, lowering his voice so Eckapeta would not hear him, in case he was wrong and she turned on him.

Eckapeta's lips twitched, but she said nothing.

"Yes, Eckapeta. Take us to your prisoner."

It was the last thing Paloma wanted to say. Of all the people in the garrison, she had a vast knowledge of the evil that the Comanche could do. At the same time, she knew their kindness and devotion to family. "Take us there," she repeated.

The sergeant led them onto the porch that drooped from disrepair on four sides of the garrison's interior. They followed him to the blacksmith's shop, where in a far corner, two men were manacled to the wall. One was a Comanche, and the other was dead.

Stunned, Paloma covered her nose with her hand and pressed up against Eckapeta, who put her arm around her.

The terrified sergeant didn't even enter the room, but stood in the doorway, gagging from the stench of bowels that had moved, probably while the dead man was in the throes of his own agony.

As her eyes adjusted to the dark, Paloma looked closer. The Comanche who glared back at her had blood on his face. She forced herself to look at the corpse who dangled from his manacled hand. His throat was bloody and she knew what the Indian had done.

"*Dios mio*," she whispered, and then felt her anger build at this needless loss of life, even if the dead man had been jailed, too. No one deserved such a death. "You should never have put this Kwahadi close to this other poor soul, Sergeant," she said.

"Wha-wha-what was I to do?" he said, his voice high and his words tumbling out.

"In mercy, free the other prisoner," Paloma snapped. She glared at the sergeant, who seemed to grow smaller with every glance in his direction. "What is it you want Eckapeta to ask him?"

"J-j-just the usual," the sergeant stammered. "Where is he from, what were their intentions, where were they going?"

Eckapeta gave Paloma a look full of disdain for the sergeant, as if wondering how such a man could be sent to a place like Santa Maria. She moved closer to the chained Kwahadi but stayed out of his reach, which had proved so deadly for the other prisoner. She spoke. No answer. She spoke again. No reply. She might as well not even have been there.

Eckapeta stepped back and looked at the sergeant, who had moved only a few centimeters closer in the small room with the big odor. "He will say nothing. I could ask all day, and he would say nothing."

"We could … could torture him," the sergeant ventured.

"He would still say nothing. He is Kwahadi," she said. "I suggest that you kill him right now."

The sergeant gasped in horror. "Think of the wrath that his fellow warriors would visit upon this valley!"

Eckapeta shrugged. "Then you never should have allowed him to be taken alive. If you kill him, his brother warriors will harm this valley. If you merely keep him in chains, they will harm this valley. If you let him go, they will still harm this valley."

"Even if we let him go?" the sergeant said, his eyes like saucers.

Paloma turned away, embarrassed to see such fear.

"If you let him go, he will know you are a weak man, and he and his warriors will harm this valley. You cannot change what will happen now," Eckapeta said.

Eckapeta watched the sergeant, perhaps looking for some clue of his intent. When she saw nothing, she sighed and threw up her hands. She spoke a few words to the Comanche, who began to sing in a high voice.

Paloma turned away. She knew what was coming. She had heard a death song before, the high-pitched wail that made the hair rise on her back and arms and turned her knees to jelly.

In one quick movement, Eckapeta grabbed a Spanish lance in the corner of the blacksmith's shop and launched it into the chest of the Comanche, ending his death song. She fixed a ferocious look on the sergeant, who quailed before her on his knees.

"You! Send an order to everyone in this little village to gather inside the garrison for protection."

The soldier said nothing. Eckapeta looked at the corporal and private who had come to find them. "Who can be in charge, if not this man?" she demanded.

"I will," said the corporal. He turned away to shout some orders. With relief, Paloma watched other soldiers obey him.

"We have to leave now," Paloma said.

"We'll have no guards with us," Eckapeta said.

Paloma took a deep breath. "Then it's a good thing that Emilio replaced our tired mounts with these horses. Marco would be angry if he knew I was riding this stallion."

A smile crossed Eckapeta's pockmarked face. "We will never tell him."

The sun hadn't entirely left the sky. Paloma knew this ride well—the one from Santa Maria, and church, and her friends to the Double Cross. Ordinarily she and Marco took the distance at a sedate pace, mostly because they liked free moments without little ones around to chat and tease each other.

With a bound that jarred her teeth, they tore through Rio Santa Maria and raced on the dirt road toward home and everything dear to Paloma, except her husband, who was probably enjoying himself in Taos. Never mind. He would be here as soon as he knew. She glanced at Eckapeta, and knew she was in as good hands. It was as if her own parents and brothers, her husband, and Toshua rode beside them. She hoped the baby inside her was too small to feel any effects from the harsh ride, but this was not the time to worry about such matters.

She knew better than to look to either side, leaving that to Eckapeta, who had come away from the garrison with another Spanish lance, this one wrested from the hands of a guard at the gate. "Just keep my babies safe," she whispered to the wind that snatched her words away. *I will think about what we will do once we are through the gates*, she told herself. *Eckapeta will get me there.*

She braved a glance around and saw nothing out of the ordinary. Her horse pounded along, lathered now and breathing audibly. She patted the animal, wishing she could let him know somehow that she would never punish him this way, if her need hadn't been so great.

"There they are!" Eckapeta shouted, pointing with the lance to a thicket well back from the road. "Use your quirt, Paloma!"

She did as the woman said, forcing more effort from her horse. Her heart seemed to beat in rhythm with her horse's stride, as she dug in her heels and wished suddenly for spurs on her riding boots.

Still there was silence. She dared a glance toward the thicket and saw the warriors, chief among them a man with a horned owl headdress, the same mask repeated on his horse. She shuddered and looked away.

And there was the Double Cross, her dear home, with its sturdy gray stone walls and gate closed, even though their neighbors teased them that all was well now in Valle del Sol, since Kwihnai had promised never to attack again.

"Don't you trust anyone?" she remembered Pepe Calderón, their nearest neighbor, teasing Marco only last week.

"Not when my wife and children are within my walls and no one has transported us to Santa Fe, where fat people live," Marco had replied. She closed her eyes and prayed that the Calderóns had forted up.

"I'm dropping back," Eckapeta shouted at her. "Don't look behind and don't stop. Crouch over your horse."

Has it come to this? Paloma thought. She swallowed tears and did as Eckapeta demanded, bending low, trying to turn herself into a horse, as the Comanches did. She clung to her horse, giving him his head because she trusted any animal that Marco had trained.

She heard the Comanches then, and the wailing sound of war put wings to her exhausted mount. As they raced toward the Double Cross, she saw the gates open and mounted guards ride out with their own lances and bows and arrows.

"Pease don't hit Eckapeta by mistake," she shouted.

She flew toward the guards, then past them into the Double Cross. Yanking on the reins, she leaped off before her horse came to a stop. She ran back to the gate and watched as Eckapeta stopped, threw her lance, and found a target. Her knife followed, claiming another victim. Then she rode for all she was worth.

The gates were barely open now, but Paloma knew what her guards were doing. As soon as Eckapeta was through, the Double Cross riders followed her. The gate slammed shut and the stout crosspiece banged down, cradled firmly in iron holders.

Eckapeta dismounted and Paloma grabbed her, holding tight. They clung to each other, then Eckapeta held her off, assessing her with calm eyes. She touched Paloma's belly.

"Is all well in there?"

Paloma nodded. "I think so. I doubt any child of Señor Mondragón is easily dislodged by a little ramble."

Forehead to forehead, they laughed, then Eckapeta gave her a little push. "Get your babies under the floor in the chapel, and your house servants. You, too."

"Oh, but …."

Eckapeta gave her a fierce look. "Little Sister, don't argue."

Chastened, Paloma put her hands together and bowed her head. "Yes, *nami*," she whispered, even as her tears came.

Eckapeta's voice was gentle then, the same voice she used when she held Claudio or Soledad. "What would Marco say if I did any less? Go, my sweet Star in the Meadow. I love you as my own."

Chapter Six

In which the Truce of God suffers

"I SHOULD GET SOME pretty bauble for Paloma," Marco told Toshua, as they walked past another row of shiny things and housewares arranged on blankets in the plaza of Taos.

"You have been saying that for three days now," Toshua commented. "I think you are the kind of fellow who chokes a coin until it begs for mercy, because you do not spend them freely."

"Guilty as charged," Marco said. He sighed and looked around at the pots, pans, iron bars, spun wool, endless chilis woven into *ristras*, silver apostle spoons, carved wooden saints, and other bits of life in the colony that he knew Paloma would enjoy looking at but would then shake her head when he tried to buy something for her. Still, he wanted her here, her touch light on his arm. He missed the smell of her—the lavender odor of her clothing, the pleasant mingling when lavender met her skin, which she scrupulously washed with olive oil soap. Lately it had all blended with her milk, which had flowed so freely for Claudio—the milk she had blushingly informed Marco needed to dry up, since another Vega-Mondragón was on the way.

He stared at Toledo brooches with Moorish design, intricate and lovely, thinking how much he liked the way Paloma leaned against him when she didn't think anyone was watching. What made such a moment so endearing was that he knew how capable she was of standing on her own. He knew that if anything ever happened to him, Paloma Vega would manage his land, goats, sheep, and cattle with great skill. With such a wife he need never fear for his children's inheritance.

"I am a hopeless case, Toshua. I miss my wife," he told the Comanche beside him.

Toshua nodded. "You *are* hopeless," he confirmed. "I watched you last night, when you thought I was asleep. You pulled that pillow very close to your chest."

Toshua laughed, a rare-enough event for Marco's ears, but evidently even more startling for two townsmen who stood by and gasped in amazement that Indians had even a remote sense of humor. Toshua gave them a sour look, which meant that almost immediately the *juez* and the Comanche were the only two men standing over the display of Toledo-made baubles. Just as well; Marco was a countryman and he didn't care for crowds.

A countryman in the company of a Comanche, probably two crimes against society in a place as dignified as Taos. At least Marco had insisted that Toshua put on the wool pants, cotton shirt, and *serape* of a servant, rather than the scraps of loincloths that both he and Toshua had worn on their way to Taos.

Toshua had drawn the line at boots or sandals, preferring his moccasins. To Marco's eyes, his friend looked not much different from other Indians around them in the plaza. He tried to see Toshua through more gentrified city eyes, and he could not deny that there was something palpably menacing about his friend, even without his lance, bow and arrows, which Marco had insisted remain behind in the public house. The knife was non-negotiable.

"I *am* a hopelessly fond husband," Marco said. "You know me too well." He became aware of a slight commotion, his hand on his knife, because that was how men stayed alive in Valle del Sol.

Governor de Anza made his stately way through the plaza. He caught Marco's eye, and both men gave each other a proper bow of respect. De Anza veered toward him, followed by a man equally well-dressed who looked like someone not long in the colony. How he knew that, Marco couldn't have said, beyond the obvious fact that the young man's eyes had no hard stare to them, no look of caution. Marco looked closer and saw disdain. *I see Taos as a big city*, he thought, *and you see it as a dunghill, stranger.*

Marco knew the governor had spent the last day in meetings, held in the refectory of the church, because he had been there for some of them, giving a casual commentary on the Indian situation in his district. The formal paperwork would follow in October, when he made his annual trip to Santa Fe. The governor's secretary had also handed him a new list of brands of missing cattle and horses.

Marco found these informal Taos gatherings vastly more useful than the formality of Santa Fe. No scribes hung around to record anything, so everyone felt free to speak his mind on any topic. The governor had listened and offered suggestions of real merit, because the man knew how to fight Comanches, unlike other governors who had come, flinched, and left New Mexico as soon as they legally could.

De Anza was a short man, but his stately bearing added five or six inches to his frame, somehow. He looked up at Marco and indicated Toshua. "This is the friend of whom you spoke, Señor Mondragón?"

"He is my more-than-friend," Marco replied. "He calls me his brother."

The governor looked from one to the other, nodding his approval. "And Valle del Sol continues to remain peaceful, because of Kwihnai's pledge to you?" He gently touched the scar on Marco's face, which the Comanche war leader had given him as a reminder of that pledge. Marco had said nothing about the scar, but news traveled fast, even in isolated New Mexico. According to Paloma, even settlers in distant places had heard how Marco and his wife and a mysterious doctor—long vanished—had saved their fiercest enemy from smallpox.

"Your Excellency, we do what we can to strengthen our ties with the Kwahadi, as you requested. We must, living where we do," Marco said, embarrassed at the attention. The younger man relaxed his air of superiority to stare at the lengthy scar on Marco's cheek where Kwihnai had peeled back the skin as a potent reminder of his own boundaries.

The governor gestured to the tribes and settlers around him. "Again we have Comanches in Taos for the fair, the first time since our victory over Cuerno Verde. At the risk of further embarrassing you, I wager we owe much of this success to you and your friend here. Keep on, señores, keep on."

"No hint of treaties yet?" Marco would have asked that question yesterday in the meeting, but there were too many others preening and clamoring for de Anza's attention.

"No hint, but I am a patient man," de Anza said. He gazed across the plaza with an expression of satisfaction. "All honor to you, Señor Mondragón! Some Comanches have returned and the Truce of God holds."

"God willing," Marco said under his breath. He came from a long line of realists, so this great trade fair in Taos still had the power to amaze him. It reminded him of the vigor of commerce, when sworn enemies would agree to do each other no harm for a ten-day period, in exchange for the opportunity to trade. For two years now, the fair had hosted Apaches, Navajo, and Utes, but no Comanches, who still smarted from their defeat in the land of the Utes by this very governor. Marco smiled to see The People now, trading with their enemies.

"Marco," de Anza began, becoming more familiar, "this is Señor Enrique Rojas, an *abogado* and *hidalgo* newly sent from the viceroy." He smiled. "If the time does come for a treaty, Señor Rojas will be the man to draw it up."

Marco bowed to the lawyer, who returned a shallower bow, telling Marco all he needed to know about the young man before him. His eyes, blue as Paloma's, and his light hair spoke of his Spanish origins as plainly as if he had strung a placard around his neck. Marco knew what *he* looked like to this man—tall, but high-cheekboned and not so fair of skin, because there had been lonely Mondragóns from the last century in New Mexico who looked on Pueblo women and found them pleasing. In the eyes of this Rojas, he would always be inferior. Marco regretted his deeper bow, then regretted his own pettiness.

"Marco, I must return to Santa Fe because business summons me," the governor said. "There is word of some unrest, from which direction I do not know. You know how garbled a report can get." Marco could tell from the amused look on de Anza's face that he had noticed Rojas' arrogance. "I leave Señor Rojas here in my stead. Let us see what he will learn today, eh?"

"I'm not a schoolboy, Your Excellency," Rojas said, perhaps speaking a little sharper than he should have, because de Anza skewered him with a long stare.

"I would never suggest that," de Anza said. He turned his attention to Marco. "I hear there are traders bringing fine horses from the cloud land of the Utes. How they get around! I have given Señor Rojas sufficient state funds to purchase some horses for my personal guard. Help him if he needs it, eh, Marco?"

Marco bowed, confident that the lawyer would allow no such thing. A glance at Rojas confirmed his suspicion.

De Anza pulled Marco closer, his arm around his shoulder in a gesture so familiar that several onlookers whispered to each other. The governor tugged Marco away for a private moment. "He's a pup and a fool, but I have to work with what Mexico City sends me. Keep him from killing anyone today, will you?"

"I can only try, Excellency," Marco said, his pride soothed by an expert politician, but also a man of no little military ability.

"I ask no more," the governor said. With a wave of his hand, Governor de Anza made his way back through the plaza, as the crowds parted like the Red Sea.

"Señor Mondragón, don't let me interfere with your valuable time," Rojas said, making an even slighter bow, now that the governor's back was turned. "You and your … well, this Indian."

"His name is Toshua," Marco said, but he spoke to the back of the lawyer, who made his own escape from less exalted company. Hands on his hips, Toshua watched him go.

"I do not think this one will live long in New Mexico," Toshua said. "In fact, if you like, I can gut him tonight in his own bed and no one will know who did it."

"Don't tempt me," Marco said, then regretted his words. "No! You know I do not approve, and neither would Paloma." There. Best to play the Paloma card.

"You ruin all my fun, Marco, you know that, don't you?" Toshua asked. His expression unreadable, he looked around at the wares of several nations. He pointed with his lips toward a pile of fabric. "Look now. I am doing what you call changing the subject."

Marco laughed. "And doing it rather well! What do you … oh, *Dios*, this is it."

Together they walked to the corner of the plaza where a crowd gathered around a weaver. As soon as the settlers saw Toshua, they backed away, leaving a path—not one to rival the governor's, but satisfying, especially after the rudeness of Señor Rojas. *Lord, smite me for pride*, Marco thought.

There it was, the perfect present for his dear wife. Marco knew his own hands were rough and he hesitated to touch the pretty shawl that appeared to be woven from cobwebs. He pointed to it. "This one, Rosario," he said to the weaver—a Tewa woman related to his first wife, the lovely Felicia.

Picking it up, Rosario carefully arranged the folds and held the shawl close to him for his inspection. "Marco, you look well these days," she said. "I hear that you have two children now, *bam*! one after the other." She leaned closer, speaking into his ear alone. "My cousin Felicia is probably smiling on you all from heaven."

"I believe she is," Marco replied, touched, because he hoped it was true.

"And that is how the world works," she told him, and rubbed the fabric against his cheek, because she knew his kind heart.

He closed his eyes in pleasure, because the merino wool, probably blended with mohair, felt as soft as Paloma's inner thighs. This winter past he had watched her nighttime nursing of Claudio in their bed, how she shivered sometimes when she pulled down her nightgown. When the new baby came, he would drape this around her shoulders for those late-night feedings. A husband had to do something, after all. A lesser man would roll over and return to sleep, but Marco, twice a husband, knew better.

He nodded to the weaver and asked the price. Rosario told him, and he pulled the coins from his pouch without any hesitation.

"See here, lover of my cousin, you know better than that!" she teased him. "Half my fun is arguing the price."

"Mine, too," he agreed, but his interest had just been captured by more commotion on a side street: the sound of many hooves. Those traders from the cloud lands to the north had arrived. They weren't a rumor, after all.

Rosario quickly wrapped the precious shawl in sturdy cotton, tied it with string and handed it to him. He kissed her cheek, which made her blush, then hurried with Toshua and others who had been waiting for the horse traders. He noticed the Mexico City lawyer in the crush, and remembered that the governor wanted horses, too. He smiled to see Enrique Rojas gather his cloak tightly around him so as not to brush against his inferiors. Toshua was probably right; this man almost certainly had a shorter future in New Mexico than anyone else in the crowd, unless something changed him drastically.

They stood under the awning of a butcher shop, watching the spirited animals. Marco's attention was quickly caught by two bays, moving in tandem. They already looked like a team, and he walked closer, wanting to catch the eye of whoever controlled this herd.

He saw two men, one older than the other—rough sorts, with untended beards and from the filth on their faces and hands, obviously not much interest in hygiene. Amused, Marco wondered what the Mexico City lawyer would make of these traders who spent more time with Indians than settlers and yet somehow managed to hang onto their hair and pertinent body parts that a man might miss.

A younger man rode closer to the portal, dirty like the others and equally bearded. Marco held up his hand. "Ho, there," he called, "is this a matched team?"

The man nodded. "Worth every *real* that old Lorenzo there is going to ask." He brushed his long hair back with filthy fingers, hair with an unexpected red shine to it, but that might have been because of all the grease. "Follow me to the grove over there and we will talk."

Marco followed the man and the slowly moving herd. He looked back for Toshua, and stopped, watching his friend, who had stepped into the shadow close to the door of the shop. His hand rested on his knife.

Marco gestured to him. "Come on! I need to strike a deal before anyone else does."

Toshua shook his head. He wiggled his hand like a snake, and pointed with his lips to just beyond the horse herd. Then he motioned for Marco to come closer.

Marco walked back to Toshua, going against the crowd that followed the horses, the lawyer among them. He stood beside Toshua and looked beyond the herd.

He counted fifteen Comanches, as travel worn as the horse traders. He looked closer and saw three children with ropes around their necks. Two of the children couldn't have been more than six or seven. Closer observation told him that the third child was no child, but a young woman. She had the look of the Ute about her, but he saw the Spanish, too, in her deeply porched eyes and full lips. The younger ones had light hair, but the older girl had hair as dark and lustrous as Felicia's. Two races mingled in her.

"Captives," he whispered to Toshua, all the while wondering why he whispered. "The first two might be settlers' children, but I do not know about the third." He gave Toshua a lengthy appraisal. "You've seen captives before. Why stand in the shadows?"

"I recognize the Kwahadi there with the horned owl headdress," Toshua replied, barely moving his lips. "I saw him in the sacred *cañón* last winter. Believe me, he is trouble. Hang back with me. I fear the worst."

Marco did as Toshua said, moving back until they stood in the door of the shop. He patted his sheathed knife and wished he had not left his bow and arrows in the public house where they slept.

He watched how the Indians with the captives waited, hanging back from the horse herd, as if biding their time until they could make the most dramatic entrance. Some instinct assured him that they had not traveled with the horse traders, considering the wary glances from the traders. He watched and began to wonder if the Comanches had followed the traders for a longer time than just this appearance at the trade fair.

"Toshua, do you think ...."

His companion nodded. "You know what will follow."

Marco swallowed the sick feeling in his stomach and wished that Governor de Anza had not left a fool in charge.

Chapter Seven

In which Marco cannot haggle, because Paloma would never forgive him

THE COMANCHES WERE EVIDENTLY familiar with the trade fair and the streets of Taos, because they ducked down an alley, riding single file but paralleling the crowd and the horse traders.

Marco made a small hand gesture to Toshua then regretted even that miniscule movement as the rider bringing up the rear glared at him. The Comanche held the rope that bound the neck of the young woman and gave it a vicious tug, a clear warning to Marco to stay well back.

The captive turned her own eyes on Marco. He could see her bare pleading from across the street, as well as long scars on her arms where she had been tortured. He knew what else they had probably done to her, and it shook him, even though he had ample understanding of just how vicious men could be to women. He made a silent vow to himself to never fear sacrificing his own life to keep Paloma and now Soledad safe.

"Don't move again," Toshua whispered, barely moving his lips. "We'll follow when they are out of sight." His eyes tracked the other fairgoers, who must not have noticed the brief exchange, so intent were they on following the horses. "Slowly now, let us join these oblivious people who would not last five minutes in *our* Comanchería."

He said it with a certain quiet pride, and Marco took heart. Their clothes and own roughness may have set them apart from the Taoseños and settlers from this softer part of the colony, but what they lacked in polish they made up for in capability. Hadn't Paloma told him, in the quiet of their bedroom, her leg thrown over him, that she never feared because he was there to keep her and the babies safe? Her absolute faith in him always seemed to add exquisite fervor to her lovemaking, and he was not a husband to quibble.

He tucked the cotton-wrapped package down the front of his shirt, wished again for his bow and arrow, and set off with Toshua at a fast walk, keeping with the crowd now and in the shadow of the portal. They came to the area just a block off the plaza to the corral where all teamsters drove their wagons and unhitched their horses. Merchants would gather, dicker, purchase, and then load the goods onto the backs of servants or slaves.

Thinking of captives, Marco looked at the three bound ones, two so young but with eyes already old. He shivered, thinking of his own babies. He knew what life was like in this harsh colony, but not until he was a father did he understand the true peril. He hoped the lawyer that de Anza left in charge would do the right thing, but he was not sanguine, which made him ignore Toshua's hand on his arm and edge toward the front.

The three traders dismounted and stood close together. The trip from the cloud land of the Utes must have instilled some discipline in the horses, because they bunched tight, too.

Several of the settlers had started forward to examine the merchandise on hoof when the Comanches rode into the gathering place. Fearful, or at least prudent, the buyers drew back. Marco counted fifteen of The People, as Toshua had said. He stared at the man with the owl headdress and the cold eyes. The Comanche raised his lance and many in the crowd stepped back. Mothers with their children moved to the rear of the gathering. Icy fingers went down Marco's back as he watched some of the Navajos and Utes melt into the background, too.

He looked for the lawyer and suppressed a smile to see that several of the town's leading businessmen had pushed him forward. Marco took a deep breath. Soon everyone would know what the man was made of. He touched the pouch tied to his own belt, hefting it, wondering.

His breath came faster when the Indian with the smallest blond boy seated in front of him dismounted. He held the rope around the child's neck loose in his hand, looking up at the boy in the saddle, then around the silent circle of people, and then at Enrique Rojas.

"I have a slave here, taken in a raid near Isleta," he said in perfect Spanish. When he said "Isleta," someone in the crowd gasped—perhaps a relative of the boy. People moved aside to allow that person passage forward, but no one took a step toward the Comanche.

The Comanche held up five fingers. "*Cinco reales*," he said in a loud voice.

The figure was preposterous; everyone knew it. Who in their cash-starved economy had such money? Marco felt the *reales* in his pouch, his heart sinking. He had only four, more than enough for his original plan to buy a team of horses, but the Comanche wanted five. He saw other mothers hurry their children away, running down a side street now.

The lawyer looked around, then at the Indian. "That is a stupid amount. You must think we are idiots. We will bargain," he began.

"No, please no," Marco whispered. "At least show him what money you have." Toshua tightened his grip on Marco's arm.

The Indian raised his eyebrows. He looked around elaborately, then yanked on the rope, spilling the child from the saddle and snapping his neck with a sound heard all around the circle. Whatever suffering he had endured at the hands of his captors was over.

Rojas went deathly pale, and tried to retreat into the circle. No one budged to let him in. He looked around in terror.

The young mixed-blood woman put her hands to the rope around her own neck, crying out when the Indian controlling it tightened the knot. "Please help me, someone," she implored. "Mary, Mother of God!"

Four reales. Marco shook off Toshua's hand and strode into the circle that grew wider as people continued to back up. He walked to the dead child first, swallowing his tears, and knelt beside the little body. He closed the boy's eyes, and made a small sign of the cross on the dusty forehead. He took a deep breath and stood up.

He knew all eyes were on him as he deliberately untied the pouch from his belt and willed his hands not to shake. He held it up, coming closer to the man Toshua had called Great Owl.

"I have four *reales* in this pouch," he announced, grateful that he was far beyond the age when his voice would squeak. "I will give all of it to you for the woman." *Please, Señor Rojas, surprise me and be a better man than I think you are*, he thought. *If Owl won't take four, please offer at least one real.*

"I asked five for a mere child," Owl reminded him. He said something in the language of The People, and the other Comanches laughed.

Marco felt the hand of death draw near to the desperate woman. "True, you did." Maybe he could appeal to the man's vanity. "I can understand that. This *pobrecito* was a Spanish child, and worth more." He looked at the young woman, who had clasped her hands together, as if in prayer. "She is Ute, perhaps? Maybe there is some Spanish blood in her, but she is not worth five *reales*. I doubt she is worth four, because all of you have probably ridden her hard."

He hated to say such ungentlemanly things, but this was a harsh bargain with men made of flint. "Four," he said again. "It's a very good offer for broken-down goods."

He stared at the Comanche, who stared back. *I will walk naked through this town before I will look away first*, Marco thought. He heard his own heart thundering in his ears. He held the pouch high, stared at the Indian, then shook the pouch so the coins rattled.

The silence that followed was broken suddenly by a sighing sound as the last air left the body of the dead child. Great Owl jerked his horse back and glanced away, reminding Marco just how superstitious The People could be. Someone shrieked. A woman moaned and fainted.

"Show me," Owl said, his voice more subdued now. He angled his horse away from the little body lying in the dust.

Marco took the coins from the pouch and held them up. He reached in the pouch again, pulling out all the smaller coins too.

"Hand them to me," Owl said, his voice softer still.

"After the girl dismounts and comes to stand beside me," Marco said, knowing this was the most critical moment in the whole, terrible affair. He listened with real relief to hear someone close by clicking rosary beads and praying out loud in Latin. *Please, Mother Mary and all the saints*, he thought. *Intercede for us here, you who sacrificed your Holy Child.*

He let out a small sigh of relief when the Indian holding the rope around the girl's neck dropped it. With a flash of brown legs, the captive leaped off the horse and ran to stand behind him. He heard her ragged breathing nearly in his ear, because she was taller than Paloma.

"The other child?" Marco said, after he handed all his horse money to Great Owl.

He turned his back on the Indian riders and took his place beside the young girl. Marco looked at the circle of fair goers, their faces so serious. The priest who had been praying came forward and knelt beside the dead child. He picked up the little one and walked toward the church, cradling the ill-used body.

"The other child?" Marco asked again. He turned around to look directly at Enrique Rojas, his eyes boring into the weak man who would now and forever in New Mexico be branded as a fool and a coward, whether those titles were truly justified or not; the man was simply too green for this harsh land. Maybe he could succeed elsewhere. "Come, señor, I know the governor gave you money for horses."

"That belongs to the Treasury," Rojas began. Someone behind him in the crowd threw a shoe. Another followed, then another. "Very well!" he exclaimed, his face the color of the red dirt plastered on the church where the priest stood with the small corpse in his arms.

Rojas' hands shook too hard for him to even open the pouch, much less remove it from his belt. One of the soldiers in the crowd slit the strings and the pouch dropped to the ground.

Great Owl laughed out loud as the lawyer groveled in the earth, picking up coins and then in his terror dropping them.

"*Dos reales*," the man said, fear raising his voice an octave or two, which made the Comanches laugh harder. Some of the people in the crowd were smiling now.

"Bring the money here," Great Owl ordered.

The lawyer sobbed and sank to his knees. Marco snatched the coins from him and walked to Great Owl again. He held the coins just out of reach.

"See here, Great Owl, I do not think this child is all Spanish either, and look, he has a shriveled arm! I didn't notice that before. This is more than enough."

Maybe he had overplayed his hand, maybe not. Two *reales* would have bought the best horse in the traders' *remuda*. He had no money for those matched bays now.

Great Owl gave him such a stare, as if memorizing his face and storing up his vision of this bold New Mexican for use in the future. *So be it*, Marco told himself. *Our lives are all in the hands of God.*

He held his breath until the Comanche shifted in his saddle and lip-pointed toward the child, who hadn't raised his eyes from the space between the horse's ears, so cowed was he.

The captor looped the rope around the child's arm and playfully lowered him to the ground as the little boy struggled to loosen the noose around his neck. Marco ran forward and grabbed him. He lifted off the rope and the boy clung to him, his arms so tight around Marco's neck that Marco thought of Soledad's farewell hug and nearly began to cry himself. He held the reeking, filthy little slave, murmuring to him as he would murmur to Claudio.

Marco stood there until another priest came forward and took the child from his arms. "We'll tend to him," the priest whispered. "May God and all the saints bless you forever for what you have done, Señor Mondragón."

"He blesses me every day, Father," Marco said. He gave the frightened child a gentle pat. "You will be well cared for, *muchacho*."

With a sigh of his own, Marco returned to the circle, faintly embarrassed at the deferential looks cast in his direction by men and women alike. The lawyer was on his feet now, brushing off his good suit and cloak and trying not to look at anyone.

"Tell Governor de Anza exactly what happened, leaving out nothing," Marco ordered him. "You can be certain that other reports are probably already winging their way toward him, so it will not profit you to lie."

The lawyer was a broken man. He nodded and left the circle, his head down, the better to avoid the scornful looks aimed at him.

Marco felt a soft hand on his arm. He turned around to see the young girl he had saved prostrate herself in the dirt at his feet, her face in the dust. Gently he lifted her to her feet then took her by the shoulders.

"I am sorry for those things I had to say," he began, "but—"

She shook her head. "You saved my life, Excellency," she said. "I will do whatever you wish, because my body belongs to you."

It was Marco's turn to blush. He shook his head. "Oh, no! Your body is yours, although it is true that I own you." He smiled, thinking of Paloma. "Actually, you belong to my wife, who is kind and gentle and needs a servant for our children, since she is with child again. Will you help us?"

Tears welled in brown eyes much like his own. She leaned forward and kissed his hands. He took her by the hand and led her to Toshua. Her hand trembled and she tried to shield herself behind Marco. He coaxed her out.

"This is Toshua, my great good friend. The only fear you should have now is if my Claudio and Soledad pester you to play with them, or make you hunt for tadpoles in the spring. Will that suit you?"

"Beyond all measure, Excellency," she whispered.

"Just señor," he told her. "In that I am firm. What … what is your name?"

"Graciela Tafoya," she said, rubbing the red mark around her neck.

"Where are you from?"

"The cloud land of the Utes. It … it is a long story, Exe … señor."

"It can wait then." Marco looked behind him, surprised to see that the Comanches had slipped away as quietly as they had come. He thought again how Great Owl had studied the very bones of his face, then put away the disquiet such an act caused him. Why borrow trouble? Wasn't there enough already in New Mexico?

"Toshua, you see a penniless man now," he told his friend. "*Pabi*, Do you think I am charming enough to talk three dirty traders out of a horse or two?"

"You can try, Little Brother," Toshua said. He sheathed the knife he still held.

"What would you have done, if Great Owl had made a move toward me?"

"He would be a dead man."

Marco looked at his empty pouch, opening it wider. "I think a moth just flew out," he joked, which made Graciela smile. He looked toward the horse traders, curious to know if they truly had been followed by that unwholesome band, and wondering if he should attempt a purchase with more money no closer than three days away at the Double Cross. They didn't look like men filled with much milk of human kindness, but all they could do was deny him.

He still stood there, watching the crowd that had followed the horse traders start to melt away, apparently no longer interested in livestock. Comanches could do that to a person. He looked toward the distant plaza, startled to see some of the vendors hurriedly packing their goods, the better to leave Taos and the Comanches behind.

A few prospective buyers, hardy types, still lingered by the horses. Marco didn't notice any of them eyeing the matched bays, so he took heart. "Come along," he called over his shoulder to his friend and his slave. "They'll either laugh me away or we'll make a deal."

Chapter Eight

In which a reeking trader is kinder than a stupid lawyer

M ARCO STOPPED SUDDENLY, WHICH made Graciela gasp and draw back. *I must remember not to startle this one*, he thought. *Do we even want to know what she has been through?*

"I will do this fast, which will probably make me a fool fit for plucking, especially with these hard cases," he said, eyeing the horse traders. He looked back at Toshua. "*Pabi*, there is something about what happened … I want to start for home as soon as possible."

Toshua nodded. "I feel it, too." He gave Marco a shove, which made Graciela gasp again. "Get those horses, if you can."

Marco walked to the matched bays, admiring the look of them. He ran his hand down the broad chest of the closest horse, which did not shy away from him or draw back his ears.

"You like what you see?"

Marco looked over his shoulder at the younger of the traders, who had put his hand on the other bay, repeating Marco's gesture. The man smiled, and Marco saw his own love for the horses.

"I do," Marco said, and made no effort to even begin the usual haggle of walking away, and arguing and walking back, and giving the disgusted headshake, the mournful look—all the tricks of trading that would take hours. He knew the trader would think him a green fool, but so be it. "I like them both. Have you trained them to work as a team?"

"I have. They are brother and sister, and work well together." The trader gave him a long look. "You are the countryman who bought the woman."

"I didn't have a choice," Marco said, faintly embarrassed. "I can use her, though."

A sour look crossed the trader's face. "Hopefully not as hard as her captors did."

"Hey, wait! My wife needs help with our two children, and next spring, our third child. I am an honorable man."

The trader nodded, and his eyes lost their hard stare, which had the effect of making him look vulnerable, if only for a second. "These Comanches! They fought us, killed one of us, then followed, just staying far enough back but close enough to keep the hairs standing up on my neck." He gazed into the distance. "God willing, we will not see them again. I'd prefer that they blend into someone else's landscape. Do you want these horses?"

"I want to use this team to pull a light carriage. My wife will travel better that way with our little ones." *Here I go*, Marco thought. "I gave away my entire purse to save that woman from death. Would you consent to trailing these horses with me back to my ranch, so I can pay you there?"

Marco watched the man's face to see if his eyes hardened again. He saw some wariness, but more interest and a little sympathy.

"Are you good for it, if I go some distance—" the trader began.

"Three days, moving fast—"

"With you?"

"I would never suggest it, if I could not do what I say," Marco assured him. "You only have my word for that, though."

The trader looked toward Toshua. "And you travel with what I think is a Comanche, who looks as though he does not suffer fools gladly."

Maybe humor wouldn't hurt. "He doesn't suffer fools at all," Marco replied.

The trader left without a word. Marco's heart sank, because he wanted the horses. *I tried*, he thought. *I suppose I can find horses closer to home and take the time to train them myself.*

He stroked the other bay this time, pleased with the way the horse whickered then pressed his great head against Marco for a moment, nuzzling like a big dog. "And you are gentle," he said softly, not wanting to be heard, because talking to a horse would only make him look like a bigger fool than he already appeared. "Paloma would have liked you."

After another look toward the trader, now standing close to his *compadres* and arguing, Marco walked toward Toshua and Graciela. He patted his empty pouch and sighed, suddenly wondering how he would pay the innkeeper, who had been highly suspicious of Toshua and had demanded a larger deposit. *Maybe I am just a foolish countryman*, he thought, with a rueful shake of his head over his own idiocy.

"Señor, you are too hasty!"

Surprised, Marco turned around to see the young trader walking toward him.

"I'll do as you wish. My *compadres* aren't exactly thrilled …." He shrugged. "I do not think you will cheat me." He gave a short, awkward bow. "My name is Diego Diaz."

"I won't cheat you. Thank you." Marco felt his face go red. "I have another problem: I gave away everything and can't pay the innkeeper either."

Diego Diaz stared at him, then laughed that throw-back-your-head kind of laugh which a tightly laced man like that lawyer would scorn. "*Everything?* Señor, must I pay your bill at the inn, too? Answer me this: how were you planning to get to wherever we're going without money for another inn or a meal?"

"Toshua and I have no trouble flushing out *conejos* or shooting the occasional deer, and who needs an inn in August, if there even were inns on the trail we take?" Marco said, striving for a little dignity. "Señor Diaz, I can see this will not work. My apologies for wasting your valuable time."

"Don't be so proud! And call me Diego. *I'll* pay your bill at the inn, and trust you to trap a *conejo*." He glanced back at the other traders, who were glaring at both of them now. "Maybe I'd like a change of scenery, myself. Shall we?"

Marco nodded, satisfied. "You'll not be sorry."

"I'm sorry now!" Diego Diaz joked. "I can't think of the last time I trusted anyone. This is a new experience."

They looked at each other and nodded. "Which inn?" Diego asked.

Marco told him.

"I'll meet you there, after I pull my kit together and get these horses." He stopped, and shook his head. "I am a fool, too! I can't leave just yet. I promised a woman near where we were attacked that I would find her husband and tell him to hurry home. *Dios*, find a man in the middle of the great trade fair! I am too susceptible to a pretty face, I suppose. This may take a while."

"We'll be at the inn, and ready. Would I know him?"

"Your guess is probably as good as mine." Diego started to where his own horse waited patiently, his reins on the ground. He stopped. "I suppose I can ask you. It was a *juez de campo*, someone we traders try to avoid."

"I can understand that," Marco said, wanting to laugh, even as his little seed of worry started to grow into a big weed. "Name of Mondragón?"

"I think that was it. Something unusual."

Marco grabbed Diego, who gaped at him, startled. "Young and yes, she does have a pretty face. Did a pockmarked older Comanche woman ride with her?"

Diego nodded. "These same Indians who sold you the woman ambushed us near Santa Maria. Only there were more Comanches. We think some of them stayed there in … where was it … Valle del Sol, to cause trouble."

"I am Marco Mondragón." He had not released his grip on Diego Diaz. "We must hurry."

"For her, I will speed along," Diego said. "Kindly unhand me."

" 'For her'? Why do you say that?" Marco let go of Diego, but not without a little shake. Surely he wasn't jealous of this smelly, bearded fellow?

Diego had already started for the traders' wagon. "She told me to go with God. No one has told me that in years. I'll see you in a few minutes."

Diego Diaz was as good as his word. Before the sun was much higher, he knocked on Marco's door. Graciela was huddled in the corner of the room, her knees drawn up to her chest. Diego looked at her first and frowned.

"Did these men hurt you?" he asked, giving Marco a look that even Toshua could not have bettered in his foulest mood.

She shook her head.

"It might be a while before she trusts anyone," Marco said. "My wife will make things good." He shouldered his parfleche and his blanket roll. "She always does."

"I already paid the bill. *Caramba*, so much!"

"No one trusts a Comanche," Marco said, his eyes on Toshua, who grimaced. "I had to pay more. I will add this to the bill for the horses."

"I told the innkeeper that I could sleep in the stable, but he didn't like that, either," Toshua said. He shrugged. "Maybe I will return and steal some horses, just to show him that he shouldn't be so rude."

Marco sighed and held his hand out for Graciela. She hesitated.

"I don't have time to wait here," Marco said, snapping his fingers. "The lady who will be your mistress needs us and I dare not delay. Come, please."

Still she hesitated, looking from one man to the other as if wondering which one would abuse her first.

Diego lifted her to her feet. "You wouldn't know friends if you saw them, would you?" he asked her, his voice kind. "Come along, and give me no grief. We haven't time for it."

The sun was warming the adobe shops and houses when they rode out of Taos. Marco rose up in his stirrups and looked back. Some of the Indian trading partners had left, perhaps concerned that the Comanches were still not to be trusted, even with the Truce of God. He noticed more soldier presence in the plaza and briefly wished he had political clout. Valle del Sol deserved better than the useless soldiers garrisoned there.

His first worry that Graciela wouldn't be able to keep up vanished the moment he helped her onto the bare back of one of the carriage horses, after apologizing for not having an extra saddle. He had made a bridle out of a rope and she held it with ease.

"Never mind, señor. I have no love for Comanches," she gave a sidelong look at Toshua, who stared back, "but they did improve my riding skills."

Marco had to admit that she sat the lovely bay with the grace of one of The People and not their captive. Her ragged deerskin tunic rode up to her thighs, and he noticed Diego admiring her legs. He reminded himself that he might have done the same, during those bad years after Felicia's death.

Diego had made a point of buying tortillas and several handfuls of dried cactus fruit before they left Taos. "Since no one here has any money except me," he said to the air, as they rode east toward the mountain passes.

A trader he may be, but he is still just a pup, Marco thought as he rode beside Toshua. He knew his own life was a hard one, but he wondered how difficult it must be to negotiate with people who could lift your hair from your head or excise parts of your body if they weren't happy with the trade. He thought of the little dead boy in the plaza and crossed himself, grateful beyond measure that his son was safely in the care of his mother.

By unspoken agreement, Marco and Toshua rode first, so they were downwind of the trader. Marco didn't think his *pabi* was particular about odor, but he had noticed his Comanche friend bathing in broad daylight in the *acequia*, so maybe civilization was rubbing off on him a little. That he bathed only when Sancha or one of the maids were hanging clothes out to dry or working in the garden wasn't lost on Marco, either. And it was only when Eckapeta was not there.

"You just do that to embarrass them," he had told Toshua once, after watching his friend air-dry himself and strut back to Marco's former office next to the horse barn.

"Why else would I take a bath?" Toshua had asked.

"To clean up?" Marco had said, knowing it was a feeble argument that he had already lost, without even understanding why.

He smiled to think of the conversation. Funny what a man will drag through his mind to stay awake in the saddle. Thinking about Paloma always worked for a long while, so he wondered all over again at his good fortune at finding another wife as sweet as Felicia. He loved the way Paloma's normally expressive face went slack after rigorous lovemaking and she relaxed into a boneless form that told him precisely how much she trusted his protection. Valle del Sol wasn't a place where relaxation trumped extreme caution, at least not yet.

In our bed you are safe, beloved wife, he thought. He chuckled as he remembered another time in their bedroom when she had stood straight up, hands on hips, splendidly naked, and asked, "Marco, do you think about me in bed with you twenty-four hours a day?"

Of course he did; he was a man. He had taken too long to reply, apparently, because she threw a pillow at him. And then another, and then sure enough, they were back in that bed. "No, only when I am awake," he admitted when they were cooling down. No reply. She was already asleep.

He leaned over to make some comment to Toshua, but stopped, struck by the intensity of his friend's gaze as he looked toward the Sangre de Cristo Mountains, the first of many passes—beautiful and smelling of lemon thistle in high summer but treacherous and avalanche-prone in winter.

"What do you see?" Marco asked in an undertone.

"It's what I feel," Toshua said simply.

Chapter Nine

In which Marco gets his wish and travels fast

THEY MOVED SLOWLY INTO the canyon. Without a word spoken, each of them began a casual, continuous sweep of his head, looking right and left, and then up as the pass deepened, searching for something out of place, something not quite right.

Before he even knew it, Marco had placed an arrow against the bow now resting in his lap. Out of the corner of his eye, he saw Diego hand a knife to Graciela.

Marco listened for the birds. Nothing. The wind wasn't even ruffling the piñon pine. All he heard was the *clop clop* of their horses' hooves.

When an eagle screamed he jumped, then looked around in embarrassment, only to notice the others doing the same thing. They all managed a weak laugh, then stopped to watch a golden eagle tuck its wings and swoop down, as swift as *la llorona*—the crying woman used to frighten children into good behavior.

Marco watched as the beautiful bird picked up speed and came so close to the earth that he knew it must slam into the ground, only to snatch a squealing rabbit in its outstretched talons and soar for a distant peak where babies probably waited, mouths open.

And that was it. The tension left the canyon as quickly as it had blown in. Small birds began to twitter again, and even the stream seemed to resume its flow.

"What happened?" he whispered to Toshua.

The Comanche shrugged. "The bad medicine decided to leave brave warriors alone. How can we tell? I do know this: Great Owl and his men are ahead, between us and the Double Cross."

Marco felt his heart thunder in his chest. "Maybe they will move north," he said, even though it sounded like a big bucketful of wishful thinking to his own ears. He wanted to bend low over Buciro and urge his mount into a three-league stride that would leapfrog them across peaks and valleys and bring them to his home, his wife, and children by tomorrow morning.

"Our women will know what to do, won't they?" he asked Toshua.

Toshua pushed up the sleeve of the heavy cotton work shirt he wore and bared his forearm. Marco looked at the crisscross of scars and what appeared to be a bite. It was a scar he had wondered about.

"When I was much younger and not so smart, I tried to corner a lion and her kittens in a cave," Toshua said. He rolled down his sleeve. "Chaa! What a fool. I didn't understand how hard mothers fight to protect their young. Let me add grandmothers, for such Eckapeta is, whether you like that or not."

"I do like it," Marco said. "Thank you. I should not worry."

"Worry all you want," Toshua said with a shrug. "I won't tell Poloma."

AFTER DARK THEY MADE a fireless camp. Marco sniffed the air for campfire smoke from other fires and found nothing. Toshua set two snares. "If Little Rabbit sees our plight and offers himself to feed us, we will skin him and cook him in the morning, when a fire is not so noticeable," Toshua said.

Diego passed around his tortillas, followed by the dried cactus fruit. When Graciela started to shiver, the trader pulled a blanket from his pack, shook it out—the stench made Marco turn away—and generously offered to share it with the young woman. He knew she must be cold, because she made no objection.

They sat close together, the canyon wall at their backs, lances at the ready, bows and arrows close by.

"Let us talk softly," Marco said. "I would know something about you, Graciela. I think you must be Ute, from the cloud land to the north."

She nodded. "My mother, yes. My father was a garrisoned soldier in Milagro," she said, naming an outpost to the north, abandoned now, that Marco knew had been even more isolated than his own Santa Maria. "When I was seven or eight, the soldiers were sent to Isleta, farther south."

"Did you go, too?" Diego asked.

She shook her head. "The soldiers were told to leave behind their country wives and children. Mama and I returned to the cloud land." Her voice hardened. She looked at Toshua. "That was where the Kwahadi Great Owl and his warriors found us nine years later, along with horses." She turned that same look on Diego Diaz, a look so hard that Marco was grateful he had done nothing except rescue her. "If it wasn't Comanche raiders, we could count on New Mexican traders to do the same thing. The Utes of the cloud land were greatly weakened by smallpox, and we were preyed upon."

"How long were you with the Kwahadi?" Marco asked.

Her long, long sigh told him all he needed to know; he wished he hadn't asked. "Four years," she said. "How is it that time can go so slowly?"

"And your mother?" he asked.

She shook her head. "She was big with child and could not keep up. They violated her and killed her."

"I saw something like that once," Diego whispered. "A baby ripped out and stuffed back in, once the men had finished with the mother." He got up and left the circle.

"Not so tough as he looks," Toshua commented. "All that beard and stink hides a younger man, I would wager."

Graciela nodded. She looked from Marco to Toshua, and lip pointed to Diego. "Tell me now: which of you is it to be tonight? All three?"

She swallowed and looked so brave that Marco's heart cracked around the edges.

"None of us," he said softly. "I told you, I bought you for my wife and children, and because I didn't want you to die. You will help my wife, because she is with child again. If I know her, and I believe I do, Señora Mondragón will teach you how to manage a household, as well. I can promise you your freedom and a small dowry someday so you can marry, if you will help her now."

Graciela's eyes filled with tears. "No man will mount me?"

"Not unless it's your idea, too." Marco swallowed his own tears, thinking how badly things could have gone for his beloved wives, because women had so little say about anything. "I expect him to be an honorable man, whoever he might be."

"It will *never* be my idea," she muttered.

"People change, Graciela," he said. "Let us leave it at that. You have heard my conditions."

She said nothing. Marco sensed that she wanted to trust him, but trust wasn't in her yet; he could tell that from the bleakness in her eyes.

"All I require is that you help my wife and children," he repeated. "If you prefer field work, I have no objections. Perhaps you can help the beekeeper. *Sí o no?*"

"I will help *la señora*," Graciela whispered. She reached for Marco's hand and kissed it.

"Very well," he said, relieved that he would not come home empty-handed to Paloma. "You will come to love my wife; everyone does."

"Will I?"

Marco looked around to see Diego standing there quietly.

"You, señor, will be at the Double Cross long enough to receive money for your horses and the inn," Marco said firmly. *So you are a cheeky fellow?* he thought. *I shall tell you what I think.* "I can tell you this, Señor Diaz: strong smells are a little hard for my wife right now. I doubt you will even see her."

Diego stared at him, then started to laugh. "I deserved that," he said, finally. He pulled out another odiferous blanket from his bedroll, wrapped it around himself, and lay down to sleep. Marco just shook his head.

"I'll watch first," Toshua said. "I also believe we should rise well before dawn and take up our journey. Great Owl and his men are in front of us, and I would rather put them behind us."

"So would I," Marco said.

Toshua shook him awake hours later, sitting back on his haunches. He looked at Marco as a cat might, patient and intent.

"Is it my shift?" Marco whispered.

"I let you sleep. It is time to ride now," Toshua said.

"That's not how we were supposed to do this. You would take a shift and I would take a shift."

"You said what you thought, and I did what I wanted."

Marco laughed softly. "Toshua, do you ever obey an order?"

"Not too often." It was Toshua's turn to laugh. "Maybe not at all. Let us ride."

They rode until daylight, taking a different trail home, this one skirting the more frequently traveled route and heading through a high pass Marco did not know. They traveled higher and higher, crested the top and started down, all before the sun was up. No one spoke.

Graciela sucked in her breath a few times when she sensed the narrowness of the trail, with its steep drop to a river far below, but she did not call out. Marco didn't know whether to credit her forbearance to the harsh school of life among The People, or to her own upbringing among the Spanish and then the Cloud People. He knew Paloma would tease out whatever information they needed about the young woman.

"You impress me," was all he said, when they finally dismounted for a rest and the remainder of Diego's tortillas.

She gave him a pleased smile, and then turned her head away, embarrassed. "I was afraid."

"So was I. I am not a friend of heights."

She pointed to Toshua. "I will wager he wasn't afraid."

"I will never ask," Marco joked.

It must have been just the right touch, because the high lift to Graciela's shoulders relaxed. She hopped down from the beautiful bay and led him toward the stream close by.

She came back quickly, minus the horse, her face flaming red.

"Is something wrong?" Marco asked.

She put her hand to her mouth. "I think Señor Diaz took to heart your comment last night. He's …." She pointed, her eyes lively, which turned her almost pretty, despite her ragged deerskin dress and thin body.

Curious now, Marco led his horse toward the water and watched, startled and then amused, as Diego, naked and shivering in the early-morning cold, rubbed his dirty arms with sand.

The trader's back was to Marco, and he saw the long scars, the kind that come from lashes with a whip, and an old, puckered scar on his side that looked like a wound from a lance—Comanche or Spanish, perhaps. Traders performed a balancing act between savagery and civilization, and hadn't Diego himself pointed out that he tried to avoid *jueces de campo* such as Marco?

"Do you think he will tell us his stories?" Toshua asked.

The Comanche had come to the stream to wash his hands, bloody from preparing the rabbit he had snared last night. Clad only in his loincloth again, he squatted by the stream and washed.

I doubt we will ever know much, Marco thought, even as he wondered where the blue-eyed trader had come from. Marco had no cause to ask. He would give the man his money, feed him a meal or two, then wave goodbye to him at the gate of the Double Cross, as a good host should. Diego Diaz would melt back into the countryside, probably to join up with his equally disreputable *compadres*. End of story, business done.

"Are you through with your shirt, Toshua?" Marco asked.

Toshua dried his hands on his loincloth. "Until the next time you make me wear it."

"Give me your shirt and I'll give it to Diego. He's a little taller than you are, but it has long tails. More to the point, it's relatively clean."

Toshua nodded and walked back up the bank with Marco. Graciela was on her haunches by the little fire that burned with no smoke. She had pushed several strips of rabbit onto a green stick and was expertly turning it over the flames, close enough to cook, but not too close to burn.

"She knows what she is doing," Toshua said. "I hadn't even built the fire yet."

He removed his cotton shirt from the *parfleche* and handed it to Marco. Tucking it under one arm, Marco walked to the fire, welcoming what small warmth it gave off, because the morning chill had not yet burned away. He thought of Diego washing himself, grateful that when he got home Paloma ·

would have a hot bath and clean clothes ready. If he was lucky—and he thought he would be since this was Paloma—she would probably even pat him dry. And since it was still Paloma, he knew he could anticipate a pleasant time in their bed, doing what made babies. Not for him, the life of a trader.

"Here, lad, it's cleaner," he said after he returned to the bank, where Diego was just standing there wet, because he had no towel. Like a dog, he shook his wet hair, and the drops flew.

After pulling on his smelly leathers, Diego fingered the good cloth of the shirt. "If I had some yucca plant, I could have washed my hair, too," he said apologetically, his head down. "It has been a while. Sometime last spring, I think."

"There's a tub where we're heading, with towels and real soap, and a bed to sleep in."

"I can't even remember when I last slept in a bed," Diego said, his voice muffled as he pulled on the shirt. "If we're lucky, we sleep in people's barns."

"Not on my hacienda. You are doing me a favor by letting me take the horses." Marco laughed. "I can even find you a straight razor to shave that bramble bush on your face."

Diego nodded and turned away. Marco knew too late how badly he had embarrassed the man. "Or you can do what you wish and not listen to me! I suppose I get this way because I have a wife who likes a bit of order around her. An obliging husband is generally a happy man."

Diego smiled, making no attempt to disguise the wistfulness in his eyes. "I'd like to save money for some land, but money is hard to come by. Maybe someday. As for a woman," he shrugged, "who wants this life of mine?"

Diego sat apart from the others while they ate, perhaps aware that although he had dunked himself in the stream, he still reeked of leathers worn too long, and that his hair was full of grease, dirt, and maybe even bugs.

I made him feel small, Marco thought. *Paloma would have handled this better.*

Chapter Ten

In which Marco hopes he has a long lifetime to improve his character

THE TRADER SAT APART from them, even after the long day of riding—not surly, not sour, but quietly sad, in a way that pained Marco and gave him more shame. Diego handed around what remained of his dried cactus and accepted his small portion of rabbit, but he was careful to stay downwind of everyone. Marco chafed inside at his own rudeness in calling attention to the young man's appearance, odor, and clothing.

I'll pay him even more than the horses are worth, plus what I owe him for the inn, Marco thought, then writhed inside at such callousness, thinking he could throw money at a problem and make it better. What was he *thinking*? Diego had cheerfully paid Marco's debt to the innkeeper and shared his food. *And I repay him with unkindness. Paloma will make me sleep in the* sala *for this.*

Graciela was far more kind. She accepted Diego's offer of a blanket on that second night and said nothing about the stench. Marco knew he should apologize to Diego Diaz, but that would only serve to remind the trader of his deficiencies, if such they were. Better to say nothing and make it up with money at the end of the journey. Even that felt hollow to Marco as he turned several times on the hard soil, trying to find a comfortable spot.

"You are becoming the kind of soft man that The People would happily prey upon," Toshua commented. "Someone could slice your other cheek and balance your face. Do you have a problem, beyond the fact that we really don't want to run into Great Owl?"

"Mostly I'm ashamed of myself," Marco whispered to Toshua, even though

Diego Diaz could not possibly hear, having deliberately chosen to sleep far away from them. "I should not have called attention to his uncleanliness."

Toshua rose up on one elbow. "You treated me kindly after you found me starving in that damned henhouse of Felix Muñoz."

"That's different! You were nearly dead. Our friend Diego is just careless."

Toshua lay down. "Or perhaps he just doesn't care."

"That's what I said."

"No. There is a difference."

THEY REPEATED THE SAME punishing day over again, rising before daylight and trusting to Toshua to guide them over unknown trails. Marco knew as well as the next man that August was still summer, but the heights they traveled more than hinted that autumn was on the way. The sky flaunted that vivid blue found at high altitude, and the sun shone, but without the heat of the lower valley. The grass had dried to the tawny shade that meant late summer and rustled as they passed.

"I believe we are ahead of Great Owl and his warriors by now," Toshua said.

Marco listened for underlying conviction but heard none, which added to his uneasiness. Nearly four years in the company of the Comanche, the man who called him little brother, had convinced Marco that his great friend knew everything. Perhaps in Toshua's world there were People who knew more than he did. It was a disquieting thought that made Marco long to see his own land and his wife and children again. Marriage and babies had turned him into a poor traveler, indeed.

As the sun began its plunge behind the Cristos, they traveled the last pass and crossed into Valle del Sol, the land of Marco's birth and the home of all that was dear to him. Marco let out a deep breath that he felt he had been holding since he left Taos. Maybe he *was* just a rough countryman, a *paisano*, the sort of fellow that townspeople chuckled about over their dinners on linen tablecloths, with fine china and silver. He knew he would never call anywhere but this harsh and unpredictable land his home.

He rose slightly in his stirrups, always eager for that first glimpse of the Double Cross, with its walls that matched the color of the surrounding cliffs. It had been built as a fortress and camouflaged by the gray stone. No *hacendado* in the district had built such a rancho, and no one was safer than the people who lived behind its protecting walls. Still ….

Marco was turning his head to make some comment to Toshua when he heard a quick whine and then a smack, followed by a groan. He turned in the saddle, his hand on his knife, to see Diego slumped over his horse's head, an arrow poking from his back.

"I was right. They're behind us," Toshua said dryly, even as he took a firmer grasp on his lance.

To Marco's relief, Graciela grabbed the trader and held Diego upright until he could manage for himself. With her help, he put both arms around his horse's neck and hung on, while Graciela grabbed the reins.

One arrow. That was all, or at least that was all anyone felt like waiting around for. "Hang on!" he yelled to Diego, and slapped the wounded trader's horse. Graciela kneed her mount and thundered after him.

Toshua had already dropped back. He motioned Marco forward.

"I can hold them off, too," Marco said.

Toshua gave him a sour look. "My little sister doesn't want a carcass in her bed!" He slapped Buciro with the end of his lance and Marco had no choice but to follow the slave and the trader.

As they thundered along, the sun dropped like a stone, leaving them in that weird twilight of late summer. "Hang on, hang on," he murmured to the trader up ahead, who was starting to list in his saddle.

Marco had to admire Graciela's skill on the bare back of a horse trained as part of a team. She rode like a warrior, leaning far out to grab Diego's shirt and attempt to keep him upright. The riderless bay pounded along on her other side, keeping pace with his sister.

And then even Graciela's skills couldn't keep Diego in the saddle. He lurched to one side, scrabbling for the horse's mane. Puzzled, shaking his massive head, the horse stopped.

Marco reined in immediately, rearing Buciro back in a punishing motion that hurt Marco all the more because he knew the worth of his old mount. "Don't fail me, Buciro," he said as he dismounted, grabbed Diego, and with strength borne of desperation, hauled the wounded man across his own saddle.

Buciro did as he was told and stayed still as a rock until Marco was back in the saddle. The high pommel prevented Marco from actually stretching the man across his lap, but he knew Buciro would not react to a strange object lying against his neck.

Graciela circled around them, her eyes big.

"Go now!" Marco shouted. "I'm following. When you get to the gates, shout, 'Santiago.' They won't recognize you and you need the password."

Graciela strained to look ahead toward the clump of trees by the cliff. "What gate? I don't …. What gate?"

"Follow me then," Marco ordered, wishing she were in front of him, but grimly pleased that she could not see the gray stone walls that blended into grove and cliff. Silently he thanked his great grandfather Victorio Mondragón, the stone mason from Jaén, España, who had insisted on such walls. Maybe if Paloma had another boy, he could be named Victorio.

Marco turned around once to see too many Indians following Toshua, who rode so low across his horse that they blended into one object. He had seen the enemy and he did not look back. No matter how many years Marco had fought Comanches, the sight could still turn his bowels to water—one more complication he did not need.

"God be praised," he whispered to see the reassuring walls and the gate closed. His guards were watching from the parapet. "Santiago!" he shouted as the night settled around them. "Santiago!"

He could hear the Comanches now, warbling their peculiar cry that was half death song and half unalloyed terror to anyone listening. He glanced at Graciela's frightened face. Perhaps she was wondering what would happen to her this time if she fell into the hands of the same Indians who had sold her to a *paisano* from the eastern side of the colony.

The gates opened too slowly to suit him, but no one was at fault. Graciela and Diego raced through, the bay following. Marco waited at the gate for Toshua.

The Comanche's horse looked riderless, but Marco knew better. Toshua was not a tall man, and given a bit to a paunch, as others of his nation. On horseback, however, there was nothing as elegant as a Comanche, and Toshua was no exception. He was flattened against his horse, his hair streaming behind him—loose as he liked to wear it. He flashed Marco a smile and made an obscene gesture as he rode through the gate.

Marco followed and the gate slammed shut. He didn't dismount until the massive beam fell into place in its iron holders and the Double Cross was as safe as anywhere in Valle del Sol.

Emilio met him in the courtyard, and called over a servant to help him drag Diego from Buciro's back.

"Careful of that arrow," Marco warned. He took a better look at Diego, who had lapsed into unconsciousness—a wise choice. The arrow protruded from the trader's shoulder, always a pesky place to doctor. The arrowhead was well dug in, which would make it a trial to remove. *What would Antonio Gil do?* Marco thought, remembering that enigmatic and grouchy surgeon who had inoculated all of the residents of the Double Cross and Santa Maria as well as many Kwahadi Comanches, then melted into the Texas plains. He would grumble, Marco knew. Still, his quarrelsome presence would have been a blessing just then. There was nothing to do but turn Diego Diaz over to the rough medicine of a talented servant.

"Carry him inside and put him face down on the bed in that room across from mine," he ordered. "Gently now. I'd like him to live."

Graciela required no orders to follow the men as they obeyed. Marco stood a moment in gratitude to an all-knowing Father in heaven who had not forgotten his devoted followers managing a precarious living in a place on the edge of Christianity. He crossed himself and went in search of Paloma.

She will be in the kitchen, he thought, *and I am so hungry.*

She was not in the kitchen. In fact, no one was in the kitchen. The great fireplace hadn't even been lit. He felt the cold logs, trying to recall the last time he had seen the fireplace with not even warm ashes. "Paloma? Paloma?" he called.

No answer. She had to be in the children's room. He ran down the hall, ignoring the groans coming from the bedroom where Emilio was just now cutting around Diego's bloody shirt. He yanked open the door to the children's room, thinking that Paloma would scold him if they were asleep and he had wakened them.

No one. "*Dios mio*," he whispered, as a rush of heat and then extreme cold spread from his head to his feet and back. His heart seemed to pound in his chest and he started to gasp for breath. *This is not going to happen to me twice*, he thought. *God Almighty would not do that to me.*

Marco leaned against the doorframe because he was suddenly dizzy. No one had lit any lamps, and no fires burned. For one terrible moment, he was back in his house eleven years ago, sitting in the dark, rocking back and forth and wailing because his wife and twin sons had died and been buried while he had been away on a brand inspection trip.

His legs wouldn't hold him, and he sat down with a thump, knocking over a vase of dried flowers that Paloma had been fussing over before he left for Taos. The thistles and cone flowers spilled onto the floor as the vase teetered on the edge of the table he had jarred. Silent, he stared as it shivered then fell on the tile floor with a crash.

Emilio looked out of the room where the trader lay, groaning louder now. Puzzled at first, his *mayor domo's* eyes softened. "Hold him still," he called into the room, then came to Marco, squatting beside him.

"Señor, señor! Now where do you think your dear ones would be, during a time of crisis?" He touched Marco's neck, then rested a warm hand on his shoulder, giving him a little shake, recalling him to 1784, and not eleven years earlier. "It is a precaution we all agreed on. Go to them, señor. We can take care of this rancid fellow. Take a deep breath now, then another."

Emilio helped Marco to his feet, then gave him a little push in the other direction. Marco stood a minute, unsure of his balance, as he breathed in and out. Embarrassed, Marco looked at his *mayor domo*, that patient man who had been through so much with him, the man who had buried his first family. He looked for derision in the old fellow's eyes and saw none.

"The … the … chapel?"

Emilio nodded. "She told me to watch for you, because she did not want you to worry, but," he looked back into the room, "we were busy, no?"

Marco nodded. "I am sorry for my foolishness," he began, but the old man took his arm and gave it another shake.

"You care and you love. That is all," Emilio said. "When you are not here, we watch them as you would. Go now."

Marco ran to the chapel. With no hesitation, he folded back the rag rug in front of the altar, grabbed the candle snuffer, and lifted the ring in the floor. The wooden flooring came up smoothly and silently. The stairs his great grandfather had built were wide enough to walk down, facing out. He felt the tension leave his body as he saw the soft glow of lamp light and smelled Paloma's good *posole*.

He continued along the brief passageway, following more lights as it widened into a room tall enough to stand in. And there they were, Paloma with Claudio on her lap, her eyes closed, her lips in his dark hair. Exhaustion seemed to radiate from her like heat. Or was it something else? Had she missed him as much as he missed her? The knowledge that she had, covered him like a benediction.

Eckapeta held Soledad, who looked up and saw him. She clapped her hands and leaped from the Comanche woman's lap. "Papa!"

As much as he adored Soli, Marco had eyes only for his wife. As he watched, she opened her eyes, blinked in the gloom, then let out a sigh. "Marco, my goodness but I have missed you."

With a sigh of his own, he sat beside her, Soli on his lap, closing his eyes in pleasure and relief. He leaned against her breast, relishing the softness of her. She was the heart of his home, his true star in the meadow.

She kissed his head. "I hope you did not worry when I did not meet you at the door."

"I did. I am a fool," he whispered.

She kissed his head again, pressing her lips down more firmly. "You are no fool. We just aren't much good apart."

Soli curled up in his lap and he leaned on Paloma. In a few months he would be able to put his hand on her belly and feel the next Mondragón. After Paloma's earlier troubles, Claudio had seemed like such a miracle, and yet here was another proof that God loved them. He was dirty, tired, and frightened at his own irrationality, wondering if the Comanche Moon would rise tonight, and here he sat under the church in his hacienda, grateful. Who could understand God's tender mercies?

"I have a smelly trader upstairs with an arrow wound that must be tended," he said finally. "I spent all my Taos money on a captive girl for you, because if I had not, the Comanches who brought her in would have killed her."

"Are you the only good man in this entire colony?" she said seriously.

"I might be," he said, not so serious. "Anyway, the youngest trader, Diego Diaz, has brought back the two matched bays I want, and I will pay him here, since I spent it all there." He nuzzled the back of his head against her breast and she laughed. "Come to think of it, we could have left him behind to die. I wouldn't have to pay for the horses."

"And you would be sleeping in the *sala* forevermore," his sweet wife told him. "Will we be safe above ground? We are heartily tired of sleeping down here."

"I believe we are safe enough. My guard is good and Toshua and I will take turns on the parapet during the night." He set Soledad aside and helped Paloma to her feet as Claudio slumbered on. "Let me carry him up the stairs and put him to bed. You might want to look in on the trader."

He raised the trap door, but stopped as a scream cut the air and wavered on, before dropping into a whimper. Paloma clapped her hands over Soledad's ears. The anguish came from the room where the trader lay. More than likely, Marco's most proficient *curandero* had just cut out the arrowhead.

Marco held out his hand for Paloma. When she was upright in the chapel, he enveloped her in a tight embrace. She clung to him, her hands splayed across his back as if she wanted to feel him everywhere and assure herself that he was home and alive and not lying down the hall in pain.

Emilio waited for him. Marco patted Paloma's hip and whispered for her to take Soledad to bed. He held his sleeping son.

"The guards are mounted," the old man said. "Keep the trapdoor open, in case the women and children need it tonight. I think you will sleep well enough." He glanced back into the room and Marco looked, too, wincing to see Graciela dabbing at Diego's wounded back with its gaping hole, now that the arrow was gone. Blood filled the basin she held and dripped on the floor.

"It's not his first wound," Marco said. "Someone shot one arrow. Only one. Why was he the target?"

Chapter Eleven

In which Paloma is certainly his better half—no surprise to Marco

SANCHA AND PERLA WASTED no time in building a fire, and soon the clean scent of piñon filled the hacienda again, and stew bubbled in the hanging pot. The babies were asleep, and Paloma was already deep in conversation with Graciela, who had done all she could for Diego. The slave stood trembling in the hall, putting her hands over her ears whenever Diego cried out.

Marco watched the process from the doorway, wincing when Diego moaned. Paloma came up behind him and put her arms around his waist. She reached lower and patted him. He chuckled and tickled her, his eyes on the men in the room who were concentrating on the patient and not the randy owners of the Double Cross, *gracias a dios*.

"I can smell the poor fellow from here," she whispered, her hands properly clasped in front of her again. "And look how long and greasy his hair is! I cannot see his face, but isn't he bearded?"

"Extravagantly so," he whispered back. "I doubt he has seen a comb or a pair of scissors in years. But he does have blue eyes. Almost as blue as yours."

"Poor fellow. Look there on his back. He has so many scars. Someone has used him cruelly." She sighed, perhaps thinking of her own scars, when her aunt took a hairbrush to her. She had told him those stories early in their marriage, but even now they made his heart sad.

When the servant finished stitching, he carefully wiped around the wound but did not bandage it. "Let the air get to it, señor," he said, as he left the room with a basin of bloody rags.

Marco tiptoed to the bed and leaned over. "Would you like something to eat?"

No answer.

"I think he is worn out from pain," Paloma said, coming into the room. "I'll check on him later."

She kissed his cheek and went into the kitchen. Marco watched his servants tend the two new horses and spent time on the parapet with his guards, looking for Comanches. Naturally, they saw none.

"Will tonight be another Comanche Moon?" he asked the guard standing nearest to him. He had heard of other Indians in American lands farther east who refused to attack at night. Comanches were not among that number. He remembered long nights from his childhood spent under the church floor, his mother praying, and his father somewhere else, probably where Marco stood now.

His eyes started to burn in their sockets, but he remained on the wall, wondering how his neighbors were faring. The last two years of relative peace from Comanches—a pledge made to him by Kwihnai in the sacred *cañón*—had made them more relaxed in Valle del Sol, even though he had repeatedly warned the other rancheros to keep up their guard.

He looked in the direction of the Castellano land grant, still unoccupied since the smallpox deaths of Alonso Castellano and Maria Teresa Moreno, Paloma's cousin. In Taos, he had asked Governor de Anza about possible settlers, and the governor just shook his head. "It appears no one is brave enough to settle on the edge of Comanchería," he had told Marco.

I understand that, Marco thought, turning his attention to the thick walls of his hacienda and the guards, alert and watching. He wondered if he would leave, if he could, and arrived at no satisfactory answer. Perhaps his roots were too deep to even consider the matter.

He heard a creak on the ladder and turned around to see Paloma. "Shouldn't you be in bed?" he asked, noting how tired she looked. How exhausting it must be to carry a baby, even one not yet much larger than a peanut.

"I'll go to bed when you go to bed," she told him.

"Even if I insist that you get some rest?"

"Probably even then," she replied, with a remarkable degree of serenity.

He knew there was no arguing with her, not with that tone of voice, so he put his arm around her. "How is our patient?"

He felt her sigh. "He just stares at the wall. I know he is awake and in pain, but he seems shy to be in our home. He even said, 'I should be in the barn,' and I told him that was nonsense. He won't turn around to look at me."

Marco's conscience did more than prick him; it walloped the back of his head. "That's my fault. On the journey from Taos, I said too many unkind things about how he stinks."

"Oh, Marco," she said softly, which was a worse chastisement than if she had yelled at him, which she never did. "Most of us are only doing the best we can. When he feels better, Graciela and I will make sure he can wash. Maybe he will allow us to cut his hair and beard."

She leaned against his chest and both of his arms went around her. "I'm sorry," he said, and meant it. "He was kind to let me take the horses with only the promise of payment at the end. And … and when he knew I had given away everything to pay that damned villain for Graciela, he even paid my bill at the *posada*. Shame on me."

"Father Francisco would order you to say a bunch of Hail Marys and make a generous act of contrition," she told him, holding him off for a moment.

"My generous act to Diego Diaz will be new clothes and new blankets," Marco said. "I promise." He pulled her close, too miserable to be at arm's length when he wanted comfort.

She nodded, and let him hold her. "You know something else?" she said finally, her voice quiet against his shirt. "The way he lies there reminds me of an old dog that Claudio and Rafael adopted, or maybe it was the other way around. I don't even know if he had a name." She chuckled. "He certainly never came when anyone called!"

He listened to her soft words, happy that she was remembering life before him, that time on her father's hacienda before everything went so terribly wrong. "And?" he prompted. This was not a story he had heard before.

"He was a medium-sized dog, much smaller than your mastiffs that patrol these parapets, but larger than my little yellow dog."

"That useless bit of fluff that now follows Emilio everywhere?"

"The one you paid my uncle an entire peso for? That one?" She laughed that low, intimate laugh that always made Marco's heart beat faster. "We don't need a dog to keep each other warm, do we? Well, the dog of Claudio's got into fights and scuffles, and romantic tangles, I am sure. He would go off to a dark corner and lick his wounds. Not even Claudio could coax him out. When he felt better, he would show up at the kitchen door for scraps."

"Did he perish from overeating?" Marco teased.

She tightened her arms around him. "He died that day in the field with Papa, Claudio, and Rafael. I … I walked just to the edge of the field, and there he was, an arrow through his heart." She pressed her head against Marco's chest, as though trying to burrow inside him. "They even scalped him!"

Marco kissed the top of her head. "That means the nameless dog must have put up a fight, defending his people, *mi Paloma*. He served the Vegas well. That's what you need to remember."

"I suppose he did," she said after a while. "Maybe it sounds silly to you, but I think Diego is licking his wounds. When he feels better, he will let us know. I don't think he is used to sympathy. I doubt there is anyone who cares about him." She kissed his chest, then backed away, the better to see him. "Are the Comanches out there now?"

"Hard to tell. I hear no strange bird calls. The horses aren't restless. There's a certain tension if The People are nearby. I don't feel it."

"Then don't stay up here too long," she told him. "The nights are cooler now, and I've been more than a week without someone to put my cold feet on."

"And maybe a little more?" he teased.

"Maybe a lot more."

Marco stayed on the parapet another hour, walking around, seeing his hacienda fortress from all angles. There were no weak spots and he knew his men. He said goodnight and walked toward his home, feeling all of his thirty-four years now.

Toshua stood outside Marco's old office by the horse barn. He gestured Marco inside.

Eckapeta sat cross-legged on the buffalo robe, a comb in hand. "Thank you for all you have done for my dear ones," Marco told her.

"They are my dear ones, too," she said, her voice as soft as his.

"Sit a moment, little brother," Toshua said.

Marco sat with them, hoping he could get up smoothly, especially when his bones ached.

"I have one thing to say," Toshua began. He turned around and sat in front of Eckapeta, who dragged the comb through his tangle of hair.

"Say on, friend."

"A warrior shot one arrow only. One!"

"No others? Are you sure?"

Toshua gave him his sternest look.

"One only," Marco said hastily, wondering when he would be smart enough not to doubt the man.

"They made a great show of following us, and yelling, but once Diego was shot, that seemed to be their only concern," Toshua said. He closed his eyes as Eckapeta tugged on his hair. "Woman! I have only one head."

She snapped out something that made Marco blush, because he knew more Comanche than he let on.

Marco thought through the silence, broken only when a piñon pine knot popped and scattered a shower of sparks.

"Diego was the target?"

"Who else? He was riding back a bit with Graciela. You and I were in no danger."

"I wonder what Great Owl wants with him? Horses? Something else?" Marco asked.

"Maybe Diego will tell us when he feels like it." Toshua shrugged. "Or he won't. Go to bed, Marco. Paloma won't stay awake forever."

She was wide awake and minus her nightgown when he finally came to bed, and he had never been a man blind to suggestion. He took his time with her, his fingers gentle on her breasts, because he knew they were sore.

She was less gentle with him, which he found nearly as gratifying as the act itself. Her urgency signaled to him that he was forgiven of all crimes and misdemeanors, or at least, that was how he chose to consider the matter. She was soft, obliging, tenacious, and fierce by turns, and he happily let her swallow him whole.

Paloma vanquished all his tension from the past week, and probably well into the next month. He relaxed and lay there at peace with his wife.

"I was frightened in that space below the chapel," she said finally. "I sang and sang to our children, and I hope they did not feel my fear."

He tightened his arm around her. "I am grateful that you did not hesitate to go to ground. Did … did Eckapeta suggest it?"

"I needed no urging from anyone," she said. "Funny I should think of this, but when I was a child, I used to stand outside with my father when lightning and thunder played. I hated to go belowground, and he knew it." She sighed. "He called me Paloma la Brava."

"You are."

"I must be, when I have babies to protect," she said, "the two we have and the third one we cannot see yet." She turned sideways and looked deep into his eyes. "Poor Diego Diaz! I looked in on him before I went to bed. There he was, gathered into a ball. I wonder, did he *ever* have anyone to look after him?"

"He told me something about a stepfather who was killed by Great Owl and his warriors not far from here. He didn't sound remorseful," Marco told her.

"He said the same to Eckapeta and me, back when I gave him the message to find you."

Marco couldn't keep his eyes open. "Then we are both in his debt. He helped you and he helped me." And then he couldn't keep his eyes shut. "*Chaa*! What did I do but insult him because of his uncleanliness?"

Paloma put her hand over his eyes and closed them. "You can apologize again to him. I think that under all that grime and hair, there might be a very good man. Heavens and all the saints know he has been good to us, for no particular reason."

MARCO LEFT IT THERE, and slept, Paloma warm in his arms. He woke up before morning, ready for Paloma again. He nearly stroked her, but her face in the early morning light showed him a woman still tired, with dark smudges under her eyes. He thought of her nights spent in the shelter under the chapel floor, alert and watching for trouble. One child to protect would have been enough anxiety, but there were three.

And each baby is equally important to you, eh, Paloma? Marco thought. He doubted that his wife gave much thought to the fact that Soledad was her cousin. *And I couldn't be nice to a broken-down trader,* he thought, still irritated with himself.

He pulled on his shirt with the long tails nearly to his knees and tiptoed down the hall. A glance in the children's room showed him two little blanketed mounds, because the air already had that chill of early fall still masquerading as summer.

He crossed the hall and peeked in, pleased to see Graciela sitting by the trader's bed, a bowl of steaming broth in hand. Diego lay sideways, babying his wounded shoulder, eyes closed, eating. Graciela looked at Marco standing in the doorway and nodded. He smiled and closed the door, glad for people in the world kinder than he was.

Returning to his room for trousers and moccasins, he admired the smooth line of Paloma's hip to her waist to her bare shoulders. He came closer and tugged the blanket over them, but not before observing the freckles on her shoulders. Once he had vowed to kiss every little dot. He had tried several times, but never got far before distracted by other enticements. She was lovely and healthy and his wife. A man could have no greater treasure.

After he dressed, he went into the hall to just stand there, staring at the door where the trader lay. He had eaten a little, and perhaps slept now, certainly marshaling his forces in the way that wounded men did. He knew what that felt like. When he had hurt himself, Felicia had always been so tender and helpful. When he returned from the slaughter of Cuerno Verde and the other Kwahadi warriors four years ago, there had been no one to tend to his lance wound. His servants had cared for him, but it was never the same. Silently he thanked Graciela and left the house by the kitchen door.

His guards, Toshua among them, stood staring into the distance on that part of the parapet that faced north and east. Curious rather than worried, he joined them. What he saw made his heart sink.

Smoke poured from the direction of the Calderón hacienda. The holdings were too far away to see flames, but smoky blackness filled one quadrant of an otherwise beautiful morning. Trouble had come to Valle del Sol again.

"We're going to have to settle this with Great Owl, aren't we?" he asked Toshua. "If we don't, all the goodwill we have earned from Kwihnai will be worth nothing."

"You have no army, only useless soldiers in Santa Maria, and Kwihnai and his warriors are far to the east," Toshua reminded him. "You know you will not take one man from the guard here, not as long as Paloma and your children inhabit the Double Cross."

"True. Sometimes a very small army is better than a large one."

Toshua nodded. "Only say the word."

Chapter Twelve

In which the trader makes a discovery

"JUST A CRISP TORTILLA with a little salt on it for me," Paloma said to Perla in the kitchen.

"That is not enough to feed a baby," Perla scolded.

"It will do this morning," Paloma replied, touched by the way the servants bullied her when they knew she was with child. The same thing had happened when she and Marco returned from their adventure in the sacred canyon to the east, and she was pregnant with Claudio. Perla and Sancha had bullied her to eat more, scolded her to sleep more, and chided her to put her feet up and rest, until Paloma could only surrender to their ministrations. It was beginning again, and their rough love brought tears to her eyes. Tears, too? So soon? *Ay de mi,* she thought with some dismay, *my body is not mine alone anymore.* Funny how that notion should make her grin through her morning sickness.

And here was Graciela in the kitchen doorway, shy to enter, even though she had already been such a help to Paloma. Paloma patted the space on the bench beside her. "Do sit down. We have been too upended to give you the welcome you deserve," Paloma said.

"I am just a slave your husband bought," Graciela said. "*Dama,* Señor Mondragón just threw that money pouch at Great Owl, so he would not kill me! He … he didn't even take out just some of the coins and toss them. It would have been enough! He gave him the whole pouch."

"I would have been ashamed if he had done any less," Paloma said quietly.

"I blush to say this, but your husband could have done anything to my body that he wanted to, but he didn't!"

Paloma couldn't help but smile, even in the face of Graciela's anguish. "I would have been ashamed if he had!" she declared this time, which brought a slight smile to the slave's lips.

I am looking at someone much like I was, Paloma thought, as she regarded the young woman seated beside her, dirty and wearing a deerskin dress so ragged that it was only fit for the burning barrel. *And what would I have wanted more than anything in the horrible household of my Uncle Felix?*

She knew. Without a word, and to Perla's shocked surprise, Paloma pulled Graciela close to her. She felt the slave's initial resistance, then felt her melt into her arms. Whatever terrors Graciela had suffered at the hands of the Comanches stepped aside, and for a moment she became just a girl again.

"I am grateful to you for helping that poor trader. All I ask of you in this house is that you help me with my children. I am with child again and I need you," Paloma said, smoothing down Graciela's tangled hair. "There now." She held Graciela away from her, seeing in her mind's eye what the young woman could become. "You will tell me about yourself, and I will tell you about me, but first, come with me."

Paloma took Graciela's hand and led her out the kitchen door and into the garden. They walked past the beans and peppers, and tomatillos, and beyond the corn. Paloma pointed to the *acequia* and the empty canal that led into a wooden shed close by.

"Marco had this made for me alone a few years ago, because I was too shy to bathe in the *acequia* after dark during the summer," she explained. "I will raise that little wooden dam, and water will flow into a metal tub inside the shed."

"How clever," Graciela said. "Do you bathe your babies here?"

"They are still small enough for the wooden tub in the laundry room beyond the kitchen. Perhaps that will be one of your chores. Here now, when the tub is full, you lower the dam again."

Paloma walked to the *acequia*, but one of the guards was already there to raise the dam. She thanked him, and walked along the plank-lined ditch as the water moved toward the shed and under the wall. Graciela hurried ahead and opened the door. They watched the tub fill with clear, cold water from Rio Santa Maria. When it was nearly full, she sent Graciela running to close the dam.

"See here? You build a little fire under the tub. Blow it out when the water is warm enough." She chuckled. "Wait a bit so you don't burn your bum, then you can lock the door and soak. Towels there, soap there."

"I have no other clothes," Graciela said, bending down to start the fire with flint and steel. In a moment, she had a small fire, which she blew on until it caught the kindling. "All I have is this deerskin."

"It's going in the burn pile, like it or not," Paloma said. She went to the door. "Watch the fire, and I'll find you something far better to wear."

"Thank you, *dama*."

Humming to herself, Paloma went into the house and to the storage room, where she took out an apron, petticoat, skirt and bodice and put them over her arm. Marco had wondered about her decision to stock the hacienda with simple clothing for the servants, or someone else in need. "My mother had a room like this," she told her husband. "She never turned anyone away." He questioned her no more.

Marco was leaning against the wall, watching her, when she came out. He hefted the money pouch in his hand. "For horses and expenses at the inn, and general acknowledgment of my stupidity. Is it enough?"

He handed her the pouch and she lifted it. "You left enough in your strong box for those shoes with red heels you promised me, and a silk nightgown?" It was an old joke between them, and she could tell he needed to laugh.

He obliged her. "*Especially* that silk nightgown! Maybe this will do for now."

From behind his back he took out something soft wrapped in cotton and tied with twine. "I got it for you in the Taos market. It's for those nights coming up when you're in bed nursing our next one, and your shoulders get cold."

With a cry of pleasure, Paloma handed Marco the clothing for Graciela and opened the package. "My goodness, it's lovely," she whispered, holding the shawl up to her cheek.

"Mohair and merino wool, knitted by one of Felicia's cousins in the pueblo," he said. "You don't mind if the red shoes wait for a while?"

She kissed his cheek. "They can wait. And we don't really need silk nightgowns."

They walked outside and Paloma saw that the men still stood and looked to the north. "Someone else?" she asked. "Oh please, not Pepe Calderón!"

"Toshua and I just returned from there. They lost a few sheds outside the hacienda, but they were forted up." He crossed himself.

"I think all of us will be more careful now. For a while," she replied.

He walked with her to the door of the bathhouse. "Will she do?" he asked, tipping his head toward the door.

"Time will tell," she said, then shooed him away.

She knocked, heard no answer, but opened the door a crack. Graciela sat in the water, her hair damp and shielding her face. Her shoulders shook, and Paloma knew she was crying. Paloma knelt by the tub and did nothing more than scrub her back.

"It's been so long," Graciela said when she could talk. "I worked so hard for Great Owl's women—carrying water, tanning hides, skinning buffalo. All they did was beat me." She shook suddenly. "Then at night, it would be one man or another." She grabbed the washcloth from Paloma's hand and stuck it in her mouth, her eyes wide with terror.

"Those days are over," Paloma said, grateful to every saint she knew of that as hard as her lot had been in the house of her uncle in Santa Fe, no man had violated her. She gently removed the cloth. "That is our pledge to you." She stood up. "Finish washing and try these clothes. I do not have any shoes for you, but when it is safe to go to Santa Maria, there is a cobbler."

She left the bathhouse, shaken to her heart's core and wondering at the great cruelty in the world. Her taste of it had been bitter, but not as bitter as Graciela's.

Marco stood by the *acequia* now with Emilio. He didn't carry the pouch, but he didn't look at peace or relieved.

She jumped right in. "Did you pay Señor Diaz?"

"I did. He is feverish, but the wound seems to be healing. No red streaks." He leaned toward her to create their own private moment in a busy hacienda plaza where a farrier bent over a horse's raised hoof, and the stone grinder rumbled as a small boy fed corn into it. The wind had picked up, setting ristras of chilis chattering as they hung by the kitchen garden.

"Check on him, will you?" Marco said. "He thinks he will be well enough to travel tomorrow, but I told him that was crazy." He gave a little laugh. "I took away his leather trousers. "He's not going anywhere."

"Did you—"

"Apologize? *Por su puesto que sí.* He just shrugged. You are right, my love: there hasn't been much kindness in his life." He patted her shoulder. "Toshua and I are going to the Calderóns again, to see if they might feel safer here, and offer our hospitality."

"Just the two of you?" Paloma couldn't help her alarm.

"You think we would take *one* guard from this place?" he asked, faintly amused. "Paloma, sometimes you are a goose."

She couldn't help the tears in her eyes, which made him look at her in a husbandly kind of way that told her without words not to fret. "Two is better than many, at times. This is one of those times." He made a small sign of the cross on her forehead, and another on her belly, gave her a pat and strolled to the horse barn, where Toshua was already waiting.

She was weeding around the peppers when Graciela, dressed and smelling faintly of lavender, knelt beside her and started weeding, too. "Mama had a small garden in the garrison, before Papa left us," she said, her eyes on the hanging peppers. "She had another one in the Cloud Land, but The People trampled it with their horses."

"They won't trample this one," Paloma said. She stood up and dusted off her fingers on her apron. "Finish this row for me, then please come inside. I will tell you about my children."

THEY SPENT A QUIET afternoon in the *sala*. It was a room not used as often in the summer as the kitchen, but it provided a quiet place for conversation. Paloma sat Claudio close to her on the floor as they sorted pinto beans from speckled Anasazi beans. Soledad joined him and sat with her ankles carefully crossed and her dress tidy, like her mother. Shy at first, Graciela joined them, and they all sorted beans. When the children lost interest and retreated to the other side of the room where a stack of colored blocks beckoned, Paloma quietly told Graciela her own story.

"My dear husband insisted on hanging those sandals over there to remind him that I was brave when I didn't have to be." She pointed to the two crossed brands, one the Double Cross, with its elaborate M and two crosses, and the equally grand star and V for *vega*, or meadow. "That is my family's brand, Star in the Meadow." Paloma ran the beans through her hands. "It's a story for another time." Paloma got to her feet and picked up the bowls of sorted beans. "Stay here and play with them. Get to know my darlings."

Leaving the beans in the kitchen with Perla, she went down the corridor to the room across from her room. She knocked, wasn't sure if she heard a muffled acknowledgment, and went inside anyway.

The smell of the man struck her first, so she left the door open, the better to air out the room. He still lay with his back to her. "Diego? Señor Diaz? I am Señora Mondragón."

"Just Diego," he said finally. "And really, you do not need to be in here. In fact, I am strong enough now to go to the horse barn maybe. Anywhere but your hacienda."

"Don't be absurd," she told him. "When you feel better tomorrow, I will have one of the men help you to the bathhouse. You can wash, and someone will cut your hair and trim your beard. We have new clothes and—"

"I don't need to be a bother!" he said with more force. He tried to move, and only groaned.

I don't care what you think you are, Paloma said to herself. *Mostly you are stubborn.* She put her hand lightly on the tight skin around his wound, stitched now with black thread. His skin was hot to the touch, so she felt his forehead, relieved to find it cooler.

"Are you in pain?" she asked. He said nothing. "Of course you are. I am going to give you some of these sleeping powders. When you wake up, you may eat. More broth?"

"Food this time, *dama*," he said. "How will I ever get better if I only drink broth?"

"A wise consideration," she said. "Here now. Let me help you sit up."

He couldn't move quickly, so she helped him. He started to protest, but she ignored him. The shadows in the room made him difficult to see, but she couldn't overlook his abundant beard and long hair, a sign of the rough men who bartered and bargained with Indians, often on the fringe of settlement.

"There now. Please sleep," she said, after she made him drink the sleeping powders. "I'll promise you my special *posole* and tortillas when you wake."

"Thank you," he whispered, as she helped him lie down. His eyes opened briefly, then closed. "Sorry to be trouble."

"You are no trouble, Se … Diego. Thank you for bringing me horses so I can take my children around in a little carriage. And thank you for Graciela."

"I didn't have anything to do with …."

That was all; he slept. Paloma watched him a moment, then left the room as quietly as she had entered it. She heard familiar voices in the courtyard now and sighed with relief. Her husband and Toshua were back.

* * *

THE MOON HAD RISEN by the time he woke up. Señora Mondragón must have opened the shuttered window—maybe to air out the room of his stink—because he could see out through the bars to moonrise. Someone was playing a guitar in the courtyard, or maybe the servants' quarters. The fragrance of piñon fires was nothing new to him, except that this was no camp in the middle of nowhere. He was in a home where people cared about one another. No one had told him that, but the evidence was all around.

Carefully he eased himself onto his back, ready to grimace with pain and stiffen. Nothing. He straightened out, stretching his legs. He no longer needed that defensive posture, the one that wounded animals and people assumed when in pain. His shoulder throbbed, but the sharpest ache was gone. He knew he was healing. Something about this home reminded him of his own home years ago, so many years that they had all run together into a jumble of good memories and harsh ones.

He needed to piss but he was unwilling to ask for help. Diego put out one leg from the sheets—sheets, imagine!—and then the other and stood slowly. Keeping his back straight, because he wasn't sure what his wound would do, he knelt down and felt under the bed until he found the pot. Relief was immediate. He pushed the pot back when he finished, and sat on the edge of the bed.

He wore a nightgown, something so alien that he nearly laughed. It was probably the property of that tall, long-nosed, high-cheeked Señor Mondragón, the same man who had come to him earlier, left a pouch of money on the table by the window and apologized for being an ass. He sounded sincere, but who could tell?

Diego's stomach rumbled. "I could eat lizards and snakes right now," he said, even though the kitchen smells suggested something far better. Snakes, horned toads, a skunk even, had served him well before. He had learned a long time ago that anything which crawled or moved could provide some sort of meat to keep a man alive. As long as he could choke it down, he would live another day.

As he sat there, contemplating his next move, Diego heard a man's footsteps. A door opened and stayed open. Diego leaned forward until he could see a sliver of a room, probably a child's because he thought he saw a crib. No, one crib and a little bed beyond it. He saw Señora Mondragón holding a small child, a boy because his dark hair was cut short. Señor Mondragón crossed in front of her. He carried another child and sat down on the floor, leaning his head against the bed where his wife sat.

Diego wished they had closed the door. The scene was private and intimate, and he had no business staring like a starving man at the nearly forgotten sight of a family preparing little ones for bed. God help him, but he couldn't look away.

La Señora started to hum. The tune was familiar to him, but he had not heard a lullaby in years. He listened, a smile on his face. What *was* that tune? And then she started to sing, and that made all the difference.

He knew the song, and he knew the words, a curious little dialect of the Canary Islands. He sucked in his breath and wiped his forehead, where sweat had suddenly popped out. His hand started to shake. "Keep singing," he whispered. "Oh, please."

It was a pleasant little lullaby. " 'Papa comes soon, from over the sea, home with a king's ransom for thee, only thee.' "

She didn't seem to know the words that followed, so she hummed them. Diego whispered, " 'He'll be here for thy saint's day, my child, my dear.' "

She knew the chorus. " 'Sleep, sleep, fear nothing, my dear. The saints are around us this day, this year.' " He sang softly along with her.

He went to the door of his room, unmindful of his bare legs. He leaned against the doorframe and took a very good look at Señora Mondragón. He had been in too much pain before, and then too embarrassed at his disheveled, odoriferous state to really look at her. He did so now, noticing her profile, as she sat holding her son. Her hair was smooth and brown. When she laughed, he knew the laugh. It was so close to his mother's. So was the profile.

Diego put his hand to his mouth to stop the sob that rose in his throat. A woman in Texas had sung that lullaby, learned from her mother who was from the Canary Islands. Mama had sung it to his little sister in their hacienda, close to El Paso del Norte. No wonder Señora Mondragón couldn't really remember the words. His mama had sung the lullaby to him, then to his younger brother Rafael, and then to Paloma, the one he knew had to be dead, killed in a Comanche raid.

Diego took a deep breath and another. He moved quietly across the hall, shaky on his feet, but moving now by some force of will that went beyond pain or suffering or any emotion he had ever known. He stood in the doorway of the children's room and opened the door wider.

Señor Mondragón got to his feet immediately and thrust his daughter behind him, the protector of his wife and children, but Diego had eyes only for the woman. She looked at him, puzzled but not fearful or defensive like her husband. Yes, her eyes were as blue as his, the eyes of their father. She was a woman grown now, and not a skinny little sister, but he knew her.

"Paloma Vega," he whispered. "See me truly."

She did as he said, looking beyond the beard and the long greasy hair, and the scar on his cheek. She swallowed and her face paled. Slowly she set her little boy beside her.

"Those words of the lullaby you didn't know," he said, as tears started down his cheeks. He sang softly, " 'He'll be here for thy saint's day, my child, my dear.' "

"Claudio? Claudio?" she asked, her voice high and strangled. Her eyes rolled back in her ashen face and she fainted, falling sideways as her husband grabbed her, his face equally pale.

"Who … who …."

He was too old for his voice to crack, but it did, anyway. "Señor Mondragón, I am Claudio Vega. I did not die."

Chapter Thirteen

In which there is another Star in the Meadow

Paloma regained consciousness with her head in her husband's lap, her children in tears, and the horse trader on the floor beside her, his head resting against her knees. She blinked, wondering for only a second what had just happened. Hesitantly, she put her hand out and rested it on that shaggy head. Washed, she knew his hair would be the same color as hers. She kissed her husband's cheek, then leaned forward and kissed the scraggly hair on the top of her brother's head. Her eyes closed as she rested her cheek where she had kissed.

"This isn't possible." She knew the words sounded perfectly clear. What came out of her mouth was that Canary Islands dialect, a language she had thrust from her mind after that horrible day when everyone died except her.

"But here we are," her brother said, in the same dialect, his voice weary with the exhaustion of his wound, but triumphant in a way that suggested he might not be a man easily discouraged. They had both been through so much. Too bad they had not been through it together.

He switched to Spanish, which banished the puzzled expression on Marco's face. Paloma sat up carefully, still dizzy, and took a squalling baby from her husband, who also clutched Soledad.

She held out her son to her brother. "We named him after you, Claudio."

"Thank you," he said, and managed a grin. "He's noisy."

"Told you he was your namesake," she joked back, eager to tease this man she'd believed dead.

She could tell he was functioning on his last bit of strength. Marco saw it, too. He set their tearful daughter close to Paloma and carefully helped Claudio from the floor where he knelt.

"You are going back to bed, Claudio," Marco said, in his *juez de campo* voice, the one no one disputed.

"But—"

"Paloma and I will get our little brood calmed down and sleeping. Let me help you across the hall. Now, now! We will join you when the children are asleep."

Claudio looked at her, mutiny in his eyes, but without the strength to do anything about it.

"I always do what Marco says, when he sounds like that," Paloma told him.

"Since when, my love?" Marco teased.

Claudio looked from one to the other. The tears welling in his eyes rolled down his dirty cheeks, leaving tracks. "Paloma, you're happy, aren't you?"

She nodded, and felt her own tears. "Never happier," she wailed, which set off little Claudio again.

"So am I," Marco told her brother. He took a more careful hold on Claudio, his arm around the man's waist.

"I still stink," he said.

"I don't care. I think your little sister will let us borrow her private bathhouse tomorrow. Whether you like it or not, the hair and beard are going away."

"I'd like that," Claudio said in a soft voice.

Paloma held little Claudio close to her in one arm, and Soledad in the other. She watched her husband and brother slowly cross the hall. Even from that distance, she saw the relief on Claudio's face when he lay down again.

Sancha peeked into the room, eyes wide and fearful, with Graciela behind her. Paloma motioned them in and explained what had just happened. The story sounded strange, even to her ears. She knew Claudio was dead, but here he was. *God is good*, she thought, hoping with every fiber of her being that her long-dead parents were somehow granted a glimpse of their son and daughter in each other's arms again, after a long and terrible time.

"Shh, shh, little one," she crooned to Claudito. In a few moments his tears stopped. He rubbed his eyes and cuddled close, still upset at this sudden turmoil in his orderly world.

Soledad burrowed close, too, but soon she tugged on her eyelashes. In another moment, she felt heavy against Paloma's belly. A finger to her lips, Sancha picked up Soli and carried her to her bed. The housekeeper commandeered Claudio next. His protest ended in a yawn, and then he slept. Paloma closed the door and darted across the hall.

Marco had found two more pillows to prop up Claudio, whose face—seen through his tangle of beard—appeared drained of all color. Whether they could blame the wound or the shock of their reunion she couldn't say, but she would have wagered her own skin was just as pale.

Weakly, Claudio patted the bed and Paloma made herself comfortable there. Marco pulled up a stool. The three of them just stared at one another, until Marco began to smile.

"It was the song?" he asked, tears filling his eyes again. "Paloma, you don't even sing that lullaby very much. What if you hadn't sung it tonight?"

She crossed herself, not wanting to contemplate the idea of them going their separate ways, unknown to each other. It could have happened so easily, because of Claudio's shame at his repugnant odor and dishevelment, and his desire to be anywhere but in the house of gentle folk. *You could have left in a few days, and I never would have known*, she thought, aghast at the idea. She reached out to touch his feet.

"Would we have known each other?" she asked finally.

"Hard to say," Claudio said after his own long silence. "You were a skinny little girl of eleven."

"I knew you were dead," she began, desperate for his story but aware of his exhaustion. "I *knew* it! How did this happen? I mean, after … after it all ended—a day after, because Mama pushed me under the bed and told me not to move—I went to the edge of the field, and there you were. I remember your cloak, red and black striped, that Mama wove."

He shook his head. "The man you saw was Jesús Perez. Remember the morning? It was cool out. He was shivering, and I threw my cloak over his shoulders."

She did remember, remembered how she stuffed her hand in her mouth and bit down so she would not cry out to see her father sliced open with his insides outside. And there was little Rafael lying next to him, eyes wide and staring, reaching for Papa, his fingers making deep troughs in the soft ground, his scalp gone.

"I looked for you, saw the cloak, and had my answer," she whispered. "I was too afraid to stay there."

Marco was too far away. All it took was one glance, and he climbed on the bed, too, holding her between his upraised knees, his arms tight around her.

"How did you alone survive?" she asked her brother. "It was God's mercy."

He shook his head slowly. "God wasn't anywhere near us that morning."

Paloma leaned toward Claudio, taking comfort from Marco's arms around her. "He was closer than we knew," she whispered. "We're still alive."

He gave her a skeptical look, then sighed and leaned back carefully, turning slightly to protect his wounded shoulder. "It was an ordinary, everyday morning," he began. "And then—how do Comanches do that?—they came from nowhere and we were surrounded. No sound. One moment they weren't there, and the next moment they were riding alongside us, not even in a hurry, just biding their time, because they knew they had us."

Paloma shivered. "It was that way at the house. I was in Mama's room, and the next thing I knew, she was pushing me under her bed, as quiet and calm as you please. They came into the house on horseback."

He reached for her hand, suddenly much younger, as though telling this terrible story had thrust him back through years of blood, sorrow, and opportunities unfulfilled. "Our parents did the best they could, Paloma," he said. "When the attack started, Papa pushed me off my horse, which took fright, reared, and fell down."

Claudio passed a shaking hand in front of his face, and he had started to sweat. Marco got up, dipped a cloth in water, and handed it to Paloma, who gently wiped the greasy sheen from his forehead and upper lip.

"The last thing Papa did was whisper to me, 'Crawl under. Hold still.' He had used his own lance to stab my horse dead, and it poured blood over me." Claudio shook his head, disbelief in his eyes. "Now he had no weapon for himself, but he saved my life. I did as he said and lay still."

"Papa would do that," Paloma said through her tears.

"I heard everything going on around me, horses and people screaming, the Comanches singing. Did … did you see Papa?"

Paloma nodded, unable to speak.

"I'm sorry. Rafael, too?"

"I didn't go into the field. I was too afraid," she said.

"I'm glad you didn't, little sister," Claudio said. "Whe … when it was quiet, I heard the raiders ripping off sca …."

"No, Claudio," Marco said firmly. "We know."

Claudio looked at Paloma. "I couldn't do anything, Sister, you can see that, can't you?"

"More clearly than you can imagine," she said. "If you had done anything, that would have been one more death that Papa didn't want. Did they leave then?"

"I'm not certain. I could feel the hoof beats of many horses around me, and then there were fewer. They were probably heading toward the hacienda."

Paloma nodded.

"The rest remained in the field, going from horse to horse, taking off saddles and bridles." Claudio's eyes were twin pools of terror now, as he remembered. "I had managed to dig myself a little breathing hole under my horse. "I held my breath and went completely limp."

He stopped, closed his eyes, and let the tears fall. Paloma wiped his face again, crooning to him as she would to comfort her brother's little namesake.

Marco got off the bed again to find and pour a small glass of the *aguardiente* they saved for special occasions and toothache. To Paloma's surprise—Marco never drank—he knocked back a glass first, shook his head in surprise at its strength, then poured another one for Claudio.

Claudio swallowed and sighed with relief. Paloma wondered how many nights he needed just such a restorative. "A raider yanked off my horse's saddle, and then I could just feel him standing there, staring down at my legs and torso." He reached for her hand this time. "Paloma, I wanted to scream and scream and never stop, but I just held my breath."

She let her breath out slowly, realizing she had been holding it, too.

"*O Dios*, he stuck his lance in my side! Pinned me right to the ground, then put his foot on my back to pull it out."

Paloma burst into tears. Marco put his hand on her neck and pulled her even closer. Perhaps driven by instinct, he put his hand on her belly to protect their unborn child from the ferocity of this story. He held her close and then reached out and held Claudio to them both.

"I know I jerked as he pulled it out. I couldn't help myself!" Claudio said when he could speak. "All I can imagine is that the Indian thought he was causing the movement with his lance." He let out his breath in a whoosh. "Then I was alone in the field. They left as suddenly as they came."

"That's the way of The People," Marco said. "I am amazed that any of us are alive in Comanchería. You just stayed there, didn't you? But you were bleeding."

"I packed my side with dirt. Didn't know what else to do. It caused a terrible infection later. Not sure how I survived that, either." Claudio separated himself from their embrace. He touched Paloma's cheek, flicking at the tears on her face. "I could see the hacienda in the distance, on fire. I saw servants running from the burning building." He closed his eyes tight. "Oh, what they did to the servants!"

"I saw them later," Paloma said. She glanced at Marco. "You can ask my husband. Sometimes, even now … nightmares." She gave her husband a long look, almost as if seeing him for the first time. "He lets me know I am not alone."

"You just stayed under the bed, Little Sister? Even when they fired the house?"

Paloma nodded. "I obeyed Mama."

"It burned down! I watched it!"

Paloma turned her face into Marco's shirt, her anguish so real, thinking now that Claudio might have been watching. *This is one of those things that does not bear thinking about*, she told herself. *He was so close, but I did not know it.* She pressed her face into Marco's shirt, breathing deep of his particular fragrance. If anything had happened differently, she would not have met this dear man who was the whole world to her now. She also knew she could never admit as much to Claudio.

"It didn't burn down completely. The *vigas* fell just so onto the bed when the ceiling collapsed, and then it began to rain, if you remember. Those beams kept the ceiling from caving in on the bed."

He nodded. "So you stayed there another day?"

"I did. I crawled out …." She took a deep breath, and another, as Marco's hand tightened on her belly. "I saw Mama. Oh, Claudio!"

"Don't think of it," Marco whispered to her. "Your mother was not suffering then. It was all over by the time you saw her mortal clay."

"I know, my love," Paloma said. She put her hand over his. "Claudio, I couldn't find a shovel to bury her and her little one." Hot tears fell on her hand again. "I found a spoon and I dug and dug until I could at least cover them with a layer of dirt."

She felt Marco shake. "You never told me that," he whispered.

"It's too hard to even think about," she said quietly.

"I never saw the dirt, or I swear before all the saints I would have searched for you," Claudio said.

"How could you have known?" she said sensibly. "You probably thought the raiders had carried me off."

"I did. You were only eleven, a useful age for a slave like… like…." Claudio looked at the door, where Graciela crouched, listening. "Like her."

"Where did you go?" Paloma asked, wanting other images to chase away the one of her mother, violated and disfigured, and still clutching the unborn baby ripped from her body.

Claudio did not hesitate to continue his narrative. He must not have wanted that image in his mind, either. "When I could stand upright, I started walking to the Borregos' *estancia*. I thought west was safer than east. What a fool I was!" he said bitterly. "It was burned, too, and full of death. I ended up crawling then. I fell into an empty *acequia*. That is where the horse traders found me a day later."

He lay back, exhausted. "The rest of my story will keep for another day. What about you, Sister?"

"I started walking south toward El Paso, but there were soldiers coming by then, and I didn't have to walk far," she said. "They took me to the Franciscans, and a few months later I was in Santa Fe with our uncle, Felix Moreno."

"That's a relief," he said.

No, it wasn't, she thought, *but you don't have to know any more now*. "My story will keep, too," Paloma told him. "You need to sleep."

"After this?" he asked, "How can I?" Even as he spoke, his eyes closed.

She touched his cheek, eager to see him with the beard gone and hair trimmed. She wondered if she would find the brother she remembered under all the layers of dirt and time and sad experience.

"He was teaching me to dance," she told Marco, as they stood close to the bed, looking down at her sleeping brother. "He was sixteen, and Papa and Señor Borrego were already talking about a wedding to unite the two *estancias*." She crossed herself. "Rosamaria Borrego was never seen again." She grabbed Marco's shirt, pulling him closer. "Husband, why do we live in this place that the King of Spain doesn't even care about?"

He wrapped her in a fierce embrace. "I am here because this land is bone of my bone and flesh of my flesh, as much as you are! If I could not watch the sun rise each morning to the east," he shook his head, "I don't know what I would do. You still love me, don't you?"

Silly man.

After checking on their sleeping children, Paloma sent Graciela to bed on her pallet in the alcove of the children's room, a neat area curtained off and private, a small place of her own. When she returned to her bedchamber, Marco was kneeling on the *reclinatorio*, his eyes closed in prayer. She came up behind him, leaned against him, and put her hands on his bowed head, giving him her own loving benediction. He relaxed, and she felt the tension leave his body.

In bed, they burrowed close together, Paloma grateful for his arms around her.

"I'll never sleep tonight," she declared.

He laughed softly. "Yes, you will."

"How do we bear this?" she asked, desperate to know.

"The same way I bore the death of Felicia and the twins, and the way you bore your own torment in the household of your uncle in Santa Fe." He'd replied promptly, which told her that Marco Mondragón—widowed and sad, then happy again—had given the matter considerable thought throughout the years. "We finally have no choice but to leave it in the hands of God. If we keep struggling, we become bitter. If we resign ourselves to His gracious will, life goes on."

"Which way has Claudio chosen?"

"Time will tell."

Chapter Fourteen

In which soap and water begin the cure

PALOMA WOKE UP HOURS later, not certain what had roused her. She listened for the children, but heard nothing. She moved slowly out of Marco's slack embrace and sat on the edge of their bed.

Before she stood up, her husband tugged at her nightgown. "Where are you going?" he asked.

"I just want to see him," she whispered.

He rested his hand on her back, then gave her a little push. "Go, then." He gave a low laugh. "I'm surprised you waited this long."

Paloma blew him a kiss and tiptoed into the hall. She peeked into Claudio's room, blinking in the low light. The bed was empty. She stood briefly in shocked surprise, wondering if she had imagined the whole experience.

She looked into the hall. There he stood, looking back at her, but leaning heavily on the carved chest from Spain. The way he stood, hunched over and stooped, reminded her of a predatory bird. She put her hand to her throat.

"You gave me quite a start, Claudio," she whispered.

"I heard someone," he whispered back. "Thought I saw him. Not a tall man. I think it is that Comanche."

"Toshua," she said. "I wouldn't doubt it." She crossed the hall and took Claudio by the arm. "We're never quite sure how he does it, but he walks these halls at night, especially if he is uneasy."

"You're not afraid that he will murder us all?"

"I used to be," she said honestly. "He terrified me. I kept saving his life, though, and he would never harm me now. Back to bed, Claudio?"

He shook his head. "I dream when I sleep. Always."

"I can give you another sleeping draught."

"No. I'd rather just sit somewhere and stare at you."

And I, you, Paloma thought. Silently, she draped his good arm over her shoulders and led him into the *sala.* She sat him down on the most comfortable bench, the one with the mohair blanket and pillow where Marco liked to rest, if ever he found a free moment. That was a rare event, indeed, with two little ones always eager to sit on him and demand stories or songs.

She heard Claudio's sigh of relief, and knew she should have just marched him back to bed. But he was still her big brother, and she would continue to defer to him.

"There now. Let me show you something."

She built a fire first. Soon the soothing fragrance of *piñon* made the weirdness of the time and circumstances seem almost normal, just another day. She lifted her old, bloodstained sandals from their nail on the wall, and took the Vega's Star in the Meadow brand down, too. She pulled up a stool to the bench where Claudio lay watching her.

He listened, eyes partly open, as she told him of her life in Tio Felix's horrible household, and how Marco Mondragón, a widower, had arrived, paid a king's ransom for a yellow dog to keep his feet warm in bed, and changed her life forever.

"The dog kept running back to me. I had to return that silly yellow dog, don't you see," she said, and laughed softly when he smiled for the first time. "Maybe I was a little bit in love. Oh, bother it, I was a lot in love!"

That was enough confession to a big brother. He didn't need to know how haltingly she had confessed to Father Eusebio that for the first time in her life she was guilty of lust. Claudio only had to watch them together for a few days to understand this greatest gift of her life.

"So you were going to follow the *juez* to Valle del Sol with that dog?" he asked, after she told him that portion of her story. "Paloma, I don't know whether to laugh or cry."

He looked as though he wanted to cry, maybe thinking of all the years she spent defenseless and on her own, making what sense she could of the bleak hand dealt her.

She thought she saw his sorrow. "Never mind, my dear brother," she said. "You would have protected me, if you could."

With the strangest amalgam of bitter and sweet, Paloma felt the years drop away until they were Little Sister and Big Brother again, sharing a mundane moment, as they had done so often on the Vega ranch. Rafael had been dear to her heart, too, but somehow Claudio had always considered her his special responsibility.

She set aside the sandals and held out the heavy brand, balancing it between them. Claudio traced the intricate lines of the star and V, his eyes filled with tears. "How in the world …."

She told him of their journey into the heart of Comanchería to inoculate The People against the ravages of smallpox, all in exchange for a devil's bargain from a mysterious doctor. "Marco found this in a cave where some Comanche raiding party had left it, probably planning to return later." She touched the shaft of the brand. "It's all that remains of our land and cattle. I think our uncle disposed of our land, but I have no way to prove anything. There is nothing left of that life, dearest."

"I suppose not," he agreed, but he didn't sound any more convinced than she felt. When had the great deception stopped bothering her? Sitting there in the semi-darkness with a man she had thought never to see again, she only knew that the cruelty of Indians and her uncle alike did not touch her heart anymore.

Claudio started in surprise and struggled to sit up, which made him groan. He stared at the open door as she gently pushed him back against the softness of mohair. Paloma turned around to see Toshua.

"Little sister, are you well?" Toshua asked.

"I am," she said. "Thank you for watching us. Have you and the guards seen any sign of Great Owl?"

"He is gone on his way to trouble others. I would speak with Marco when he is awake."

"I will tell him."

Toshua stood in silence another moment, then left as quietly as he had come.

"He calls you 'little sister,' too," Claudio said, and he did not sound happy about it. "After what happened to our parents, our brother, what have you turned into? Do I *know* you?"

His words might have stung, if spoken years ago, but not now. Her time of struggle, of learning to cope with The People so visible in her life now, had vanished like smoke. What had ruined her childhood had no hold on her womanhood now. What would Claudio understand?

"In your travels, have you seen a flower growing through a crack in a rock?" she said. "There's no reason why it should, but it does."

"I don't understand. Each year, the struggle grows harder." He took a deep breath. "I looked for you in every Indian village from here to Luisiana and then I gave up, because it hurt too much to keep trying. I don't know how I feel about anything now."

"You will come to understand. I've turned into a wife and mother and friend," she told him. She couldn't help the catch in her throat. "And now a sister again! What was hard is now soft. We have both walked down dark halls, but different ones." She put her hand on him, then leaned forward and rested her head on his chest. His good arm went around her, after a hesitation that brought tears to her eyes. He didn't trust her yet; she wondered if he ever would.

"I fear your story has not reached a happy moment yet, my dear brother," she whispered. "Stay with us and I know it will."

"Easy to say, Palomita," he said and she heard the strain in his voice. "We have both been used hard and lost so much."

"I know. I know. Can we leave it in God's hands for a while?"

"That One who didn't care what happened to us?"

Poor man. Paloma sat up. "Yes, that One," she told him. "You can probably say what you want about Him, and He'll understand. Try it for a while." She kissed his bearded, dirty cheek. "I'll sit here while you sleep, Claudio. Claudio?"

She set the heavy brand on the floor, ready to watch all night, protecting her brother from demons she could not see.

*   *   *

CLAUDIO WOKE IN THE morning to the sight of Marco Mondragón slumbering where Paloma had sat last night, his head forward on his chest. He lounged there at ease in a nightshirt that had seen better days, his legs hairy and bare. He needed a shave, but he was a handsome man with a capable look, even in slumber.

He must have known Claudio was staring at him, because Marco opened his eyes. He didn't say anything, but sat there with an air of morning stupefaction, combined with a curious confidence that made Claudio smile a little. Marco looked like the kind of man who might be getting a little soft around the edges because he had a wife who took care of him—a man who didn't mind that a bit.

"Where did you put my sister?" Claudio asked. He didn't mean to sound so sharp. What was going on in his mind?

"She's back in my bed," Marco replied. "She needs her rest. Are you comfortable enough?"

He was, actually. The lingering odors of piñon had been replaced by kitchen smells far superior to anything concocted out of doors in the harsh life he was used to, traveling from settlement to settlement, or tribe to tribe. It struck Claudio that he hadn't been inside a house of any substance since the Vega *estancia* near El Paso, his own home.

His shoulder throbbed, but the edge of pain was gone. He wanted eggs and chorizo and then a long, long soak in a hot tub: two luxuries that until yesterday seemed so remote as to belong on Mars. Both were nearly in reach right now, and it warmed his heart, even as it confused him.

Claudio lay there, arms crossed on his chest, as a curly-headed boy wearing a much smaller nightshirt peeked into the *sala*, his eyes wide.

Marco held out his hand. "Claudito, we may have to call you something else, because this man you see is also Claudio."

"My name?" The little one settled himself into his father's lap.

"Your name. This man is Mama's brother."

The boy turned his face into Marco's chest, suddenly shy.

"Hungry?" Marco asked Claudio. "I am. Let me help you into the kitchen." He stood up, his son in his arms. He gave the child a gentle swat on his hinder parts, set him down and sent him on sturdy legs down the hall. "Go get in bed with Mama, but don't wake her."

Marco watched him go, and Claudio saw all the fondness on his brother-in-law's face. "Used to be Paloma and I could stay in bed until the sun was up. That was before children."

Marco looked down at his own bare legs. "I'll help you into the kitchen after I get on some clothes. Sancha has standards."

To Claudio's amusement, the *juez de campo*, a man of power and influence, scratched himself in a place that might make Paloma roll her eyes. He slapped the top of the door frame and ambled down the hall, returning soon enough in leathers, a cotton shirt, and moccasins. A robe was draped over his arm.

"Stand up. I'll help you into one sleeve and pull the other over your shoulder."

"Will I meet standards?" Claudio teased. This crazy place where Paloma lived was working some magic on him.

"I think so. Sancha has a soft heart for a hungry man."

"I still stink," Claudio said, without any embarrassment this time.

"Not for much longer."

"I'll need some help with my bath. Do you have a servant who won't mind?"

"I'll help," Marco said. "I still owe some penance for being an ass."

"Oh, no, I—"

"Now *you're* being an ass! Be careful, or Paloma will wash her hands of both of us."

Marco said it in such a straightforward way that Claudio knew he would be foolish to take offence against his brother-in-law. He let the man help him into the robe, struck to his heart's core that in less than twelve hours, he had acquired a sister, a brother-in-law, and a niece and nephew. He couldn't help his sudden sob that seemed to come out of nowhere, leaving him ashamed of his weakness. *Please, don't think I am a weak man, Juez*, he thought.

Marco, all kindness, seemed to know what to do. "I don't mean to hurt you," he said, glossing over Claudio's sudden emotion and blaming it on pain instead of anguish of a different sort. "I'm not much good with hair, either. Paloma usually cuts mine. Thank you, Sancha." Marco reached for the cornmeal porridge with its green chilis that Sancha handed him, and picked up his spoon. "Just set that in front of Claudio. He can manage. Claudio, this is Sancha Villareal, my housekeeper. Sancha, Our Father has blessed Paloma with a brother again. Thanks be to God."

That was it: no fanfare, no emotion, just a simple, calm acceptance of his presence that allowed Claudio no chance to feel strange or set apart like some nine-day wonder. He could feel the Double Cross opening its generous arms to enfold him.

Claudio ate slowly, savoring the corn pudding and chilis, seasoned with a sprinkle of cinnamon and sugar, just the way Mama used to make it. Without even trying, he could see Paloma's fine hand in the kitchen of Marco Mondragón. He looked around at order and neatness, then back at the man who ate beside him.

"I'm tired," Claudio said simply, but it was exhaustion of an inward sort, the kind that ground a man down until he didn't care anymore.

"I know," Marco said just as quietly. "I've had that feeling."

Claudio finished breakfast in silence, unwilling to let down his guard, not after years of fear and overwork, but unable to resist the great kindness of the man beside him. He made no objection when Marco put his arm carefully around his waist, pulled him to his feet, and walked him through the kitchen garden and into a shed where a trough of water waited for him. *O Dios*, there was even hot water.

Marco pulled off the nightshirt and helped Claudio into the water. "Too hot?" he asked.

Dazed now, unused to help, overwhelmed, Claudio shook his head. He sank down slowly, careful to keep his wounded shoulder out of the water. To his embarrassment, he just sat there and stared like an idiot.

"I can take care of myself," he managed to say.

"I doubt it," Marco replied.

Out of the corner of his eye he saw Marco remove his own shirt and leathers. He rolled up his underdrawers and soaped a washcloth.

"If I get my clothes wet, Paloma will scold me," he explained, as he began to wash Claudio's chest. "I like to keep her happy."

Claudio sat there like a wooden figure while his sister's husband told his own story, how his first wife and twin sons had died in a cholera epidemic while he was away on a brand inspection trip.

"I'll admit now that I was on my way to ruin. After eight dreadful years, each one worse than the one before, I met your sister. She had been used pretty hard by your uncle. Not the way Graciela was used, but cheated from your land and cattle and made to work too hard by people who should have loved her." He shook his head. "She's so short."

"I noticed. My … our parents were both tall."

"I think the Morenos deprived her of food right when she most needed it to grow," Marco said, and Claudio heard the anger in his voice. He even scoured Claudio's skin with more fervor, until he noticed he was hurting him. "Sorry!"

"I'm surprised such treatment didn't stunt more than her growth," Claudio said.

"Something burns inside Paloma," Marco told him, after long thought. "I take no credit for it. There is some passion, some purpose that kept her whole and kind, so kind, even to her cousin—your cousin—Maria Teresa Castellano, the real mother of our Soledad. Teresa was so cruel to Paloma."

Claudio saw his brother-in-law's embarrassment, and knew he was not a man to speak frankly of such personal things. *You must know I need to hear this*, Claudio thought, and it humbled him.

"Paloma told me last night that Soledad is actually our cousin."

"Soli is, but you will never know that, if you choose to compare how Paloma treats her little cousin and our own child," Marco said. Claudio heard all the fervor and love in his brother-in-law's voice. "To us, Soledad is our daughter, as surely as if we made her ourselves. That will never change."

"Have you any idea how lucky you are, Señor—"

"Marco, only Marco. I know full well how lucky I am."

For one irrational moment, Claudio hated the man who was helping him. Why should Marco Mondragón's life have been so easy? He repented immediately, thinking of Marco's losses. He sat there, dazed by his own unkindness, in water getting dirtier by the minute as years of grime came away. He could blame the rough men who saved his life and then exacted their own tolls, or he could look to his own sins.

"Paloma turned me into a good man again, before I was ruined forever," Marco said, his eyes on the washcloth. "My God, but I love her." Apparently it was Marco's turn for a self-conscious laugh. "Hold up your arm."

Marco told Claudio next about his neighbors and the stupid soldiers in the garrison at Santa Maria. Keeping up a steady conversation, he continued to scrub away years of grease and grime, while Claudio just sat there. As he slowly regained control of himself, Claudio wondered if his brother-in-law had the slightest idea what else was washing away, too. Of course he knew, Claudio decided. The *juez* was nobody's fool. Before Marco finished a third washing of his hair and beard, Claudio was smiling.

"Let me help you up," Marco said. "One more good soaping and then I'll pour clean water over you, because the stuff you're sitting in would make Paloma gag."

Claudio nodded. "She was always particular about herself and her clothes. You would think that with two brothers she might have tried to be a boy and compete with us, but not Paloma."

"No. She's very much a woman," Marco said. "You should have heard her when she found a mouse in the kitchen last winter! I swear she climbed right up my back."

They laughed together. Marco poured cold water over Claudio, which left him gasping, then opened the spigot in the bottom of the tub. "See here?" He pointed to a smaller trough to take away the used water. "It drains into the kitchen garden. Paloma's idea."

Marco dried himself and dressed, then tossed a dry towel to Claudio. "Put it around your waist. I'll get some clothes for you, and then I'll turn the women loose on your hair."

After Marco left, Claudio sat down on the stool. He held out one leg and then the other, pleased to see them clean. His beard still itched, but he knew that any lice still alive after Marco's ruthless application of tarry soap would soon meet their fate. He imagined that his little sister had a fine tooth comb she knew how to use.

Claudio stared at the wall, wondering if a man, perhaps him, with no hope and no prospect of anything except overwork and ill-use, could change into something else overnight. He had no intention of giving God any of the credit, so he was left to wonder at the possibility.

Marco returned with wool pants and a cotton shirt. He winced when Claudio winced, as the rough cloth touched his stitched wound.

"Come now, Brother, it is your turn with the ladies. I hope you are not too attached to your beard and hair almost down to your waist."

"Ruthless, are they?" Claudio closed his eyes, nearly overcome with even the hint of a joke. He took Marco by the arm. "I am not used to anyone doing anything for me. Here I sit like a bump in the road. You must think me a weak man."

"You're a tired man," Marco said as he opened the door. "I know what it is like to not care, and maybe even to wish that you could just lie down and die." He crossed himself. "Every step you take requires effort and you see only bleakness ahead." He put his arm around Claudio, still careful with his shoulder. "Am I close?"

Claudio nodded, unable to speak.

"With the horse traders, you could brawl and wench and cheat people and drift around. No one cared what happened to you. After a while, you thought you didn't care, either."

"I didn't."

"You're certain of that?" Marco asked.

"I should know myself." Claudio felt a sudden burst of anger. "What makes you so smart?"

"I have known desperation." Marco took him by both shoulders this time, but gently. "Brother, your fortunes have changed. I know it. Paloma knows it. *You* need to believe it." He startled Claudio by kissing his forehead. "That is the hardest leap of faith there is."

Chapter Fifteen

In which Soledad is puzzled by grownups

HER BROTHER WAS SITTING on a straight-backed chair in the kitchen garden, his eyes closed, his face turned up to the sun. Paloma watched him through the kitchen window, suddenly shy. She leaned back against her husband, whose arms automatically circled her. "Do I even know him?" she whispered.

"He's had a hard life, riding with rough men," Marco said. "Even then, Claudio Vega was kind to me, trusting me with horses and paying my bill at the inn."

"That is what our father would have done," she said, and knew the answer to her question. "I know him." Paloma looked at the fine-toothed comb in her hand.

"It looks sort of puny for the task ahead. Sancha, what do you think?"

Early in her marriage, on Marco's advice, she had started asking Sancha her opinion. The housekeeper had come with Felicia when she married Marco. At first Paloma had asked her advice, just to assuage any pain at seeing another take her beloved Felicia's place. Now it was a matter of habit, nurtured by the reality that Sancha did know best.

Sancha joined them at the window. "He looks better. I know he must smell better. Still, that is a lot of hair."

Sancha stood another moment, then snapped her fingers. She went into the storeroom and returned with shears—serious shears, the kind to tackle thick layers of fabric.

"Use these. Put a sheet around his neck and just ... just whack off his hair until it is shoulder length, like the hair of this man behind you. Then use that little comb. Do the same with his beard."

" 'This man behind you?' " Marco asked with a laugh. "Sancha, am I in your *libro negro*? What did I do?"

Sancha gave him a terrible stare. She jabbed a finger toward his chest. "Paloma threw up this morning. It is *your* fault."

Paloma leaned against the bad man, hoping that in some comfortable ring in paradise, Felicia could look down and nod with approval how thoroughly her own Sancha had become the champion of her husband's second wife.

"We won't blame him entirely, Sancha," Paloma said as she took the shears. "I had something to do with this turn of events, too. Could I ask you to get me an old sheet?"

Sancha left the room grumbling, and Paloma turned her face into her husband's chest and laughed quietly. "All *your* fault that my skirts won't button in a few months, and I'll be forced to set over the buttons on my bodices," she whispered. "I'll show you! I'll make you buckle my shoes for me when I don't bend so well."

They laughed together. Marco kissed the top of her head, gave her a pat on her rump and went into the garden, where Toshua stood now, eyeing her brother Claudio, who was returning stare for stare.

"Oh, dear. Claudio, you will have to learn as I learned," she said, looking through the wavy glass at the three most important men in her life. "Don't bear him a grudge, Toshua." There was no way the Comanche could have heard her, but he looked squarely in her direction. "Yes, you, Toshua."

Feeling the need for an ally and a better barber, Paloma went down the hall to her children's room, where Graciela had just finished braiding Soledad's brown hair into an intricate design.

"My dearest, you are lovely!" Paloma said, clapping her hands.

Soli twirled around, trying to look at the braids, until she fell into a giggling heap next to Claudio.

"Graciela, wonderful," Paloma said. "Is this a design from your cloudland home?"

The young woman nodded, her eyes lively with the praise.

"Could you fix mine that way sometime? I have no skills along these lines."

"I can, *dama*," Graciela said.

"Do this for me now," Paloma said. "Let us go to the kitchen garden where you will help me shear my brother's hair and beard. He is a wild man and I do not even know where to start."

"Shall we take these wild ones with us?" Graciela asked, and she held out her hand for Soledad.

"Most certainly! Come, Claudito. I have a digging spoon and you can build a ditch next to where the peas used to be."

He took her hand, skipping ahead, tugging her after him, until Soli stopped him. "Ladies walk slowly," she told her little cousin/brother. "Like this."

Paloma felt her heart grow a size or two to watch Soledad clasp her little hands together at her waist, just as she did. She thought of her cousin, Maria Teresa Castellano, and all her spite and meanness. Soledad was none of that, because she never saw it in her own young life. *I could not give you a kinder present, cousin*, Paloma thought, as tears tickled her eyes. *She is my treasure, as she might have been yours.*

Hands on his hips, her small son watched them both, walking slowly side by side. "That is not fun," he declared, and skipped ahead of Graciela, into the kitchen and out the door, banging it behind him.

Soli tugged at Paloma's skirt. "Mama, I would rather run, too."

"Then run, my love. You have years and years to become a lady," Paloma assured her.

"You see how I need your help, Graciela," Paloma told the slave as they walked into the kitchen. "They will only get livelier, while I get more awkward." She looked out the window to see little Claudio just staring at his namesake, whose face was still turned to the healing sun.

"Look at him. I wonder how long it has been since my brother just sat in the sunlight."

He opened his eyes when they came into the garden. His face was rough and weathered, and old eyes looked back at her. Somewhere under all the layers was her brother. Paloma said a prayer, the same one never far from her mind and heart since he walked into the children's room last night, singing Mama's Canary Island lullaby: *Oh, how I thank thee, Lord.*

Graciela took charge of the sheet, wrapping it around Claudio's neck and knotting it firmly. There would be no room for the most elusive louse to make a getaway. He made little strangling noises, which small Claudio imitated, staggering into the onion row and collapsing on the dried-up pea vines. In another moment he was digging around the yellowed vines. Seeing two other spoons in the row, Paloma knew it was time for a reckoning before Sancha started to wonder out loud what was happening to the family silver, and whether or not that trickster Señor Coyote was whisking them away.

"He looks just like his father."

Paloma smiled at her brother. "Then he will be a lucky man someday. Graciela, is it tight enough? I won't have my brother escaping, not after all these years."

She meant it as a joke, but her tears came anyway. Seeing them, Claudio reached for her hand and she clutched it.

"Where else would I possibly want to go?" he asked quietly. He turned her hand over and kissed it.

Soledad watched, her eyes narrowing. Paloma looked at her, wondering about her daughter's bright mind and what went through it. "What, little one?"

"Does Papa *know* about this man?"

"He does," she said seriously, as her brother laughed, "and he will not mind. Soli, Claudio is *my* brother, like little Claudio is your brother." She pointed to her son, busy creating a network of *acequias* in the bean row now. "Someday maybe Claudito will kiss your hand."

Soli made a face. "I will have to wash it."

"You might change your mind," Claudio said. He looked back at Graciela. "Graciela, whack this bramble bush."

Paloma took a seat on a stool that her thoughtful husband must have placed there. She watched as Graciela's capable hands gathered her brother's hair, clean but tangled, into her hand, and with a sure stroke, began to cut through the mass. It fell away in bunches.

Soledad laughed when the wind took Claudio's hair and blew it around the garden. "Mama! In the spring, the birds will make nests!" she exclaimed.

And life goes on, she thought, watching the hair fly, seeing it through her daughter's eyes. *In the spring there will be another baby as Marco and I continue to build our own nest in this hard valley*. God's goodness to her filled her heart. Thank heavens Claudito demanded her attention just then, with the need for water to pour into his network of *acequias*.

When she came back to the garden from the kitchen with a pitcher of water, Graciela had evened off Claudio's hair, brown, now that all the grease and dirt were gone. Paloma added water to her son's little canals, then stood beside Graciela. She ran that fine-toothed comb through her brother's hair, catching what lice remained.

"Once a week, a bath," she told Claudio.

"Are you serious?"

"Never more so, Brother," Paloma assured him. "Now hold still for your beard."

Claudio put his hand up. "I sort of like my beard," he began, his voice tentative.

"You can 'sort of like' a lot less of it," Paloma said firmly. "Graciela, trim it close. If we like it, we might let it stay."

He frowned at Paloma. "There was a time when you did what I wanted," he said.

"I am not eleven," she replied and glared back.

They stared at each other. His lips started to twitch first, at least what she could see of his lips under his sprout of beard. She started to laugh.

Graciela gaped at them both as they laughed. Little Claudio left his miniature irrigation ditches among the bean vines. Wide-eyed, Soledad looked from one adult to the other. "I'm going to find Papa," she said in her most Paloma-like voice, which made Paloma double over helplessly in mirth.

"Are we in trouble now?" Claudio managed to gasp out, as Soledad started for the horse barn, every inch of her charged with purpose, from the set of her shoulders to the resolute swaying of her little dress.

"We are and it's your fault," Paloma said. "Hmm, perhaps I have been threatening her with Papa a little too much. She sounded so much like me!"

"Aha! Definitely your fault," Claudio said promptly, nothing but merriment in his eyes now. The tired look, the haunted gaze was gone, at least for a moment, as they laughed in the kitchen garden and Graciela just shook her head.

"Let's wait a minute, and see if 'Papa' comes," Paloma said, when Graciela raised her arms to begin the next phase of Claudio's rehabilitation.

He came, taking his time, and already with a grin on his face. He carried Soledad, who appeared to be telling Papa what she thought. Toshua followed behind. Amused, Paloma thought it quite remarkable just how many servants suddenly seemed to have business near the garden.

His grin a wide smile by now, Marco carried Soli into the kitchen garden and spoke to her. "My dearest, you say they were scolding each other and laughing?"

Soledad nodded her head emphatically.

"Being really silly?" he asked.

Soli took her father's face in her hands. "Papa, Mama never acts like that."

"Good thing Soli is asleep late at night and doesn't hear," he whispered in Paloma's ear.

"Hush!" she whispered back, her face hot, but not before Claudio's shoulders started to shake.

"I told you it was your fault," her brother said, which made Marco laugh out loud.

Soledad sighed and looked from one to the other. "You are not helping, Papa," she said, with all the solemnity of *dos años y medio*.

"No, I am not," Marco said. He kissed her cheek and set her down. "Mama and her brother like to tease each other. Don't you tease little Claudio now and then?"

"Yes, but that is different," Soli insisted.

"How?"

Paloma could see that the complexities of the argument were nearly beyond her daughter—nearly, but not quite.

Soledad drew herself up, folded her hands carefully in front of her waist and declared with great dignity, "*We* are little. *They* are not."

"You have me there, Soli," Claudio said, as Paloma turned her head into Marco's shoulder and laughed. "Let's make your mother go inside and behave herself."

Soledad nodded. "Who will cut your beard? It has to go." She lowered her voice. "Mama is right about that."

Even Toshua smiled. "I could take my knife to him," he told Soledad.

"You might frighten him. It must be Graciela," the child said.

Paloma looked at Graciela, who had been watching the whole exchange with wide-eyed wonder. It touched her heart to see the slave grow suddenly serious. A wistful look came into her eyes. Paloma touched her arm.

"Graciela? It appears I have been banished to the house. I am relying on you."

The slave nodded. Tears pooled in her eyes and Paloma understood what she could not say.

"Take us as we are," Marco said simply. He clapped his hands together. "Soli, you had better help Claudito with that … that muddy road?"

"*Acequia*, Papa," Claudio said patiently. "We need more water."

"And that is the truth of life here, son," Marco said. "Sancha has water for you in the kitchen. Come, Paloma. You need to remember your manners. This might mean a visit to the *sala*."

Soledad's eyes widened again. "The *sala*? Papa! She'll be good."

"She always is. Almost always." Marco turned to Claudio. "Off goes the beard."

"*Sí*, Señor Mondragón. I would wish to avoid the dread *sala*."

AFTER THE NOONDAY HEAT of the kitchen garden, the *sala* was cool and inviting. Paloma had no objection when Marco steered her toward the bench where Claudio had spent most of the night. He sat her down, sat down beside her and swung her feet up into his lap.

Toshua had followed them into the *sala*. He squatted on his haunches by the bench. Paloma looked from one to the other.

"What are you two planning?" she asked.

"She knows us, too," Toshua said.

"I only marry smart women, same as you," Marco said promptly. He took off her shoes and rubbed her feet. "Toshua and I are going to ride into Santa Maria tomorrow. I want to see what happened there, if anything." He stopped.

"When are you going to get around to telling me that you and Toshua are going to track Great Owl and see where he goes?" she asked, feeling a hollow spot in her middle.

"I told you she was smart, Toshua," Marco said. He ran his hands over her instep. "I haven't decided. Paloma, I don't know what Great Owl is up to. Was he just after horses when he came here before Taos? Why did he shoot at Claudio? And why did he stop?"

"You fear he might endanger what little peace we have earned from Kwihnai?" she asked.

"I fear it greatly." He rubbed her ankles now. "We've worked hard to maintain peace here in Valle del Sol."

"Whatever you do, I must come, too. After all, he shot at me."

Paloma looked at the doorway and let out her breath slowly, her eyes wide, her heart remembering.

Claudio must have convinced Graciela to leave him a close beard. Paloma sat up, her eyes on her brother, but seeing their father. Papa always told Mama he liked a close beard because he had tender Spanish skin, which always made her laugh; she was more Spanish than he was.

And there he stood, close beard, his eyes so blue, as blue as hers, his head tipped slightly to one side, just like Papa. Paloma bowed her head and closed her eyes. Marco's arm went around her waist and she leaned against him.

Claudio came closer. He knelt in front of her. "Paloma, I never thought this moment would happen," he said, choosing his words so carefully, as though he walked them through a briar patch. "I never thought we would be together again." He swallowed and looked at Marco. "Please bless me. It's been so long, and I don't even know if I believe anymore, but please …."

Marco made the sign of the cross on Claudio's forehead. "You, too, must take us as we are."

Chapter Sixteen

In which Marco explains brothers and husbands

THE MEN DID NOT go to Santa Maria the next day, and not even the one after that, not with so much field work to be done as August drew to a close.

The only thing that happened was Eckapeta's disappearance. One day she was there, playing with her grandchildren—for such they were—and the next she was gone. Paloma asked Toshua.

"She will find Kwihnai and they will talk," Toshua said. "If he has something to tell us about Great Owl, she will bear the news back here."

"You don't worry when she rides alone?" Paloma asked.

They were sitting on the low wall by the *acequia*. He put his arm around her, something he had never done before, something that made Claudio, sitting on her other side, give a start and look away. She turned her head toward Toshua.

"To what purpose?" the Comanche questioned in turn. "Worry is a great failing among you Spanish. Go rub your beads. Better yet, go find your man and rub him."

She had laughed softly, well beyond letting her good friend embarrass her, especially when he was right. She could tell that Claudio didn't quite understand yet, but time would change him, as it had changed her.

To Paloma's relief, Marco said nothing more about tracking Great Owl. She knew her man well, though, and was certain the idea had not left his mind. In the years since the death of her parents and brother, she should have known better than to borrow trouble from a different day. The brown robes had taught her that sufficient was the day unto the evil thereof. If the Franciscans hadn't taught her, she should have known it anyway. Still, she worried, and she knew it was because of her children, helpless little ones. Every breath she took, she breathed for them.

That's what it is to be a citizen of this poor colony, she thought a few mornings later, as she lay in bed and listened to her husband's light snore. She turned on her side to watch his slow breathing and the way his fine-veined hands rested on the coverlet, wide open. She thought of her brother across the hall, and his nightmares. She remembered her own, and the relief she felt that Marco was there to cover her closed eyes, moving so rapidly, until she was at peace again.

There had been no one to give Claudio peace. Too often his hands balled into fists as he slept. She knew because she was already conditioned to hear her children in the night. Somehow, her brother became part of her nighttime stewardship. He had only been with them five days, but she went to him when he cried out and sat with him, holding his hand until he relaxed in sleep again.

Whether Claudio knew she was there or not, she could not say, except that her heart sank the night he called out, "Mama!" Tears on her face, she held both his hands that night.

When she came back to bed, she woke up Marco, the words spilling out of her about the sorrow that had driven the sleeping Claudio Vega back so many years into another world, one before her birth, when he was a young boy.

Tucked close to her husband, Paloma felt her own heart finally stop its racing. She knew who she was and where she was, and she thanked God and all the saints for her good man.

She knew her words had disturbed Marco, because he did not return to sleep immediately. "Paloma, what did you do when you had nightmares in the house of your uncle in Santa Fe?" he asked.

"Do? Do?" she had asked in turn, uncertain what he meant.

"You know, when you had nightmares."

"No one ever came into my room. It was just me and the Comanches." She shuddered. "Some nights it seemed as though they rode around and around my bed."

She felt his huge sigh and happily let him pull her closer. She debated whether to tell him any more, but he was her husband. "For the first year, when I had those nightmares, I crawled under the bed and into the farthest corner, as I had crawled that day when everyone died."

"*Dios mío*," Marco whispered into her neck.

"I felt safe there," she whispered back. "That is why I don't begrudge a moment sitting with my brother. I wish someone had sat with me."

She lay still now, debating whether to get up—morning wasn't far off now—or sleep as long as she could. She knew this early-morning meditation would be her only free time all day, because that was the nature of life on the Double Cross. Soon she would be outlining daily tasks for the house servants, tending her children—thank God for Graciela's help—and helping out where Marco needed her. Better to lie there and just enjoy the comfort of food enough, shelter enough, love enough. Too many had far less than she.

She thought about her children in the next room. Sometimes at night before they slept, she heard their drowsy conversation, their giggles, their shared secrets, even with their still-rudimentary language. Marco usually went into their room to remind them that night was the time to sleep. She had to laugh into her hand when he thought he spoke quietly and told them to whisper if they wanted to talk, so Mama wouldn't hear. "She needs her sleep," he whispered on more than one occasion. "Why, Papa?" Soledad had asked, and he had replied, "You'll know soon enough," which seemed to satisfy the child.

At peace with herself, she rested her hand on her belly. Her waist had not yet begun to expand, and most mornings started with her kneeling over a basin, but she felt the same serenity she had known with her first pregnancy. This side of love was one of God's great mysteries.

She knew her husband's body well. In a moment of candor—she who was modest—she had told him how she loved to look at the two of them joined together. He had smiled and sat up from her body. "Look all you want," he had said, gazing deep into her eyes, then down to where they were still coupled. "I like it, too."

At moments like that, she thought of her parents, and hoped they had been as happy as she was now. *We cannot know*, reason told her, but her heart disagreed.

She lay still, thinking of the day's tasks ahead. Thank goodness all the candles were made for the coming year, and the wool they were keeping for household use had been spun and balled into tidy skeins. When winter's bitter cold and blowing snow made the Double Cross seem like the last Christian outpost in the world, she would stay warm by the fire, a child on each side of her, as she knitted caps and mittens and socks. By then, the baby would be moving. She wondered what Soledad would do when she put the child's hand on her belly to feel movement within. *I'll find out*, she thought. *And what will I tell her, this no-daughter-but-so-daughter of ours?*

Paloma decided this would be a good day to walk with Graciela and the children beside the *acequia*. She had noticed how Graciela seemed to start with every sudden sound, and how she continually looked over her shoulder. More than two men in the kitchen at the same time nearly reduced her to tears.

Paloma understood, thinking how frightening it must have been to be at the mercy of women demanding her labor during the day, and men claiming her body at night. Only God's mercy had spared Paloma that indignity.

Sancha had also whispered that food was disappearing from the bread safe, something that hadn't happened before Graciela arrived. Paloma understood this, too. She had tried to squirrel away little scraps of food in the Moreno house, but all that earned her was humiliating exposure and a beating. Paloma thought back to those days. Even knowing she would be thrashed, she felt compelled to steal, because she was eleven and on her own in the world, and a girl had to eat. And so she understood how her brother cried out for their mother.

"Patience and time," she said out loud, which woke up Marco.

He turned sideways, light brown eyes looking into blue ones. "Eight years, I shared my pillow with no one." He touched her cheek. "Now, mostly it's just you, but sometimes it's Soli and Claudito as well. Do we need a bigger bed?"

"No. We'll just crowd together like pine nuts in a basket," Paloma said.

"Patience and time, eh? Who are you worrying about now?"

"Graciela. Sancha tells me she has been stealing food. I am reluctant to chastise her, because I know something about her fears." She inched closer, because the morning was cool. "Claudio's wound is better, the wound we can see, at least."

Marco sat up. "I'll give him something to do today. I was planning to ride to Santa Maria with Toshua. I will invite him."

"You'll be careful?"

He nodded and got out of bed, dressing quickly as she lay there watching him, enjoying just another few minutes off her feet. She swallowed because the basin was starting to summon her. She must have made some noise, because Marco grabbed the basin, pulled her into a sitting position and set the basin in her lap. He held back her hair as she vomited, then poured her a glass of water. She sat cross-legged as she drank.

"Better?"

"In a few months," she joked. "Must you go to Santa Maria?"

"I must. I hate to leave little Santa Maria at the mercy of that garrison. I should have been there sooner, especially since we do not know what mischief Great Owl has done in the village."

"Ah! You tell me not to worry, and you worry about Santa Maria," she said, getting out of bed. She pulled on her *camisa* and was looking for her petticoat, when Marco came up behind her and pulled her close.

"As *juez de campo*, I get paid to worry," he growled into her neck, which made Paloma laugh, then cover her mouth, not wanting to wake the children.

Once dressed, Paloma followed Marco into the kitchen and then the garden beyond. He stood there and she looked where he looked, to see Toshua standing on the parapet, facing north.

"He has been doing that all week," Marco told her. "He won't say why."

"He tells me not to worry, and yet he is worried. Is it for Eckapeta?"

"I think not. He knows how resourceful she is. I think he knows there is trouble in the north, from the land of the Utes."

"They will harry us, too?"

"Hard to say. The Utes were our allies when Governor de Anza led us against the Comanche Cuerno Verde in '79," Marco said. "Does Great Owl seek to gain their trust, or does he plan to work carnage among them? I should find out."

"Why you?" she asked.

"That has always been Governor de Anza's special charge to me, since we form the eastern boundary of New Mexico." He put his arm around her and walked toward the *acequia*. "We've done well, thanks to Kwihnai, but now we have trouble."

"Very well," she told him. "Enlist Toshua and ask my brother. He is well enough, and I can tell he is bored."

Claudio perked up immediately when Marco invited him along to Santa Maria. In answer to Marco's question about his shoulder, Claudio patted it and didn't make a face, although Paloma couldn't overlook the sudden sweat on his forehead.

"Are you certain?" she asked.

"*Claro,*" he replied promptly. "Can I help it if you keep your house too warm?" He wiped his forehead with the back of his hand. "I need to ride." He stood back and looked around the high-walled plaza where she felt secure. "I'm not used to being enclosed, Paloma. In fact ...." His voice trailed off.

She knew what he was going to say. Only five days with him after years certain that he was dead, she realized that she did not know this man. They had both grown up. She said it for him. "In fact, you are not so certain that you belong here."

Claudio gave her a look of surprise mingled with relief. "*Claro.*" He kissed her cheek and hurried toward the house. She watched him go, noticing with dismay the extra spring in his step.

Graciela watched her children in the kitchen garden, where Sancha had set them to work picking beans. "No one is too young to help a little," Sancha had told her. Paloma went into the horse barn, where she had last seen Marco. He was saddling old Buciro, so she came up behind and put her arms around him.

"Something bothers you," he said.

"How do you know?" she asked.

"Because you're quiet." He chuckled and it was the kindest sound. "And correct me if I'm wrong, but does my back feel just a little wet now? What's the matter, dearest heart?"

"Claudio doesn't think he wants to stay here," she mumbled into his shirt, feeling like a disagreeable child. "All these years, and he isn't sure!"

Marco turned around and took hold of her hands. He kissed each palm, then set her hands against his chest. "Give him a little room, Paloma. Where has he been these past years?"

"On the plains, traveling here and there with smelly traders, pretty much living the life that every man would enjoy, I suppose," she said. "Even you! Don't deny that you like stripping down to a loincloth."

"It's pretty comfortable, Paloma," he teased. "You should try it."

"I would flop and not be so comfortable," she said, which made him throw back his head and laugh. "Oh, stop it! Does no man ever really want to be domesticated?" She pointed to herself. "But *I* am here!"

"To my great satisfaction," he told her, and gave her the look she remembered from the first time she saw him, something he probably wasn't even aware of: an appraisal, followed by a slight nod, as though he had found something that had been missing.

"You've seen me when I return from a trip. I never ride my horses hard, do I?"

"Never," she agreed.

"Why is it that I pick up my pace when I see the walls of the Double Cross?"

"You love your home?"

"I do. I always will," he admitted. "Mind you, Paloma, those long eight years after Felicia died and before you and I … I rode slowly because there wasn't anyone waiting for me. Now I hurry up because I know you will be standing at the gate, practically jumping up and down, but holding your hands so tight together because you are a Spanish lady."

"Oh, I don't…" she began, then blushed. "Well, yes, I suppose I do."

"I know I'll hear about puppies, or Soledad's cough, or Claudito's new tooth, or what damage the hail did to your peas. You'll scold me because I look tired or too thin, or smell bad, though not as bad as your brother, and—"

"That is so unimportant," she began, but he put his fingers to her lips.

"Then why do I crave it? I know that I will hear the latest news, that Soli and Claudito will sit on me and demand horsey, that you will have my favorite meal cooking—"

"I have that meal ready for days, because I'm never sure when you'll arrive," she said.

"I will pray that night in my own chapel, kiss my children goodnight, and lie down in my own bed with the finest wife a man can have." He put his hand on her waist and started walking her out of the horse barn. "I do like to ride the plains with Toshua, but Paloma, I know where I live, and I know who I love. Let's just let your brother be Claudio."

"All those years—"

"We can't change them." He stopped walking and put his hands on her shoulders. "You can do one of two things, Paloma, as I see it: you can whine and cry and hang onto him, or you can give him a kiss goodbye and assure Claudio that he is always welcome here."

"Put that way, you make it simple," she told him, but with reluctance. She threw up her hands. "I know! I know! You are only going to Santa Maria, so why am I behaving this way?" She put her hands on her hips. "When did I turn into a problem?"

"Probably the morning after we started this baby," he said with a grin, then put up his hands and laughed harder when she slapped his head. In another moment she was laughing, too.

Chapter Seventeen

In which Paloma soothes and Marco insists

IT PAINED PALOMA'S HEART to watch them ride away, even if it was only to Santa Maria. She smiled and waved at her husband, brother, and Toshua only because Claudito was in her arms and if she cried, he would start to wail, and then Soledad would join in. She remembered how gentle and dignified her mother was, the perfect Spanish lady, and wondered if she would ever approach such perfection. She felt cross and hot, wanted to throw up, and her breasts were so tender.

There was Graciela to consider. In the excitement of Claudio's return, Paloma knew she had neglected to acquaint the slave with her role in the greater scheme of life on the Double Cross. What better time than now, with the servants busy about their tasks. The day was warm enough for her little ones to splash in the *acequia*, after Emilio dammed it to allow water onto the crops beyond the walls. What remained flowing into the courtyard would safely entertain them for hours.

The matter was quickly accomplished. "I had been planning to water the peppers one final time this very morning," Emilio said. "Let them play."

Paloma smiled at Claudito's eagerness to discard his clothes and leap into the shallow irrigation ditch. "You are so much like your father," she said, as she tossed in wooden boats. She helped Soledad from her clothes and took the more cautious child by the hand, raising her own skirts and settling her into the cool water. In a few minutes, she was splashing Claudito and chortling about it.

The water did feel good. Paloma tucked up her skirts and sat on the brow of the ditch, letting her bare legs dangle in the water. She motioned to Graciela. "Sit with me."

The slave did as she was bid. What else could she do? Paloma thought a long while before speaking. She had grown used to her role as wife of the *hacendado*, but her years of near-servitude would never allow her to injure anyone with either words or blows. There was no need to mince words with a slave, but she did, anyway.

"Graciela, I value your help," she began. "Marco teases me about never asking for anything, but believe me, I did ask him to find me help with the children, when he went to Taos. True, we have servants, but they already have other tasks."

"Señor Mondragón surely did not know what a high price he would have to pay," Graciela said, and Paloma heard her remorse. "I will never be out of his debt."

"He did what had to be done."

"No one else came forward," Graciela told Paloma. "To see those people staring at me, and to know in my heart that I would be the next to die …." She shuddered, unable to continue.

"This is why I thank God every night for the goodness of the man I married," Paloma said, blushing because she was raised to be circumspect, especially around servants. "He gave all because he was not about to take a chance that it would not be enough." She laughed. "Between you and me, this is the same man who paid an entire peso for that little yellow dog over there."

Graciela gasped in surprise. "Surely not!"

As the children splashed each other and squealed over water bugs, Paloma told Graciela her own story, including the part about the meddling priests of San Gabriel making sure that the dog was let loose, which meant that she would have to return it to the rightful owner.

"Those two priests plotted and planned that I would do exactly what I did—start to walk to Valle del Sol from that place where Rio Chama meets Rio Bravo," Paloma said. "I was already in love with that man with the light brown eyes. I'll admit it now." She touched Graciela's shoulder, saddened as the slave flinched. "Here, in this place, we help each other."

Graciela sighed and looked away.

"Until you do believe it, let us do this: tonight, you may take as many tortillas as you like to bed."

Graciela began to weep, which made the children look up in surprise. Paloma put her finger to her lips, and they returned to their play.

"I … I can't help myself," the slave whispered.

"I did the same thing in the house of my uncle, when I was sent there at the age of eleven after my parents died," Paloma said. "I was beaten for thievery.

We don't do that here. Take as many tortillas as will make you feel safe."

"No one will mind?"

"Not a single person."

* * *

MARCO KNEW HE WOULD never dare tell Paloma how happy Claudio looked to be in the saddle again. The smile started on his face as soon as the gates of the Double Cross closed behind them.

"If it's too much for your shoulder just yet, you can turn back."

"No, no, I am fine," Claudio assured him. "Paloma would never understand how nice it feels to be out from behind walls."

"No, she would not," Marco said, amused. He grew serious quickly. "There was a time when your sister was adventurous, but not with babies now. And that's the way I want it, too. We have far more at stake."

"I do understand," Claudio said. "I thought maybe someday I would find some land and a wife, but the longer I lived the horse trader life, the less I considered it."

"Do you intend to go with the horse traders?" Marco asked, wondering just how Paloma would manage news like that. *Please tell me no*, he thought.

"I wish I knew," Claudio replied. His expressive face, so like Paloma's, showed his amazement at the events of the past few days. "I was just going to follow you here, get the money and rejoin my *compadres*. Now I have a sister again, and apparently the Comanches want to kill me."

"Are you so certain?" Toshua said from Marco's other side. "If they had wanted to kill you, they would have."

"I have wondered about that myself," Claudio said. "Was Graciela the intended target?" he joked, and Marco laughed.

Toshua rode ahead. When Claudio believed himself far enough away, he said, "Marco, I do not feel easy with that man."

"Neither did your sister at first. Nor I, to be sure."

"Then why—"

"Is he part of our life now? As Toshua saw it, Paloma kept saving his life, and he felt obligated, as a man of honor would." Marco shrugged. "He became our friend, and so did his wife."

"I'll never trust him."

"Never is a long time, Claudio. You also never thought you would see your sister again, did you?"

At least Claudio had the good grace to laugh at himself. "Let us leave it there for now."

To Marco, Santa Maria looked much the same, a weary little outpost of brave people who deserved better than to be guarded by nincompoops.

He noticed some burned outbuildings, much as he and Toshua had seen at the Calderón hacienda. The fire had taken a small grain field, too, damage so minimal that Marco wondered what game Great Owl was playing. He remembered Comanche raids from his childhood, ones that gave him nightmares. This was small pickings, indeed.

The great gates of the garrison were open, with two guards looking more curious than alert. *We have been lulled into complacency*, Marco thought.

He asked that they be taken to Sergeant Lopez, and the guard wasted not a minute, mainly because Marco already knew everyone was terrified of Toshua. He glanced at the Comanche, who sat tall and glared at the soldiers who were casually trying to flatten themselves against walls and disappear through doorways.

"You could look a little less frightening," he told his friend.

"This is not my frightening look," Toshua replied.

"Have I ever seen that look?" Marco joked.

"No. The only ones who will ever see that look will be those who attempt to harm Paloma or your children."

Marco took a deep breath, grateful down to his stockings that Toshua was his friend. "If someone tries to harm *me*?"

"You can take care of yourself, Little Brother," Toshua told him.

I may have just received the greatest compliment of my life, Marco thought, suddenly humbled to the dust. "Thank you, my friend."

Claudio appeared to recognize the private who ushered them to Sergeant Lopez's office.

"Do you know him?" Marco asked as they walked down the portal to a room Marco had visited many times. In earlier years, there was a lieutenant to serve the garrison, but not in recent memory.

"Yes. He was the only *soldado* who showed any initiative when my *compadres* and I were set upon by Great Owl."

"I don't think he recognizes you."

"How could he?" Claudio asked. "I look less like a tumbleweed and more like a Spanish gentleman now."

"More Spanish than I, certainly," Marco replied.

Sergeant Lopez surprised Marco by his sobriety. He sat behind his desk, a shrunken man with bags under his eyes and his nose deeply veined, testimony to too much drinking. Marco wondered at the state of his liver, and saw illness now, not drunkenness.

He rose unsteadily when Marco entered the room, and somehow managed a short bow without toppling over. Marco reached across the desk to steady him. "You need a doctor," he said.

"Where would I find one, señor?" the sergeant asked. "Here we are on the ragged edge of our sovereign's domain. Do sit down." He leaned closer, his eyes on Toshua. "Does he need to be here?"

Marco tried not to smile. "You could ask him to leave, Sergeant."

"Oh, no, no." The sergeant's pale face reddened. "He'll be fine. And señor, you are—"

"This is Señor Claudio Vega, my wife's brother," Marco said. "You might remember him as Diego Diaz, who came to your attention a few weeks ago after that skirmish with the Comanches."

"I don't recall …." The sergeant looked away. "I … may have been ill."

Marco heard a sound behind him like someone turning a laugh into a cough. He looked and there stood the *soldado* who had shown them into the sergeant's office, at attention by the door. To Marco's further amusement, he gave the *juez* a slow wink.

"I'm certain that was it," Marco said smoothly. "Perhaps that was why no one from this garrison made any effort to visit my hacienda to see how my wife and children were, when you knew I was in Taos. And why you didn't visit the Calderón hacienda when Comanches burned some of the outbuildings. I certainly hope for the sake of this district that you feel better soon."

The sergeant passed his hand in front of his eyes. "Señor, I have fifteen men in this garrison, where there used to be thirty."

Marco remained silent, watching the sergeant shrink even smaller. The man ran his hand around his dirty neck cloth, eyes darting here and there as if searching for an answer in a corner of the untidy room.

"The Comanches are gone now, and nothing much of consequence happened," the sergeant said at last.

"I am grateful," Marco said, "but I can't help but think that Great Owl was curious to know what *you* would do, if he attacked with any warriors. Obviously he has his answer by now. What will you do when—I do not say if—he returns to Valle del Sol with more warriors?"

"You promised us that Kwihnai would keep us safe," the sergeant whined.

"I promised you that *Kwihnai* would not attack us, and he has not," Marco snapped. "Great Owl needs to be rooted out and destroyed before he can turn more warriors to his path. I need men from this garrison to help."

Another silence, one longer than the first, told Marco everything else he needed to know. He stood up, put his hands on the desk, and leaned across it, which made the sergeant lean back until he was in danger of toppling from his chair.

"Will you give me *anyone* to help?"

"I dare not," Sergeant Lopez whispered.

"I will go with you."

Marco turned around to see the *soldado* looking at him, his gaze level and in no way subservient. "You? One soldier?"

"*Sí*, Señor Mondragón," he replied quietly, but with a certain flair that did not hint of subservience. "If I may say, this looks like one of those campaigns that either needs hundreds of troops, or maybe four or five."

"What makes *you* so wise?" Marco asked. "You, a mere *soldado*?"

"It's not wisdom, señor," he replied, still calm, still unfazed. "It's logical common sense."

"We'll take this one," Toshua said.

"You can't just take …. I have to give permission and I won't," the sergeant said, in his first show of strength in the whole dreary interview. "Private Gasca, leave now! I will deal with you later, you rascal!"

Toshua turned to face the sergeant. He stared at him like a rattlesnake would watch a pack rat, and then walked closer, never taking his eyes from the sergeant's face. Slowly, slowly, Toshua took out his knife. His eyes wide and staring, Sergeant Lopez watched the knife. He closed his eyes in what Marco interpreted as a close approximation of mortal terror.

"We want him," was all Toshua said.

The room suddenly filled with a fierce odor that made the sergeant bury his face in his hands. "Take him! Only leave!" the sergeant said, unable to raise his face to the other men, humiliated.

Toshua nodded. "I think this one is truly ill. He reeks of something, but it is not—what is that you call it?—ah, he is probably not contagious."

"Sergeant Lopez, I will take very good care of my army," Marco said. "Go change your *pantalones*."

The four men walked from the room and out into the clean air of the courtyard. "Toshua, you have a disturbing effect on this garrison," Marco said, which made Private Gasca tug on his upper lip, his eyes merry. "And you, *soldado*, do enlighten us as to just who you are. *Soldado* seems to be a misleading rank."

Private Gasca drew himself up and saluted. "*Soldado* Joaquim Gasca, formerly *Teniente* Gasca of the Royal Engineers." He grinned. "I build things."

Wonder of wonders, Marco thought. "And you somehow got in trouble, lost your commission, and ended up in my backwater district?"

Private Gasca nodded, his expression dreamy. "She was a lovely woman, so willing in bed, or on table tops, or rugs, but, *ay de mí*, the wife of my *coronel*."

Toshua shook his head. "If you had been one of The People, you would be minus those parts that make you a man. And the colonel's wife would have no nose anymore."

Marco looked at his brother-in-law, whose mouth was open in amazement. "Will he prove useful, Claudio?" he asked.

Claudio shrugged. "Who can tell?"

"I can tell," Marco replied, suddenly hopeful that this visit to Santa Maria's garrison had not been in vain. "You're bored, aren't you, Private?"

"To pieces," Gasca said. "You'll promise me adventure?"

"We're on the prowl for a Comanche, who now that I think of it has some money of mine. I overpaid him for a slave. We'll tell you more as we ride."

"And this gentleman?" Gasca asked, indicating Toshua.

"I'd rather lose you than him," Marco said frankly. "In or out?"

"In. This garrison is far too slow."

It came as no surprise to Marco that the corporal in charge of all matters equine issued *Soldado* Joaquim Gasca—a Catalonian from his name, and they were always trouble—a nag that looked like it would be walking on its knees soon.

Private Gasca gave the animal a sorrowful pat when he returned from gathering together his few possessions. "Could one of you take my bedroll and someone else my gun and clothes?" he asked. "If I climb on Old Ancient of Days here with anything more than my own weight, he'll drop dead."

Claudio obliged, and Marco took the gun. "We'll go slow," Marco said. He stopped their peculiar expedition with a motion of his hand.

"One thing more, Joaquim," he said, "and make no mistake about this: I have a lovely wife and she adores me. If you even look at her funny, I will gut you myself from throat to genitals and blame Great Owl's warriors."

"Only if you get to him before I do," Toshua said. "I have better methods to make him suffer. He'll plead to die before I am done."

"And imagine what *I* have learned, riding with horse traders for twelve years," Claudio said. He shook his head. "Not pretty."

Gasca looked from one man to the other. "It appears to be unanimous that I must behave myself. Very well, señores, if that is the price of adventure…."

Chapter Eighteen

In which Paloma becomes the perfect hostess to more smelly men

"Señora, Emilio does not know who these riders are."

Sitting at the kitchen table, Paloma looked up from her contemplation of the basin, her great companion these days, where she had discarded a wonderful noon meal of turkey and *posole*. She wondered why there had to be trouble, when she was feeling aggravated that Marco the *juez* had so thoughtlessly got her with child again.

"Sancha, all I want to do is die, and we have visitors?"

"I am not certain what they are, but Emilio is worried."

Paloma put aside the basin. "I had better check then," she said. She rinsed her mouth and wiped her lips. Deciding it was uncharitable to blame Marco entirely for the state she was in, she went outside. After all, no one had forced her to take off her clothes and cavort naked.

Emilio motioned her to the parapet. She felt some small appreciation for that same rascal husband, who had insisted that the ladder be replaced with a shallow staircase, just for her, since as he put it, "You like to know what is going on." She climbed the steps, grateful for the handrail.

"You're pale, *dama*," Emilio said. "I would not have bothered you, but look."

He pointed to the west and handed her his telescope. Paloma propped her elbows on the ledge and looked. First she saw only a cloud of dust and felt the familiar tightening in her belly that meant Comanches.

"You have called everyone in from the fields, have you not?"

"Ah, yes. Can you tell …. My eyes are old, señora."

She handed back the telescope. "Just keep the gates closed. We'll know more when they get closer, although I do not think they are Comanches. The People never create clouds of dust."

"No, they do not," Emilio agreed.

She stayed where she was, and looked into the courtyard below, where the field servants had gathered. Graciela sat close to Claudio and Soledad as they played with blocks on the porch. They were building walls, which touched her heart. Someday, if Marco continued working his quiet diplomacy with the Comanche through Kwihnai, perhaps there would be no need for walls.

She rested her arms on the parapet, watching the approaching men. In another minute she sighed with relief. "These must be the horse traders, Emilio, probably looking for Claudio. We will open the gates to them."

And so it was that Paloma was standing in the courtyard when the gates opened and the rough men rode inside. She stood there, her hands folded in front of her, watching them.

"Do get down, señores," she said with a gesture.

They remained in the saddle, looking around at the guards on the parapet. "Where is Diego?" the older man asked.

At least she thought he was older, but who could tell with all the hair and beard? She remembered his broken-down sombrero and the red bandanna pulled tight around his hair, which spilled out anyway, from her last look at them in the cemetery at Santa Maria, where they buried the one killed by Comanches. Her stomach began to churn because she could smell them from where she stood. *What have you horse traders against a good wash, now and then?* she thought.

"He is not here."

The traders looked at each other. "I told you," the younger man said to Red Bandanna. "He's taken the money and run."

"He has not," Paloma said. "And he is not who you think he is."

"How do you know so much?" Red Bandanna asked, his voice rising, belligerent in tone. He edged his horse closer to Paloma but she stood her ground. "*You*, just a woman."

All it took was a glance at the guards on the parapet, who to a man nocked arrows in their bows and aimed them at the horse traders.

"I have a lot of friends here," Paloma said calmly. "Back up now, señor, before you get at least one arrow through your throat."

After a glance around, he did as she said.

"Much better. Please dismount. My servants will care for your horses in the barn."

With another look at each other, not so aggressive this time, the traders did as she said.

"I can tell you everything you need to know about Diego Diaz. Wasn't that what you called him?"

"What are you saying?" Red Bandanna asked.

"I know he is not Diego Diaz, and so must you. It could be that I wish to know more," Paloma said, curious what they could tell her about their discovery of Claudio, found bleeding in a ditch.

"You assume a lot," Red Bandanna said. "Perhaps we will not tell you anything."

"Suit yourselves," she replied. "Do you know whose hacienda's this is?"

"A *cabrón* who leaves a pretty wife alone?"

Paloma raised her eyes to the parapet again, with the same results as before. Almost. One of the archers let loose an arrow that landed right in front of Red Bandanna.

The trader froze. "Beg pardon," the archer called down from his vantage point. "Careless of me."

Oh, you men, Paloma thought, grateful beyond words for Marco's guards, who suffered fools no more gladly than did their employer. "Mind your tongue, señor! You are the guests of this district's *juez de campo*, Marco Mondragón." She wondered how such news would affect men who dallied on both sides of the law.

She had her answer in the more tentative looks the men exchanged. "We can leave right now," Red Bandanna said. "We'll wait for Diego somewhere else."

"You'll wait right here, and while you wait, my housekeeper will supply you with towels and soap." She pointed to the *acequia*, wondering where all her bravado was coming from. "When you are washed and clean, I will serve you wine and *biscoches* in the *sala*, and you will learn what I know about Diego Diaz."

Both traders gasped and stared at the irrigation ditch as though it had suddenly turned red, like the Nile of Moises' tale in Exodus. Red Bandanna glared at Paloma, which meant that another archer had to apologize for accidentally letting loose his arrow, this one coming so close to grazing the man's hair that he turned pale under all his dirt.

"So careless," the archer murmured, shaking his head. "What will Señor Mondragón say?"

"Gentlemen? The water isn't too cold. Possibly there will be more than just wine and *biscoches* waiting for you in the kitchen when you are clean. Oh, thank you, Sancha."

Paloma took the towels and bowl of soft soap made from yucca and set them by the *acequia*. She turned, all serenity, and went into the house, taking her children and Graciela with her. Sancha and Perla giggled by the kitchen window.

"Señora, you are a brave lady!" Graciela said.

"Not really. I cannot abide strong odors right now, but I want to be a good hostess. Their clothes will still stink, but at least the smell of piñon in the kitchen will mask some of that."

While the horse traders bathed in the *acequia*—Sancha laughed so hard she had to turn away from the window and sit down—Paloma fed her little ones, sang to them, and left Graciela to lay them down for a nap. She wondered where her courage was coming from and hoped Marco would hurry home; then she prepared a meal that would take some of the sting out of her treatment of rough men unused to civilization.

The traders must have found clean shirts from somewhere deep in their horse packs, and even a comb. When they came through the kitchen door an hour later, the results were evident, right down to their slicked back hair, still damp and now restrained with rawhide thongs.

"Please be seated," Paloma said. "Here we have turkey mole, *posole*, tortillas, and Anasazi beans, the best I know." She gestured to the table and they sat. "One moment before you begin." Paloma made the sign of the cross and asked a quiet blessing on the food. "And keep these sons of thine safe on their journeys," she concluded. "There now. Take whatever you would like."

Red Bandanna looked a little shy, now that he was clean. "We didn't … didn't mean to frighten you," he said in a voice as soft as hers. "We're not used to this."

Paloma cast aside her own shyness. No reason they should think that she was such a martinet to all visitors to the Double Cross. "I must be frank, but it is this way, señores: I am with child, and strong odors are difficult for me right now. Thank you for indulging my whim. The *juez* will appreciate it, too."

Suddenly shy themselves, the men looked away. To her amusement, Paloma noticed that neither man stopped eating, even though her candor had embarrassed them. There was hope for such men.

"What are your names, please?" she asked.

"Your husband is really the *juez de campo*?" Red Bandanna asked.

"He is, but he is sometimes inclined to overlook misdemeanors in districts other than his own."

"In that case, I am Lorenzo Diaz. Paco Diaz was my late brother, and this is Rogelio, my …." He looked at the younger man. "What are you?"

Paloma stared down at her *posole* and tried not to laugh.

"I was your slave, but you said that after seven years or so, I'd be free. Has it been seven years?"

Rogelio's eyes were earnest, but vague enough to make Paloma suspect he was a little slow.

"Not quite yet, Rogelio," Lorenzo said, after a long tug at his beard.

"How much longer?"

"Eight or nine months," Lorenzo said with a vague wave of his hand. "You have other plans? Does the viceroy in Mexico City want your opinion on land grants?"

"No …." Rogelio said doubtfully, which told Paloma all she needed to know about the slave's mental acuity. Perhaps Lorenzo Diaz's carelessness with dates was less self-serving than it seemed, its goal being to keep someone like Rogelio alive in a dangerous place.

"More tortillas, please," Lorenzo said. His gaze met Paloma's and he winked, which sent her back into her napkin, because she wanted to laugh.

Paloma recovered and moved the covered dish closer. "There is *flan*, too," she told them.

"I do not remember the last time I had *flan*," Lorenzo said. "My mother used to make it." He sighed, and glanced at Rogelio. "You probably don't think I even had a mother."

Rogelio shrugged, his eyes on the *posole*, which Paloma moved closer, too. He nodded his thanks, and she saw the unhappiness in his face. Maybe he understood more than Lorenzo thought.

When they finished the *posole* and tortillas, Sancha brought in the *flan* with an unexpected flourish. She set it, all quivering and fragrant, with burned sugar and rum, in front of Paloma, who dished out generous helpings. They were rough men and just barely clean, but their appreciation for what was an ordinary meal touched her heart. She doubted they had a home anywhere. Hadn't Claudio said something about not being under a roof since their family's own roof near El Paso?

While they ate, she told them Claudio's story. Rogelio listened and nodded, his attention more taken with the *flan*, but Lorenzo put down his spoon and stared at her.

"*You* were in that burnt out hacienda?"

"That would depend on when you found Claudio. After a day under the bed, I set out for El Paso, and some soldiers found me."

"We never saw any soldiers," Lorenzo said quickly. Paloma doubted they ever hung around anywhere long enough for troops to arrive.

"Claudio told me he was bleeding in a ditch from that lance wound," Paloma said, and swallowed, feeling her brother's pain all over again, and her own distress as everything she knew disappeared in blood and fire.

Lorenzo surprised her by covering both her hands with his. She did not pull away, even though Rogelio's eyes were wide and his mouth open. She doubted he had ever seen much tenderness in the horse trader before.

"He nearly died, señora," Lorenzo said. He gave her hands a squeeze and let go, after sending a sour look in Rogelio's direction. "We couldn't take him to the Franciscans in El Paso, where they have an infirmary."

"I was there," she said, and put her hand to her mouth as the implication struck. "I was there! If only you had …." She stopped, remembering her own childish promise to herself not to endlessly revisit the event, because the pain was too great. It was greater now, because she and Claudio had found each other. "Why didn't you?"

Lorenzo looked away. "We were in some trouble with the law in that district. Some horses that weren't strictly ours to trade."

Paloma nodded. She picked up her spoon again, but Sancha's delicious *flan* had lost its taste. "What's done is done. I'm just grateful you saved my brother's life."

"We took him to some Apaches, who cleaned out that hole in his side. He had packed it with dirt to stop the bleeding, and there was pus and matter." Lorenzo shuddered. "The Apaches knew what to do. We left him there and then came back for him, and he stayed with us. My brother Paco had lost a son and wife in a Comanche raid, so he called him Diego, after his dead boy."

"Claudio said he looked for me every time you came to a village."

"He did, though he would never say why, or who he was looking for. Finally, after years of that, he stopped."

They sat in silence. Finally Lorenzo slapped his hands on his knees and stood up. "We'll wait outside."

"You're welcome to sit in the *sala*," Paloma said.

"No, *dama*. We're used to being outside. We feel hemmed in here, even though your hacienda is lovely."

"At least sit in the *galería*, señor," she told Lorenzo. "I would not consider myself much of a hostess if you just stood outside in the hot sun. Sancha will bring you wine and *biscoches*."

Lorenzo made an awkward bow, which Rogelio didn't even attempt to imitate. She walked them to the front door, even though Lorenzo protested that the kitchen door was good enough for them. "We're not exactly *hidalgos*," he told her, embarrassed.

"You are to me," she said simply, and gave a more elegant bow, grand but not showy. "Thanks to you, I have a brother again."

Chapter Nineteen

In which Claudio makes stupid plans

"I KNOW THOSE HORSES," Claudio said, as they approached the open gates of the Double Cross. "My friends have arrived. I hope they did not frighten Paloma."

Marco rode slightly ahead. Claudio noticed that the nearer they came to the Double Cross, the faster he urged his horse.

Toshua, that Comanche he knew he would never trust, must have noticed the quizzical look on Claudio's face. "He does that. His first wife and twins died while he was gone on a brand inspection trip. I don't think he even realizes that he is nearly at a gallop. He worries."

"Even now?"

Toshua looked around him elaborately. "Has your colony suddenly become safer?"

Trust a Comanche to make him feel like a fool without even breaking a sweat. Claudio ignored him, as much as a man could ignore a Comanche, and glanced at Joaquim Gasca, who seemed to be observing the Double Cross through an engineer's eyes.

"Hard to find, eh? I did the same thing," Claudio said, riding closer to the private or lieutenant, or whatever he was. "Quite a marvel, isn't it? The gray stones make it nearly invisible."

"Without a doubt," Joaquim said, "although I can see one improvement that would make it even safer."

"Don't hesitate to tell Marco then, when he slows down," Claudio joked, then flinched at the gallows look that Toshua threw his way. "Someday he has to realize that Paloma is safe inside, doesn't he, Toshua?"

"You have never loved a woman, have you?" was all Toshua said, before he neatly put wings to his own horse.

Claudio watched him. As much as he hated Comanches, he could never ignore the elegant way that someone not so tall and with a bit of a paunch could turn into Pegasus, almost.

Claudio rode beside Joaquim, his eyes on the horses grazing outside the stone walls. "I wonder: do you think these traders would take this superannuated nag of mine in exchange for one of those beauties?"

"Highly unlikely," Claudio told him. He edged his horse closer to Joaquim so he didn't have to raise his voice. "I believe several of these horses sort of fell into Lorenzo Diaz's hands in Isleta, where I was supposed to meet up with them, after I collected my money from Marco."

Joaquim twisted in his saddle to regard Claudio. "You do realize that Señor Mondragón is a *juez de campo*?"

"*Claro!* If they have spoken to Paloma, they know, too. I have a feeling that my *compadres* will not want to linger overlong at the Double Cross."

"What will *you* do?"

It was a good question, one that Claudio had not resolved in his mind. "I honestly do not know. Don't tell my sister, please."

"You would actually leave with these horse traders, when you have a better way before you here at the Double Cross?" Joaquim asked. "This is the finest land grant in Valle del Sol!"

"It doesn't belong to *me*. Horse trading is what I have known for years," Claudio said.

"You know the Mondragóns want you to stay," Joaquim told him. "I mean, *I* would, if the boot were on the other foot. Nobody cares what happens to me, and here are these good people, *your* people."

"What would I do here? Work for Marco? Become a farmer? Raise sheep? I know I'm a good horse trader."

"You can't change?"

Joaquim shook his head and turned away, coaxing his pathetic mount into a stumbling trot, leaving Claudio alone with the traders' horses, quietly cropping grass and ignoring him, too.

You handled that well, idiot, Claudio thought, angry at himself. He thought he might sulk a bit outside the walls, but his horse knew where the barn was, and where there would be grain, and went forward of his own accord.

"Traitor horse," Claudio said. "Are you part of a conspiracy to keep me here?"

His horse had nothing to say, so Claudio let him lead the way through the open gates where archers watched from the parapet.

The sight that met his eyes made him rein in, and stare in amazement. "Paloma, only you could do this," he said softly.

Marco had dismounted and was standing next to Paloma in a typical pose, his arm around his wife's shoulders and his son on one hip. Nothing unusual there.

What made Claudio's eyes nearly pop from his head was the sight of Lorenzo Diaz, horse trader and ramshackle adventurer, sitting meekly in a chair with a towel around his neck as Graciela sheared him like a sheep.

His heavy beard, where probably countless little creatures had dwelt for years, was gone, revealing heretofore unknown scars and a bit of an underbite. The slave was working on Lorenzo's hair now, combing and clipping until it was shoulder length like Claudio's own.

Amazed, Claudio turned his attention to Rogelio, a slave still, probably because no one could remember the terms of the original agreement of his servitude and he was none too bright. Rogelio had been skinned first, his hair tied back neatly now with a black bow, probably from Marco's clothing chest. Without his whiskers, he was handsomer than Lorenzo by far. Rogelio kept stroking his face, as though unable to believe what had happened to him.

Lorenzo, you old fart, Claudio thought. *You probably made Rogelio go first, to test the water.*

Lorenzo looked up and hailed him. "Diego—no, no, Claudio—Señora Mondragón says I am *un hombre muy guapo y elegante*!"

Paloma turned her face into Marco's shirt and laughed. "I never said that, Lorenzo! I possibly mentioned that you might be sought after by the ladies now."

How did she do that? Claudio wondered, stunned by his little sister's skills. In all the years he had known that hard man, Lorenzo had never taken a bath, figuring that occasional rainwater and dips in whatever river they forded was enough for any man. Lorenzo had whacked at his beard now and then, sawing with a knife, but never with such skill as Graciela exhibited as she combed and cut.

"Lorenzo, are you planning to give up trading and become *un hidalgo*?" he teased.

Lorenzo gave him such a look then—three parts disgust and one part pity. "Your sister kindly asked us to bathe because strong smells trouble her right now, in her family way."

My shy sister said that? Claudio asked himself. "And the hair, too?"

He shrugged. "One thing led to another until I found myself sitting in this chair with a towel around my neck."

"Lorenzo and Rogelio are so kind," Paloma said. "I never met two more obliging gentlemen. Look how fine they are now." She stepped away from

Marco's loose hold on her. "A few more minutes, and I will call you to dinner."

"I hope there will be more *flan*," Lorenzo called after her.

Claudio shook his head. *Flan?* This from the man who had no qualms about eating anything that crawled and didn't fight back too hard? Claudio distinctly remembered a dinner of javelina, eaten raw because they were starving.

Good God. Clean a man up, promise him good food, served on china plates, and probably a bed with real sheets, and he becomes a stranger. *I don't know you*, Claudio thought.

He stared at the hacienda, home to charming strangers, one of them a sister he had given up for dead years ago. The skinny, spunky child had turned into a poised Spanish gentlewoman who reminded him vaguely of the mother he tried not to think of, because his last view of her gave him nightmares for years.

I could leave tomorrow with Lorenzo and Rogelio, he told himself. He looked back at the open gate, which he knew would close at dusk or sooner, given any hint of danger. His heart started to beat faster at even the thought of such confinement, he who had spent so many years on the plains, dodging Indians, starving and feasting in turn, selling horses or stealing some. He knew he had turned from a young man of principle to a man who didn't mind the occasional theft. He could overlook a multitude of sins now that would have troubled him greatly when he was still the son of Pedro Vega, landowner and captain general of the El Paso del Norte District.

Claudio couldn't have said when he had changed, except that it must have come on gradually. There was no one moment when he woke up, looked at his reflection in a tin pan or still water and said, "Well, here is a rascal."

Paloma had no idea. For the past few days and nights, she had sat by him, listened to him, and even hugged him for no particular reason. His little sister's kindly nature had blossomed into thriving womanhood, made sweeter by marriage to an excellent man.

On the other hand, Graciela seemed to know him for what he was: an adventurer with few scruples. Her astuteness did not surprise him. He saw bedraggled slaves like her in every marketplace, in every Indian camp. Their lives were usually short and harsh, with death a relief. It had been his observation that such ill-used women either became hardened and suspicious or shrinking ghosts.

Graciela was different. He could tell from subtle changes in the week or so he had known her that the Double Cross was working its magic on her. He knew she had been stealing food; now Paloma made sure that Graciela took tortillas to bed with her. The result was a relaxing of the slave's shoulders. She no longer started at every strange sound. Just last night, he had heard her tell

Paloma in a quiet voice that she did not need any extra food. He even thought he heard her singing, but that could have been Paloma.

He knew he owed Graciela a great debt for keeping him in the saddle after the Comanches shot him. She had been fearless in her protection. He thought about it now, as he stood so indecisive outside the house. He had not expected her to help him. No one had helped him with anything in ever so long that her protection in a dangerous situation had the power to amaze him.

A person could get soft, being around people like Graciela and Paloma, and even Marco, Claudio decided. He could let down his guard or remain alert, suspicious, and dependent on no one. There was only one logical choice for him.

He watched Graciela put the final touches on Lorenzo Diaz's impressive transformation into a man still several rungs below Marco Mondragón's gentility, but not on the bottom of the heap anymore. He remembered Graciela's sure hand on his own hair and beard, and the level way she looked at him full on, comparing sides, snipping a bit here and there until she was satisfied. Her hand on his shoulder, however briefly, had felt so friendly. It pleased Claudio to see Lorenzo's beaming smile as he took off the towel around his neck and handed it to Graciela with a certain flourish.

Claudio lost his own smile as he watched Marco stroll casually to the gates and stand for a long moment, staring at the horses acquired somehow in Isleta. Out of the corner of his eye, he saw Lorenzo stand up straighter, watching Marco, too, which made Claudio's heart sink. Their business was a shady one, at times. By keeping in motion and trading on the fringes of the colony, they managed to stay ahead of any scrutiny from other *jueces de campo. I will be surprised if we are still here by morning*, Claudio thought. There, he had said it: we.

It won't break your heart, Paloma, if I leave, he rationalized to himself. *I'm not meant to live confined, and you have so much here to keep you occupied. You won't even know I have left.* "You won't miss me," he whispered, trying out the traitor words. He winced at the sound and knew he was turning soft already.

He heard the dinner bell. Paloma had sent Perla's little grandson into the kitchen garden to ring it to summon the house folk to meals and later, everyone to evening prayers.

He wanted to go inside, but Marco was walking around the small herd now, looking closer at the brands.

Lorenzo nodded his thanks to Graciela and walked toward Claudio slowly, not wanting to attract Marco's attention. "Do you think if Rogelio and I are gone before daybreak, it will be soon enough?" Lorenzo whispered to Claudio.

"He's a smart man, but Señor Mondragón is also our host," Claudio whispered back. "No later than daybreak, and I am coming, too."

"Don't be a fool, Claudio," Lorenzo said, his voice mild and patient for a change, as though the Double Cross was beginning to lull him into complacency, too.

"I don't belong here," Claudio said.

"You are so certain of that?" Lorenzo asked.

Claudio had second thoughts in the kitchen. The table nearly groaned with slabs of beef, turkey, boiled eggs sliced in half and sprinkled with hot peppers, and mounds of bread cuddled up next to a bowl of butter. He smiled to see the imprint of a little finger dragged through the butter, remembering Paloma's own love for butter and the tears it caused when Mama scolded her.

With gestures from Marco, everyone was soon seated. Graciela led the little ones, protesting, from the kitchen. Marco called her back and set Claudito on his lap, with Soledad next to Paloma. Graciela retreated to the great fireplace, where Perla handed her bowls of food and pointed where they should go.

Lorenzo stood in the doorway, all shaven and shorn and nearly unrecognizable. Marco waved him to a spot next to Joaquim Gasca, who was unabashedly admiring Paloma. A long, hard stare from Marco ended that admiration. To Claudio's private amusement, the private-lieutenant-royal engineer prudently directed his attention to the plate of chorizo and beans waiting circulation to the left.

Toshua sat on Marco's other side, confirming Claudio's suspicions about the Comanche's place at the Double Cross. The Indian ate with no conversation, then got up suddenly halfway through the meal and went to the kitchen door.

A woman stood there, someone Paloma obviously knew, too, because she was on her feet and in the woman's arms. *Paloma, how can you?* Claudio thought in dismay.

The Comanche woman smiled at Toshua and kissed Paloma's forehead. Claudio noted her pockmarked face and missing fingers, but he could not ignore the genuine pleasure in her eyes upon seeing Paloma.

They stood in quiet conversation for a few brief moments. Claudio glanced at Marco, who smiled at the woman.

"Join us, Eckapeta?" Marco asked. "There's room here by Paloma."

The woman shook her head. "It was a long ride," she said, her Spanish as good as Toshua's, the man who must be her husband.

She spoke softly to Toshua, her hand on his shoulder. He picked up several tortillas from the table and a pot of *posole* by the fireplace.

"When you have refreshed yourself, Eckapeta, would you and Toshua join us in the *sala*?" Marco asked, returning his attention to the massive hunk of beef on his plate.

She nodded, and left as quietly as she had come, Toshua right behind her with the food. Paloma returned to her seat beside her husband, rested her head against his arm for a moment so brief that only a brother would have noticed, then made sure Soledad had more beans on her plate.

"I always feel better when she is here," Paloma said to Claudio.

"I don't know how you can, Little Sister, after what you saw all those years ago," he replied, and winced inside when the conversation stopped entirely.

He could have kicked himself at the look of sadness in her eyes. *I should never have reminded her of Mama*, Claudio thought in misery. He nearly made apology, when he realized with a worse start that her look of sorrow was directed at him. She wasn't remembering Mama; she was feeling pity that he had never moved on. He stared at his plate, certain now that he would leave in the morning. He didn't know this sister.

Marco moved into the sudden conversational chasm by nodding to Perla. "I believe we are ready for your most excellent *flan* now."

The other diners leaped to fill the awkward pause. Joaquim Gasca took another tortilla before Perla's little grandson began to clear the table. Lorenzo spooned down the rest of his *posole* and cast a longing eye on the turkey platter that Graciela was removing on Sancha's orders.

Looking like the benevolent host he was, Marco eyed them all in that leisurely way of his. He did not fool Claudio for a minute. His eyes rested on Lorenzo, who had the spoon to his open mouth.

"Señor Diaz, what say you to dessert in my office? It's just down the hall. Graciela, you take my place here and help little Claudio, because he loves *flan* almost as much as his mother. Excuse us, my dear." He looked at Claudio next, and there was nothing soft in his eyes this time. "You come, too. We three have a matter of business, and it won't wait."

Claudio got to his feet and took his bowl of *flan*. He felt old, sour, and his shoulder hurt. He dared a look at his sister, whose eyes were still filled with concern for him. She opened her mouth to say something to him, he was sure of it, but Soledad demanded her attention and the moment passed.

I am failing her, he thought in misery. *Or is she failing me?*

Chapter Twenty

In which Claudio disappoints nearly everyone

MARCO KNEW THERE WERE days when the Council of the Indies of King Carlos III did not pay him enough to be *juez de campo*. This was going to be one of them.

Carrying his bowl of *flan*, he ushered Lorenzo and Claudio into his office. He had moved from his office by the horse barn when it became obvious that Toshua needed a place for Eckapeta to stay when she visited, and Paloma needed his help, with her infant cousin and their baby on the way. The house had too many empty rooms, so it made perfect sense to turn an unused bedchamber into an office. It made even more sense because Paloma kept his office tidier than he ever had.

He had found her here late this afternoon, looking through his correspondence from the governor and the list and descriptions of missing cattle and horses. He knew from the frown on her face that her discovery hadn't pleased her at all.

Without a word, she pointed to the entry listing three missing horses from Isleta and their brands, the same brand he had noticed on Lorenzo Diaz's horses tethered outside his own gate. He promised her he would deal with the matter, which didn't lessen the frown.

"I wish I hadn't even looked," Paloma told him.

She looked so distressed that a hug was in order, even in an official government office. And then another hug, because Governor de Anza was a long way away, followed by a lingering kiss, because King Carlos probably never gave New Mexico a thought.

"Paloma, if you hadn't looked, I would have," he said to console her. It might even be true.

"They're smelly and probably rascals, but I like them, Marco," she told him.

"I do, too," he assured her, "but there is a point of law here."

"Be merciful," she pleaded, then kissed his ear.

Now was not the time to recall such pleasant things as a kissed ear. Marco gestured to the chairs. Rogelio, who had tagged along, crouched in the corner. Marco moved behind the desk to take his usual place, but sighed and pulled the chair usually reserved for Paloma and set it in front of the desk. He sat close to his guests, who looked more worried than hungry now.

He reached behind him to the loose papers on his desk and put them in Lorenzo's lap.

No fool, Lorenzo finished the *flan*—first things first—then took a look at the papers.

"I picked these up from the governor when I was in Taos," Marco said. He sat back and gave Lorenzo the hard stare that usually reduced horse thieves to silence. The thing was, he didn't mean it this time. All the events involving Lorenzo Diaz and the man's now-dead brother and the horse trading in Taos had landed Claudio Vega back in his sister's life. How could a husband be angry about that?

But as he had told Paloma, the law was the law. He had sworn in Santa Fe before God that he would uphold all the laws, even the silly ones. Except when he couldn't, because the Council of the Indies had no idea what went on in the Valle del Sol District.

"Those horses are inside my own horse barn, now that the gate is closed," Marco said, then slammed his hand on his knee. "*My* barn! And I am this district's *juez de campo!*"

His dramatic gesture would have been more effective had he slammed his hand on his desk instead of his knee. At least his bowl of *flan* was safe on his desk.

"Señores, I know those are stolen horses," he said.

Lorenzo gazed back, so innocent. Claudio looked less innocent. Rogelio in the corner started to whimper.

"The last thing I want to do is arrest you," Marco admitted. "In a roundabout way, you have reunited my brother-in-law with my dear wife. The husband in me wants to just wave you on tomorrow and forget I ever saw you."

"Listen to the husband," Lorenzo said.

Marco was a man of some rectitude and considerable honor. He called every scrap of his will and reason into play then, just to keep from leaping to his feet, grabbing Lorenzo by what was left of his hair and slinging him around the room. It was one of those moments, thankfully far apart, when he wished he were Toshua and could just slice off half a yard of skin, or scoop out a testicle, and have done with it.

He counted to ten, then counted again. All the while Rogelio was sniffing by the door, wiping his nose on his arm. *Thank goodness Paloma doesn't have to look at that right now, in her delicate state,* he thought, mostly to take his mind off the harm he wanted to do Lorenzo Diaz, horse thief.

Marco did the time-honored thing and sidestepped the matter, because a larger crisis loomed, a personal one. "Here is another matter, Lorenzo: Claudio gave me a bill of sale for a matched team of bays. Is that bill of sale a forgery?"

"Absolutely not," Lorenzo replied firmly.

Marco would have believed him, except for that tiny moment between question and answer when Lorenzo's steady gaze flickered as he glanced toward the ceiling. A less experienced *juez de campo* wouldn't even have noticed. Marco had interrogated many a liar, and Lorenzo Diaz was one more in that long line of rascals and cheats.

"You're telling me the truth?" Marco asked again, knowing that the answer would be the same, and that he was about to become poorer. But honor was honor, and he could prove nothing.

"Would I lie to a *juez de campo*?" Lorenzo asked. This time he mastered the little flicker toward the ceiling.

"Many have," Marco said. He stood up and went to his desk drawer, where he counted out the sum owed for the team eating hay in his horse barn now. He was going to miss them when he returned them to their owner. He handed the money to Lorenzo, then took out a smaller amount and gave it to Claudio.

"Brother, thank you again for trusting me enough to pay my bill at the inn."

Claudio accepted the coins, but his face was troubled. *You look so much like Paloma,* Marco thought. *Would that you ran with a better crowd.*

"I forgot to look, and the bill of sale is in my room. Where did you buy that wonderful team of bays?" Marco asked Lorenzo.

"The ranch of Señor José Vasquez," Lorenzo said promptly, without any eye waver. "In the valley of Pojoaque."

I can return them when I go to Santa Fe this fall with my wool clip, Marco thought. *I hope I am paid well for that wool clip.*

And that was all the business he cared to conduct with horse thieves. He closed the drawer where he kept his money and locked it, pocketing the key. "Lorenzo, I will not keep you any longer," he said, not bothering with a bow, because the rascal deserved none. "I expect you to return those three horses eating in my barn to the man in Isleta, where you stole them."

"Señor, I never …." Lorenzo began.

Marco withered the horse trader with a look. "You have been paid for the team I now own. We have no more business. I expect you to be gone by daylight." His own stare at Lorenzo did not waver. "I have the power to arrest you and seize this property you claim you acquired honestly, but Lorenzo, I do not have the heart."

He stood by his desk until the men left, then sank down into his chair again, kicking himself for his folly. He looked up to see Claudio standing in the doorway. Marco just shook his head.

"Marco, did … did you want me in the *sala*, too?" Claudio asked.

I wish you were an honest man, Marco thought, but Paloma will never hear otherwise from me. "Yes, I do. Let's walk together."

"I'll be there in a minute," Claudio said, not meeting Marco's gaze. "Time for a piss, you know."

"You won't even walk with me," Marco said softly, as Claudio hurried away, his head down.

Sick at heart and determined not to show it to his wife, Marco went to the *sala*, where he heard laughter from Joaquim Gasca, who was probably entertaining Paloma. The man had no scruples, either. *I am surrounded by idiots,* Marco thought, *and I am chief among them.*

Her eyes merry, Paloma patted the tall chair next to hers. They were the only chairs in the room, so everyone else sat on the adobe outcroppings from the wall, padded with Pueblo blankets and frankly more comfortable than the chairs. But the chairs represented power, something he needed just then. To his personal gratification, Toshua and Eckapeta sat on the floor close to Paloma.

He smiled at the two of them, suddenly struck by something he hadn't considered before. Whenever Paloma was in a room with strange people, Toshua always stood in front of her or close by. And here was Eckapeta, too, as watchful as her husband over that which Marco held most dear. He felt himself relax. No matter how many scoundrels came his way in the course of official duties, Paloma was safe. His pummeled heart started to beat again.

"Eckapeta, please tell us what you learned from Kwihnai," he asked with no preamble, because he wanted this day over, and consolation of a personal nature from Paloma.

"I found Kwihnai in the summer camp," she said, skipping right to the heart of the matter, too, even though Marco knew how much The People liked to draw out a story. But then, Eckapeta always had a secret sense for personal feelings. He blessed her in his heart.

"I told him what Great Owl had done, and how he had shot at our Claudio." *Our Claudio. Our Claudio could use some scruples*, Marco thought.

She gave Marco a sharp look, which made prickles run down his back. Could the woman read his mind?

"I asked Kwihnai for help to find Great Owl and destroy him, but he will not commit any warriors." Eckapeta spoke in a calm voice, but Marco heard the undercurrent of disdain. "He knows Great Owl is out to disrupt any attempt at peace, but Kwihnai wants to see how things go."

"That implies he will be watching us," Marco said. "I understand this, so do not frown, Eckapeta. Kwihnai's walk is more hazardous than ours."

"Between two Comanche forces," Joaquim Gasca said. "Maybe I should be like my sergeant and never volunteer for anything."

"Change your mind?" Marco asked, almost wishing he could change his.

Joaquim shrugged. "You can't imagine how boring life is in Santa Maria, señor. Perhaps I will be a hero."

"We will be an army of three," Marco said.

"Four, surely," Claudio said. "I am coming, too."

"Please remain here with your sister and Eckapeta," Marco told him. "I saw how you were wincing on that ride back from Santa Maria, and that was no long trip. There will be hard traveling into the cloud land of the Utes. You still need to heal."

Marco wanted to say more—how he did not entirely trust Claudio, because of the matter of the stolen horses. He also knew he would face Comanches without a weapon before he would humiliate Paloma with her brother's failings in front of these people. "Remain here, Claudio."

Claudio shook his head. "I want to go with you!" he said, louder this time.

"And I want you here. *You're* the one Great Owl tried to kill," Marco said, his voice rising as well. Paloma put her hand on his arm.

"You'll make me stay behind walls with the women and children?" Claudio challenged. "Paloma, you don't need me here, do you, not with all the archers and guards around this place?"

"Well, I …" she began, "I would feel safer if you were …."

Claudio stood up and left the room. Marco listened a moment until the door to his bedchamber banged shut.

No one spoke. Paloma's face had gone white. Only Joaquim seemed uninterested in the family drama that had just unraveled. He stretched and stood up.

"Are we leaving early, señor?"

"As soon as we can," Marco replied. "Your room is the next one down the hall, beyond what I am certain is a closed door now. We will ring the bell for prayer in the chapel soon. You are welcome to join us."

Joaquim ambled to the door. "Señor, El Padre Celestial and I worked out an arrangement years ago: I don't bother Him and He lets me alone. Good night."

At least his servants did not fail Marco. He knelt with them, and with his daughter and her wiggles through the Rosary, and then his prayer for his family's protection while he was away. His heart opened wide as his little son, also kneeling occasionally with Paloma, repeated his words under his breath, then crossed himself in strange directions while Paloma tried not to laugh.

Serious as usual—who ever knew what she was thinking?—Graciela knelt behind Paloma, ready to take either child, counting her fingers because she had no beads. Marco reminded himself to ask Paloma to give her the old rosary she had received when she came to Valle del Sol as a new bride. He had given Paloma a beautiful ebony Rosary for Christmas, a Rosary for the dignified matron that she was now, when she remembered to be dignified.

His prayer was hurried, because the children only had stamina for worship in short doses, but he prayed from his heart for God's protection on them all, as his little army prepared for what, Marco did not know.

Marco continued his prayer in his bedchamber, while Paloma and Graciela prepared the children for bed. He knelt at his *reclinatorio* and tried to pray. He hoped the saints didn't take offense, but he felt more peace listening to his wife and children. She was singing a lullaby, and he knew from experience that the sleepy children were arguing about bed as their eyes closed.

Paloma went right into his arms when she came into their chamber. "A long, long day," she whispered in his ear.

"Too long for you and me to have a few minutes of tipi time?" he teased, reminding her of their sojourn among The People.

"Heavens, no," she told him. "Only a few minutes?" She shed her clothes without any more conversation and shook her head when he went to extinguish the lamp by their bed.

He blew out the lamp anyway, but opened the shutters. "Full moon tonight, Paloma. I always look better by moonlight."

She laughed and gathered him close in bed. "You're my lover," she whispered in his ear. "Don't think of anything but me for a little while."

He didn't. She was easy to satisfy, and then to satisfy again, because Paloma Vega was his lover, too, his constant, his star in the meadow. She turned her face into his arm when she cried out, so her satisfaction would be for his ears only. Their empty house was full now and he felt no need to entertain the guests.

She didn't want him to leave her, so he stayed where he was until his rump cooled off. "Autumn is coming, my love," he told her finally, as he reached for the bedding and pulled it over both of them. "My ass gets cold."

"Your language," she said in that gruff voice he loved so well, the one usually reserved for times like this. She began to massage his cold rump against her, until she began to sigh again, and turned her face into his arm. "My goodness. I *thought* I was tired."

"Tell me truly, Marco," she said finally, when he had settled himself beside her. "Am I a freak of nature?"

He laughed softly and pulled her close. "No! You just love me a lot."

She laughed, too. "I do, you know," she said, the words sounding almost shy to him. Her modesty after a wild romp never ceased to amaze him. Paloma Vega was a lady through and through, except when she was just a woman. And that was the magnificent paradox of his wife.

He hoped she wasn't too tired for what he thought of as their drowsy time, when problems of the world were solved, and issues aired and put away in the sleepy fashion of lovers.

"I told Lorenzo to leave tomorrow and return those three horses you were wondering about to the man in Isleta he stole them from," he told her, as he stroked her hair. "You were right."

"I wish I hadn't even looked," she said, her fingers tugging gently at his ears. Somehow she had figured out how much he liked that.

"It's worse. That matched team I bought from Claudio in Taos? Stolen, too."

He heard her intake of breath. "They're so beautiful. But isn't the bill of sale over there on your clothes chest?"

"Forged. Lorenzo told me they were legal, but I could tell he was lying."

"You didn't call him on his lie?"

"How could I do that?" he asked her, as she rubbed his chest. His sigh sounded enormous in the quiet room, until he realized she was doing the same thing. "I feel that I owe the horse traders a bigger debt for sending Claudio to us, no matter how inadvertent that was. I paid Lorenzo, but I will return those horses to … to … Señor José Vasquez in Pojoaque Valley when I take my wool clip and brand records to Santa Fe in a month or so." He rested his hand on her belly. "Go ahead and say it: I'm a gullible idiot, and many pesos poorer."

Paloma pressed her hand over his. "Push down gently right there, and you will feel the tiniest little package."

He was happy to oblige her and change the subject. She was right. Just a soft touch and he let go of the day's cares. More important business than brands and money was going on inside his wife.

He thought she slept then. His eyes started to close, too, but she brought his hand up to rest between her breasts. She was so soft there. His slim Paloma had been replaced by a woman with smooth curves, and he liked this one even better.

"Claudio isn't so happy here, is he?" she asked in a small voice, almost as if she didn't want to hear her own words.

"He told me on the way to Santa Maria that he doesn't like living behind walls."

She sighed again, then raised his fingers to her lips and kissed them. "When you return, let's think of ways to make him happier about Valle del Sol." She put his hand on her neck, and Marco knew she was ready for sleep then. "There's land here, and maybe he'll find a lady to court." She started to say more, but the day finally caught up with Paloma Vega.

MARCO WAS STILL IN the grip of sleep hours later. Through the fog of morning, he heard a rooster, and another, and then a scream so loud and heartbroken that he was out of bed in one motion. He looked back to apologize to Paloma for scrambling over her like that, but there was only a pile of blankets where she should have been.

Another scream, and then wild sobbing, and he knew without opening the door what had happened. "Damn you, Claudio," he whispered as he grabbed his nightshirt and pulled it over his head.

Paloma lay against the open door to Claudio's room, weeping. He knelt beside her and gathered her close, even as their children began to cry in the other bedchamber, startled from their sleep. He didn't need to confirm Claudio's absence. Whether three hours, three days, or three years had passed, empty rooms all felt the same.

He held his sobbing wife close to his heart.

Chapter Twenty-One

In which Marco does his duty, even if King Carlos doesn't pay him enough

THE HORSE TRADERS HAD taken Marco at his word. They were gone before daylight, Claudio with them, plus the three horses under discussion last night, and the matched team, as well.

Startled to see his master in a nightshirt with his hair wild, the night guard stammered out what had happened. "They … they were as nice as you please, and said you had told them to leave early, because the days were getting shorter." His eyes were wide and worried. "Was that wrong? Forgive me, señor!"

"No, no," Marco replied, stung by his own words. "I told them exactly that."

"Your … your wife? Is she …. Señor, we could hear her!"

There was no sense in lying. "Her brother left with them, and she is devastated," he told the guard.

He told the same thing to Toshua and Eckapeta, who had come to their door of his former office, Toshua with lance in hand. "I can bring back Claudio," Toshua said, his voice hard and tight.

The last thing Marco wanted was for a Comanche with murder in his heart to go after a confused man. "We can't keep him here against his will," Marco said. "I must go back to Paloma."

Eckapeta touched his arm. "My grandchildren?"

"Go to them. Paloma needs me right now."

And here I stand in my nightshirt, Marco thought, as he hurried back to the hacienda, Eckapeta right behind him. At least Paloma was still on their bed, where he had left her. He closed the door and crawled in beside her, holding her close as she cried and then slept, exhausted.

When he knew she had surrendered to deep sleep, he got out of bed, dressed and went across the hall to Claudio's empty room. *How could you do this to your little sister?* warred with *We both knew you were confused and unhappy.* He sat on Claudio's bed. "I was lost and you found me," he said, looking across the hall to the bedroom he shared with Claudio's sister. He looked down at the rumpled sheets on which he sat, testimony to a poor soul tossing and turning and unable to find any peace. "You were lost and no one found you, Claudio. Were we too late?"

He lay back on Claudio's bed, his moccasined feet dangling over the edge, and stared at the ceiling. He could remain here and let someone else lead this little expedition to scout out Great Owl. There was certainly plenty to do. The harvest was nearly over, and the cattle had been rounded up and brought down from summer pastures. What remained was to decide which ones to take to the Santa Fe market, along with his wool clip. Governor de Anza would entertain him and he would turn over his brand records and taxes he had collected to the *fiscal primero*. At most, he could devote two weeks to hunting Great Owl, or just ignore the man and hope for the best.

But there was no one else to take up the task.

"Yes, and Great Owl will attack the Utes closest to us, and perhaps cajole or force them to join him and come against our settlements," Marco told the ceiling. "There goes any chance of peace. Damn, but this is a dilemma."

He heard the door across the hall open and turned his head to see Paloma looking at him. He blew her a kiss, hopeful. She returned his kiss, then looked toward their children's room. He knew Graciela and Eckapeta had taken their little ones to the kitchen for mush and raisins.

She must have known it too, so she just stood in the doorway in her nightgown and disheveled hair. Her eyes were red with weeping, but she was the most magnificent woman he had ever seen.

She padded across the hall on bare feet, closed the door behind her and climbed onto Claudio's bed. With a sigh, she rested her head on his stomach.

"I wish I understood," she said simply.

Marco touched her hair, combing out the tangles with his fingers. "It is God's mystery," he said finally. "There you were, two young ones who survived a terrible ordeal. You wound up in Santa Fe in the household of your uncle and were treated abominably."

She nodded, then turned sideways so she could look at him. "Go on," she whispered.

"I suspect that Claudio wound up as practically the possession of Lorenzo and Paco Diaz, men too easy with the law."

"Claudio knew better!" Paloma protested.

Marco put his hand over her mouth. "Hear me out, wife," he said, relieved when she kissed his fingers. "I have been part of rescues of colony children stolen by Comanches or Apaches. Even a Ute tribe. They should loathe their captors, eh? Small children like ours—God forbid—I could understand little ones transferring their allegiance to Indian parents. But older children? Children who would have been the age you lost your family all those years ago? I don't understand it, but some of them come to love the very people who stole them." He sighed. "Maybe someone much smarter than I am can explain this odd thing someday, but I have seen it. Claudio identifies with the horse traders now. He only feels safe with them."

"He never gave us a chance!"

"He certainly did not." Marco pulled Paloma closer until they were breast to breast. "Here is the oddest part of all: what happened to you could have made you sour and bitter, but it didn't. There is something in you that would not succumb to foul treatment."

He enveloped his wife in a tight embrace. "Paloma my heart, I was on my way to turning into Claudio when you came into my life with that yellow dog. I had given up! All I wanted was a dog to keep my feet warm. I owe you a debt I can never repay."

They clung together until Paloma heaved a shuddering sigh. "My love, I was only a day away from giving up, too, and just returning to Santa Fe and my relatives. Adventures aren't all that fun, are they?"

They laughed together.

"What … what made the difference?"

She thought a long moment, rubbing her cheek against his chest. "Something inside I cannot explain. Why doesn't Claudio feel as I do? We were reared by the same parents."

Marco raised himself up on one elbow to see her better. "Was Claudio happy?"

"Well, certainly," she began, then stopped. She flopped on her back and stared at the same ceiling that had given Marco no answers earlier. "No, no, he wasn't. I've tried so hard *not* to remember that morning, but another piece is coming back."

"Let it."

She touched his heart then by putting his hand on her belly, as though to protect their child within from what she was remembering. He knew it was an unconscious gesture, but it told him everything he ever needed to know about Paloma as a mother, and if he wanted to flatter himself, her idea of him as a father.

"He and Papa had been arguing for some time. Claudio was sixteen and desperate to join the army. Papa said no, of course. Papa always said, why would you do that when there was this hacienda and land grant? I didn't like it when they quarreled."

Her voice sounded small, like a child's. She hesitated, as if resisting another memory.

"Go on, Paloma, tell me," he whispered. "I'm keeping our baby safe."

"The last thing I remember him saying to Papa … oh, I can't."

"You can. You're safe, too."

"How could I forget this? Claudio said, 'There are times I wish you were dead, Papa.' " She shuddered. "Papa just laughed. He knew Claudio was joking. I remember that Papa put his hand on Claudio's head and gave his hair a friendly little tug, and Claudio put his arm around Papa. All forgiven."

"And then?"

"They all died." She sucked in her breath, and he pressed more firmly on her belly. "Marco, do you think Claudio keeps remembering that argument?"

"I think it highly likely. Imagine that much guilt."

They were silent then, twined in each other.

"I know he was happy to find me," Paloma said.

"Of course he was, but there is this war going on inside your brother."

"Do you think he will ever return?"

"I am certain he will, Paloma," Marco said, and meant every word. "He'll show up when he feels like it, visit a while, but then he'll leave again."

Paloma gave him a long look. "Unless he can find a reason to remain, my love."

She slept again, but peacefully now. Marco stayed with her.

Paloma woke up to the noisy rumble of a stomach—hers. Marco was snoring softly in her ear, just tickling it enough to wake her up, if her stomach hadn't.

"I am hungry," she whispered into that ear.

He opened his eyes. "Come to think of it, so am I. We haven't slept this late since we were newly married."

She sat up, hands flying to her hair, which by this hour was usually smooth in a low bun on the back of her neck. She looked down at bare legs up to her thighs, hoping that no one had decided to blunder into Claudio's room and see her in such disarray.

She looked around the sparse room, wondering if she could find a brush, and found something better. She pointed it out to Marco, who was closer. "Over there. Is that a note?"

He got up, reached for the folded paper, and spilled out a handful of gold coins. He read the note and started to smile. "Maybe Claudio isn't so far off the mark. It's addressed to me. Listen: 'Señor Mondragón'—ah, the penitent sinner!—'I am returning the team to José Vasquez in Pojoaque.'—well, well—'It was easy to steal back your money from Lorenzo, for he is a heavy sleeper. Tell Paloma I am a fool and that I love her. Claudio.' "

"I would like to wring his neck," Paloma said, then managed a smile. "I would!"

"I don't doubt it," Marco told her. He went to their room and returned with her hairbrush. "Turn around. I can do this for you, and then I think I had better get my carcass to the horse barn. We still need to find out what Great Owl is up to."

She closed her eyes when he began to brush her hair. She knew she had the power to weep and rail and carry on and keep him from this scout for Great Owl, but she understood his duty.

"How long?" she asked when her hair started to crackle and he stopped.

"Two weeks, perhaps a little more. I know you will feel safe here with Eckapeta and my guards. I want to know where Great Owl is. Winter is coming, and I doubt he will act before spring."

She stood up, and staggered, but he was right there to steady her. "Crying makes me red-eyed and dizzy," she said. "I think I will not weep anymore over Claudio, that rat."

He laughed and clapped a brotherly arm around her shoulder as he steered her toward their room. "That's my girl!"

Paloma stopped at the door. "I am wondering … why did Great Owl sell Graciela for money? He didn't want to barter, did he? I am naïve, indeed, but why do Comanches want money?"

"I have wondered that myself, because I have seen many barters for captives. There is only one reason I can think of, and that is partly why I want to find that rascal. It didn't occur to me any sooner than last night, but I think he might want to buy guns from the French. The governor told me of such suspicions—a word here, a word there."

She absorbed that bit of unwelcome news. "And then?"

"That's the rub. Is he planning to shoulder aside Kwihnai, or destroy the cloudland Utes, or try to gain their alliance against us? And if there are French in our Spanish domain, where are they? The whole thing makes my head ache."

He helped her dress, because she couldn't seem to concentrate on anything.

She borrowed one of Marco's hair ties and gathered her hair low on her neck, not taking time for a bun. It was easy enough for her to go calmly into the kitchen, greet her children, and help Graciela give them their breakfast.

"Mama, you scared me," Soledad told her as the little one sat on her lap.

"I didn't mean to, my love," she said. "It's just that my brother has left without saying goodbye and I was so sad."

In that wise way of children, Soledad stared at little Claudio. "When he is naughty to me, I might not cry if he left."

Paloma laughed and hugged Soledad. "I remember times like that, too, with *my* brothers."

She smiled at Marco over Soledad's head. "And you, señor, had better prepare your little army. If Eckapeta, Emilio, and a host of excellent archers and guards cannot manage in your absence, then we are too cowardly to live in Valle del Sol."

There was no denying the relief in his eyes or his good humor. "Señor, is it? Should I sleep in the horse barn when I return?"

"Only if you prefer smelly barns to me," she teased back. "I will miss you most awfully."

She meant both statements, and reminded him again an hour later when she and their little ones knelt on the hard ground by the gate while he made the sign of the cross on each forehead and blessed them to be safe. Then she was in his arms with no tears, and a whacking great kiss that made Joaquim Gasca laugh out loud, and Toshua turn away, because he was a gentleman.

Children in tow—Soledad and Claudito both looking like thunder clouds because they wanted to ride with Papa—Paloma climbed the steps to the parapet. The little family watched the three horsemen until they were small specks against the enormous sky.

Chapter Twenty-Two

In which Claudio is more penitent than usual and Lorenzo is equally firm

L EADING MARCO'S STOLEN TEAM of matched bays, Claudio did not look forward to catching up with the horse trader and Rogelio. Lorenzo would certainly thrash him. Several years had passed since his last beating by either Lorenzo or the late unlamented Paco, but Claudio knew how Lorenzo felt about commerce, legal or otherwise.

Maybe it was the haircut, or the barbering, or even the bath. All Lorenzo did was frown at him. Since it was Lorenzo, this was no ordinary frown, and probably would have totally cowed an entire generation of gently raised children from a big city like Taos. As it was, Claudio only felt relief.

At least until Lorenzo opened his mouth and did not even mention the team in tow. He went right to the matter of Paloma. "Claudio, you fool," he said, his voice still conversational, which of itself made the hair on Claudio's back stand on end. He would have preferred the shouting Lorenzo, the man he knew. "You have a wonderful sister, an honorable brother-in-law—even if he is a bit picky about the law—all the food you could want, and I saw how that slave Graciela looked at you." Lorenzo gestured around the wider world of New Mexico. "Why on earth are you following us?"

Graciela looked at me? Claudio thought, startled. He halted the team of bays. *Dios*, but they were trained well. "I don't know that I want to stay at the Double Cross. Besides, I feel the need to return this team to Hacienda Rumaldo."

"Since you gave the money back to Señor Mondragón—"

"And *you* told him the team came from Pojoaque Valley," Claudio challenged. No sense in holding back now, since Lorenzo hadn't beaten him to a pulp yet. "Imagine Marco's embarrassment, and probably his lifelong irritation, if he took these lovely beasts to Señor Vasquez and earned a blank stare in exchange, because they aren't his? Or were you just planning not to return them?" Claudio looked down at his saddle horn. "Lorenzo, things get complicated when we do either right *or* wrong."

Lorenzo stared at him for a long time. Claudio thought he might be choosing his words with extraordinary care. It wasn't even noon yet, and Lorenzo continued to surprise him. Maybe that bath had washed the crusty stuff around the trader's conscience. What about his own conscience?

"Claudio, you're turning into an amazing amount of trouble," Lorenzo said.

"*Me*? Paloma's the problem," Claudio said in his defense, though it sounded weak to his clean ears.

Lorenzo ignored his outburst. "We'll return the team to old Señor Rumaldo's pasture, although I don't doubt for a minute that someone else with fewer scruples than we have will just steal them again."

Claudio smiled at Lorenzo's artless declaration. "We are horse traders and we do a little *paso doble* all around the law. One step here, one step there." Might as well admit it. "I think I'm getting tired of the dance." Claudio waited a moment. "Are you?"

"No!" Lorenzo declared, even though Claudio thought he heard the tiniest hesitation. "What I *am* doing is getting tired of *you*, Claudio. After we return the team and someone less principled steals them, Rogelio and I are going to escort you back to the Double Cross."

"And if I don't want to go?" Claudio challenged.

"Rogelio and I will either garrote you with a nice thin piece of wire and dump your stupid carcass here for the buzzards, or we will tie you up and drag you back to Paloma. Your choice."

"That's no choice!"

"I knew you would see it my way."

* * *

As far as Paloma could tell, the only advantage in having Marco gone for any length of time was the opportunity to eat more cooked onions that usual. Even before they were married, he had warned her of what happened to his inner workings when he ate too many cooked onions. She liked them, so his absence meant more onions in the food.

That wasn't enough reason to wish him away, however, so mostly she felt glum waking up in the morning with no man beside her. True, she could lie in bed with her hands behind her head and think about things, but she missed Marco.

True, there was more room in the bed for Soli and Claudito, if they woke up early enough to join her. She knew they missed their father, too, although she had to smile on the first morning when Soledad looked under the bed and peered inside the massive clothes press, then crawled into bed with all the resignation of a Christian martyr and none of the grace.

"You know Papa never hides in those places," Paloma said to her daughter as she cuddled her close.

"I was hoping," Soledad said with a small sigh that went right to Paloma's heart.

Even Emilio's offer to drop the gate in the *acequia* and leave a little water to splash in met with a sorrowful shake of Soledad's head.

After one long day of unhappiness, a consultation with Perla followed by a visit with the beekeeper resolved at least some of Soledad's misery.

"If this doesn't cheer her up a little, then there is no remedy," said the practical Perla to Paloma and Eckapeta as they watched Soli stare out the kitchen window. "Come, child," the cook said. "You need to pay a visit to Cipriano." They looked out the window together. "See? There he is, talking to Sancha. And see what is in his hand?"

"Honey?" Soledad asked, perking up.

"Yes! Bring it here and you and I will make something wonderful."

Soledad darted out the door, forgetting that she was a lady and should walk everywhere. Perla looked at Paloma, and her glance bordered on conspiratorial.

"Would that we had a remedy for what ails Sancha," she said in a low voice.

"What can you mean?" Paloma asked.

"Señora, Sancha has been moping ever since Lorenzo rode away."

"Lorenzo?"

Perla came closer. "At this very window, Sancha took a good look at Lorenzo while he was bathing in the *acequia*." Perla rolled her eyes, which made Eckapeta laugh.

"Bigger than Big Man Down There?" Eckapeta teased in turn. "Eh, Paloma?"

They were all laughing when Soledad walked back into the kitchen, her eyes on the full jar of honey in her hands. Solemnly, she held it up to Perla, who, still smiling, poured it into a well-seasoned pot and swung it back over the low coals. She handed Soledad another jar. "Take your Mama with you to the spring house and measure me just this much cream," she said, putting her finger against the jar more than halfway up.

"Mama, what is she planning?" Soledad asked as she skipped alongside Paloma to the spring house.

The stone-lined room, set three feet below ground level, smelled sharply of curing cheese and curdled cream. Paloma measured out the cream and handed it to Soledad. "Perla will want you and Claudito to stretch out some honey sweets."

Soledad gasped, her eyes wide. "Mama! All this because I am sad?"

"Yes, you scamp! I expect you to be much more cheerful when the honey is pulled and cut into little bites." She kissed Soledad's hair, breathing in the fragrance of summer sun and thinking how quickly August had faded away.

The mother in her had something else to say. "And don't start to think that if you are sad we will make candy every time."

"I will never do that, Mama," Soli declared, eyes wide, voice solemn.

"Never?" Paloma asked, amused.

Soli gestured for Paloma to bend closer. "I might try it on Papa just once."

"You are a scamp!" Paloma said, giving her a gentle swat on her skirt. "I will warn Papa."

Soledad mustered all her dignity, which apparently was considerable for one so young. "A girl has to try, Mama."

"I suppose she does, dearest," Paloma said, remembering a few such moments with her own mother. Suddenly Paloma missed dreadfully the wisdom Mama could have shared with her own children. "I believe I did, once or twice."

"Did your mama give you a swat?"

"Certainly! Now hurry on before I give you another."

Her heart full, Paloma watched Soledad skip ahead, happy now, even though the cream jar was in some danger. Standing by the spring house, her hands pressed together, Paloma whispered, "Mama, if only you could see my dear ones."

With all her heart, she wanted Marco beside her. Marco would listen, then gather her close, assuring her that somehow, at least in his personal theology, their departed ones knew and understood. She thought of her brother, wherever he was, sad that he did not know how she felt. *Please come back, Claudio*, she thought. *If you do not, go with God.*

Standing on chairs, but only as close to the fireplace as Paloma would permit, both children watched as Perla slowly stirred the honey and cream. When the time was right, she added a pinch of ground chilis, which made Claudito take a swipe at his mouth.

"Just like his father," Paloma whispered to Eckapeta. She took the Indian woman's hand and tugged it to her cheek. "Why wouldn't Claudio stay?" she whispered.

"He does not like or trust Toshua and me," Eckapeta said, with no hesitation. "It is more, though. I think that deep down in a hidden place, he is sad he could not protect you from the raiders."

"It was so long ago," Paloma said, her eyes on Soli and Claudito, almost dancing in their eagerness to begin pulling the *miel y leche*. "So long."

"Not to Claudio," Eckapeta said.

"What a waste," Paloma replied. She stood up and put her arms around her children, watching Perla work her magic. "Marco told me my brother would return now and then." She rested her chin on Soli's head. "I hope that is often enough for me."

She glanced at Sancha, wondering when she had become so self-centered that she did not notice the housekeeper was pining, too. *Lorenzo?* And there was Graciela, standing like a shadow by the door, her eyes on the children, because they were her stewardship. The girl's frown, however, told Paloma there was something more she'd been missing. She turned to Eckapeta.

"Why are you the only woman in this kitchen who is not mournful?" she asked her great good friend.

"I don't live in yesterday or tomorrow," Eckapeta told her. "None of The People do. We don't even have words for it. I live right now."

I may have just learned something, Paloma thought, as she spread a little olive oil on the wooden table so Perla could pour out the hot, thickened mass. Paloma enlisted Graciela to take the children outside and walk them around until the honey cooled.

"But why is Graciela moping?" Paloma asked.

Eckapeta shrugged. "Maybe you need to pay more attention to her and think less about your own problems, even if she is just a slave."

"That is not something you should say to our *dama*," Sancha scolded.

Eckapeta gave the housekeeper a sharp look. "I say what I want."

"I should handle today's problems only?" Paloma asked. She could placate Sancha later.

Eckapeta nodded. "I will walk the children around outside until the *dulce* cools. Ask Graciela to help you straighten up the children's room."

Paloma gestured to Graciela, who had only gotten as far as the kitchen garden with the children.

"I have neglected everything in the last few days," Paloma said to Graciela as they made Soledad's bed together, then tidied the room. After they finished, she sank down on Soledad's bed and patted the spot next to her. "Sit down."

Graciela sat, calmly enough but always with a level of tension that puzzled Paloma. *We treat you well*, she thought. *What more is there?*

She could only try. "Sancha tells me that no tortillas are missing now."

"I have lost the need for extra ones," Graciela told her simply.

Paloma decided to come right out and ask. The children would be back soon and clamoring for her attention in the kitchen. "Is something troubling you? I would like to know, because I have been where you are, and no one cared."

Graciela shook her head decisively, but too soon. "Nothing, señora." She managed a false laugh that fooled neither of them, from the way the blush rose higher on the slave's face.

You are no good at lying, Paloma thought. She said nothing more. If Marco could listen to Lorenzo, know he was lying, but pay him anyway for stolen horses because he was a gentleman, she could leave Graciela alone.

"Well, then, we had better return to the kitchen," Paloma said. "Soledad and Claudio will probably stage an overthrow of the hacienda if we are not prompt."

Graciela nodded, but stayed where she was a moment more. Paloma regarded her from the doorway. *I must try to learn more*, she thought.

"If there is something I should know, please tell me," Paloma said, trying once again. "I care not so much for myself, but if the matter involves a loved one, I need to know, don't I?"

Graciela pressed her lips in a tight line and shook her head, even as her eyes seemed to send another message.

So the matter rested for another day. The honey candy helped relieve Soledad of any anxiety because of the absence of her father, and Claudito was happy to follow in his sister's footsteps. Paloma conferred each morning with Emilio, concerning the day's duties as everyone prepared for the coming winter, even as the sun shone hot and long on the dry land. The grass in the pastures had cured to tawny yellow, nutritious for cattle and sheep alike. The lambs born in the cold of February had arrived at the adolescent swagger of almost-sheep.

Daily she consulted Marco's journal, where for many years in his meticulous print he had recorded each day's duty. She smiled over his little doodles in the margins. Early ones had been of lambs and chickens. After they were married, the doodles changed to slim women and even one erect phallus, which told her all she needed to know about her rejuvenated husband. Her smiles deepened as she came across a man and woman tangled together, and then on pages closer to today, babies.

The doodles since their marriage were a relief, compared to the ones dating back to the time of his first wife's death. On one page, after recording a concoction to treat scours, he had drawn three small crosses. Two pages later, he had drawn his own face, with cheekbones more prominent, eyes hollow, wide and staring. Then no doodles for several years.

"Now is better," she said out loud, turning to today's entry. She thought a moment, then drew a fair rendition of Soli and Claudio splashing in the irrigation ditch. After another moment's thought she drew a profile of herself, one not so slim, and with the barest hint of another baby inside.

"Do men ever think of anything but women?" she asked Eckapeta that night, when the children were in bed and she was visiting her friend in Marco's former office. She told Eckapeta about the little drawings and they had a quiet laugh together.

"That is your answer," the Comanche woman said.

"I mean, I think about household duties and children and cooking," Paloma said, perplexed. "I could go all day without thinking of Big Man Down There." She laughed again. "But I don't!"

"And there is your answer again."

Someone knocked on the door just as Paloma rose to leave. Quicker than thought, Eckapeta slipped her knife from its scabbard and motioned Paloma behind her.

"What?" Eckapeta asked, and not in a kind voice.

"Is … is la señora there? Emilio here."

Eckapeta stepped back and Paloma opened the door. "Yes, Emilio?"

Emilio gave her a mystified look. "Señora Mondragón, the horse traders are back, and you won't believe who is with them."

He gestured for her to follow him and she did, Eckapeta close behind, knife in hand, ready for anything.

Paloma walked with him to the gates that had closed again. Three of her servants were leading horses to the barn and there stood Lorenzo and Rogelio. Attached to Lorenzo by a rope, and with a noose around his neck, was her brother Claudio.

Chapter Twenty-Three

In which someone spills overdue beans

"Here! I don't want him," Lorenzo said, handing her the rope. Claudio gazed mournfully back at her. Every angry word she had wanted to fling at him vanished. She took the rope, loosened the noose, and lifted it over her brother's head. Without a word, she kissed his forehead and he dropped to his knees.

Paloma knelt down, her arms around him. Gradually, hesitantly, he put his arms around her. He mumbled, "Wrong of me," and then something else too indistinct for her ears.

"Doesn't matter. You're my brother." Firmly, she raised his chin until they were eye to eye. "You can come and go as you please, but don't you dare just leave again without telling me."

"You sound like Mama," he told her, his eyes no less bleak.

Her heart lurched. "I expect I do, Claudio." She took his arm. "Come on. Let's go into the kitchen." She gave Lorenzo and Rogelio her narrow-eyed, dare-you-to-disagree look. "All of us."

"It's late. We can sleep in the barn," Lorenzo said, but Paloma knew feeble resistance when she heard it.

"And where would my manners be?" she scolded, figuring Lorenzo, crusty man inside and out, was less vulnerable than Claudio right now. "You'll sleep where you slept when you were here before. It may be late, but there is always something to eat in my kitchen."

She sat her brother at the table, deeply aware how beaten down he looked. When everyone was seated, she opened the bread cabinet and took out two of Perla's large round loaves baked only this morning. Deftly she sliced the bread while Sancha, in her robe with her hair in braids, rubbed her eyes in the doorway, then moved into action, reaching for a bowl of butter and honey. Soon the men were eating. By the time anyone looked up, there was hot chocolate whipped to a froth, with just a pinch of chili powder and precious vanilla.

"Tell me now, whoever wants to talk," Paloma began. "What is going on?" She looked from Claudio to Lorenzo. "Either one of you, and soon."

Rogelio spoke, to her surprise. "Claudio returned those bays to Señor Rumaldo. He made us do it."

"But I thought ... Marco told me that the bays belonged to a *hacendado* in Pojoaque Valley," Paloma said. "I believe the Rumaldo hacienda is two days south of us, and not west through mountain passes."

"We lied about Pojoaque," Rogelio said. He looked at Lorenzo, who glared back. "*Dama,* we lie about a lot of things." He hung his head then, a child in a man's body.

"Thank you for the truth, Rogelio," she said simply. "Have some more bread and honey." She looked at Lorenzo then. "You still have the three horses that belong to someone in Isleta."

Lorenzo threw up his hands in self-defense. "Señora, are we giants with seven-league boots? I thought it best to return Claudio."

"But you *will* return the horses?" she asked, knowing she was starting to sound as relentless as Marco, the *juez de campo.*

"Yes!" he said.

"Yes, what?" Sancha demanded.

"Yes, Señora Mondragón," Lorenzo mumbled.

He raised his eyes to Paloma's, and she saw the worry there, which made her heart beat faster. "Señora, I cannot help but think that your husband and his little army might need a few more recruits." He glanced at Claudio. "Let him tell you more." He jabbed his chest and pointed to Rogelio. "As for us, we will go north tomorrow and find Señor Mondragón."

"With stolen horses?" Paloma asked, exasperated.

"We prefer to think that they have entrusted themselves to men—us— who will treat them with the consideration due to fine horseflesh," Lorenzo said with some dignity.

Paloma couldn't help her unladylike snort. Lorenzo took her smooth hand in his rough one, leaning closer. "There is more afoot here than we know. Can you tell us his route?"

Paloma squeezed his hand, suddenly not concerned about the impropriety. "You worry me."

"You should be worried," Lorenzo replied and Rogelio nodded.

"They … they were going to skirt the foothills of the Sangre de Cristos, and take the little pass into Valle San Luis. Do you know it?"

"Ute country, Kapota Ute. We know it."

"Are you on any kind of good terms with the Utes?" Paloma asked.

"Hmm. If their memories are short," Lorenzo replied. "We, uh, try not to trade with the Kapota Utes."

"I wouldn't doubt it," Paloma said with some asperity. "From what Marco tells me, the Kapota Utes are as adept at horse stealing as you are."

Lorenzo winced, as though Paloma's clipped words were splinters of glass thrown at him. "Let us say we are almost even, in that regard."

What is the matter with some people? Paloma asked herself, then took several deep breaths for control, when she really wanted to bean Lorenzo with a cooking pot.

The other side of that tarnished coin struck her. "But you're willing to help Marco?" she asked. "Truly?"

He still had hold of her hand, and he gave it another squeeze. "Señora, you have been kind to us. We leave in the morning." He glared at Claudio. "But *not* with that one."

Claudio said nothing. He closed his eyes and leaned forward until his cheek rested against the table. "Paloma, forgive me."

"Forgiven," she said. "You as well, Lorenzo, even if you are a scoundrel. Go to your rooms now."

"Me?" he asked, all innocence. "I am a businessman. Nothing more."

"Then may all the saints protect us here in Nuevo Mexico," Paloma replied. She inclined her head toward the rascal, wondering just when it was that life and its lessons had changed from black and white to gray. "You are going to help my husband, and for that I forgive thousands of sins."

"We'll leave early," Lorenzo assured her. "Before breakfast, even. I want to get to the shelter of the foothills."

"No one leaves here without breakfast," Sancha said.

Paloma stared at her quiet housekeeper, seeing her for the first time as just a woman, and not the faithful servant who had followed young Felicia to the Double Cross when she married Marco, young then, himself. *I do not even know how old you are*, she thought, *or if you had a dream or two of your own.*

"You are so kind, Sancha, and I am grateful," she said, pleased to see her face light up at such small praise. "I am not at my best in the early morning, these days."

Lorenzo released her hand, and turned his attention to Sancha. "We'll be ready." With a slight, self-conscious bow to Paloma, the two rascals left the kitchen.

Paloma patted Claudio's shoulder. "Come now, Brother. Whatever you have to say can wait until morning. I am tired, even if no one else is."

"I am more tired than you know," he told her, getting up.

"I have some idea," she said gently.

She walked arm in arm with him down the hall, stopped at the door and kissed his cheek. "Go to bed. We'll talk in …."

He took Paloma's arm and pulled her into the room, closing the door behind them. She suddenly wished for Eckapeta's watchful presence, then reminded herself that this was her brother.

"What, Claudio?"

"Has Graciela said anything to you about what happened when the Comanches shot me?"

Paloma shook her head. "She is efficient in her duties, and the children love her, but she says little."

"Nothing?" He gave her arm a shake.

"No." Paloma pulled her arm away. "No, but several times she has looked at me as though she wanted to say something. What is this?"

He sat on the bed. "As I was trailing the horses toward my *compadres*, alone and with time to think, I became more and more certain that after I was shot, Graciela said something like, 'That was meant for me.' At least, she might have said that." He rubbed his shoulder.

"Why in the world would she imagine that the devils who had just sold her would shoot her?" Paloma said, with a slow shake of her head. "You must be mistaken."

"I'm not convinced, but I'm too tired to reason through the matter," Claudio said.

"Don't worry." Paloma kissed his forehead. "I meant what I said, *hermano*. Come or go, as you will, but don't sneak away."

* * *

HIS STOMACH FULL, HIS conscience bruised but not battered, Claudio Vega slept well, waking hours later to sunshine in his room and the sweet fragrance of sage bundles drying outside his window. He tried to put both hands behind his head, but his wounded shoulder wasn't cooperating yet. Never mind; one arm was good enough.

He sank a little deeper into the pillow, trying to remember when he had felt this relaxed. The feeling was different from the relaxation induced by grinding on one whore or another. He tried to analyze the sensation, but nothing in recent memory came to mind.

He did something he usually tried not to do, and let his mind drift back to those days on the Vega ranch, before his world erupted in blood and fire. He had shared a room with his younger brother Rafael, who liked to talk. Because

Claudio never considered the early morning a good time for conversation, he started waking up early before Rafael, just for the solitude.

He remembered mourning doves, and the occasional owl. Mama and Papa might be talking softly in their room next to his. He had time to spare, time to think, time to make plans for his future, which he had hoped would include the army, even though Papa was opposed to it. He wanted to see more than the ranch, more than El Paso. Mexico City was four months away. San Antonio was closer, but directly through Comanche country, as well as the domain of the Apache, and the cannibal Tonkawas.

Anything had been possible, early in those long ago mornings, before everything changed. Still, he could not deny a pleasing and wholly unexpected return of optimism. He lay on a comfortable bed in his sister's house, with the fragrance of sage close by, and the inevitable *piñon* odor from the kitchen fireplace. A man could probably travel the world and know New Mexico just by the smell.

He looked around the little room, with its colorful Pueblo rugs on the floor, walls of deep blue halfway up, and then white to the ceiling. There was a crucifix nailed to the wall at the head of his bed, and a clothes press, ornately carved and probably from Spain. Everywhere he looked he saw order and cleanliness. He let the peace of it sink into his dusty heart and closed his eyes again.

When he woke again, the sun was much higher in the sky. He heard Paloma talking to her children across the hall, and laughing. His sister was happy, content, and the wife of a good man. The determined child who possessed a deep well of courage perhaps greater than his own had kept herself alive through a massacre, followed by a famine of food and love from selfish relatives, to blossom now as a cherished wife and loving mother. If Claudio were a smaller-minded man, he could have resented her good fortune. Now it made him smile.

He dressed quickly and followed his sister and the children down the hall toward the kitchen, moving quietly behind them because he wanted to enjoy looking at these relatives he never thought to see again, or meet. He wondered if Paloma had any idea how much she resembled their mother, who was taller but as graceful as her only daughter.

Paloma turned around at the kitchen door and motioned him toward her. "I hope you are hungry," she said. "Sancha made an enormous breakfast for Lorenzo and Rogelio, and there are eggs and sausage for us, too. Perla is baking more bread now and it will be ready soon."

His mouth began to water at just the idea of hot bread. He knew there would be butter and honey on the table. He could make a little bowl shape in the soft bread to fill with butter and honey, then fold it over and enjoy the goodness. A man could grow to like this.

He sat next to Soledad, and nearly dropped the cup of hot chocolate that Paloma handed him when the child gave him a swift kick under the table. Eyes narrowed to slits, she put her face close to his. "That's because you made Mama cry when you went away."

Amused more than injured, he glanced at Paloma, whose mouth had opened in astonishment. Her eyes narrowed then, and she picked up Soledad and carried her into the hall, where Claudio heard a series of spanks, and a wail that diminished in volume as its owner retreated to her bedchamber, probably ordered there by Mama Mondragón.

Little Claudio, seated on his other side, shook his head. "*I* missed you," he said, leaning against Claudio's arm. "Mama missed you."

Claudio put a comforting arm around his little namesake, who cuddled close. "Do you think your papa missed me?"

Claudito considered the question. "Maybe not so much," he said, which made Claudio laugh.

"My daughter," Paloma said, her face red, as she came into the kitchen again. "I think it will be a while before she becomes a lady."

"You have a staunch defender, Paloma," he said. "My shin will probably heal."

"Oh, you!" she teased in turn. "I told her to stay in her room until she is penitent. It might be a long day, because she is stubborn."

By now her small son sat on Claudio's lap. "Don't be sad," he said, hoping to make the child smile, because he had suddenly turned serious. Claudio whispered teasingly in his ear, "Did the chickens and goats miss me? The bees in the hives?"

Claudito giggled. "No!" He seemed to give the matter real thought. "I think Graciela did. She has been crying and crying each night."

Paloma sat beside her son. "Claudito? Why didn't you say something?"

His shrugged, the complexity of the situation beyond his years. "You were too sad to bother."

"I am never too sad or too busy for you, my son," Paloma said firmly. "She cries every night?"

The child nodded. Claudio looked at Paloma over his head. "Finish your breakfast, Claudio," she said. "I will find Graciela."

He looked down at the half-eaten sausage remaining, and the one egg slowly hardening, his appetite gone. "Stay here with your son," he said. "This has gone beyond mere curiosity."

Chapter Twenty-Four

In which Claudio looks deep inside

C LAUDIO THOUGHT GRACIELA MIGHT still be in her little alcove in the children's room, so he made that his first stop.

Soledad had flopped back on her bed, arms and legs wide apart, staring at the ceiling. Her eyes filled with tears when he came into the room.

"I am truly penitent," she whispered to him as she sat up, brushing down her skirt and crossing her legs at the ankles, a nicety Paloma had undoubtedly taught her.

He struggled not to smile and managed to keep his face neutral. "Soli, I shouldn't have left the way I did. It was bad-mannered of me."

"Aha! I was right!" Her momentary triumph faded as she looked at him. "But I shouldn't have kicked you. Mama says you are having a hard time, and I should be kind."

Her sincerity touched Claudio's heart. He remembered another little girl, unhappy because she could not keep up with her brothers, who had dumped their clothes in the *acequia*. The punishment had been an hour on her knees in the chapel, praying for Santa Maria to forgive her sins, followed by another hour by the laundry tub, washing their muddy clothes. If anything, Paloma had a softer heart than Mama, he told himself, and then chuckled. Of course, Mama had two rascals for sons who didn't mind teasing their little sister.

He put his arm around Soledad. "I will pledge to behave myself, as long as you will, too."

Soledad nodded. "We could make a vow," she said.

"It will be enough if you kiss my cheek and I kiss yours," he told her.

She kissed his cheek. "I'm sorry."

His heart full, he kissed her cheek. "I promise not to make your mama cry again."

"Mama said I should make a good curtsy to you," Soledad said. "I have been practicing, because Mama says every girl needs to know how to impress men."

The innocence of her answer, and what it told him about his sister made Claudio smile. He wondered if he should warn Marco that Paloma was highly skilled in the management of men, and decided against it. Marco probably knew exactly what he had gotten himself into by marrying Paloma Vega. "That would be nice," he told her.

Soledad stood by her bed and held out her skirts. Her curtsy wobbled, and a frown of great concentration drew her eyebrows together, but she dipped and rose, then clapped her hands.

He rose and bowed to her, remembering long-ago lessons and better times. "There now. We are both penitent, and I require your help to find Graciela."

"Does she need to curtsy to you, too?" Soledad asked as he opened the door and ushered her out of misbehavior jail.

She might, he thought. "I just want to talk to her."

Soledad took his hand in the hall and he found himself being towed toward the kitchen, where Paloma was just wiping off Claudito's face, over protests.

"Don't struggle, *mi primo*," Claudio said. "Your mama is wise beyond her years." He gave Soledad a little push forward. "Soledad and I have reached an agreement. She gave me quite a curtsy, Sister."

"You are sincere in your apology?" Paloma asked, kneeling in front of her daughter and looking her in the eye, which Claudio thought was a wise touch.

Soledad nodded. "I will be kind to your brother."

Paloma enveloped the child in a gentle embrace, and kissed her. "Will you help my brother find Graciela?"

"Yes, Mama."

"Go look for her then," Paloma said. "My brother will come in a minute."

They both watched Soledad dart from the kitchen, followed closely by her little brother. Claudio took Paloma's hand and kissed it. "Soli told me you said every girl needs to know a good curtsy to impress men. You sound a bit calculating, dear Sister."

She only laughed and gave him a little push. "We women have so few weapons in our arsenal. We control no property. We have no say in government." She gave her belly a pat. "Our bodies don't always belong just to us. A little charm goes a long way, in getting what we want."

"Is Marco on to your scheme?" He teased.

"*Claro que sí*! I decided years ago that if I were so fortunate to marry—the matter was in some doubt—it would only be to a smart man." She touched his cheek. "Go find Graciela, you smart man."

He knew a compliment when he heard one, even though he had heard none in years. "As smart as Marco Mondragón?"

"Time will tell."

Soledad and Claudito amounted to no help at all. They had started looking in the kitchen garden, but had been waylaid by what must have been yesterday's play, a series of roads around mounded piles of dirt with dead pea vines stuck here and there to resemble trees and a mountain pass. Soledad looked up.

"Mama said Papa and Toshua are going through mountain passes. We are going around the mountain to surprise the Utes," Soli explained. "We are bringing more food and horses to Papa."

He watched them a moment, saddened that their play was so serious. Children on the frontier obviously didn't know the pleasures of a solitary ride through the hills, or even the delight of visiting neighbors from *rancho* to *rancho* without taking along an armed guard.

"Soledad, do you have a tea set for your dolls?" he asked.

"My dolls would like that," she told him, "if we were not so busy helping Papa."

Someday, he thought, *someday*.

He passed through the garden, wondering where *he* would go, if he were Graciela and wanted to avoid unpleasantness. He looked in the smoke house and then the henhouse. No Graciela. He decided against the horse barn, since servants and guards were always coming and going.

He tried Paloma's bathhouse next, and there she was, huddled inside herself, worry written on every line of her face, her body poised for flight, even though there was nowhere to run. "Graciela," was all he said.

She leaped up, but he stood in front of the door. Her eyes were wide with terror, telling him much about her treatment among the Comanches. Staring at the terrified slave, Claudio knew why his sister seemed to possess a double measure of serenity and kindness. Somehow Paloma had overcome the greatest fear on the frontier: that Comanches had the power to ruin lives and destroy otherwise rational minds, even when they were not around.

He realized with amazing clarity that he was still trapped in that fear, and so was Graciela. He saw it plainly for the first time since the raid that destroyed his life, but hadn't destroyed Paloma's.

He could ask Paloma how she had managed this nearly impossible feat, but he already knew her answer, as unpalatable as it seemed to him. He could almost hear her telling him, *Claudio, dear brother, I came to know The People. That is what we must do in New Mexico, if we are to survive as a colony.*

"I will never hurt you, Graciela," he told her. He took a bucket, upended it, and sat down in front of the door. "But I am not leaving until you satisfy my curiosity about Great Owl."

"I have nothing to tell you," she said, her voice flat.

"I have all day to wait," he replied. "While you're mulling over whether to trust me, or whether you are afraid of Great Owl while living in the safest hacienda on the frontier, let me give you this to think about: I distinctly heard you say, after I was shot, 'Meant for me.' I wasn't the target. You were."

She shuddered and shook her head. "You couldn't have heard me. You were in shock and pain."

"I *did* hear you. Tell me why Great Owl wanted to kill you? He had just sold you for a lot of money. I hate Comanches, but they know good business. He had what he wanted."

She shook her head again, reminding him of Soledad—stubborn, willful Soledad.

"Do you even understand why Señor Mondragón and the others have gone after him?"

Another shake, but less vehement. At least she was listening.

"Great Owl is a renegade. He is out to destroy the tentative peace feelers that Kwihnai, a powerful chief among the Kwahadi, is sending out through Señor Mondragón. My brother-in-law thinks that French traders might be involved, but I do not know."

He watched her face as he spoke, and saw a flicker of something. "How are the French involved, Graciela?" he asked.

She said nothing, even though she started to shake. The French were involved.

He gave his imagination free rein, because he was desperate to know what was going on. His own hard life had made him cynical. He thought he didn't care for anyone, but he knew how wrong that was. He cared deeply what might happen to the good people of the Double Cross.

"When the French came to Great Owl's village, if they did, did Great Owl give you to them to share, while they were in camp?"

Graciela began to weep, and he had his terrible answer. Remembering the times he, Lorenzo, poor dead Paco, and Rogelio had shared a terrified woman between them, he felt shame so great that he turned away.

When he could bring himself to look at her again, her face was chalk white. "You needn't turn away in your disgust," she told him, her voice barely loud enough to hear. "Don't you think I feel enough shame for both of us?"

"Oh, no, wait," he burst out. "That is not why I turned away! Graciela, I have been as bad as the Frenchmen, to my eternal shame. It's not you."

"There were three men, there to forge a deal for weapons," she said in her small voice, her eyes on the dirt floor. "Until then, I thought I was past caring …." She let her voice trail away. She turned around and faced the back wall. "Three. All night." Her voice sank lower. "When one finished, another began."

What could he say to that? He heard her weeping, even though she tried to muffle her tears. Other men probably slapped her when she cried as they violated her, until all she could do was try not to cry, which would make them angrier. *God forgive me*, he thought. *I was no better than they*.

He thought a long moment. He knew better than to call on God or any saints for help, because he wasn't certain there was anyone above him in a distant place called heaven. What to tell this beaten-down woman, hardly more than a child herself? He could only speak from a confused heart, one bruised more than his shin where Soledad had kicked him this morning.

"It's like this, Graciela," he began, slowly sorting though a mound of words to find the right ones. "It sounds crazy, but something happens to people when they spend time at the Double Cross. They get better."

His words sounded stupid to his ears, but Graciela stopped weeping. He waited while she blew her nose, and then squared her shoulders, a gesture so courageous that his heart felt funny.

"I can't explain it. Lorenzo could have killed me when I took that stolen team back to the rightful owner, or he might have beaten me senseless. What did he do? He brought me back here. This place is a magnet."

"But you left. You did, and la señora cried and cried," Graciela said. She turned halfway, until Claudio saw her profile.

"I never said I wasn't stupid," he admitted, pleased to see a tiny half smile on her face.

He thought a little longer, and felt another rush of understanding. "Maybe this is it: Paloma and Marco treat us as though we are already the wonderful people they want us to become."

She turned to face him. "How do they know what we can become?"

He shrugged. "It's a mystery to me."

"What should I do?" she asked after a long silence. "You *are* right. I see Comanches everywhere."

She shook at the thought and he reached out to touch her arm. She pulled back, and he withdrew his hand.

"Tell us what you know—me and Paloma and Eckapeta."

She shook her head. "Not Eckapeta."

"Very well. Tell me and Paloma."

Graciela rose slowly to her feet. He watched her smooth motion, entranced by the idea that such a graceful woman was well-named. He had been in enough Indian camps to see female slaves, none of them like Graciela.

He left the bathhouse, calling over his shoulder, "Come with me." He hoped she'd decide to follow, or at least not bolt for the open gate. And where would she go? Like most women, she had little choice in life's fortunes. He didn't look over his shoulder, not wanting her to think he was a weak man. Graciela already knew he was a fool. There was no need to impress her, since she had seen him with a noose around his neck.

Paloma stood in the kitchen all alone. "The little ones are with Eckapeta in Marco's old office," Paloma said, indicating that they should sit around the table. "We won't be disturbed."

Without asking, she put a plate of *biscoches* on the table and poured wine.

She sat and folded her hands in front of her on the table, turning her attention to Graciela.

"My husband told me that he, Toshua, and Joaquim Gasca were going to cross the Cristos and move along the foothills into the high land of the Ute Kapotas. They want to find out what Great Owl is up to. What can you tell us, Graciela?"

Claudio glanced at Graciela as Paloma spoke, noting how she flinched and looked around at the name of Great Owl.

Paloma must have noticed, too. She leaned forward, her eyes deep pools of kindness. "Great Owl is not here, Graciela. He has no power to hurt you in my home. If my husband has enough information, he can stop Great Owl before all chance of peace is gone and the frontier explodes again. I need to know what you know, and I need to know it now."

Chapter Twenty-Five

In which Graciela looks deep inside, too

Cᴌᴀᴜᴅɪᴏ ᴍᴜsᴛ ʜᴀᴠᴇ sᴇɴsᴇᴅ Paloma's agitation. He moved closer to her on the bench. "Sister, when the Comanches shot me, I distinctly heard Graciela say, 'Meant for me.' Help us, Graci."

It was just the smallest nickname, but Graciela looked up at him, her eyes less frightened.

"My father used to call me that," she said.

Paloma had lived long enough on the frontier to know what was expected of her. She reminded herself that Graciela was half Ute, and Indian conversation had certain rules.

"Tell me about your father, Graciela," Paloma said. "You said he was a soldier."

The slave nodded. "Mama is, was, Kapota Ute from near the White Mountain. Do you know it?"

Paloma shook her head, but Claudio spoke. "Oh, yes, I have been to White Mountain to trade horses. In the San Luis Valley."

Just a wisp of a smile came and went from Graciela's face. "Trade or steal?"

Claudio gave just the same smile. "Depending. And so did the Kapota people."

"Papa met Mama in the presidio of San Felipe, near Ojo Caliente, or what used to be Ojo," Graciela told them. "She was kitchen help in the *capitán's* house and Papa was a corporal. I was the oldest of three." She stopped and looked down at her hands.

"Are you a cook, too?" Paloma asked, when all she really wanted to do was demand to be told what the slave knew about Great Owl. "Perhaps when my little ones are older, you might help Perla, who already complains of creaky bones."

"I would like that," Graciela said.

"Did the garrison pull out?" Claudio asked.

Her face clouded as she nodded. "Governor Mendinueta said none of the country wives and children could go to Santa Fe."

"He could have been kinder," Paloma murmured.

Graciela shivered and looked away. "Where was kindness in any of this, señora?" She sighed and rubbed her shoulders, even though the room was warm.

Paloma made just the smallest gesture, but it was enough. Graciela got up quickly and sat beside her with no hesitation. "We are three survivors," Paloma said, looking from Claudio to her. "You went back to the White Mountain?"

"Yes, we four."

"Where are…" Claudio began, and Paloma clamped her hand on his leg. *Don't you know, Brother?* she wanted to ask, but she didn't need to; he understood and patted her hand.

Paloma slowly put her arm around Graciela's shoulders, hoping not to frighten her, but to understand the terror of what must surely have come next. Graciela tensed, then relaxed.

"Who is your chief?" Claudio asked, to Paloma's relief. He seemed to finally understand the roundabout course she was taking.

"He is called Rain Cloud. He took us in, because he and Mama are related somehow in that Indian way that no one but Indians understands, I think." Graciela smiled. "My little brothers and I really didn't fit in at first. I think we have always been more Spanish than Ute." She touched her neck. "I once had a necklace with a cross," she said, her voice wistful. "I don't remember which Nurmurnah man snatched it from my neck."

She pressed her lips tight to keep from crying, and squinted her eyes into tiny slits. *I used to do that,* Paloma thought. *Anything to keep Tia Moreno from hitting me, if I dared to cry for my family.*

"So there you were," Paloma said, tightening her arm around the slave, who was starting to shiver uncontrollably. "Another log on the fire, please, Claudio."

Graciela smiled her thanks at Claudio, who blushed, to Paloma's amusement. "Do either of you remember when that new governor chased and killed Cuerno Verde many leagues north of here?" she asked him.

"I do." Claudio made a face. "Lorenzo and Paco even considered joining with the soldiers and settlers—and Indian allies—but they didn't. That would have been too much patriotism to suit them." He looked at Paloma. "You must think me a disgrace to the Vegas."

"You survived and so did I," she said simply. "And so did Graciela. I consider *that* the remarkable achievement."

Graciela turned her face into Paloma's shoulder. "Go ahead and cry," Paloma said. "You think we have not cried?"

She did, and when she was finished, she wiped her face on Paloma's apron, when Paloma held it up to her. She seemed to understand what she needed to say then, and the story came out.

"As you probably know, the Utes allied with Governor … Governor …. He was there in the plaza briefly before your husband bought me."

"Governor de Anza," Claudio supplied. "Graci, we know that the Utes were brave and true, during that hunt for Cuerno Verde and his Comanche raiders."

Graciela held herself a little taller. "They were, but oh, the retribution came later, after the soldiers were gone. Great Owl—he is Kwahadi Comanche—swooped down on us, and my life changed yet again." She took a deep breath. "Mama and my brothers. Gone. I was four years with The People." Another breath. "I cannot tell you what they did to Mama and my brothers."

"It has been done to us," Paloma said quietly.

"Then how can you …." Graciela stifled her outburst, her eyes fearful again.

"Both of you listen," Paloma replied, her voice firm. "I have come to know The People. Do I understand all the Comanches? No, but the ones I know, I love."

"I doubt I will ever get to that place," Claudio said.

"Time and patience. Tell us more, Graciela. Marco and I have both been wondering why Great Owl insisted on money for you, and not barter. Marco suspects the French are involved."

"Money for guns," Graciela said. "Señor Mondragón is right." Her voice hardened. "Those … those three Frenchman came to smoke pipes and plan for a shipment of muskets."

"From where?" Claudio asked. "All of Texas and Luisiana belongs to Spain now."

"I don't know. I do know that the Frenchmen wanted money," Graciela told them. She took a deep breath. "I heard Great Owl say that the little boy he tried to sell first in Taos was just to test the crowd."

"*O Dios*," Paloma whispered, thinking of her own little ones.

"I heard him say that no matter what anyone offered, the result would be the same. Great Owl suspected that if he killed that child and then offered me, someone would pay a large sum." Graciela looked down at her hands. "He calls that the weakness of the whites. They don't like to deal in death."

Silence ruled in the kitchen as Paloma absorbed that much cruelty. She glanced at Claudio, his lips tight and eyes small, too. *You are not as hardened as you would like us to believe,* she thought.

"But why would he track you and try to kill you?" Paloma asked. "I don't understand."

"I do," Claudio said, after a long moment. He spoke slowly, as if piecing his idea together word by word. "Graci, do you think he assumed that Marco was a Taoseño, and would not know him as a Comanche troublemaker over here so close to Comanchería?"

"I think it very likely," the slave replied. "Until this last time, during my years with The People, Great Owl has never been here."

Paloma did her own piecing together of the story that now involved her husband. "No man from Taos who bought you would think of tracking Great Owl." She took a deep breath. "Because you know where Great Owl is likely to be, don't you?"

Graciela nodded.

"He and his warriors must have watched us leave and head east through the mountains," Claudio said, speaking softly as though all the Comanche warriors were gathered outside, pressing their ears to the walls. "That had to upset his plans. Marco was no Taoseño. He had to assume that Marco knew what was happening on the frontier. Great Owl couldn't risk you telling him anything."

Graciela nodded again, still unable to speak. The terror was back in her eyes, her shivering greater. Paloma felt the slave try to burrow close, so she put both arms around Graciela.

"All he had to do was shoot you if he could, so you would never give away his hiding place," Paloma said, "or his plans with the French."

"And even if he missed you, he knew you would be too frightened to say anything," Claudio continued.

Graciela covered her face with her hands, her breath coming in little gasps.

Paloma kissed her cheek, remembering again with frightening clarity that awful day when the eleven-year-old Paloma Vega huddled under the bed in the burning building, nearly frightened into insanity by the Comanches.

"They don't even have to be here to terrify us," Paloma said finally. "Even now, I still dream …." She looked at her brother. "I know you do, Claudio. What else?"

"Need you ask? I reach for a big bottle of *aguardiente*. What do you do, Paloma, when it happens now?"

"I am lucky," she said simply. "Marco holds me close and covers my eyes with his hand."

A pine knot spat in the fireplace, and they all jumped. Claudio was the first to speak again. "They rule through fear and we are still afraid." He reached across Paloma to touch Graciela. "Will such fear ever go away?"

No one had an answer. They clung to each other. Paloma made herself think through the whole matter. "Great Owl has the money now, and he must have arranged a rendezvous with the French for guns. He will cause all the trouble he can. He will ruin any chance of peace that Kwihnai wants and Marco has been working for."

"Not if we find Marco and the others and stop the French," Claudio said.

"Or find Great Owl's summer camp first," Paloma said. Then she put words to her fear because these two people knew exactly what was at stake. "Governor de Anza had an army when he defeated Cuerno Verde."

"Some eight hundred men, counting Ute allies," Claudio said. "We will have … let's see … seven brave souls."

"Seven?" Paloma asked.

"I am counting Graci, too," he told her. "We need her."

He reached across Paloma again and took Graciela's hands in his own. She did not pull back. "We must do this. You need to stare down your fear and come with me."

"How can I?" she asked, drawing back into Paloma's embrace.

"By the doing of it," Claudio told her. "We'll travel by night, we'll hug the foothills, we'll trap rabbits and eat raw meat if we have to. I am not the tracker that Toshua is, but we will find Marco."

"I will be forever grateful, if you do," Paloma told him. "Should Eckapeta go along with you?" *Please tell me no*, she thought. *Please.*

Perhaps he read the reluctance in her eyes. Or he might be a true son of Pedro Vega, brave man who died too soon. Even more likely, he was the brother she knew would always protect her, even if he was not there, by leaving a Comanche warrior as formidable as her husband, Toshua.

"Eckapeta stays here, Paloma," he said with no hesitation. "I rather doubt she would leave you alone with the babies, no matter how many guards and archers surround the Double Cross."

Paloma didn't hide her sigh of relief. "You will always protect me, won't you?"

His face clouded over. "I could not protect you earlier, but I have another chance now. Graci, I will guard you, too, and I need you."

Graciela bowed her head and her voice became soft. "Pray God you will not do me damage."

"Never," he replied, his voice as soft as hers.

What he did next did not even startle Paloma. As she watched, her heart full, Claudio knelt on the kitchen floor and bowed his head. "Gracious God, defend us," he said, his arms stretched out to encompass the Double Cross and everyone within its sheltering walls and those beyond. "Protect us from all danger. May the saints watch over us and all we hold dear: our families, Holy Church, King Carlos, peace to our lands and chattel."

She had heard this ages-old declaration once before, when they were small children. Papa had come to El Paso to serve as commanding officer of the frontier outpost's garrison. He had married their mother, widowed young and childless, possessor of a land grant. Years later, on orders from the Viceroy in Mexico City, he had been chosen the district's *capitán-general*. In the Ysleta Mission Church, Papa had knelt before the archbishop and repeated that very oath, his sword lying in front of him.

Claudio had remembered it all. As Paloma held her breath with the enormity of what dear, battered Claudio was doing, he took out the dagger at his waist and laid it at Paloma's feet.

"Bless me, Sister," he whispered. "There is no archbishop and your husband who should do this is far away now. I crave your blessing."

Paloma rose to her feet and put her hands on Claudio's head, wishing she could remember the archbishop's words. It was too many years ago, and she had been so young. She knew what to do, because her love for her brother filled her heart.

"May God and all the Saints protect you and Graciela Tafoya, soldiers defending my home and protecting my husband," she whispered. "Do all you can to defend the fragile peace we are forging here on the frontier. And do no harm to the innocent." She leaned forward and kissed his head, then made the sign of the cross with her thumb on his forehead, his cheeks, and his mouth.

He rose to his feet and held her close. Paloma whispered into his chest. "Come home safe to me, Claudio, you who were lost and now are found. And bring my dear ones home, too."

"I vow to you that we will."

"When do we leave, Señor Vega?"

"I am Claudio to you, for we are *soldados*, Graci," he said. "We leave now."

Chapter Twenty-Six

In which another small army sets out to do impossible things

THEY STAYED ONLY LONG enough for Sancha and Paloma, her face so serious, to sling carne seca, hunks of sweet cactus, yesterday's tortillas, and a wineskin into a cloth bag. Eckapeta contributed one of her deerskin dresses with thigh-high slits for easy riding and dared Graciela to turn it down.

A few words from Paloma with Emilio at the horse barn produced a mare for Graciela, a gift that made the slave smile. "I will be your friend," she said to the horse, who tossed her head and whickered back, evidently understanding.

Claudio saddled his own horse Bueno, grateful Marco didn't know that the black had been acquired from an obnoxious *ranchero* near San Mateo two years ago who had cheated Lorenzo just one time too many. At least, that was what Lorenzo had claimed, and Claudio had overlooked it, as he had overlooked too much. Claudio had learned through hard experience never to look too closely at any horse dealings of the Diaz brothers. That they hadn't gone anywhere near San Mateo in the intervening years reinforced Claudio's own suspicions about the transaction for Bueno.

"Do you like to ride, Graci?" he asked the slave.

He liked how she dimpled up simply from his little nickname. "I do," she told him. That was all. She was not a talkative woman.

Something about her suggested real intelligence. He discounted her complete dread of Comanches, because only fools would not be afraid of The People, and Graci was no fool. He needed an ally on this trip. He looked at her, so pretty in that deerskin dress, and decided that he also needed a friend.

He couldn't even remember his last actual friend. Probably it had been Rafael, his younger brother.

There in the horse barn, he pulled out a rudimentary map that Paloma had drawn, indicating which of the passes through the Sangre de Cristos Marco had said they would travel. He knew the massive San Luis Valley well enough, but he wagered that Graci knew it better.

He beckoned her closer and she came toward him, slightly hesitant at first. Maybe on this little trip she would understand that he meant her no harm. Or maybe she would always be wary of men. *Every experience changes us,* he thought, wondering if his own experiences had changed him for the better. He doubted it supremely.

"We'll travel along this western slope of the Cristos," he said. "We'll hang close to the sheltering trees and brush. When can we reasonably expect to see the Kapota Utes and Rain Cloud?"

She pointed close to the large X Paloma had drawn, which he knew was La Blanca, a hulking mountain that seemed to rise out of the valley floor, but which was really just a jog in the Sangre de Cristos.

"That's scarcely more than a pass away from where Governor de Anza first encountered Cuerno Verde five years ago," Claudio said. "Marco told me he was wounded there, three days before the final battle."

"The Kapota will be near there, or maybe a little north," she said.

"On the eastern slope, we might see Comanches," he said. "I have never doubted Ute bravery, but that seems so close to danger, especially with women and children. Why there?"

"It's good land with many deer and elk," she said. "And no, you should not doubt the bravery of my people."

Well, I've been told, he thought, pleased the slave was not so beaten down that she had no spark left in her. He had seen too many hollow-eyed women discarded by Comanches.

Paloma had divided the food into two pouches. She handed one up to Claudio and the other to Graciela, who smiled her thanks. A blanket apiece came next, followed by bow and arrows given to the slave.

"I'm not good with these," Graci said, as she accepted them.

"Then carry them as extras for me," Claudio told her as he put his arms through the loops for his arrow case and slung his bow. "Do you want a knife?"

She did, which Eckapeta furnished, tucked in a beaded sheath and strung on a deerskin belt. Graciela nodded her thanks, still wary of the Comanche woman, and tightened the belt around her middle.

There was nothing left to do but blow a kiss to Paloma as she stood by herself at the open gate.

"Two years ago, I would have ridden with you," his sister told him. She patted her still-flat belly gently, which told him she had already established a rapport with the latest Mondragón within. "Too many other responsibilities now. Still, give Marco a kiss for me."

"I will, but not on his lips," Claudio teased.

"Oh, get going," she said in a gruff voice. "And go with God."

If He can keep up, Claudio thought. He motioned to Graciela, and they began their journey to find Marco, or maybe French gun dealers, or maybe Great Owl himself. He avoided thinking about the sketchiness of his plan.

"We're going to keep moving off this plain," Claudio told her. The sun was high overhead and it was no time to start a journey, but he felt a gnawing uneasiness, knowing that Marco, the damned Comanche, and the foolish royal engineer were out there somewhere between catastrophe and trouble, and he owed his sister for her kindness to him.

"The Palo Fechado Pass will bring us out near Taos and—"

"You don't want to go there," Graciela said. "I know a better way."

"A Comanche way?"

She shot him a venomous look and he knew she hated The People as much as he did. "A Ute way! We are no strangers to these mountains. Follow me. We'll camp high tonight. Is your horse surefooted?"

He could have objected. He could have protested. He could have said that women like Graciela Tafoya didn't know anything, but he was a smarter man than that. Besides, when she rode ahead of him, certain of a trail he could barely see, he liked the way her hips swayed in the saddle. A man couldn't see that, if he led.

She wasn't fooling. They left the main trail—the tried and true way to Taos between towering mountains—and angled through a series of low foothills. They didn't seem to be rising at all, just weaving back and forth among tall grass and then hills. The air grew cooler, and he found himself breathing heavier.

He watched the slave ahead of him. She rode with casual grace, her back straight but her hips loose, blending with her horse. The rise and fall of her shoulders told him that she was not breathing heavily. The weight of his own mortality struck him. What was he now? Twenty-eight?

"How old are you, Graci?" he called ahead, the first thing he had said in hours.

She turned around and put her hand on her horse's cruppers. "Twenty-two," she said with a slight smile. "Maybe you should ride into the mountains more often to strengthen your lungs, and leave the horse thieving to your *compadres*." She returned her attention to the miniscule trail she followed.

I think I've just been insulted, he thought with real amusement. "Why does everyone think that Lorenzo Diaz is a horse thief?" he asked. "Now and then he does true business."

He saw her shoulders shake, and knew he needed to hang around with better people. *Caramba*, maybe even Lorenzo knew it. Hadn't Lorenzo brought Claudio back to his sister with a noose around his neck?

An hour passed, then another. He was hungry, thirsty, and needed to piss in the worst way, and still Graci continued her slow, steady climb into low hills that were turning into more challenging heights.

"Stop a minute," he said finally, and she did. She dismounted with such considerable delicacy that she revealed nothing to anyone who might be curious. Not him, of course. *I am still a bit of a gentleman*, Claudio thought, as he took only a tiny look.

Without a backward glance, she walked to a clump of bushes. He turned away and took care of his own business, dousing some rabbit brush and finding great relief in so simple an act.

"Some wine?" he asked when she returned to her horse, smoothing down her deerskin dress.

"For me, too?" she asked, and he remembered she was a slave. He had forgotten, watching her sure movements and the way she took command—a slave bought by his brother-in-law.

"Yes, for you," he replied quietly, handing his wine skin to her. "Graci, we're partners here. You are saving me from going miles out of the way."

She drank her fill, then handed it back. "May I have some tortillas?" she asked.

"You don't even need to ask. *Carne seca*, too."

She took what he handed her, ate, and didn't ask for more. "Just tell me when you're hungry," he said.

She nodded, but he knew she would never say anything. As they continued on the trail, winding higher now, he thought of what Marco had told him about Paloma, how even now, she never asked for anything. With a start, Claudio realized that he never did, either.

They continued long after dark, guided by Graciela's sure sense of direction. He hinted that they could stop at any time, but Graci only ordered him to go a little farther. "There is a small meadow soon, and a stream," she told him.

She was right. Claudio dismounted gratefully, stretching his good arm above his head and gingerly rubbing his other arm.

Like the good horsewoman he knew she was, Graci tended to her mare, leading her to the stream for a long drink, sitting beside her until she was done. She led the docile animal to the best patch of grass and hobbled it there. She didn't leave the horse right away, but stayed and chatted, nose to nose, so softly that Claudio could not hear. Of course, he wasn't intended to be part of the conversation.

Claudio cared for his mount while Graciela toed the grass until she found a comfortable place for her blanket. She plunked her saddle next to the spot and just sat there until he got the food from the leather bags. As before, she took what he offered her, shook her head over any more, then walked into the bushes for a moment. After she returned, she went directly to her saddle and blanket, rolled up in it and lay there quietly, her knees drawn up close to her chest.

The next day was much like the first, with Graciela leading the way until they reached the highest point in their passage and started down. He made no attempt to ride beside her on the narrow trail, grateful for her calm competence.

They regained the valley floor in the dark, but he knew precisely where they were. Graciela had saved them two days of travel and kept them away from Indians and settlers alike. He doubted she had said six words.

Her silence had ceased to bother Claudio. He wondered what she had been like around her mother and brothers, and tried to imagine her as a laughing young woman, with ideas and dreams of her own. He wondered about his own dreams, not even certain when the last one had guttered out like a spent candle and left him in the dark.

They were riding side by side now through the scrub brush and stunted trees, so common a sight in New Mexico. The day had been warm, and the piñon resin gave off its familiar odor. The moon had risen, but he was tired down to his bones. Maybe he could stay awake if he talked. Of course, that would only work if someone answered him.

"If you could do anything you wanted to, Graci, what would it be?" he asked.

She gave him a squinty look, her eyes nearly disappearing, as though she disapproved of his question.

"Just curious," he mumbled, feeling like an idiot.

"I have no answer," she said. "That's not something you think about, with Comanches." She gave an involuntary shudder.

She must have felt she owed him more conversation than that. "Wh … what about you?" she asked.

Up until that very moment, he had no answer, either. A few times at the Double Cross, he had tried to imagine himself as a *hacendado* like Marco. His thoughts had dribbled off into nothing, because he had no idea what that meant. Life was trading or stealing horses, hurrying away to stay unfettered by a district *juez de campo*, hanging around the edge of a trade fair or even a horse sale, watching the oily-tongued Lorenzo make his deals. Life was having enough to eat, finding a warm spot in a snowstorm—a barn if they were lucky—and once in a while paying for a woman.

He had watched Marco and Paloma tease each other, laugh, cuddle, play with their children, or just sit in the *sala*, Paloma's feet usually in her husband's lap so he could massage them. An outsider, he had still felt the warmth of their devotion to each other, and truth be told, their affection for any unsuspecting houseguest who happened to wander by—him, for example.

"I don't have any plans either," he told Graciela, even though it was a lie. Sitting there in the growing cold, a blanket around his shoulders, he knew he wanted more. More of what he wasn't certain yet, but more of what had been his lot, so far.

He found the camping spot and lay awake a long time after he thought Graciela slept, staring up at the familiar planets and constellations, a traitor to his words. He had assured Paloma that he preferred being outside, and not hemmed in by rooms and high walls. He stared at the stars, cold and unblinking and huge at their high altitude.

"I want a roof over my head, kind people around me, good work to do, a family," he whispered, secure in the certainty that Graciela slept.

"I do, too," he heard her say most distinctly, from the distance of her own blanketed burrow.

He closed his eyes in embarrassment, kept them closed, and soon he slept.

In the morning, she made no mention of his drowsy conversation, but neither looked the other in the eyes. They had reached the end of their dried beef and tortillas, but there were cactus chunks to chew on. Tonight he would make a snare for rabbits, or watch for unwary deer. Failing that, snakes weren't so bad. He could dig a hole against a boulder—plenty of those—and shield a small fire from any other riders.

He watched Graciela shivering in her blanket as she doggedly chewed on the dried cactus. She had said last night that she wanted something better, too. *I wonder if either of us will know it when we see it,* he thought.

They sat in silence as the sun rose on the enormity of San Luis Valley, trapped between two massive mountain ranges, a high and dry desert. The Rio Bravo stretched in the distance, lined by cottonwood trees. After dark tonight they could strike across the valley toward the river and fill their nearly empty wineskins with cold water.

Two days more would see them to White Mountain, where they might find Utes. Failing that—and if they felt particularly invisible—Graci could lead them to Great Owl's stronghold. What had seemed like a good idea, sitting around the table in Paloma's kitchen, now seemed foolish beyond words. What they really needed to do was find Marco and his miniscule army. That way, they could all be foolish together.

But just for now, Claudio took a deep breath of piñon-scented air. He breathed in and out, seeing his puffs of air in the crisp cold of an early September morning. Gazing across the high, wide valley, he felt an unexpected emotion, one he almost didn't recognize. Graci was in his line of vision, so he admired the high plain, and the erect back and handsome profile of a born horsewoman.

He wondered, not sure, if what he felt was hope.

Chapter Twenty-Seven

In which Marco's little army follows a smoky trail

MARCO REMEMBERED SOMETHING FATHER Damiano, head of the abbey at the junction of the *rios* Bravo and Chama, had told him about pilgrims on a journey. "You gather any group of people together, and there is always someone who complains," he had told Marco, who at the time was barely out of his boyhood.

The Mondragóns had traveled from the Double Cross to Santa Fe, to take the annual reports and bring along a puny wool clip from a disastrous year. Continual Comanche raids and a Comanche moon that never seemed to set had ground them down. A hungry winter stared back at them, but his father's records had to be carried to Santa Fe, no matter what.

But here had been Father Damiano, bringing them hot bread and butter, good mush and mutton. Other travelers had filled the refectory, and sure enough, Marco heard one of them complaining.

"There is always one," Father Damiano had told him. "Always."

Not this trip, Marco decided. Toshua never said much, but Joaquim Gasca had proved to be a remarkable conversationalist.

Marco had a question for Joaquim first. "You said that there was one thing I could do to make the Double Cross safer. Care to divulge it?"

"With pleasure," the private/lieutenant of royal engineers, or whoever he was, replied. "If you erect two stone bastions diagonally located on two corners of your parapet, they would offer your best archers an unparalleled view of two outside walls, without exposing themselves."

"Why not one on each corner?" Marco asked as they rode along.

Joaquim shrugged. "Why bother, unless you are a slave to symmetry? I'll design it for you when we return."

"What will I owe you in exchange for your service?" Marco asked, contemplating the waste of a talented man, busted down to a private in a shabby garrison, all because he could not keep his breeches buttoned.

"Simple, señor: Use your influence to get me out of the army, where I am utterly useless. Or at least get my rank back."

"I haven't that much clout," Marco replied, both impressed and amused with the working of Joaquim's nimble mind.

"You have that much, and more," Joaquim replied promptly, which suggested to Marco that the man had been thinking about the matter for some time. "Just think: when we return with Great Owl's scalp, and all sorts of firearms and ammunition that the French tried to sell to him, Governor de Anza will let you do what you want."

"You mean the mythical French traders?" Marco asked.

"No myth," Joaquim said, with something of command in his voice now.

What a poor private you must have made, Marco thought. "How do you know this?" he asked.

"I pay attention, Señor Mondra—"

"Just Marco. Tell me more."

Joaquim needed no encouragement. "I took it upon myself to keep Sergeant Lopez's desk tidy, which mostly amounted to throwing out wine bottles," Joaquim explained. "I, um, happened to see a directive about rumored French traders from far to the north, selling guns to tribes as they drifted south."

"Sergeant Lopez never mentioned that to me," Marco said, wondering what else the poor, stumbling-drunk sergeant had never mentioned.

"Between you and me, I doubt he will be alive when we return," Joaquim told him.

Marco crossed himself. He thought about Joaquim Gasca and his obvious ambition. *Joaquim, my wife would tell you that anyone can change*, he thought. "If what you predict is true about the sergeant, how would you run the garrison? It will never be an important *presidio*."

"No, but it can be disciplined and orderly, with troops riding out on regular patrols, even if only five or six soldiers at a time." He smiled at nothing in particular, as far as Marco could tell. "See there, maybe I like order and symmetry, too."

"Then I will see what I can do, Joaquim."

They followed the eastern slope of the Sangre de Cristo Mountains some distance, then crossed the range on a Comanche trail, according to Toshua, who told them stories of raiding parties as they sat close together around small evening fires.

"Do you miss that life, Toshua?" Joaquim asked one night after the wineskin had been passed around one time too often.

God knows Marco would never have asked such a question, but he did want to know what Toshua would reply.

"I admit I wouldn't mind a good raid, now and then," Toshua said, after another swig. He held out the wineskin and gave it an owlish stare. "This is worse that tizwin. But I like to have my wife nearby, and I like to be near Paloma. You, too, Marco. Sometimes, anyway."

"Only sometimes?" Marco teased.

"The way I see it, I can solve a lot of your problems with Valle del Sol people, if I can torture them and kill them. But no, you won't let me. You will never know the satisfaction of drawing a knife around a squirming man's head, and yanking off his whole scalp, plus ears. Rip. Squish." He yawned.

Marco and Joaquim stared at each other. Marco put the wineskin away.

ANOTHER CHILLY NIGHT AND warm day followed. Toshua shot a deer, and they gorged until their bellies were full. Lazily over that night's campfire, they argued the merits of packing along the rest of the raw meat, or leaving it some distance away for grizzlies. The grizzlies won.

"We are an army with no ambition," Marco said the next morning as they saddled up and continued trailing close to the foothills. In the distance was Mount Blanca, still with a trace of last winter's snow on top. Marco doubted it would last the week.

Toshua stood with his hands on his hips, gazing at the mountain. He pointed with his lips. "See that smoke?"

Marco strained his eyes. "No."

"Utes. The village of the man you seek, Rain Cloud." He stared again. "Or maybe not. Rain Cloud is usually to the north by now, hunting the buffalo, getting ready for winter." He shrugged. "We will see. He should not be here."

They set out across an empty plain of short-stubbled grass, brown after furnace blasts of summer sun, even at this high elevation. Hawks swooped and glided on air currents, looking no more filled with purpose than the men riding far below them.

Marco sensed that something had changed. Toshua rode ahead now, alert, his head on a continuous swivel. A few times he patted his quiver, as if to assure himself it was there, and full of arrows.

Joaquim didn't seem to notice. He breathed deep of the clean air and chewed on a piece of jerky.

Or maybe he did have concerns. "Marco, how is it that you don't seem a little apprehensive to be approaching a Ute camp?"

"They allied with us when Governor de Anza took his soldiers and settlers like me to track Cuerno Verde and kill him, back in '79."

"I was still dallying with the colonel's wife in La Havana," Joaquim said. "I'm sorry. Go on."

"I know Rain Cloud," Marco said, his eyes still on Toshua, even farther ahead now, having kneed his horse into a gallop. Marco tapped Buciro with his spurs and quickened his own pace, deeply aware how wide this open valley looked and how vulnerable they really were.

"I was wounded in that first battle," he explained, looking over his shoulder at Joaquim. "A lance in my ass, if you must know."

Joaquim laughed. He had put spurs to his horse, too.

"Rain Cloud got an arrow in his leg, a bit more dignified. We were laid out side by side in camp. That's a good way to get to know someone," Marco said.

"You speak Ute?"

"Enough. His Spanish is pretty good." Marco stared ahead at that visible smoke that he knew was more than a morning campfire. He dug his spurs into Buciro, aware that his faithful horse would require no more encouragement to break into a run. He stopped Buciro alongside Toshua, who was waiting for them.

"There is trouble in the Ute camp. If it is Great Owl trouble, I am not riding in first, to face angry Utes," Toshua said.

"Toshua, you can do anything," Marco said.

Toshua gave him a look, the one that made him wonder if Toshua was deadly serious or toying with him. "Now and then, I wonder why Paloma married you."

"So do I, Toshua. Wait in that clump of trees. I'll go alone."

Mount Blanca loomed to the north now, but he knew the little pass because even though wounded himself, he had escorted Rain Cloud and other injured warriors home after the second battle and Cuerno Verde's death. Rain Cloud had told him this was a favorite place, with a spring and sheltering cover.

He heard voices before he saw the camp, and knew the Kapota women were slashing their arms and screaming their sorrow. The keening began low, then grew higher and more frenzied until the screams reverberated inside his skull. He came closer and sucked in his breath to see the aftermath of the raid. The brush shelters were smoldering mounds now. Untended children cried because their mothers had been slung over horses and carried away, probably as Graciela had been abducted four years ago.

He turned away at the sight of older women dead in terrible ways. One struggled in her death throes, her feet digging into the ground. His glance fell on Rain Cloud, squatting in the dirt by one of the women.

Her face was battered beyond recognition, but Marco remembered a kindly Ute woman who fed him, too, when she came to care for Rain Cloud. *A husband shouldn't have to see such things,* he thought, filled with a wrenching combination of anger and grief. *Why in God's name do I live here?* he asked himself, not a new question. God must be weary of hearing him whine.

Their faces menacing, other Utes started to gather around him. Marco prudently dismounted and squatted close to Rain Cloud. He swung the light cloak he had been wearing from his shoulders and covered the naked body before them.

"Great Owl did this?"

Rain Cloud nodded, his eyes bleak. "We came back from hunting elk, Marco." His eyes welled with tears. "We had enough meat to get us through the winter."

"Has Great Owl molested your village before?"

Another nod, this one slower, as if it took all of Rain Cloud's energy. The old man put his hand on Marco's arm. "It is time for us Kapota to move toward the setting sun to other mountains. The bears have left us behind. It is an omen and we must follow our brothers the bears."

"I have two men with me, one a soldier and the other a Comanche— Toshua, a Kwahadi, but my friend and brother. May I motion them in, if they will be safe here?" Marco asked.

"We have heard of your Comanche." Rain Cloud spoke to two of the mounted warriors. "They will go with you to escort them in. Three of you? Only three?"

Marco nodded, dread sinking lower into his stomach like sour beer. "We are a very small army, aren't we?"

Chapter Twenty-Eight

In which Claudio remains a perfect gentleman, so Graciela does not stab him

Two riders in a large and lonely valley, Claudio and Graciela continued to hug the western slope of the Cristos. The absence of buffalo suggested that Utes or Comanches had been hunting and scattered the herd. Claudio wasn't too proud to scare away buzzards from one carcass that had been shot to eat right then on the hunt, probably while other hunters raced on to overtake and shoot more. The best parts were gone—the heart, liver and haunches—but they salvaged enough back meat for a good dinner that night, one that made Claudio hold up his hand in protest when Graciela tried to offer him another chunk.

"Is this how you eat, when you are with the horse traders?" Graci asked.

He had built a small, hot fire in the shelter of a cliff overhang, probably a cutbank years ago when the river had reached much higher. The Rio Bravo was as changeable as a woman who hears bad news and edges away, not for days or weeks until the pout is over, but for years.

"Yes, we eat like this. *Javelina* is the worst."

Graciela made a face. "Have you eaten skunk?"

"Tastier than you might think."

The slave put down the small bone she had been gnawing on. He had marveled to himself that anyone could look ladylike gnawing on a bone, but Graci did. "Did you like that life?"

She had never asked him a question so personal, and it touched him. In their brief time together, Paloma had asked such things, but she was his sister. Graci had no particular reason to be interested, but she was. Outside of

Paloma and Marco, he couldn't think of anyone else who cared.

"I thought I would always trade horses." He paused at the look on her face. "All right, then! Steal horses sometimes. Lately, I am not so certain."

"Señor Mondragón seems like the kind of man who would offer help," she said. "I know that la señora doesn't want you to leave."

He knew it, too. Head against his saddle, he lay back and considered the stars, neutral observers of the human drama that played out beneath them. It struck him that he used to be a neutral observer. Now that he had found his sister, there were decisions to be made, the possibility for heartache, responsibilities. He suspected these were just the irritations that some men ran away from, because life alone was surely simpler. But was it as much fun?

He glanced at Graciela, pleased that she didn't seem to mind listening. "Funny, isn't it, how life seems to plod along, one day much like the one before, until we get to thinking that nothing will ever change? Then it does."

"Here we are, on an empty plain," Graciela said, staring at the stars, too. "I wonder … how far ahead do you think the others are?" She pulled her blanket tighter around her shoulders and shivered.

"They had two or three days on us," he said. He watched her as she clenched her jaw to keep from shivering.

Claudio looked away, ready to roll into his blanket and tough it out until morning, as he had the night before—in fact, as he had on most nights of his life since the raid.

He made the mistake of looking back at Graciela, with her tense jaw and squinting eyes. He had seen the fear in them when he doused their little fire, but she had said nothing.

He couldn't credit what he did next to any particular show of benevolence, since that was not his nature, in recent years. He looked at Graciela, saw someone cold and took his chance.

"Graci, you can sit there and shiver until daybreak, and I can do the same thing, but that makes us foolish."

"Wh … what do you mean?" she asked.

"Just that." He stood up and shook out his blanket. "If we put our blankets and … and ourselves together, we'll be warm. That sounds pretty good to me."

He waited. He saw the fear in her eyes, and her rapid intake of breath. Best be straightforward. "If I had wanted to take you, I could have done that our first night on the trail. I'm bigger than you are and I'm stronger."

She nodded, her eyes wide, but the fear receding, replaced with wariness.

"It may come as a surprise to you—and maybe to me, too—but I'm a gentleman," he told her. "For too many years I forgot I was, but that's what I am. That's how my mother and father raised me, same as they raised Paloma to be a lady."

A long silence followed. He was about to call it a bad business and wrap up in his blanket again when Graci cleared her throat. "Only if we lie back to back," she said.

"Suits me, Graci. I'm tired of being cold." *And alone, and broke, and hopeless*, he wanted to add, but he didn't. He had some dignity remaining.

Graci stood up and held out her blanket. Businesslike, he told her to lie down again and face away. She did, and he lay down beside her, spreading both blankets around them, which felt like heaven on earth. For one small moment, he wondered why Paloma hadn't given them more blankets. Marco had ridden out with two blankets, plus he wore a *serape* over his wool shirt.

He pressed his back against Graciela's and tucked the blankets around him. He heard Graciela do the same. He started to chuckle. *If I get back alive, I am going to ask my little sister if she gave us one blanket each on purpose*, he thought, even though he was pretty sure what Paloma would say.

"What's so funny?" Graciela asked.

"I'll tell you later," he said and faked a yawn. "Too tired now."

He lay there beside the slave, a woman he would have taken without a qualm only a few weeks ago. He was conscious of the tension in every muscle of her back. She sighed, and the tension lessened. In a few minutes, she slept, her breathing even and deep. He listened, closed his eyes, and slept, too, finally warm in body and heart.

IN THE MORNING, CLAUDIO thought Graciela might shy away from him, but he underestimated her. After he built another small fire, she deftly shoved more buffalo chunks on last night's toasting stick, cooked it until the meat was hot and smoking, and gave him more than his share. He tried to protest that she should divide it equally, but she narrowed her eyes and dared him.

To top it off, she rummaged in her saddle bag and pulled out two linty lumps of honey candy, giving him the larger piece. He brushed off the lint.

"From where did this appear?" he asked.

"Señora Mondragón made some candy to placate Soledad," she said, popping her piece in her mouth. "I stole some."

"Paloma told me you weren't stealing tortillas anymore," he said, enjoying the rare treat, but willing to tease her.

"No tortillas." She shrugged. "This was different." She laughed, a soft sound muffled by her hand covering her mouth. "And what do you know, I forgot I had it. I *forgot*." She said it again, with wonder in her voice, as if she understood, for the first time in a long while, that she had enough and some to share. She was wealthy.

He saw it all in her pretty face and smiled back. They were two conspirators now, not just a beaten-down slave and a battered horse stealer, dragging sins and misdeeds on chains he could not see. The knowledge warmed him as much as the blankets and her body heat.

After another day of riding, mostly in silence, they ate what remained of the buffalo meat, drank from a river that anyone else would have called a stream, and bundled up together.

"Tomorrow we will be near a favorite camping area for Rain Cloud," she said, when Claudio thought she slept. "It is a place he likes to leave the women and children while the warriors hunt the valley for elk and deer, sometimes buffalo."

"Great Owl's camp is near, too?"

"Over the mountains, toward the Staked Plains. I will show you and Señor Mondragón, when we find him."

"It will be safer if you draw a map and remain with Rain Cloud's women," he said.

"Oh, no. I am coming with you."

He turned around until he was facing her back. She heard him move and turned around, too.

"It's too dangerous. Marco will just send you back."

She started to cry, weeping silent tears, the kind of tears he understood. He had cried enough of them, after the Comanche raid, when he found himself in the hands of rough men who would only tease and humiliate him.

"Graci?"

"I have a daughter in Great Owl's camp," she managed to gasp out before another wave of sorrow covered her. "I have to find her."

"Child of a Comanche?"

It sounded stupid and naïve when he said it, and he could have kicked himself. But that wasn't necessary, because Graciela Tafoya kicked him.

"What other baby could it be?" she hissed. "She was not the first, but she is the only one who lived!"

He did the only thing he could do, which was hold her tight as she sobbed. Claudio thought she might pull away, but she burrowed into him like a small animal. Thank God he was too smart to wonder out loud why a Comanche captive would want such a child. He held her close, remembering a horrible day when Lorenzo and Paco had been hired to return a Spanish captive to her people on a *rancho* near Tesuque.

She had run to them with a child in her arms, which Lorenzo had wrenched from her and tossed back to the gathering of sullen Apaches, prisoners themselves now, courtesy of Governor Mendinueta. She had screamed for the child and sobbed all the way to Tesuque. When they passed through the village only six months later, he learned she had been dead for weeks, her heart broken, or so her Spanish family said. Lorenzo just shook his head.

Claudio had nightmares, new nightmares piled onto old ones, until he never wanted to close his eyes.

"We'll see what we can do, Graci," he said and his words sounded so lame.

"That sounds like no," she said quietly. "I am tired of hearing no."

She turned around, her back to him again. He did the same, wondering why Paloma had allowed him to roam around off the Double Cross, since he obviously had no brains and no heart. *When this is done, I swear I will go back to my horse traders*, he thought. The notion gave him no comfort.

At some point in the long night, perhaps triggered by Graciela's revelation, he had the nightmare he so dreaded, the one where he saw the torn body of his mother, clutching his unborn baby brother. Usually the dream morphed into the sight of that baby thrown by Lorenzo, end over end so slowly, back to the Apache prisoners, as its mother screamed and tried to reach for it with abnormally long arms. Instead, the sight of his mother was blocked from his vision as a young Paloma walked in front of him. He called to her, and she kept walking, unhearing and unseeing, until she was out of sight on what he knew was the road to El Paso.

It seemed so real that he called again, wanting her to turn around and wait for him, as he buried his mother with a teaspoon. She walked on and eventually disappeared, as the dream turned into the more familiar terror, with the Comanche captive and her long arms.

And then it was over. He lay there in a sweat, someone's cool hand over his eyes, pressing down. "Graci?" he whispered.

"Who else would be here?" she whispered back. "I'm not very happy with you right now, but no one needs to cry out like that. Go to sleep."

He did as she said, and remembered nothing more until morning. When he woke up, Graciela was kneeling by the cold campfire, slicing bits of cactus into smaller bits, somehow making it look like more. She hummed as she sliced, and he marveled at the resiliency of women. He took a deep breath and another, enjoying the silence. There was no Lorenzo to curse at Rogelio and thrash him for being slow, or childlike, or in the way. This was better.

"I don't think men understand women and babies," Graciela said, with her back still to him. "Let us leave it at that."

A coward, where delicacy and tact might be called for, Claudio was happy to agree.

They started into another morning on the wide plain, and he could have kicked himself again for leaving the shelter of the mountains. They should have started out during the night. The moon was nearly full now, and they could have traveled in more safety than in this broad sunlight.

"Graci, let's wait," he said, when they had hardly begun their day's journey.

She had ridden ahead of him, probably grateful to distance herself from an idiot. She looked back at him, then beyond him, and gasped. He turned around in surprise, and watched in horror at a cloud of dust in the distance.

The air was calm, so he could not say it was wind blowing dust. *It's over*, he thought.

"Di … di …didn't you say that Rain Cloud's men were hunting buffalo?" he asked.

"It's not buffalo." She edged her horse closer, whatever quarrel she had against him gone, at least for now. Or maybe for always, if the dust cloud turned into Comanches.

"There is nothing we can do," he said calmly. He pulled an arrow from his quiver, surprised how steady his hand was. "I'll shoot as long as I can."

Her face was set and brave. She took her knife from its sheath, and turned to him. "It's funny. I started to make some plans, even while I was tending Señora Mondragón's little ones. Maybe it's better not to have plans."

He could think of nothing to say to that. He leaned over and kissed Graci's cheek. "I think you're a fine woman," he told her, and meant it. No point in telling her that he had started to plan, himself.

They faced the dust cloud that all too soon materialized into horsemen. As Claudio wiped his eyes and readied his bow and arrow, he squinted to improve his aim, and saw what looked like a wagon. Three men were bouncing along on the wagon seat, as someone suspiciously like Rogelio rode the off horse of the team pulling the wagon. He put down the bow and told Graci to sheathe her knife.

She stared at him, her hand still tight around the knife handle.

"No, I mean it," he told her. "Take a good look."

She did, and he heard her relieved laughter.

Calm now, Claudio felt his racing heart slow down. *Oye*, too much of this terror was going to turn him old before his time.

Lorenzo Diaz slowed his horse, waving his sombrero to dispel some of the dust he had raised. "What are you doing here?" he hollered.

"I could ask the same of you," Claudio said. He stared at the wagon as Rogelio came closer, then slowed the horses, grinning like the fool he was. Claudio looked at the men on the wagon seat, took in their bound hands and legs tied together. If one had fallen off, all would have tumbled to the ground.

His mouth open, Claudio looked at the long boxes in the wagon bed, and smaller metal boxes.

"You found the Frenchmen," he said. "They *do* have weapons."

Lorenzo nodded. He patted his chest. "Paloma tells me I will be a hero."

"Paloma?" Claudio asked. "*Paloma?*"

"She told me to do the right thing and help Marco."

"And you actually *listened* to her? You didn't just grab the guns and run to the nearest shady dealer? Lorenzo!"

Lorenzo leaned forward, his eyes bright, his face dusty, but his smile unmistakable in its kindness. "Claudio, Claudio, you should listen to women sometimes. I've never been a hero before and Paloma thinks I will be good at it."

Chapter Twenty-Nine

In which Lorenzo is surprisingly righteous

L ORENZO WOULDN'T HEAR OF stopping for a brief parlay. "We have work to do, lad. Paloma made me swear an oath to be a righteous man and think of others."

He prodded his horse into motion and Rogelio did the same with the wagon. His head crammed with a thousand questions, Claudio rode beside the horse trader.

There wasn't any glow of sanctity about the dirty fellow that Claudio could see, but Lorenzo assured him that every man should go about doing good, now and then. "That's what Paloma told me." He dipped his head, and Claudio stared at the spectacle of a shy Lorenzo. "Sancha even mentioned it."

Now he understood. Sancha. "Lorenzo, you amaze me," Claudio said. He knew his amazement would pass, and probably Lorenzo's sudden righteousness, too, but here they were and Lorenzo was in a great hurry to find Marco. He turned to Graciela, whose amazement mirrored his own.

"Are we close to the Ute camp? Perhaps they have seen Marco."

She nodded, and pointed with her lips like an Indian. "That small range to the south of the big Blanca," she said. "There is a pass. You'll see."

He did see. They rode steadily on. He heard one of the trussed up men arguing with the other in a language he did not know. It wasn't French. Soon the three men were shouting at each other. He heard some familiar words— why was it that curses on other tongues were so easily learned?—and suddenly knew this was English.

"They're not French," he said to Lorenzo as they pounded along.

"Two of them are," the horse trader replied. "They came down from the north."

"The *north*? You can't be serious," Claudio said.

Lorenzo just glared at him, and Claudio knew something had changed. Only weeks ago, any contradiction would have earned him a slap across the face. Claudio wondered if he could credit Sancha with this transformation of a brutal, sour, dishonest man. Lorenzo had mentioned Paloma; perhaps she was the author of this good behavior. He glanced back at the arguing prisoners. Maybe all three could take some credit.

"There is something wrong."

Lorenzo and Claudio both looked at Graciela. "Name me something right about this fools' trail we are traveling," Lorenzo snapped.

"I mean it," Graci fired back. "Rain Cloud and his warriors should have noticed us by now," she said. "We are so close to the pass, and they are not here."

"They've just moved somewhere else," Claudio said.

She shook her head with some vigor, and gave him that stare that women so easily mastered, the one that asked, *Just how foolish are men?*

"We gather chokecherries here. This is the time and the place. Something is wrong."

"Should we turn away from the pass?"

She gave him the second stare women mastered to perfection. This one asked, *Do I have to think for you, too?* She rode ahead of them both, leaving Claudio to wonder just how men and women ever got close enough to mate, produce babies, and continue mankind.

* * *

"THERE ISN'T MUCH MORE we can do here, *nami*," Toshua said to Marco. "Those who are going to die have died, the restless spirits have settled down, and Great Owl is still out there somewhere."

Marco nodded and wondered how to convey even a tenth of his unease to a man who felt no fear. *Have I become a coward?* he asked himself, even as he knew the answer. He had become a husband and a father, and he did not relish taking chances. Only his duty to distant King Carlos—and more important, a promise to Governor de Anza—kept him from bolting home.

He looked around the Ute camp, tidier now, but eerie in the absence of many children and young women. In an orgy of grief, the survivors had burned the brush shelters that hadn't already been destroyed by the Comanches. With tears and wailing that kept the hair on Marco's neck and arms erect, they had washed the desecrated bodies of the older women and the babies too young to serve any Comanche purpose beyond mutilation and violation, then wrapped them in shrouds.

Silent, Marco and Joaquim had helped take the shrouded corpses into the mountains, carrying the dead to rocky places. Toshua's aid—Comanche aid— had been politely but firmly refused by Rain Cloud. They dug a deep hole and placed the bodies within, piling back the earth and stacking rocks.

The bereft men stood in long silence. Some chopped off their braids. All wore the sleepy-eyed expression so familiar to Marco, the one that said, *I cannot close my eyes without seeing my dear ones.* The Utes were exhausted in mind and body, and some were weak from letting their own blood when they really wanted to kill Comanches.

They had ridden back in more silence. The air hummed with their silence, even the birds paying respect and the wind holding back any rustling of the quaking aspen, already starting to turn yellow.

But they rode with warriors, who were never fools. Farther down the trail at the spot where the pass could be seen, several men gestured to each other and spoke in low tones. Marco rode closer. "What do you see?" he asked in Ute.

He looked where the warrior pointed. Winding their way up the mountain was a strange sight: a wagon in the lead. No, there was a white man in front, followed by more familiar people—one a relative he hadn't thought to see again. *I swear I'll thrash that rascal for making Paloma cry*, he vowed to himself.

"*Dios mio!*" he exclaimed. "Joaquim, it is Claudio and Graciela, and I don't believe this, but also that rascal Lorenzo."

His Ute was fair, but not up to complexities, so he signed to the warrior in the lead, the one already nocking arrow to bow. "Friends, and something more," he said, in case his signing wasn't as good as it used to be.

With a highly skeptical look, the Ute rested his bow and arrow on his lap. "I am willing to kill anyone right now," he told Marco.

"Not these. At least, not now," Marco said, understanding him perfectly.

They arrived in camp just before Claudio came in, guiding his horse with his knees and holding both hands up in surrender. Graciela rode beside him. Marco watched the expectation on her face turn to worry. She dismounted slowly and walked to Rain Cloud, who held out his arms to her. He wrapped her in his embrace and they swayed from side to side as he tried to explain what he could not explain. Whatever greeting she had anticipated after four years a captive of the Comanche turned to less than dust as she mourned in the ruin of the Ute village.

Marco watched Lorenzo, whose face registered no shock at the obvious signs of a successful Comanche raid on a peaceful village. Lorenzo Diaz, damn his soul, had lived too long on the frontier.

On the other hand, Rogelio stared in shock and disbelief. His lips even started to quiver. The three men tightly bound on the wagon seat seemed to draw together even closer. Marco looked at the wagon, with its load of long boxes, and shorter boxes and powder kegs. The rumor was true. The French were ready to do business and further disrupt the frontier.

Marco nearly turned to the warrior with the bow and arrow in his lap and ordered him to start shooting. Why in heaven's name were the French interested in poor, wracked New Mexico? Wasn't life hard enough already? Why did the battles of wars begun in distant lands have to be fought here? *I will never understand kings*, he thought.

"Señor Mondragón?"

Marco looked up from his tight fists to Lorenzo, who held out a folded sheet of paper to him.

"Read this, señor," the old scoundrel urged. "Your wife …."

Marco snatched the paper, his heart hammering in his throat. *Please, please, nothing wrong there*, he asked God. He scanned Paloma's familiar handwriting. As all good wives did, here on the edge of Comanchería, she assured him first that all was well. His breathing slowed and he continued, reading of the two Frenchman and one Englishman that Lorenzo had actually apprehended farther north and then brought to the Double Cross, along with cases of firearms.

He couldn't help smiling as he continued. "I am certain we have Sancha to credit for Lorenzo's sudden honesty," he read. "Did you ever think Sancha would blush? Not I."

He kept reading, barely mindful that the others had dismounted and dragged the prisoners from the wagon seat. "They came from far, far to the north, a place called the Mandan Villages. They are intent on stirring up trouble, which besides good food, the French are famous for," Paloma had written.

He smiled again, wondering if she had made them bathe. Ah, this woman of his! He read her conclusion, which professed her love and worry in equal parts, and then other sentences she had added in even smaller print at the bottom. The smile left his face.

"How they got here alive, they would not say," Paloma continued. "How they plan to leave, no comment. You have Toshua, and he has ways to loosen tongues, so you must find out more. Something terrible is going on."

Paloma had added a note on the back: "My love, I think one of us had better learn some English. I fear there will be more of these people."

Chapter Thirty

In which Marco deals with scoundrels and retains his honor

"W ERE THEY GOING TO use these guns against us?" Rain Cloud asked Marco, after he dismounted. "Should we just kill them now?"

The Ute chief had spoken in Spanish. Marco heard one of the prisoners suck in his breath. He looked at the other Frenchman and what must be the Englishman, who appeared puzzled, nothing more.

"How many languages do we need here?" Marco asked Rain Cloud.

He knew Rain Cloud would not fail him. After all, a wounded man doesn't lie beside another wounded man without learning a few home truths. Rain Cloud gave him a slow wink, one the prisoners could not see, and appeared to consider the question. Marco felt some gratification to see sweat break out on two foreheads. The Englishman appeared clueless.

"*My* Spanish is good enough, and we only need one Frenchman who speaks Spanish," Rain Cloud said. "I don't care about the Englishman. I have met a few Englishmen. I do not like them, or Americans, either, if such he is. Two of these prisoners are expendable. That one and that one."

The Frenchman who spoke Spanish translated this into French for his fellows, who quickly looked as stricken as he did.

"I have no use for men like you, who would deal in death and leave our children and wives at the mercy of Comanche renegades," Marco said to the two expendables who had dropped to their knees. "Tell them that."

"I think they already know." The Frenchman bowed. "I am Jean Baptiste LeCroix, a trader like these, um, gentlemen of yours." He indicated Lorenzo and Rogelio, who watched with some interest.

"They're wretched worms, much like you," Marco said. He could almost feel Lorenzo bristle, but the trader wisely said nothing.

Perhaps Jean Baptiste LeCroix thought to ingratiate himself with Marco, the man with the power. Who knew what a Frenchman thought?

"What about this one?" he asked, pointing to Claudio. "Is he a wretched worm, too? And this woman, unless you all take turns with her?"

Big mistake, Marco thought, and moved out of the way. *Fool. You should have left it alone.* As Marco expected, Rain Cloud whipped out his knife and filleted a strip of skin from Jean Baptiste, who screamed and clutched his arm. The chief gathered Graciela close. As Marco did *not* expect, Claudio stepped forward, grasped the dangling, bloody strip and ripped it off the rest of the way, to the prisoner's further anguish.

"Claudio is my brother-in-law," Marco said in his most conversational tone, when the Frenchman stopped screaming. "I wouldn't advise any more hard words about him. My wife loves him. And Graciela? She has some standing in this tribe, as you might have just learned. Certainly more than you have. Do not try to impress me."

The other Utes had gathered around, probably happy enough to take their minds off their own miseries. Looking as terrified as his two companions now, Jean Baptiste knelt in the dirt beside them.

Marco turned to Rain Cloud, who had wiped off his knife and returned it to its sheath. "My friend, before we do anything else to these upstanding citizens of one country or another, I would like to know just what they are doing here."

Rain Cloud nodded, suddenly the perfect host. "We could all sit down right here and discuss this."

"Please, before God, I am bleeding to death!" Jean Baptiste said, but softly this time. Possibly he could see that he had no more standing than an earthworm. Lesson learned.

"It won't come to that," Marco said in his most cajoling voice. He pointed to his cheek and its lengthy scar, put there nearly two years ago by Kwihnai himself as a reminder to stay away from the sacred canyon of the Kwahadi. "It'll give you good stories to tell. At least, it will if you live much longer than today."

Jean Baptiste sobbed out loud. Rain Cloud shook his head. He gestured to one of his warriors, who threw down what looked like an old rabbit skin. Jean Baptiste pressed it against his wound.

"Good. Rain Cloud, let us just sit here in a circle and find out a few things."

They sat down, Marco next to Rain Cloud, and Toshua next to Marco, who couldn't help noticing how Graciela and Claudio seemed to find each other and sit close. Lorenzo and Rogelio squatted by the prisoners.

Marco turned to Lorenzo. "Señor Diaz, tell us how you found these worthless men."

"We were north of the Double Cross, on our way to find you," Lorenzo said. "I honestly think they were lost."

"Imagine. And you took them to Paloma—Señora Mondragón? I own that I am surprised, Lorenzo." He couldn't resist. "Could it be that you have designs on my housekeeper?"

He had to give the old scoundrel credit. Lorenzo drew himself up, two spots of color burning in his cheeks. "I never met a better woman, excepting your own wife, of course."

"Of course." Marco stared hard at the prisoners. All three had gone pasty white. The Englishman was even beginning to drool. Paloma did that before she had to find a basin, but he thought the *inglés* could just vomit in his own lap. "I do hope they were polite to my wife."

Lorenzo tisked his tongue. "There was a fourth one, another Englishman, who thought he would be insolent to so fine a lady." Lorenzo nodded to Toshua. "*Your* wife dispatched him with one stab."

None of the prisoners would look up. Toshua grunted his approval. "She would do that."

"I hope my children did not see any of this," Marco told Lorenzo, who shook his head, and continued his narrative.

"I asked la señora what to do, and she told me to find you." He laughed and clapped his hands, which made the prisoners start. "And here we are!"

"I commend you, Lorenzo," Marco said. "You could have taken those guns and I would have been none the wiser." He leaned toward the horse trader. "Paloma will be proud of you, too, and more to the point, so will Sancha." He assumed mock anger. "Do you mean to deprive me of my housekeeper?"

"If I can," Lorenzo said cheerfully.

"We shall see," Marco said, quietly pleased, even as he wondered about Sancha's taste in men. *You're a fool, Marco,* he scolded himself. *Paloma decided you were the man for her. Who can know what an otherwise rational woman thinks?*

He kicked Jean Baptiste's boot. "Attend to me! Where are you from and why have you come to sell guns to Great Owl?"

Marco looked at Toshua, then back at them. "I advise you to tell me the truth." He looked next at Rain Cloud. "I have certain resources here."

Jean Baptiste drew a long, shuddering breath. "We are from the Mandan Villages."

"Which are—"

"Far to the north, on the Missouri River."

"A long way to go for mischief," Marco said. "Are you French?"

"From Canada."

Toshua snaked out his hand and yanked on Jean Baptiste's bloody arm. "Señor Mondragón to you!"

Jean Baptiste sobbed out loud. "I was born in Montreal and I work for the North West Company, señor," he babbled. "It is a British company."

"The British? They are going to great lengths to foul things so far south."

"There are agents among the North West Company," Jean Baptiste said, his face even whiter than before. "Agents of the crown." He looked at the Englishman. "Some of the *ingleses* aren't yet certain which side of the fence they belong on. Tell them where you are from, David."

"David Benedict, sir. I am from St. Louis, Missouri."

Jean Baptiste translated. "David is British, I think, and American when it suits him."

David Benedict said nothing. Marco already saw death in his eyes.

"All of you are working so hard to keep the Comanches busy in New Mexico," Marco said. "Why? We are a poor colony. I will admit that Spain is on the decline here. What could we offer you?"

Jean Baptiste gave him a sharp glance, then he looked into the distance. Perhaps he saw his own puny influence coming to an end. But he had to try, apparently. "Blame the British. Think how much they lost last year when the Treaty of Paris was signed." He made an elaborate gesture. "A whole continent!" He sidled closer until Marco wanted to back away in disgust. "They want to cause as much trouble as they can for you Spaniards."

I don't think like empire builders, Marco told himself, *but I can try*. "Let me guess: you have been selling guns all along the way from the Mandan Villages. On the Missouri River?"

Jean Baptiste nodded.

"How, if I may ask?"

He tried to sidle even closer, and Marco put up his hand.

"The British crown sent agents among all the tribes, promising muskets for money," Jean Baptiste said. "Some came here. And there are Frenchmen in Canada willing to play the game, too. Anything to disrupt the Americans." He made a sorrowful face. "I fear Spain is just in the way."

Marco wanted to laugh at the Frenchman's obvious attempt to turn himself into a valuable resource, the kind who was kept alive to sing his self-serving melody to the viceroy in Mexico City and not left to die in some dry canyon in poor New Mexico.

"How did you do this?" Joaquim said, looking like a man interested and friendly. "You must be clever, indeed."

Jean Baptiste turned his attention to Joaquim. Marco glanced at the other Frenchman and saw nothing on his face but disgust. Marco smiled inside. *I am the hard man and Joaquim is the kind man. And you are a fool to fall for that, Frenchman,* he thought.

"We started out a year ago with guards and eight wagons of muskets," Jean Baptiste said. "We dropped off guns, and some of the guards rode to St. Louis with the money."

"What a clever plan," Joaquim said.

Jean Baptiste seemed to relax, which made him the only happy person for miles around.

"Ah, St. Louis! Nature's perfect city," Joaquim said. "I congratulate you on finding a place that I would consider a den of thieves. I have to wonder if any money ever got into the proper hands."

Jean Baptiste's eyes clouded over as he realized the ragged man in the ill-fitting uniform was playing with him. He turned his attention back to Marco.

Marco had no plan to make the man comfortable. "So here you are, with no guards, and one wagon left. Why no guards?"

"Smallpox, señor," the Frenchman said mournfully. "The rest ran away."

"Wise of them," Joaquim said.

Marco shook his head. "You are at the end of the line. How exactly do you plan to get back to St. Louis?"

"We plan to ask Great Owl to provide us with an escort north to the land of the Pawnee," Jean Baptiste said.

Joaquim burst into laughter. "The *Comanches*? You think they will *help* you?" He slapped Jean Baptiste on the back, then doubled over as mirth rendered him helpless. "Oh, my! Helpful Comanches? Marco, have you now heard everything under the sun?"

It wasn't funny, but it was. "I would almost give a year of my life to watch you ask Great Owl to assist you," Marco said. He laughed until tears came to his eyes. "Don't you know *anything* about Comanches?" he managed to gasp.

Rain Cloud's laugh started as a low rumble in his throat. The other Kapota Utes looked at one another and shook with silent laughter at first. When they laughed, Jean Baptiste turned deadly pale. Everyone was making fun of him.

Marco held up his hand, and the laughter stopped. "You will not sell guns to Great Owl."

Marco had to give David Benedict a silent *bravo*. The Englishman knew it was over, but he was going to die with dignity. He stood up.

"Others will come after us, señor," David Benedict said quietly, in Spanish so poor that even Toshua winced. "We are the first."

Why us? Marco thought. *We live a hard life that your kind will make harder.* "I no longer doubt you, Señor Benedict. But right now, and in this place, *you* will not sell those guns to a terrible man." What he said was complex, so he waited for Jean Baptiste to translate.

David Benedict nodded and knelt in the dust again, done. *You're a brave one*, Marco thought.

He looked the prisoners over. He was a man of honor, kind when he could be. He watched three pairs of eyes trained on him, knowing that a lesser man might get some thrill from such power over life and death. Marco felt nothing but distaste at what he had to do, but he was not a man to shrink from duty.

"Stand up, you three," he said, with Jean Baptiste continuing to translate. Of the prisoners, Jean Baptiste had no fear in his eyes. He knew he was safe because Marco needed him.

He reached forward and took David Benedict by the arm. "You will stay alive. Translate, Jean Baptiste, damn you! I know a priest who lives where the Chama joins the Bravo. He speaks English. I will take you, David Benedict, to the governor and you will tell him about the English and especially the Americans." He looked at the two Frenchmen, staring at them long and hard. "I have no use for the French."

Both men sank to their knees again, then farther, pressing their foreheads against the dirt, groveling. *We want so much to live*, Marco thought. *God help me, I do not want to do what I must.*

He took out his dagger. "Tomorrow there will be a battle. We are few, compared to Great Owl, but he cannot have those guns. You are an encumbrance because I cannot trust you."

"Spare us!" Jean Baptiste pleaded.

Here is the dilemma, Marco thought. *I am Christian gentleman. I cannot order other Christians to their death. God help me, I cannot.*

Toshua grabbed Marco's arm. "Let us remove them for now. We must decide soon, but another hour will not matter."

Marco nodded.

"You need me!" Jean Baptiste cried out, as Rain Cloud took his arm in a surprisingly gentle grasp and started pulling him from the circle.

"No, I don't," Marco said. "Spain is fading in this land I love so well. But face this fact: so is France." He pointed to David Benedict. "*This* is the real threat. However, I am a Christian man, and cannot deal out justice so readily."

Chapter Thirty-One

In which Joaquim Gasca finally uses the education his parents probably paid for

WHEN TOSHUA RETURNED, HE laid a hand on Marco's shoulder. "The two Frenchmen are dead," he said simply.

When Marco opened his mouth to protest, Toshua added, "I knew you did not have the heart for it, but it had to be done. I did not want you to return to Paloma with their blood on your hands. For me, I don't mind."

"You didn't torture them?" Marco asked.

"No," Toshua said. "I did as you would do. Chaa! Am I becoming a Spanish man? They died quickly."

"Now what will we do?" Joaquim asked.

"Patience, my friend," Marco told him. "Graciela, in all of this, I never asked why you are here, and even you, Claudio." He peered closer at his brother-in-law. "I had not thought to see you anytime soon."

"I brought him back to Paloma with a noose around his neck," Lorenzo growled, sounding remarkably like an injured parent. "Some people don't know when they are well off."

"You, Graciela?" Marco asked, not wanting to laugh at the stubborn look on Claudio's face. She swallowed and he saw the fear in her eyes. "I won't hurt you," Marco added.

"It's not you, señor," she whispered. "I am so afraid of Comanches."

"She came anyway," Claudio explained, pride in his voice. "Tell him, Graci."

Marco noted the little endearment, and the way Graciela moved closer to Claudio. "I understand what it is to be afraid of Comanches, whether you can see them or not," he said gently. "That is their greatest power over every Spaniard in New Mexico. Please, Graciela."

She took heart and stood straight. "I can show you where Great Owl's village is. I told Señora Mondragón and she said I had to tell you. None of you will find it without me."

Marco could have kicked himself then. Great God in heaven, why had he not demanded that Jean Baptiste tell him where Great Owl planned to meet the French arms dealers? Great Owl would never bring them into the village, with his women and children.

"I am a fool," he said bitterly. "I should have asked that miserable interpreter where the trade was to take place!"

"No matter," Joaquim said in his breezy fashion. He turned to David Benedict and spoke in English. "Where will the trade take place?"

Marco stared at the royal engineer. "I had no idea you could be so useful," he said. "Where on earth…. How—"

"I began my engineering days in La Florida, where there is a considerable English presence, mostly unsanctioned," Joaquim said. He twirled his forefingers around his ears. "There was a time a few years ago when England and Spain were allies. War makes me dizzy! I have always been good with languages," he concluded modestly, which made Marco laugh out loud.

David Benedict folded his arms and set his lips in a tight line. Marco didn't even bother to glance at Toshua. "Joaquim, you might suggest to our prisoner that this is no time to be stubborn, or think that by holding out he will get better terms than a visit to Santa Fe. He is lucky to be alive."

Cheerful, Joaquim spoke to Benedict, who ignored him. Joaquim shrugged. He took Graciela by the arm and handed her off to Claudio, who led her away from the circle. Benedict eyed the two of them, his frown deepening. The morning was cool, but beads of sweat slid down his temples.

Toshua took out his scalping knife, turning it over several times, as if trying to figure out which edge was sharper. He strolled casually to a woodpile. As everyone watched, probably not one breath drawn among all of them, the Comanche searched until he found a long splinter. Carefully, he pared it down even further, until the end was needle sharp.

Toshua took his time returning to the circle. A gesture, and two of Rain Cloud's warriors grabbed Benedict's arms. Toshua held the sharpened splinter at Benedict's waist, then slowly lowered it, tapping it here and there as the American started to breathe fast.

A word from Toshua and the warriors pushed Benedict's legs farther apart.

"No! No!" the American screamed. He spoke rapidly to Joaquim, who held up his hand to stop the Comanche. Toshua turned to Marco, a question in his eyes.

"Joaquim, tell him that we will have the entire truth, or I will not stop Toshua," Marco said.

A few rapid words in English and Joaquim nodded. "He will speak the truth."

Desperate, Benedict gulped and spoke slower. He lost control of his bowels and his humiliation was complete. Marco felt his heart go out to the Englishman or American or whoever he was. If any of them survived, Benedict would go to Santa Fe, spend some years in prison in Mexico City, then return to St. Louis, or wherever he felt safe from Comanches. He would tell his tale of near mutilation, and shove fear deep into every man he spoke to. Marco knew he was watching the birth of terror. David Benedict would never be free from fear again.

"Toshua has a knack, hasn't he?" Joaquim asked, his voice not so breezy this time. He spoke to David Benedict in English.

Benedict's voice was tight and urgent. The words spilled out of him. At a gesture from Toshua, the warriors released Benedict, who fell to the ground in his own filth.

"Should we, um, do something for him?" Joaquim asked Marco.

"No. Just leave him there," Marco replied, more shaken than he wanted to acknowledge. "This is not a game we are playing."

Marco felt unexpected pity as he watched the defeated man in the dust. Benedict had drawn himself into a tight ball now. Marco wondered how many nights the man would jerk awake from a terrible nightmare in just that position. Marco looked around at the solemn faces of the others, Hispanic and Indian alike, wondering how long *he* would call out in fright from the same nightmare. Thank God Paloma would be there to soothe him.

"Where is the meeting?" Marco asked Joaquim. He turned away from the man Toshua had reduced to quivering *flan*.

Joaquim pointed to Dos Hermanos, two peaks rising from the Sangre de Cristos. "Between those two, tomorrow when the sun is directly overhead."

Hands on his hips, Marco stared across the valley, toward the Cristos. "We will be there at daybreak, watching." He called to Lorenzo, who hurried over, giving a wide berth to the sobbing man. Rogelio trotted behind, as loyal as a hound, though probably not as bright.

Her eyes averted, Graciela joined them, Claudio's arm tight around her waist. Marco thought he would never smile again, not after what he had just witnessed, but here he was, smiling to see them.

Marco looked around this smaller circle, these people he trusted. "Graciela, the purchase of firearms will take place at noon tomorrow between those two peaks. Do you know them?"

"Yes, the Two Brothers," she whispered, her voice barely audible. She pointed beyond the more southerly peak. "That is where Great Owl's village will be located. It is high and hidden."

"How certain are you that Great Owl will be there?" Marco asked.

"Positive, señor," she replied firmly. "Great Owl always camps there. Who does he have to fear?" She gestured in a sweeping motion as graceful as her name. "There is a pass uniting the two sites."

"Even better," Marco said. Next he turned to Lorenzo. "Answer me honestly now." He gestured to Benedict, still curled so tight. "Let him be your bad example of someone who thinks he will lie."

Lorenzo gulped and nodded.

"Have you ever dealt with Great Owl?"

"Once," Lorenzo said, with no hesitation. "Of course, I had a long beard then and long hair. I didn't smell as sweet, either. He has never seen me looking *this* handsome."

"Would you truly like to be a hero for Sancha?"

Lorenzo colored, dipped his head like a little boy, then nodded, while Rogelio whooped. The sound was cut short by a backhanded slap, but Rogelio still grinned.

"Would you pretend to be a French trader?" Marco asked Lorenzo. "You, too, Rogelio."

"Only if I know there are some of you looking down on me, and hopefully ready with bows and arrows and maybe even some firearms. We don't need to sell him *all* of them, do we?"

Joaquim's eyes narrowed. "Why are we selling him any muskets at all?"

"I want my slave money back."

"You surprise me, Brother," Claudio said.

Marco turned to Graciela. "You would let someone as foolish as my brother-in-law hold your hand?" He turned hard eyes on Claudio next. "If he somehow survives what we are planning, I do not want him to have one single centavo to purchase more guns."

Marco turned to Joaquim, who stood watching this whole exchange with amusement. "You there, my royal engineer. Did your professors teach you how to foul up a firing piece?"

"No, no! I learned that in a bar in La Havana, Cuba," Joaquim replied. "Saved my life, I think. Certainly that part that David Benedict nearly lost."

Marco looked around this smaller circle, wondering when it was that he had become a leader, and not just a *juez de campo*. There were probably *jueces* all over New Mexico who checked brands, registered them, collected taxes, and minded their own business. Why was he not among that number?

He gestured for Rain Cloud to join them, wishing he could erase the sorrow from his old friend's eyes. He remembered with painful clarity the three days and nights they had lain side by side five years ago, wounded after the first battle with Cuerno Verde. He remembered the taste of the buffalo and wild grass stew that Rain Cloud's wife had fed them both, as she scolded them in her gentle voice for taking so many chances. She was dead now, and must be avenged.

"My friend, how many warriors have you?" he asked.

"No more than twenty, I regret to say."

"Get your men, and listen to what I propose."

He waited while Rain Cloud gathered his warriors—Kapota Utes who sometimes allied with the New Mexicans, and sometimes with Comanches, depending on how the wind blew. They filed into the growing circle and sat down by their chief, silent.

Marco squatted on his haunches. "Here is what I want to do." He pointed with his lips to Graciela. "You know this little one. She and her mother lived among you until four years ago, when Great Owl swooped down, silent as the bird that is his totem."

Everyone nodded. He had their attention. "Tomorrow at noon, Great Owl, our common enemy, will buy guns from French traders."

"Toshua and I killed the traders," Rain Cloud reminded him. He looked over his shoulder at Benedict. "And this one is worthless."

"I know," Marco said. "May they burn in hell. Lorenzo, stand up."

Surprised, the horse trader did as he asked.

"Lorenzo here, a hero in many parts of New Mexico, will pretend to be a French trader."

Marco smiled inside as Lorenzo stood a little taller and struck a pose. *If I didn't know you better, I would be impressed,* he thought.

"But guns—" Rain Cloud began.

"Tss, tss, tss," Marco cautioned. He indicated Joaquim Gasca, a thorough-going rascal who had richly deserved being broken down to private. *We work with what we have,* Marco thought. "*This* hero is going to fix those guns so they will not fire."

"That will be magic," Rain Cloud said, and looked at Joaquim with more respect than anyone had assigned such a scoundrel in recent memory.

Marco drew in the dirt with his dagger, forming the Two Brothers and that jog in the Sangre de Cristo Mountains as they continued south, then handed his knife to Graciela. She knew what he wanted, and drew a line from the Two Brothers over the hump of the Cristos, and partly down to the eastern side of the mountain range.

"Here is the danger," Marco said. "I will not try to fool you. I would like five of your warriors with me, as we watch our hero Lorenzo sell bad guns to Great Owl, who will probably have brought many of his warriors with him. I say 'probably,' because I do not know."

"Who can know these things?" Rain Cloud said philosophically.

"Who, indeed? Not my God and all his saints, nor your totem the bear, who knows so much and gives you his wisdom. At the time we are making our trade, you and the rest of your warriors will strike Great Owl's camp with its women and children." He looked around at the men, who were now listening intently. "Some of you will probably be able to rescue your own women and children."

They all sat in silence, everyone considering the plan, a plan of ifs. Marco looked from face to face, weighing what he saw. Governor de Anza's words echoed in his mind and heart: "We have to work together to live in this land."

"The traders will make the deal and leave the guns that will do them no good. Rain Cloud, I will depend on you to allow at least one person on horseback to escape," Marco told them. "This person will surely race to alert Great Owl that his women and children are in peril."

"It will be his turn to suffer!" one of the warriors shouted. The others shouted, too, and David Benedict whimpered.

"When the message has been delivered, Great Owl and his warriors will ride toward their camp, which you and your braves will already control. We will fire on Great Owl from the cliffs' heights, because we will have kept some of the good guns for ourselves. We will kill as many as we can, but you must be ready to fight the ones who slip through."

To Marco's chagrin, Rain Cloud stood and gestured to his warriors. They followed him from the circle without a word. Joaquim made a sound of disgust. Marco shook a finger at him, demanding silence.

"They are thinking about it."

"You know these people, don't you?" Joaquim asked.

"I do." He leaned toward the royal engineer. "If you expect to remain alive in this colony, you had better come to know them, too." He looked at the Utes, standing close together, talking and gesturing. "And do you know something else? I like the Kapota Utes."

But had he convinced these beaten people that they could yet avenge a terrible wrong? Marco closed his eyes, tired down to his toes, wanting nothing more than to crawl into his own bed and hold Paloma close. *I have become so simple*, he thought.

He opened his eyes as Rain Cloud and his warriors returned to the circle. "We will do this thing," the chief said. He sighed and looked to the western mountains. "When we are done, we will move to the more distant cloud mountains where the sun sets." He shook his head. "I fear our friend the bear has already begun that journey."

"Not yet," Marco said. "He's licking his wounds. He will roar again. He will roar tomorrow."

Chapter Thirty-Two

In which the bear roars

"WE HAVE NO TIME to spare," Marco said. Soon even the few surviving women and children were helping lift the heavy boxes from the wagon to the ground. Joaquim pried off the lids and stood a moment, staring down at the beautiful muskets; then he barked out orders, very much the royal engineer again.

He sent Claudio for small twigs. "Straight and narrow," Joaquim ordered.

Claudio looked for Graciela to help him. He swallowed a lump in his throat to watch the slave dip a partially burned cloth into a buffalo bladder filled with warm water. She pulled away the burned part, wrung it out, and knelt by David Benedict, who still lay on the ground, trying to make himself smaller.

Benedict closed his eyes in evident relief as she wiped his grimy face, her touch so gentle. Gradually Benedict straightened out and allowed her to clean his chest and his private parts. He started to weep again, this time in humiliation, while she cleaned his filth as kindly as if he were a small child Claudito's age.

Claudio came closer in time to hear her say, "Just do as you are told and you will live. I am a slave, and that is what I do."

"I don't speak his language," Graciela said to Claudio, embarrassed. "He knows a little Spanish, but very little, I think."

"He feels your kindness," Claudio assured her. "You're the one nice thing that has happened to him in an awful day."

"Sometimes how we speak is more important than what we say," she replied. She folded her hands in her lap, and didn't even look at him. "What I do is this, Claudio: what I wish someone had done to me." She looked up, and he saw her kindness directed at him, as if everyone else in the battered clearing had suddenly disappeared. "If you do that, too, you'll be happier."

He tried to think of some scathing rejoinder, some careless answer, but none came to mind. Graciela Tafoya spoke the truth.

He saw the moment as a choice. He could ignore her or he could respond. Something told him—maybe there was a God—that his response would rule his life from this moment on, no matter how long or short it was. No one living on the edge of Comanchería had any guarantee.

Not caring who was watching, he knelt beside Graciela Tafoya. As David Benedict watched from worried eyes, Claudio leaned forward and touched his forehead to Graci's. That was all he had the courage to do. He sat back on his haunches and watched her face as she pinked up, then gave him a smile so blinding that the sun should have just given up and gone away, a poor loser.

"Be careful in the work of this day and tomorrow," she said, and he heard herald angels clearing their throats and giving each other a note before breaking out in hallelujahs.

Together they led David Benedict to a grassy spot. Graciela put his ruined trousers beside him. She pointed to the stream and made rubbing motions. Benedict just stared at her stupidly.

"I fear he will not last long in New Mexico," she said, with a shake of her head. "I do not trust him, but someone in St. Louis might miss him."

"It's that easy?" he asked. "I just do good things?"

He had no business wrapping his mind around such a subject, not with Joaquim on his knees by the muskets, and Marco and one of the Utes coming back to the clearing with clothes that the Frenchmen had worn, and Rain Cloud and his men whistling for what horses remained. He stared in further amazement as Lorenzo and Rogelio cut out five of their stolen horses and led them toward the Indians—Lorenzo, who never gave anything to anyone without exacting some sort of payment. He took her by the hand.

"You do good things," she repeated. She nudged his shoulder and held out a handful of twigs. She covered his hand with hers, twigs and all. "Claudio, every morning, even when things were so awful, I hoped that maybe this day, it would be different. And now it is."

She startled him further by kissing his cheek. "Don't think so hard. Take these to Joaquim."

BY EARLY AFTERNOON, JOAQUIM had driven slender twigs into the touch holes of four crates of muskets, keeping back two each for the men who would be watching above the rendezvous site. Graciela had carefully daubed a bit of soot in each hole to hide any hint of bare wood. Joaquim had pawed through the crates, snatching up all the vent picks so no one could remove the twig, if they happened to notice.

Marco did everything the engineer demanded, marveling to himself how someone previously dedicated to wine and women could take command when the situation warranted. If they survived this admittedly foolhardy attempt, maybe he would see if he really had enough influence with Governor de Anza to request that Private Joaquim Gasca be returned to his rightful rank. Crazier things had happened.

A superstitious man, Lorenzo Diaz had been reluctant to don the clothes worn by one of the dead Frenchmen. He changed his mind after Toshua grabbed him by his chin and stared long and hard into his eyes. "I took his clothes off him before I killed him," Toshua snapped. "Don't be a baby."

In a short time, Lorenzo was peacocking about, reminding Marco of Paloma in a new dress, one with shape and style and no drawstrings to allow for a growing belly. He still owed her a pair of red dancing shoes. If he survived tomorrow, he would get her those shoes. *Funny what a man thinks about, when death is a distinct possibility.*

Marco watched in pleasant surprise as Joaquim continued his relentless efforts to prepare them all. Lorenzo was less than pleased to find Joaquim digging through the little cart that Rogelio drove, which carried their few possessions. He turned nearly apoplectic when Joaquim pounced on three bottles of rum in deep green glass. As Marco held Lorenzo back, Joaquim popped the corks, took a sip and then poured out the rest.

"Why?" he demanded. "Why?"

"Because I can make excellent *bombas* out of these with the loose powder." Joaquim dug deeper as Marco started to laugh. He yanked out a shirt and made the mistake of sniffing it. "Or we could just throw this at Great Owl."

On Joaquim's directions, Marco wrapped the three bottles in the reeking shirt and stuffed them into his saddlebags. The altered muskets went back in their crates, with eight working firearms set aside. For lack of any other container, Marco emptied out his extra clothes from his parfleche and carefully poured most of the black power into the leather case. Graciela stuffed several large rocks into the powder keg, smoothing over the black powder until the level rose closer to the top again.

Soon there was nothing left to do except go. Stuffed full of good advice, Lorenzo and Rogelio left first, accompanied by a Ute warrior to guide them. "Yes, yes," the horse trader assured Marco. "We will hug Montaña Blanca like a one-centavo whore and this Kapota will lead us through that saddle in the mountains, so we can come at the Two Brothers from the north."

"Don't take any chances," Marco said.

"Everything we are doing is a chance, señor," Lorenzo reminded him. "If I don't return, tell Sancha … tell Sancha …."

"What?" Marco asked.

"That I went to my death thinking of her and smelling sweet."

"I will do that," Marco said, as he admired his own control. *You smelled sweet two weeks ago, you old rascal*, he thought. *One bath needs to be followed by another.* "I will," he repeated, grateful for the courage of the men he rode with, even if they did smell ripe.

Afternoon shadows settled in the San Luis Valley as the wagon and riders disappeared into the distance. Soon sheltering night would come. Rain Cloud and his warriors left next, accompanied by Claudio and Graciela. Marco feared for her, but there wasn't a safe place with any of the parties. Rain Cloud and his warriors would ride through the night through mountain passes Marco didn't even want to think about, because heights were not his best friend. Revenge and sorrow fueled them and he did not doubt they would succeed.

"She has her reasons for riding with Rain Cloud," Claudio told him, and they sat close together on their horses. "Did you know … she had a baby with the Comanches, a girl about one year old now."

"She wants her child," Marco said. Only a few years ago, he would have heard that news with real distaste. Now he just hoped she found the little one. He put his hand over Claudio's hand on his pommel. "Help her all you can."

That wasn't enough. Marco rode to Graciela. "Know this: Lorenzo is going to deal in muskets with Great Owl, a truly evil man. If he succeeds, he will get my money back that I paid for you. When he does, you will not be my slave anymore. You may do as you please. Granted, Paloma will still need your help, but I can find someone else to take your place, if you have other plans."

"I have never made a plan in my life, señor," she told him.

"Then it is high time you started."

It warmed his heart that she turned to look at Claudio, who was talking to Toshua, unaware of her glance. "Go with God," he told her.

"Wait!"

Marco turned around to see David Benedict on his feet, holding both his hands high.

Joaquim guided his horse closer to the man, who still trembled and gave Toshua a wide berth. They spoke, and Joaquim turned to Marco. "He doesn't want to be left behind."

"I had forgotten him," Marco admitted. "What should we do?"

"You're the leader," Joaquim said, with faint surprise.

"I think you have become our leader," Marco said, inwardly pleased with how Joaquim's face lighted up, even as he shook his head in denial. "Well, then, we are co-leaders," he said. Leaning closer, he added, "But I believe Toshua rules us all."

They laughed together. "I say we take him," Joaquim said. "We have another horse. Perhaps he will be useful."

"If he doesn't betray us." Marco contemplated the frightened man. "Let him know that if he does anything to put us in harm's way, I will turn him over to Toshua."

"That should do the trick," Joaquim said. "My own bowels get loose just thinking about it."

David Benedict had joined his hands together in bare pleading. "Very well," Marco said. "Let him know that if something happens, he will be two or three days dying."

Joaquim translated. Benedict nodded. Marco had never seen eyes so desperate. "We all want to live," Marco said. "Tell him that, please."

They galloped into the dusk, Toshua in the lead, ranging ahead. Marco and Joaquim rode side by side, with David Benedict next and the Ute warriors bringing up the rear.

"This could be a disaster of monumental proportions," Marco commented to Joaquim.

The royal engineer shrugged. "I hope not. I'd like to build those bastions for you at the Double Cross, and—you won't believe this—I've even been thinking of ways to make the Santa Maria garrison a spit and polish outfit."

Marco threw back his head and laughed, loud enough for Toshua to turn around and make an obscene gesture. "I'd better be quiet," Marco said, dabbing at his eyes.

"It can be done," Joaquim said, sounding more than a little defensive. Marco had to bite the inside of his mouth to resist commenting on his partner's transformation from regimental disgrace to San Miguel the Archangel himself, complete with sword and halo.

"Marco, what do you want to live to do?"

"Sit beside Paloma when she gives birth to the next Mondragón," he said, with no hesitation. "And see our three children grow old."

"Then let's get to it," Joaquim said. "We have a colony to protect."

Chapter Thirty-Three

In which plans must change

Thank God for the *Ute warriors*. When Marco shook his head at the narrow path so high above the Rio Conejos, the one called Deer Bones dismounted, took hold of Buciro's bridle, and led the way. He kindly told Marco to close his eyes. "There is no shame in this fear," Deer Bones told him. "You are not a Cloud Ute."

"I am a terrified *ranchero* from Valle del Sol far away and below," Marco told him with a shaky laugh. Deer Bones just patted his leg.

Marco closed his eyes as directed and found himself leaning toward the rock wall. Embarrassed, he managed another laugh as Buciro plodded steadily on, led by the Ute on foot. "Go ahead, call me a coward! I am earning it."

"I would never call you a coward, not the man who shrouded my mother for burial when my father Rain Cloud could not bring himself to do it," came the quiet reply. "We will always be in your debt."

"She was good to me at a hard time in my life," Marco replied. "I did not know she was your mother."

"Then do not call yourself names that are not true. We're nearly through the worst part."

In Marco's opinion, they were through only the first of many worst parts, as the little army threaded its way into the Sangre de Cristo Mountains. He had spent his lifetime nearly in the shadow of their comforting bulk, and he traveled the well-known passes as a matter of course. This was different; these were trails only Indians or desperate men would use.

Think of something pleasant, Marco told himself, and he did, remembering the birth of their first child, his and Paloma's. In the hardest moments, Paloma had fixed her blue eyes on his light brown ones, bearing down in agonizing silence until he told her, for the Lord's sake, to cry out if it might help.

"Only if Soledad is far from the house," she had gasped, a mother already to another woman's child, and tenacious in her love for her small cousin.

When Buciro stumbled and then righted himself, Marco closed his eyes even tighter, thinking only of Paloma. How she cuddled close to him on cold winter mornings, flung her arms wide in the summer, usually taking more than her share of their bed. Paloma nursing Claudio, and leaning back in relief when her milk drew down. Paloma teaching Soledad how to walk like a lady. Paloma with her hair spread on their pillow, her head thrown back in ecstasy. Always Paloma. If he had to die on this mountain pass, or fighting a renegade intent upon scuttling Kwihnai's tentative peace overtures, Marco wanted Paloma's name on his lips. Others could petition saints or El Padre Himself; Paloma was his life and light.

"Open your eyes, señor. We are through the pass."

Marco opened his eyes to see the kind smile of Deer Bones, shy almost, much like his father, who was even now making his own precarious way toward Great Owl's village. Or perhaps Rain Cloud had been surprised and *his* little army lay dead. If only there were some way to know these things.

Marco looked around, grateful to be alive. He lifted his eyes toward the plains, where the sun was rising. To some, it was only Thursday, with nothing out of the ordinary in store. Here, in this isolated colony, it was a day when a victory might make his homeland a safer place. He chose not to consider defeat.

He doubted King Carlos would ever hear of the day's events. He would never know about a *juez de campo* charged with making peace in a dangerous place. Suddenly, as though a cosmic fist had slapped his head, Marco understood clearly that his allegiance was not really to some distant king. It was to his colony alone. He was a New Mexican, not a Spaniard. He felt a swell of pride, followed by humble gratitude. What had just happened? He watched the sun rise over his country, his home, his mountains and streams, his loved ones, New Mexicans all.

"Señor, if I must say, you look like a man suffering from either advanced epiphany or unspeakable indigestion," Joaquim joked, guiding his horse alongside Marco's, as Deer Bones raised his hand in greeting and edged away.

"Nothing so profound as indigestion," Marco teased back, too abashed to tell anyone except Paloma about his advanced epiphany. He gestured to Deer Bones. "This excellent man got me through the mountains. I was as poor a leader as you can imagine. I'm surprised I did not foul myself. Now, Joaquim, it is your turn to lead us. Tell us where to place ourselves, and what to do."

Joaquim nodded and sat a little taller, even though Marco knew he had to be as tired as all the rest. The royal engineer gestured the others into a tight circle, where they dismounted, stretched, turned around to relieve themselves, then looked at him, ready for orders.

He spoke to a small man, unusually short for a Ute. "Tall Grass, here we are between the Two Brothers, the rendezvous. We have trees to shelter us, but we are still so high. What should we do?"

Marco smiled to himself. Whether he knew it or not, Joaquim was conducting a council of his officers, asking advice and actually listening. He had the makings of a fine leader, provided he could keep his breeches up.

"Tether our horses here among the trees, and move down the mountain," Tall Grass said. The Ute pointed to clumps of faraway sumac bushes. "We can hunker down behind those and wait."

Joaquim looked at Marco and raised his eyebrows in a question.

Those bushes might shelter someone the size of Soledad, Marco thought, appalled. "It's not enough shelter."

"It is for me and the Utes," Toshua said. "Marco, you eat too much."

"Guilty as charged," Marco said. "I'm also taller than any of you, except David Benedict." He looked at Joaquim, a question in his eyes.

A little smile played around Joaquim's lips and his eyes were bright, almost as if he were enjoying their predicament. Marco couldn't help but think that such an expression was a natural fit for a man who raised hell in Cuba and Mexico City before being broken down from *teniente* to *soldado*, the lowest of the low. Damn the man; he was probably enjoying this.

"We'll manage," Joaquim said, licking his lips in anticipation, if the gleam in his eyes meant anything. "Toshua, you and the Utes will get as close as you can to the valley floor behind those sumac bushes. Marco, you and I and David Benedict will prepare another little surprise. Marco, get out those bottles. I pray God that parfleche of black powder didn't bounce off your horse."

As Joaquim's plan began to unfold, Marco had no doubt that El Teniente Gasca could manage the presidio at Santa Maria, given the opportunity. Luckily, Lorenzo's rum bottles had survived their jostle in his saddlebags, probably because he had wrapped them tightly in the horse trader's foul shirt. Some of the black powder had spilled out, but Joaquim just shrugged.

The scheme faltered immediately. Joaquim swore in disgust. "I need a funnel," he said. "In God's name, just a funnel!"

Marco felt in the inside pocket of his doublet. He fished out the letter Paloma had written to him and given to Lorenzo. He twisted it into a funnel and Joaquim slapped his forehead.

"A scoop, a scoop," he said next. "Make that appear now, will you?"

Marco chuckled and reached into the same pocket, this time pulling out the little note Paloma had tucked among his clean socks. He handed it to Joaquim, who read it and rolled his eyes. Marco felt his face grow hot.

"I had a wife once, Marco, if you can believe that," Joaquim said. "After a year or two, she never wrote *me* any love notes. What power do *you* have?"

"This is not the time," Marco mumbled, still the reticent *Hispano*.

Joaquim directed Marco to put the paper funnel in the bottle opening. He creased the other paper and carefully scooped black powder into the funnel.

"How much powder?" Marco asked.

"Enough to make a very loud bang. One more scoop. That is good. Fill the other two bottles. Set them upright. We need wicks now."

"Part of Lorenzo's shirt?" Marco asked.

"Takes too long to burn."

As Joaquim stared at the rum bottles, his chin in his hands, David Benedict picked up the paper funnel. He tore it in half, rolled it lengthwise, and stuck it in the first bottle. With a grunt of interest, Toshua unwrapped a length of sinew from his lance. He handed it to Benedict, who backed away from him in terror at first, then took it, careful not to touch Toshua's hand. He fastened the paper wick inside the mouth of the bottle. He repeated the operation, using Paloma's smaller note on the last bottle, then sat back and folded his arms, satisfied.

"*Muy bien*, David," Marco said.

Pleased, Benedict spoke to Joaquim. " 'I can throw a long distance,' he says," Joaquim repeated.

"We need fire. Here is my flint and steel," Marco said, pulling out a small pouch.

Joaquim took out his own, and David Benedict shrugged. He jumped and cried out when Toshua tapped his arm and handed him a flint and steel.

"I think he will never like The People very much," Toshua remarked.

"Toshua, no man likes to have his privates toyed with," Marco said.

Toshua astounded him by bursting into laughter. "Tell that to Paloma!"

If his face was red before, it was on fire now. David spoke to Joaquim, probably demanding to know what was so funny. He laughed, too. The Utes spoke Spanish, and they gave up any pretense of solemnity. Deer Bones even flopped back on the grass, wheezing as he laughed. Joaquim had a snort-laugh that sent them all into more helpless paroxysms of mirth.

"Maybe we needed that," Marco said, when the laughter died down to a weak chuckle, and finally just a snort here and there.

Then it was all business. They shared their *carne seca* and bits of cactus. Marco gave the rest of his dried meat to Deer Bones, pleading a full stomach, and the Ute did not argue. Out of the corner of his eye—no sense in humiliating the man—Marco watched him share with the other warriors and wolf down the rest of the meat. *It's going to be a hard winter, my friends*, Marco thought, remembering the ruin of the Ute village, and their winter preparations destroyed or stolen. *Better you do go west with Bear.*

The sun was nowhere near high overhead, but they all knew better than to wait around. Joaquim gathered them again. "Go with Toshua to the sumac bushes," he directed the Utes. "Just wait. Lorenzo will come and make the deal for firearms. If they demand a demonstration, he has two good muskets."

Two working muskets, Marco thought, aghast at their flimsy plan. *It seems we had one good brain among the eight of us, to think up that scheme.*

But the time to second guess had come and gone. He listened with the others.

"I told Lorenzo to stay where he is when the deal is over," Joaquim continued. "Above all, not to move forward. At any time, if—pray God *if*— Rain Cloud has attacked their secret stronghold, we should see someone riding toward Great Owl for help. That's when we attack them."

"Suppose that villain Great Owl decides to kill our horse traders?" Toshua asked. "I could not watch that without attacking Great Owl right away rather than later."

The Utes nodded. Everyone looked at Joaquin.

"Then we will throw our *bombas* and fight." He turned to Marco. "Use your flint and steel to light your *bomba* at the last moment. Throw it immediately, or you will become a distant memory to Paloma. If there is time and we are still alive, fire your muskets. Ah, good, Marco, you have your bow and arrow, too."

Juaquin translated his instructions for David Benedict, who appeared as intent and serious as the others. Toshua shook his head. "I have heard sillier plans, but I do not recall when that might have been."

"We are working with what we have," Joaquim said with a smile.

David Benedict raised his hand. He spoke slowly and in earnest to Joaquim, who pursed his lips and then nodded. Turning to Marco, Joaquim said, "Is there any powder left in your parfleche?"

Marco lifted the flap, now powdery with black residue. "Several good-sized handfuls. Why?"

"David wants to sow it in the field like grain, just beyond the farther of the Two Brothers. A well-placed shot will set it on fire. Think of the added confusion."

Marco handed the parfleche to David. With a nod, the man started down the hill. They watched him walk with a purposeful stride toward the plain.

Toshua motioned to the Utes to start down the hill toward the sumac bushes. He looked back at Marco, then walked toward him. Marco watched him, remembering the desperately thin man tethered in the henhouse of a madman, so close to death but saved by Paloma. He thought of the Comanche brave stepping in front of him when they reached the wintering quarters of The People in the sacred canyon, protecting him and Paloma from sure death. His heart full, Marco thought of Toshua sitting cross-legged on the buffalo robe in his old office by the horse barn, singing to little Claudio and Soledad. All of a sudden he wanted to grasp every fleeting moment and hold it close for just another second or two.

"I don't want to die today," Marco said frankly.

"I don't, either. We are close to some sort of peace between your people and mine. I feel it. I'd like to see it, same as you." Toshua put a gentle hand on Marco's shoulder. "But we will die bravely, if we must."

Toshua was not a tall man. Marco bent down and kissed his forehead, then each cheek. "Go with God, my friend. May you always have a horse to ride."

He had never seen tears in Toshua's eyes before. As Marco watched in silence, his heart too full to speak, Toshua wiped the tears spilling from his eyes and touched their wetness to Marco's forehead like a benediction.

"And may Paloma and your children be forever with you."

Marco swallowed. He clapped Toshua's shoulders and gave him a little push down the hill. Toshua gave him a backhanded wave and joined the Utes.

"Look there!" Joaquim said, pointing to the first of the Two Brothers on their left.

Marco took a deep breath. Lorenzo and Rogelio bounced along in the wagon carrying the faulty firearms, right on schedule. Marco looked down at the sumac bushes. Nothing. The Indians had vanished.

By now, David Benedict was back beside them, breathing heavily, the empty parfleche in his hand. In silence, they each loaded their two muskets, and made sure the flints were securely in place. Marco rested the muskets on his shoulder and picked up the *bomba*. Joaquim pointed down the hill to the last sheltering trees.

Without a word, Marco moved into place. He sank down, making himself as small as he could, and watched Joaquim, that worthless soldier, and David, an agent for a foreign power, settle themselves at equal distance from each other.

A million doubts ran through his tired brain, tugging on his mind like little impatient children dancing about, demanding and whining. What if this doesn't work? What if Rain Cloud is already dead? What will I tell Paloma if Claudio is dead? Who will tell my darling if *I* am dead? What if Great Owl chose a different rendezvous?

He leaned against a tree and looked across the valley. Lorenzo and Rogelio had stopped the wagon. He watched them get down and stretch, then look around. Marco knew they would never see the Indians by the sumac bushes.

He prayed they would know everyone was in place, then he turned the matter over to God and San Miguel. He had done all he could. The faulty and foolish plan was ready. He settled down to wait, keeping his eyes on the low hills to the south, knowing that sooner or later, Great Owl and his warriors would come out of a pass—which one Marco did not know—and the dance of death would begin.

The sun reached its height and began a slow descent, with no sign of Great Owl. Marco felt his heart plummet into his boots. He leaned forward to see Lorenzo and Rogelio lounging in what shade the wagon provided. Toshua and the Utes were still invisible. For a small moment he felt alone and afraid. The terror passed; perhaps Paloma had just said his name out loud.

The smile died on his lips. He took a deep breath and watched Comanches, so many Comanches, file out of a pass. Even from the distance, he saw Great Owl's headdress. "Good God," he whispered, and started counting. He stopped at twenty, but there were twice that number. His face went cold and then hot and he felt a great pain beyond anything he had ever known.

"Paloma, if our baby is a son, name him after me, and tell him I was a good man," he whispered to the ground that he knew would soon claim him. "If a daughter, name her Maria Rosa, because I like it. And you? Oh, Paloma. No red shoes. Forgive me."

He took another deep breath and the panic passed. He looked at the sky, then at the aspens farther up the slope. He would like to have heard water flowing one final time. A hawk wheeled high above and he thanked God for one last pretty sight.

"Thy will be done, Father," he prayed.

Chapter Thirty-Four

In which there is singing

FEELING LIKE A MAN standing outside his own body, Marco watched the long line of Comanches cross the plain toward the wagon and the horse traders. He saw Lorenzo tip the beret of the dead Frenchman at a rakish angle. Marco wished Sancha could see what a brave man looked like.

Great Owl and his men made a slow progress from the pass to the rendezvous. Marco said one final prayer, thanking God for his life, and asking for a miracle similar to loaves and fishes, where the few multiplied into many. He made himself small in the grove and rested his first musket against his raised knees.

He watched the trade, the little figure of Lorenzo opening one of the musket cases and taking out one firearm after the other. Great Owl made a gesture, and Lorenzo prepared the musket to fire. The bang echoed between the Two Brothers.

Marco sucked in his breath when Great Owl made the gesture again. *Please, please, no more demonstrations*, he prayed, knowing the only useable flintlock left was Lorenzo's own personal weapon that he kept behind the wagon seat. He closed his eyes when Great Owl made the gesture a third time.

A third time, the sound reverberated across the plain, but Lorenzo must have aimed in a different direction. Marco opened his eyes and sucked in his breath. Lorenzo had to have fired his own personal weapon, and was now defenseless. He had also aimed right at the field David had sowed with black powder. Flames roared into the air between the Comanches and the route to the pass.

Holding his breath now, Marco watched as Great Owl flung something at Lorenzo. He sighed with relief when Lorenzo caught Marco's own money pouch, tossed more than a month ago across the plaza in Taos to save Graciela's life. He leaned forward to see Great Owl gesture again, this time to his warriors, who swarmed the wagon, grabbing weapons from the open box and pulling out the other crates, as the grass fire spread closer. "Get your guns and move away," Marco whispered.

The grass of late summer was paper-dry, but there was not much of it. The flames that had sprung up in a terrifying whoosh burned out quickly. It seemed like ages, but surely not more than a matter of minutes before the crates were empty, and the deceptively full powder keg and metal box filled with lead bars to melt into bullets were also in Great Owl's possession.

Everything fell apart.

As Marco watched in horror, one of the milling warriors yanked poor Rogelio off the wagon seat and skewered him with a lance. Lorenzo dived under the wagon seat as the horses reared and bolted, running in a tight circle until the wagon tipped over.

Two warriors fell from their saddles as Toshua and the Utes began their silent work with bow and arrow. Whatever surprise gained ended quickly as other braves started up the slope toward the sumac bushes.

Just as quickly, David stood up and threw his *bomba*, which exploded right over the largest group of Great Owl's warriors. Marco couldn't help his smile at the screams of terror from Comanches, those fearsome Indians who usually made others scream. He struck flint to steel and lit his own *bomba*, felt a flash as his eyebrows singed off, and lobbed the missile directly at Great Owl.

Wincing from the pain, he watched as the rum bottle turned end over end, then exploded high in the air. More braves screamed as the glass shards cut deep into their flesh. Crazed, three horses ran back toward the pass, stopping to buck and whirl until not even their profoundly skilled riders remained on their backs.

Calm now, Marco steadied his rifle and willed the black smoke to blow away from the scorched land. He took careful aim and fired. He was no musketeer, but he watched in grim satisfaction to see a man suddenly grab the space where his arm used to be.

There were still too many warriors and now they turned their attention on their clump of trees, throwing themselves from their horses and crawling up the slope. Marco fired his last musket just as Joaquim lit the final *bomba*.

Instead of throwing it, Joaquim rolled *la bomba* down the hill, where it exploded with a roar just in front of the Comanches on the slope. Marco pulled all his arrows from their quiver and set them in front of him. He let loose one after another, silently thanking his long-dead father, who had insisted Marco practice and practice until he was in tears and his arms ached.

Still they came. He shot his final arrow and took out his knife. "Paloma, I have loved you," he whispered, ready for the final stroke before everything ended. He prayed only that he would not mind the pain when whatever warrior grabbed him, circled his scalp with a knife, and yanked off his hair before he died.

He crouched behind the tree and waited for death. The shouts and yips of the Comanches filled his brain and he waited in the black smoke.

And waited. Even though his ears rang, he knew his overheated imagination told him the sound was retreating. He shook his head to clear it, and listened.

He heard other shouts and yips, but from a direction that puzzled him. He stood up and swatted at the smoke like an idiot, desperate for a clear view of the plain.

God granted his wish. God blew and the smoke whooshed past him. He took a deep breath and coughed until one more cough would have expelled his lungs. He dropped to his knees at the sight before him.

More Comanches filled the plain, but they were riding in hard from the east, riding into Great Owl's warriors and striking them with an audible smack. He looked to his left to see both David and Joaquim on their feet, staring, too. Farther down the slope, Toshua rose. He looked up at Marco and made a wide and elaborate sign for horses, his hand vertical followed by his other hand forking the vertical hand.

"*Claro, claro*," Marco shouted in understanding, and gestured to Joaquim and David to follow him up the hill. They pounded up the slope to the larger tree line, where they had tethered their mounts. He swung onto Buciro and gathered as many reins as he could handle, leaving the rest to Joaquim and David. Starting down the slope, he leaned far back to stay in his saddle and realized that old Kwihnai and his Kwahadi warriors had ridden to their rescue.

Marco watched in silence as the Kwahadi Comanche methodically decimated Great Owl's renegade Comanches. He felt strangely at war within his heart to see the Comanches fight each other. Part of him rejoiced, the part that had seen the suffering of settlers, including Paloma and Claudio. Another part, hopefully the part he listened to the most, made him yearn for peace to come from this battle. True, the Spanish were interlopers upon the land that The People had ruled for years, but even the Comanches had come from far to the north and driven out other tribes living on these plains. What belonged to whom?

Surely there comes a time when peace begins to make more sense than continual warfare. *Is this the time?* he asked himself. *Let it be the time, dear God in heaven.*

Tall Grass lay dead behind a tiny sumac bush that wouldn't have hidden a chicken, stretched out and staring at the sky with eyes that saw nothing. Marco noted with fierce satisfaction that he still wore his hair. Deer Bones was even now reaching for his own horse, as were his remaining companions.

Holding his breath, Marco stared hard for Toshua to materialize, to rise up and raise one eyebrow and then the other in a way that Paloma called creepy. He would have given the earth to see his friend. He looked around, determined that no enemy would take Toshua's scalp.

He turned fast, knife in hand, when someone tugged his sleeve. Deer Bones put up his hand.

"You know better than to think Toshua is among the dead," the Ute chided him. "I'm surprised at you. Look."

Marco looked where Deer Bones gestured. Relief covered him like warm rain to see Toshua striding toward the overturned wagon, carrying his lance. Marco kneed Buciro into motion again, Toshua's horse following behind.

There was no help for Rogelio, whose scalp was gone, and both ears. Marco winked back tears as he dismounted and helped Toshua and two of Kwihnai's men right the wagon.

There lay Lorenzo, curled up into a tiny ball, no mean feat for a man as tall as he was, and a hero besides.

"You better touch him," Toshua said. "I am a Comanche. I know you think we all look alike."

"I don't now," Marco said. "Good God, who convinced Kwihnai to help us?"

Toshua shrugged.

"Lorenzo? Lorenzo?" Marco said. He gave the horse trader a little shake. "It's Marco."

"Not opening my eyes," Lorenzo said. "You could be a Comanche trying to fool me."

"I suppose I could be," Marco said with a laugh, he who had never planned to survive this day, let alone laugh again. "Do you want me to tell Sancha that you weren't so brave?"

That was all Lorenzo needed. With a groan, he straightened, then sat up when Marco held out his hand. In a gesture he didn't expect, Lorenzo put Marco's hand to his cheek, then kissed it. "I couldn't save Rogelio. Everything went so fast. Did … did you see what happened?"

"I saw him die with a lance through his chest, but I was some distance away," Marco said. He patted Lorenzo's cheek and Lorenzo released his hand.

"He threw himself across me. That lance was for me," Lorenzo said simply. "He is your hero." He looked up at Marco. "Would to God I had treated him better throughout his life."

"I doubt he would have wanted you to change anything," Marco told him. "He had a home, and food, and work to do. Remember that instead."

Lorenzo nodded, then bowed his head against his upraised knees. Marco turned away to allow him to grieve, then turned back again and took Lorenzo's arm. "I have to know something. Forgive me, but tell me, how did you know to fire the grass with your last shot?"

Lorenzo looked from Marco to Toshua, puzzled. "Toshua told me."

"How in God's name?" Marco asked. "He was hiding in the sumac bushes."

Lorenzo patted Marco's head as if the *juez* were a little boy. "Surely you saw him crawl from the sumac bush, tell me, then crawl back."

"No, I didn't see a thing," Marco said. "Not a thing."

Toshua patted his head next. "You're not a very observant man. I just counted coup on you."

He walked with Toshua to Kwihnai, who sat on his horse with its beaded leather mask, looking more sinister than all the hounds of hell. Marco fell to his knees, bowed his head to the earth, and stretched out his arms in complete submission. "I will never forget this day."

"Good," Kwihnai said, practical as always. "Up you go now. We have a job to finish, you and I."

Marco stood up and walked beside Kwihnai's horse to a clump of Kwahadi warriors. He smiled to see the husband of Paloma's good friend Kahúu, whose sister's baby Paloma had carried on her back through the sacred canyon, and returned with tearful reluctance to the warrior who smiled at him now. He held up his hand.

"How is your small daughter?" Marco asked. "Paloma will want to know."

"She is healthy and makes us laugh," the warrior said. Marco realized then that he did not even know his name.

The circle of Kwihnai's warriors opened, and there lay Great Owl, naked and stretched out on the ground, pinned there by arrows through his palms and feet. Swallowing his revulsion, Marco stared hard at the renegade who stared hard back at him, his lips curled in defiance.

Kwihnai leaned down and handed Marco his lance. "He is yours to kill. We do not need his kind of trouble, if we plan to make peace some day."

Marco took the lance. *God forgive me*, he thought, as he plunged it deep into Great Owl's heart.

The air itself seemed to explode with the high-pitched wails of victory from Kwihnai's men. He listened to the throaty warble, a sound he never thought to hear so close and remain alive. He wanted to warble, too, but he didn't know how. Maybe Toshua could teach him.

He listened to the high sound, then looked up in surprise, certain he heard a woman's voice, pitched even higher.

There she was on horseback—Eckapeta. Toshua stood beside her, his hand on her leg. Marco stepped over Great Owl and stroked the nose of her horse.

"You did this."

"Paloma told me to ride like the eagle flies to Kwihnai, and convince him to help you. I argued back that I would not leave her and the babies, but she won." Eckapeta shook her head. "I must be losing my powers."

Marco pressed his face against her horse. "I lose a lot of arguments to her, my dear friend, and thank God for that."

They all looked around at another shout, this one of warning, and then purpose, as two of Kwihnai's warriors wheeled their horses and started at a dead run toward the south end of the Two Brothers.

A single figure on horseback had left the cleft in the mountains and rode toward them. Marco shaded his eyes with his hand, watching as the lone figure seemed to hesitate, then turn back to the cleft too late. With a shout, both warriors shot their arrows. Neither missed.

"That is the cleft you must follow," Toshua said.

Marco mounted his horse and looked for the remainder of his little army—Joaquim, David Benedict, Deer Bones, and the two surviving Utes. And there was Lorenzo, mounting the pony that must have belonged to Tall Grass.

Marco turned to Toshua. "Not you, my friend?"

"No. This is the time for the Utes. We will leave them alone, too. Eckapeta?"

With a wave of his hand, Toshua started toward Kwihnai. Eckapeta appeared to be arguing with Toshua, to Marco's amusement. He had an idea what the heated discussion was about, so he waited.

Eckapeta turned her horse. "You will see us in the spring, when Paloma gives birth, if not sooner!" she told Marco, after a hard glare at her husband. "I will bring a new cradleboard."

"Then go with God, my dears," Marco said, and made the sign of the cross over Toshua and Eckapeta, and every warrior who had saved his life.

Kwihnai kneed his horse forward. With strength Marco would not have credited to a man past his prime, the Comanche pulled the lance from Great Owl's body and handed the bloody thing to Marco. "Take this and do more good. Give it to that bearded man in your big city who fights so well. Tell him we will think about peace. We will come to Taos next year to trade and discuss the matter."

"I will tell Governor de Anza," Marco said. "Kwihnai, thank you for my life."

"Don't waste it."

Chapter Thirty-Five

In which Claudio makes his own peace

A HARD LIFE IN the mountains and on the plains of New Mexico had not prepared Claudio for the sight of Ute warriors, weary beyond belief but with vengeance burning inside, as they fell upon a sleeping village of Comanche women and children.

He hung back in shock as the men tore into each lodge and dragged out struggling women and silent little ones, trained from birth to make no noise under any circumstances. He held his breath for the slaughter to begin, but nothing happened. Confused, he looked for Graciela, who rode beside Rain Cloud now.

The two of them sat side by side as the Utes rousted out every occupant of brush shelter and tipi, from infant to elderly. His heart lightened as Ute warriors took their own wives and big-eyed children away from their captors. Some of the warriors were not so fortunate. They stood with heads bowed beside their horses.

Claudio understood then why there had been no sudden death. He watched as Graciela dismounted and stood in front of the Comanche women and children. He knew what would follow, after she found her half-Comanche daughter.

They had arrived at the camp just as the sun was rising, when many faces were still in shadow. Graciela scanned the gathering, hands pressed to her mouth. She walked with sure-footed grace to a woman in the back row, who had thrust a child behind her.

"Cecilia," Graciela said softly. "Come, my dear." She knelt and held out her arms as a naked child rubbed her eyes and yawned. "Cecilia, or Rabbit, whichever you will."

The captive woman made a half-hearted grab at the little one as she toddled forward, then threw herself into Graciela's arms. Fearful, the woman dropped her arms to her sides and bowed her head, but not before a Ute warrior with no family knocked her over with his horse. The other Comanches stirred restlessly, mothers holding their own children tight to their bodies.

Rain Cloud nodded his approval. "Claudio, take the Ute women and children down by the river. Sit there with them until all is quiet here."

"I am not a coward," Claudio said quietly.

"I know that," Rain Cloud replied. "You are a Spaniard and you will not want to witness what will happen here. Go now."

For one strange moment, he did not want the Utes to kill the Comanches, people he had hated too long. These were mostly women and children, and his heart rebelled, even as his head reminded him that he was one Christian among many Utes set upon revenge who wouldn't mind slaying him, too, if he interfered. *When did I change?* he wondered to himself, even as he moved to do as Rain Cloud demanded.

Claudio dismounted and gathered Graciela close. "Cecilia, is it?" he whispered.

"I only called her that at night, when the Comanches could not hear me," she whispered back. "I spoke to her in Spanish, but I doubt she remembers it. I have been several months gone, after all."

The Comanche women began their death song. Her child tight against her body, Graciela ran toward the river with the rest of the Ute women and children. They huddled there together, Claudio standing with them, alert and watching for trouble, as the work of death began. He noticed an old Comanche on horseback, riding to alert Great Owl and his warriors, just as Marco and Toshua had hoped would happen. Flinching at the sound of death, Claudio wondered at Great Owl's arrogance, so confident of his success with the weapons dealers that he left his camp unguarded.

Claudio sat with his back to the women at the river, unable to bear their hollow eyes. Probably no more than a week had passed since Great Owl's thugs had captured them and the few children allowed to live, but they had suffered greatly. As the Ute warriors worked their destruction, Claudio hoped everyone's wounds could heal, those both seen and unseen like his own.

The sun was past its zenith when silence finally ruled the Comanche camp. He waited for the crackle of fire and the odor of burning bodies to signal the end of the carnage. A few more minutes, and the Utes made their way to the river, first to wash the blood from their hands and bodies, then for the lucky few to reclaim their loved ones.

Feeling like an old man, Claudio slowly walked back to the camp and its great bonfire of shelters and bodies. He sucked in his breath and put his hand over Cecilia's eyes as the overpowering heat and flames worked their will among the dead.

It wasn't enough. He picked up the little one and turned her face into his shoulder. Graci walked beside him, her face averted, too.

He wanted nothing more than to leap on his horse, take Graci with him and ride fast away from all death and vengeance, and blasted hopes. On horseback last night when Graciela led the way, he had ridden for a time beside Rain Cloud. The sun had not quite left the sky, so Rain Cloud stopped every so often to look around, as if imprinting the cloud-high mountains on his mind.

"You're really going to leave these cloud mountains?" Claudio asked. "Even if we defeat Great Owl?"

"Even then," Rain Cloud said. "There comes a time when a man is too old for this much sadness." He said nothing more.

Maybe even a young man can reach that time, Claudio thought now, as he stared at the ruin around him.

Graciela was made of sterner stuff, apparently. Still clutching her child, she spoke to Rain Cloud. He nodded and patted her shoulder. A few words to one of his warriors, and Claudio held out his arms for a woven bag filled with dried meat and chokecherries, small and deep purple, that the Ute women had probably been gathering when the Comanches struck. A bag of dried bugs and roots completed Rain Cloud's parting gift.

"Do this for us," Rain Cloud ordered. "If you see only Comanches, ride fast and warn us so we can flee. If you see victory, stay with your own people. Graciela, too."

"Shouldn't Graci decide whether to stay with you?" Claudio asked, looking at the woman and her child sitting alone.

"With a Comanche child, she has no place among this people. Go now." Rain Cloud gave him a little push, not a cruel attempt to drive him off, but a firm reminder to hurry along.

They backtracked through the pass, Graciela holding her daughter on her lap, bound together with a wide strap. He rode beside them, glancing at the little girl, who finally began to smile at him, then giggle and turn away.

The trail was easier to follow in the daylight. He led the way, motioning Graciela to fall back as their hidden trail over the mountain joined the larger trail to the plains, the one Great Owl's warriors had taken. *I cannot just wait at the mouth of the pass*, he told himself. *My brother-in-law is down there. Paloma would never forgive me if I did nothing.*

"Stay here. I am going down."

"But Rain Cloud said …."

He ignored her, his mind clear of everything except his love for Marco Mondragón and Paloma Vega—the one still new to him, the other loved and lost, and found again. If Marco lay dead on the field, Claudio would fight his way back to the Double Cross and help his sister carry on. He had thought only a few days ago that family ties were a nuisance bent on suffocating a man. What a fool he had been.

His thinking had changed because he loved Graciela Tafoya. She was as bruised and battered by life as he was. She might not even want him in her bed for a while. He smiled to think of his mother's favorite *dicho*: "Patience, and shuffle the cards." Mama had said that often enough when he was young, impatient, and quarrelsome, picking fights with Rafael and Paloma until they ran off in tears. He hadn't understood that irksome *dicho* then, but he understood it now. Time was all he had, besides love. If love couldn't walk hand in hand with patience, what was it worth?

He looked back at Graciela standing there with her arms folded and anger in her eyes at being left behind. He blew her a kiss, something Paloma did each night before she closed the door of her children's room. He looked closer. The angry look was gone, but her arms were still folded. *Patience, Graci*, he thought.

He rode out of the pass and into sunlight already beginning to soften as afternoon shadows lengthened. Hardly breathing, Claudio stared at a mound of bodies on fire. The surrounding field was burned black. He rode through weeds stinking of smoke, counting the living.

That new patient heart began to beat again when he saw Marco, and then Joaquim, and even David Benedict, a man Claudio thought would never survive such a day. There was Lorenzo, leaning on a shovel. Claudio looked for Rogelio, his tired mind finally comprehending that Lorenzo and the shovel told their own tale.

He stopped his horse as two Comanches rode toward him, lances ready. He held up his hands. "Marco Mondragón," he shouted. "Help me here."

Deer Bones was closer. He signed to the Comanches. They lowered their lances and turned away, loping back to the main body. The Ute gestured for him to come closer.

"You've won a great battle," Claudio said, looking around. He watched some of the Comanches ride east, their lances dripping with bloody scalps. Looking closer, he thought he saw Toshua, and was that Eckapeta?

"My father? Does he live?" Deer Bones asked.

"Rain Cloud is well and so are the others. Some found their wives and children," Claudio told him. "Do you—"

Deer Bones shook his head. "All dead. My father will lead us west now, and we will begin again." He looked over his shoulder. "Tall Grass has gone singing bravely to his ancestors, but two of my friends and brothers remain. We will ride to Rain Cloud."

He leaned closer and touched Claudio's arm. "This was a good work. Your brother is a brave man."

"He is, Deer Bones. When you reach the mouth of the pass, you will see Graciela Tafoya. Tell her to ride down here." He chuckled. "She wasn't happy when I left her there, but I think she will come."

Deer Bones raised his hand in farewell. Claudio watched the three Utes until they were out of sight. Still he waited, hoping to see Graci. No Graci.

He came close to the battered wagon with empty crates still scattered around it. Joaquim and David tossed sabotaged muskets on the fire, which caught and crackled and soon became unrecognizeable.

Hands on his hips, Marco smiled at him. His face was blackened with gun smoke, which made his teeth a brilliant white. Claudio looked closer. His brother-in-law was missing a tooth, but that wasn't all; his eyebrows were gone, probably singed off in what must have been a desperate struggle to stay alive.

"All is well with Rain Cloud?" Marco asked, after Claudio dismounted and grabbed him in a fierce embrace.

"As well as any man can be, who has lost so much," Claudio said.

Marco clapped his hand on Claudio's shoulder. "Come home with me?" he asked.

"If you want me to," Claudio said. "I trust you will not put a noose around my neck."

"No noose. In fact, let me make a proposition." He looked beyond Claudio. "You found your little one, Graciela? Give thanks to God."

Claudio turned around to see Graciela riding toward them. *God is good*, he thought. Perhaps he should also apologize to God for thinking Him callous and uninterested in the ways of man. Paloma could advise him about such matters.

Graciela nodded, eyeing Marco with wariness. Claudio walked to her side and held out his arms for Cecilia, who surprised him by holding out her own arms. He held the child, wondering what Marco would say, but not wondering too hard. He was beginning to understand the *juez de campo*.

"She has beautiful eyes, Graciela," Marco said. "Please tell me that Soli and Claudito will have a little friend. Think of the fun!"

Graciela let out a sigh that went on and on. She dismounted with Marco's help, and threw herself into Claudio's arms. To his surprise, and then complete gratification, Claudio Vega discovered that he could hold a child and a woman at the same time.

THEY SPENT THE NIGHT camped as far to the south of the Two Brothers as they could travel before complete exhaustion ruled. Marco insisted that Graciela and her daughter sleep in the wagon, and Claudio told his brother-in-law that would do for him, too.

"So that's how it is?" he asked Claudio when the two of them moved away from the fire for final relief.

"I believe it is," Claudio told him. He finished his business and buttoned his trousers. "Marco, I'm not so certain what to do now."

"Get in the wagon with them, as you so boldly said."

"She is still irritated with me for leaving her alone in the pass."

Marco buttoned his trousers, laughing softly. "It's a cold night and she only has one blanket. Get in the wagon."

"I finally know good advice when I hear it," Claudio said to Marco, who slapped his back. "You should congratulate me."

He crawled in the wagon. Marco was right; the night was cooler. Probably in the morning there would be a film of ice on the water bucket. He yawned.

"I only have the one blanket," he heard from Graciela. He tried to gauge the frostiness level in her voice. He knew he was still a babe in the woods where women were concerned—the kind of women that a man didn't pay for, leave before daybreak, and worry about catching diseases from.

"Would you share your blanket?" he asked.

"Yes, if I can put Cecilia between us," Graciela said. "It's a cold night for September."

"Yes, last year it was warmer at this time. Maybe there will be an early winter." He lay down, disgusted with himself because he was talking about the weather. *Ay caray!*

Graciela spread her blanket over the three of them. Cecilia was already asleep, folded up like a little flower. She might be Soledad's age, or a little younger. There would be dresses for her at the Double Cross, and maybe secrets to share in the years to come. They would gang up on poor Claudito, so Claudio hoped Paloma's next baby was a boy. He smiled into the dark. *I am making plans*, he thought.

Graci had made no comment, but at least she was facing him. He hoped she would speak, but the silence lengthened until he heard her even breathing. Maybe tomorrow night. He closed his eyes.

"Graci, I have absolutely nothing but my horse and the clothes on my back. I left my blanket with one of the Ute women," he told her sleeping form. "I have bad dreams, and even Lorenzo says I do not talk enough. There are days when all I have is a beating heart."

"That is all you need, really," she told him.

Claudio sat up in surprise, then lay down quickly, because he was letting in the cold air on Cecilia. Had he really said that? Surely he had simply thought it. He nerved himself to look at Graci. Her eyes were open and he saw no fear there. He wasn't certain what else he saw, except that he had seen that same look in Paloma's eyes, when she sat with Marco. Maybe it was love, and maybe he was tired and wandering in his head.

"We … we'll need to think about it," he stammered.

"If you still need to think about it then do so," she replied, generous and patient at the same time.

Cecilia lay between them, but Claudio stretched his arm across the child just to touch Graci. She must have had the same idea, because their hands met in the middle. They twined their fingers and rested them on the sleeping child.

Claudio knew he would never go to sleep now. He closed his eyes and slept.

Chapter Thirty-Six

In which matters are settled to nearly everyone's satisfaction; no, everyone's

WHEN HAD THE GROUND *become so hard?* Marco asked himself as he stretched and groaned, the morning sun in his eyes. Two more nights with his bones on the cold ground, and then there would be Paloma. He had lost his sense of adventure. All he wanted was his wife and children and a good pot of *posole*.

His memory also wasn't what it used to be. "I must be getting old," he told Claudio, as they squatted together around a pathetic fire that Joaquim had started. "Last night I started to tell you about a proposition. Remember?"

"Barely," his brother-in-law said.

"It's a simple proposition. Governor de Anza has been too busy to assign anyone to the land grant that used to belong to Alfonso Castellano. It is more than that: no one has been brave enough to willingly settle in Valle del Sol. Don't know what they're afraid of."

He heard Claudio's laugh, touched in his soul because Paloma and Claudio were so much alike, left too young to struggle on their own through desperate circumstances. They had few wants and made no demands, because harsh life had instructed them not to expect anything. He reminded himself again to get red shoes for Paloma.

"I have to go to Santa Fe in a month, as part of my duties as an officer of the crown. I want you to come with me and claim that land grant for your own."

Claudio stared at him, his mouth open. "You're serious?"

"I never joke about land and cattle. Yes or no?"

"Yes, but—"

So like Paloma, Marco thought. "I know, I know: you have no cattle, no sheep, no horses, no house, no servants."

"That about covers it. At the moment I don't even have a blanket."

They had reached the wagon. Marco leaned against it, tired even though the sun was barely up. "I have all those things in abundance and I will share."

Marco would have given the earth right then for Paloma to see her brother's face. A host of emotions crossed it. Marco said nothing, only watched and held out his arms, his heart full. Claudio grabbed him in a fierce embrace. "Marco, your sister told me not so long ago that I overthink matters. Maybe it is a man's bad habit, because you do, too."

Claudio nodded. Before Marco could stop him, he knelt and kissed Marco's hand. Marco raised him to his feet and took him by the shoulders. "No more horse trading, no more thieving. Marry that woman in the wagon and allow Paloma and me to help you."

"I had better," Claudio said simply. "Graci has the blanket."

HAVING COME FROM THE north, Marco Mondragón's ragged little army passed through Santa Maria first and not the Double Cross, and learned of Sergeant Lopez's death. Wielding powers he suspected he did not possess—but which he also knew the governor would not dispute—Marco informed the leaderless *soldados* that El Teniente Joaquim Gasca was their new commander.

"You will obey him in all matters upon pain of my serious displeasure," Marco told the assembled soldiers. He had no idea how much serious displeasure he was capable of, when all he wanted to do was go home, bathe, and throw himself face down on his bed.

He left David Benedict with Joaquim. "I wouldn't trust him for a minute," Marco whispered. "Tell him this fable that Toshua checks the jail periodically. That should remind him not to run away, although where he would go, I could not tell you."

Joaquim translated and David shuddered. He spoke, and Marco could tell it sounded like a question. "He wants to know if you are taking him to Santa Fe to face the governor and prison," Joaquim said.

"Tell him prison can wait," Marco said, knowing that even an enemy agent, English or American, could change, especially now that he understood what New Mexicans were capable of. A man with David Benedict's talents didn't need to languish in prison. Marco had no doubt that the English in Canada or the Americans in St. Louis would try again to create mischief. They could just try it somewhere else.

"Tell David I want him on the Double Cross later this winter. Paloma and I need to learn English."

Joaquim translated and David nodded. "*Muy bueno*," David said.

"*Bien*," Marco corrected. They would *all* be busy this winter, apparently.

On Marco's request, Joaquim's first order was to send a *soldado* on a fast horse to the Double Cross to let his dear ones know that all was well and he was on his way. Lorenzo had insisted on keeping the wagon that now represented the last remnant of the ragged southern end of an enterprise to stir up trouble among the Indians. It was slow and creaky and about to disintegrate, but Lorenzo was a hero, after all.

So it was that Marco and Lorenzo and Claudio and his newly acquired family traveled together the last miles home. Feeling uncomfortably like a father counseling his son, Marco rode in the wagon with Lorenzo for a few miles, interrogating the older man about his intentions for Sancha Villareal.

"I … I thought maybe I'd see if she might go walking with me by the *acequia*," Lorenzo stammered, his face flaming red.

"At that rate, you'll be too old to impress her on your wedding night," Marco snapped, exasperated. "Marry her soon, but only if you promise me and Paloma that you will become a respectable husband, bathe once a week, and treat her well. No more wenching and horse stealing."

Lorenzo opened and closed his mouth and said nothing. Marco took that as an excellent sign. "I have need of a herdsman, Lorenzo," he continued. Life among two-year-olds had taught him to temper demands with sweets. "I pay well. I know you are good with livestock, but they better damn well be *my* horses and cattle, and no one else's! Yes or no?"

"Sheep, too?" Lorenzo asked.

Marco slapped the side of the horse trader's head and started to laugh. "Sheep, too, you … you *pendejo*! And chickens, ducks, and turkeys. Goats. Are we perfectly clear?"

"We are, señor."

"Good!"

He stepped from the wagon seat onto Buciro, who had been matching his stride to the wagon team's. Marco watched the team, thinking of the miles the horses had churned up during their long journey on the edge of the frontier. "Lorenzo, I believe this team that has come all the way from the Missouri River is as smooth-walking as the stolen horses you foisted on me."

Lorenzo looked them over with the eye of a professional. "They're not as handsome, so no one will probably steal them from you."

"You should know, since you're the best horse thief around. Remember that Sancha won't love you if you misbehave. I will claim them as contraband of war."

He rode beside Claudio and Graciela next. Cecilia sat in front of Claudio now, her eyes earnest as she grasped the high pommel.

"I believe she thinks she is in control of your horse," Marco whispered to his brother-in-law.

"I'll let her believe that."

He edged his horse between Claudio and Graciela and reached inside his doublet. "Here you are, Graciela." He leaned over and set the money pouch in her lap.

"This is not mine," she said.

"It is if I give it to you," he replied. "You are free. I hope you will marry Claudio because he needs a good wife."

"Even a wife who is a little worse for wear?" Graciela asked. "Some men wouldn't consider me a prize."

"No one around here. Ask Paloma: we already see you as we hope someday you will see yourself."

He looked away, the better to give her time to collect herself. If she had any questions, Paloma probably had answers.

Thank God for Claudio. "Graciela Tafoya," Claudio said, "I have a beating heart."

Marco had no idea what they were talking about. Obviously it wasn't his business. When he fell behind, their horses came together. Claudio leaned over and kissed Graciela.

"That is a good start," Marco said.

Claudio, man of doubts, wasn't quite done. "Marco, do you really have room for us in the hacienda? It's starting to fill up. Provided I get that land grant, I still have to build a house."

"*We* have to build a house," Marco corrected. He smiled at Claudio, a man with as many faults and failings as himself who was about to be greatly improved by a wife. "Until then, we'll add another bed to the children's room, and you and Graciela can have your old room. When the new baby comes, I might have to reclaim my office by the horse barn."

"Are we a bother?"

"You are a blessing."

THEY ARRIVED AT THE open gates of the Double Cross as the sun was setting. Paloma stood there, a child holding each hand. Her smile lit the evening lamps.

"O God, I am blessed above all men in New Mexico," Marco whispered.

A mere month ago, he would have raced ahead to be first. Now he sat on his horse and ushered Lorenzo and his team through. He sat there, an idiot grin on his face, as Sancha Villareal, his dignified and proper housekeeper, ran to the wagon, put her foot on the wheel and pulled herself up next to the horse thief, trader, and general bad man. She murmured something not intended for any ears but Lorenzo's and kissed him soundly.

"Another good start," Marco said. He gestured Graciela and Claudio through next, smiling even wider as his brother-in-law handed a sleeping child down to Paloma. She kissed Cecilia, then handed her to Graciela, who stood beside her now.

Again more words passed that Marco could not quite hear. He watched a brother and sister hold each other close, then laugh, and add Graciela and her half-Comanche child to their embrace. Close together, Claudio Vega and Graciela Tafoya followed Lorenzo and Sancha through the gates.

Finally it was his turn. Marco dismounted and grabbed Paloma in such a fierce hold that she squeaked in protest and reminded him that the Mondragón he couldn't see yet wasn't used to bear hugs.

That didn't explain why she held him so close to her body, but he already knew that logic escaped her when they embraced, as when they did other things. And here was Soledad, joy of his heart, demanding to know why he had no eyebrows. He kneeled down to hug her, which meant Claudito climbed onto his back and rested his head against Marco's neck with a huge sigh of welcome.

He was home.

Epilogue

Tired, so tired. Still, after supper Marco had children to cuddle, talking all the while with Paloma. As he held his little ones, she just sat beside him and watched, sizing him up for weight loss, or injury, or some other sign of his ordeal. He wanted to tell her there would be nightmares, but she would know soon enough, and be there.

Marco knew his intelligent wife saw something in his eyes, because her hand went to his thigh and she moved closer to him. In another moment, she leaned against his arm, her eyes closed, which made him speculate how difficult it must be to stay home and wait.

"I love you, Paloma," he whispered.

"And I, you," she said. "I do not like myself when I worry."

What could he say to that? He kissed her and felt her sigh.

Paloma still had the power to amaze him. When the children were in bed, she took him by the hand and walked him to the *sala*. Touched beyond words, he stood in the doorway as she took down her brand from its place next to his on the wall.

Marco followed her down the hall as she went to Claudio's closed door and knocked. "Paloma, you are magnificent," he said.

Bless her, she was also practical. "This is the right time," she assured him. "A few weeks ago, no. Now, yes."

Claudio opened the door. His eyes fell on the Star in the Meadow brand, too long unused, and he swallowed.

Paloma held out the heavy brand with both hands. "Marco tells me you will be going with him to Santa Fe soon to see about the Castellano land grant. Here. What better brand than this one?"

Claudio took it from her. "It's not Vega land," he began, but she put her fingers to his lips.

"*Al contrario*," she chided him gently. "It will be." Paloma put one arm around Marco, her other hand against Claudio's chest. "I doubt we can restore what is lost, but what is land, compared to family?"

Claudio leaned against the door frame, at ease now and smiling at his sister. He tried to speak, but his eyes filled with tears. He set down the brand and held out his arms for both of them. He looked over his shoulder, spoke softly, and Graciela joined them.

The four of them stood close together, no words needed.

Paloma broke the spell in her sweet way, looking at Marco, her expression earnest. "My love, do our parents really know that Claudio and I are happy?"

Marco wondered how many times Paloma would ask that of him. He was no theologian, but he had faith in his answer, because it put to rest his own sorrow. And if she asked again, what did it matter? In turn, she would be there each night to comfort him through dreams not of his choosing. He had his strengths; she had hers.

"They know, my dear ones. Of this I am certain," he told the brother and sister. "How, I could not tell you. I leave that to Him. Will that do?"

Paloma nodded, her face hidden against his chest. His heart told him she smiled.

Bryner Photography

A WELL-KNOWN VETERAN of romance writing, **Carla Kelly** is the author of thirty-five novels, numerous short stories, and four non-fiction works. She has been writing for years. Her first novel was a three-sentence, typed mystery titled, "The Old Mill," written when she was six years old. Her novels are considerably longer now.

Carla is the recipient of two RITA Awards from Romance Writers of America for Best Regency of the Year; two Spur Awards from Western Writers of America for Best Short Fiction; and two Whitney Awards, one for Best Romance, 2011, and another for Best Historical Fiction, 2012. She also received a Lifetime Achievement Award from Romantic Times.

Carla enjoys writing historical fiction, which she sees as a byproduct of her study of history. In addition to her works centered on the American West, she has written many books featuring the Royal Navy during the Napoleonic Wars.

Carla and Martin Kelly live in Idaho Falls, Idaho. Look her up on: www.carlakellyauthor.com.

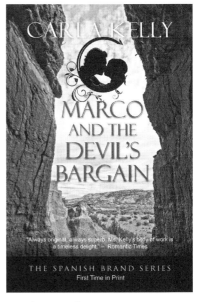